SINISTER JUSTICE

Visit us at www.boldstrokesbooks.com

By the Author

Final Departure

Sinister Justice

SINISTER JUSTICE

by
Steve Pickens

2018

SINISTER JUSTICE
© 2018 BY STEVE PICKENS. ALL RIGHTS RESERVED.

ISBN 13: 978-1-63555-094-8

THIS TRADE PAPERBACK ORIGINAL IS PUBLISHED BY
BOLD STROKES BOOKS, INC.
P.O. BOX 249
VALLEY FALLS, NY 12185

FIRST EDITION: JANUARY 2018

THIS IS A WORK OF FICTION. NAMES, CHARACTERS, PLACES, AND INCIDENTS ARE THE PRODUCT OF THE AUTHOR'S IMAGINATION OR ARE USED FICTITIOUSLY. ANY RESEMBLANCE TO ACTUAL PERSONS, LIVING OR DEAD, BUSINESS ESTABLISHMENTS, EVENTS, OR LOCALES IS ENTIRELY COINCIDENTAL.

THIS BOOK, OR PARTS THEREOF, MAY NOT BE REPRODUCED IN ANY FORM WITHOUT PERMISSION.

CREDITS
EDITOR: JERRY L. WHEELER
PRODUCTION DESIGN: SUSAN RAMUNDO
COVER DESIGN BY TAMMY SEIDICK

Acknowledgments

Special thanks to Jerry Wheeler for once again making the editing process easy and painless, and to all the talented folks at Bold Strokes for their hard work and help in getting Jake into print.

Dedication

For Ang, my beautiful friend, who is never afraid to drag me back to reality—frequently by my ear.

And, always, for B.

Chapter One

Once upon a time in a quiet little village named Arrow Bay lived a handsome young man and his loving husband. They lived in a neat little house with a trim green yard filled with flowers and Japanese maples. In the front yard grew an ancient apple tree, its boughs laden with fruit turning bright red in the late September sun. In the breeze, golden leaves from two old maples drifted across the yard languidly like gilded pages from a book of fairy tales. A smart-looking beagle lay asleep in a patch of sun at the base of the tree, while the handsome man raked up the leaves. Every time he raked up the leaves, more and more drifted in from the beautiful old trees next door, so many that the handsome young man thought he'd never finish, that he'd rake and rake until the end of time, like Sisyphus pushing the large boulder up the hill for all eternity, only to have it come rolling back down. Rake and rake and rake...

"Samuel Patrick O'Conner," said Jake Finnigan, shaking a warning finger at his bearded husband, "If you don't stow it right this second, you're going to be working out here alone." The Bigleaf maples from the Crenshaws' house across the street showered another wave of golden leaves across their front yard.

Sam laughed, unable to help himself. Jake stood scowling, his blue flannel shirt tied across his waist, the sun glistening off his biceps.

Sam found himself thinking how good Jake looked in his work boots, faded jeans and a white T-shirt that clung to his muscular torso. He knew the two hours a day Jake spent working out with weights and exercise equipment were not out of vanity, but out of his desire to eat junk food and fight off the "fat kid" stigma he'd suffered all through his childhood.

"Just for that, kiddo, you're on the hook for dinner tonight," said Jake. He tossed his rake aside in disgust. "Oh, this is hopeless. Until the wind shifts back to the west, I'm not even going to bother."

"We're lucky, actually." Sam dropped a small gardening shovel into the loop of his work pants while peering over the chain link fence next door. The yellow house had red shutters with hearts cut into them, and a concrete walkway leading to the front door flanked by ceramic figurines of the Seven Dwarfs. Strewn about the creeping myrtle were Bambi, Thumper, Flower, and some frog that neither Sam nor Jake had ever been able to pin to any Disney film. Currently the entire yard was almost totally obscured by a healthy layer of elephant-ear sized maple leaves the color of butterscotch.

"Brother," said Jake, shaking his head. "Poor Al and Phyllis. They're going to catch hell for that."

"Isn't much old lady Weinberg can do about the leaves. Those trees are on the town's heritage list. They're well over two hundred years old." Sam buttoned up his blue flannel shirt against the chill.

"I know. I love those old trees. Except for the three weeks a year when they shed their leaves." Jake walked over to the apple tree, patting Barnaby, the couple's beagle, on the head. Ella Fitzgerald began singing "It's De-Lovely" from the radio they had propped up against the tree.

"Well," said Sam, returning to the flowerbed he'd just planted. "That's that for now. We'll have plenty of 'Blushing Bride' tulips come spring."

Sam glanced around the front yard, with its tidy flowerbeds on either side of the walk and the boxes full of late fall flowers on the porch.

"I know what you're going to say," said Jake, retrieving his rake.

"We've got to do something with that backyard," replied Sam.

"At least we got rid of that damn boxwood."

"True, but that blackthorn behind the garage is going wild, and you know—"

The sound of a black '99 Lincoln Town Car pulling into the driveway next door cut him off. The garage door screeched as it opened, making both Sam and Jake grimace. The Lincoln jerked forward into the garage. The engine gunned twice, spewing a cloud of black exhaust. With a final rumble it cut off. A moment later, the car door opened, then slammed shut. The sound of heels on concrete echoed from the garage. An angular woman with a monochrome pineapple of steel-gray hair popped out of the doorframe. She paused, ogling her yard with beady eyes before letting out a short grunt, the cuff of her gray tweed coat flapping about her ankles. Leona Weinberg turned her hatchet face from her yard, looked briefly at their house then across the street where the maples shed another wheelbarrow full of leaves across her property.

Jake and Sam immediately went back to their yard work, pretending not to have noticed the arrival of their neighbor. Leona stomped around her yard, kicking leaves and cursing under her breath. "Son of a mongrel dog, no good heathens, mealy mouthed, caca, dang blamed inconsiderate no good so-and-so's."

Barnaby woke from his slumber and started barking. Sam stood up and shouted, "Quiet, Barnaby, sit!" The dog responded at once and sat back down on his patch of earth under the elderly Red Delicious apple tree. It was not, however, quick enough for Mrs. Weinberg.

"You keep that dog quiet, Mr. O'Conner or I'll have the law on you!" she shrieked from across the chain link fence.

Jake threw down his rake. "Listen, you—"

Sam kicked Jake in the shin.

"Ow! What the hell did you do that for?"

"We'll keep him quiet, Mrs. Weinberg." Sam was grinning, perhaps the worst, most plastic grin he'd ever seen in his life. Jake burst out laughing.

"I don't see what is so funny, Mr. Finnigan. And would you please turn that devil music down!" she barked, just as Sarah Vaughan came on singing "Poor Butterfly."

"Devil music?" said Jake, irritated. "That's Sarah Vaughan!"

"I know who it is. And I know what station it is coming from. Turn it down, or—"

"You'll have the law on us. Yes, yes, I know," said Jake, going back to his raking.

"Jake…" Just then, Phyllis Crenshaw pulled her white Dodge into her drive, parked, and got out, waving at Sam and Jake as she retrieved the mail from her box. A gentle, generous woman of about forty-five, Phyllis had short-cropped blonde hair framing a heart-shaped face with dimples. She wore silver-rimmed glasses over sparkling blue eyes. Phyllis Crenshaw had a hearty laugh and was thoughtful and intelligent, with a wonderful sense of humor. She worked for the ferry system, which was where Jake had met her, and the two had become quite chummy.

"Afternoon, fellows!" she called. "Beautiful day, isn't it?"

"It is," said Jake. "How's life on B watch?"

"Going well. Julie Crawford is out, she had her baby—"

"Mrs. Crenshaw," interrupted Leona Weinberg. "What are you going to do about these leaves?"

"Which leaves, Mrs. Weinberg?"

"The leaves your filthy trees dumped all over my yard. What are you going to do about them?"

"Do? Well, nothing. God seems to have wanted them there or he wouldn't have had the wind blow that way," she said, winking at Jake and Sam. Sam had to bite the inside of his cheeks to keep from laughing.

"You have a lot of gall bringing up God when you attend that heathen church in town."

"And you have a lot of gall bringing up leaves to me when you have a gardening service attend to your yard. You should give them a call. Good day to you, Leona," said Phyllis. She got back in her car, waving to Sam and Jake, and drove up the rest of the length of her driveway.

"Well, I never!" cried Leona Weinberg.

"And you never will, either," said Jake under his breath. This time Sam wasn't able to contain his laughter and instead erupted into a coughing fit.

Leona Weinberg stared at them with her beady pig eyes and whirled away, stomping up the walkway to her front door and assaulting it with her keys before throwing it open and disappearing into the depths of her house.

Another gust of wind blew in from the southeast, showering High Street with a shower of golden leaves. Sam and Jake laughed until their sides hurt.

Chapter Two

After spending that afternoon working in the yard, neither Jake nor Sam felt like cooking. As the sun slipped lower on the horizon, they showered and dressed, then jumped into Jake's electric blue PT Cruiser and headed down to the Bitter End Bar and Grill.

The Bitter End, named after the nautical term for the free end of a rope or chain on a vessel, was the type of place locals flocked to loyally but until recently tourists hadn't discovered. The ones who did their homework stumbled on to something the locals of Arrow Bay had known for decades: the Bitter End served the best food and drinks in town. Aside from basic burgers and French fries, the Bitter End served an abundance of fresh fish, salmon, mussels, and local seafoods along with fresh pies made with locally picked berries, homemade ice cream and cakes, fresh baked bread and doughnuts. Word of mouth usually kept the place almost always packed to capacity from the moment the doors opened until closing time.

That Wednesday evening, however, the restaurant was only at about half capacity. Jake and Sam sat at their favorite table just to the left of the end of the bar. Jake ordered a Jameson and Pepsi and Sam a Green River soda. They greeted their friend, the Bitter End's best bartender, Caleb Rivers, with a hearty hello. A barrel-chested man about thirty with arresting opalescent blue eyes, short goatee, and cropped brown hair, Caleb also had nicely defined biceps and pectoral muscles under a black Bitter End T-shirt that neither Jake nor Sam had ever seen him without. Of medium height and graced with a bashful, engaging smile and personality, Caleb had legendary bartending skills. He knew the most obscure drinks, and Sam and Jake's repeated efforts to stump him had led to them both downing some fairly toxic concoctions.

Caleb was straight but not the least bit narrow-minded. Over the years, a casual acquaintance had become a very strong friendship, Jake and Sam offering sage advice and sympathy concerning Caleb's never-ending series of short-lived relationships with a profusion of women.

He brought their drinks over and sat down at the table with them. "Evenin', guys. What brings you out on a Wednesday?"

"The fundamental inability to come up with anything interesting for dinner," replied Jake, taking a sip of his drink. "Excellent as always."

"Thanks. It's so difficult to mix whiskey and cola together."

"I could have said you were skimping on the Jameson but decided to be polite."

"That's because you feared being smited for lying."

"That's smote," Sam corrected him.

"Okay, smote. And I wouldn't be so cocky for someone who's in check."

"What?" Sam exclaimed, alarmed. He turned to the chessboard that sat at the corner of the bar. Caleb and Sam had a game going at all times, sometimes lasting for months. Sam hopped off the chair and went over to the chess set, pushing his glasses up his nose while scowling down at the board.

"Pretty quiet tonight," Jake said.

"Town council meeting. Wait until about nine thirty when everyone comes in for a drink after that bunch of cut-throats is finished."

Jake rolled his eyes. "God, now what?"

"Wilde Park. Longhoffer is determined to plow the sucker under."

Jake looked aghast. "What for?"

"Oh, just what Arrow Bay needs. A big name box store cluttering up the waterfront."

"Can they even do that? I mean, Wilde Park is right up against a residential neighborhood, not to mention the channel!"

"It's zoned commercial at that end," said Sam, returning from the chessboard. "Longhoffer does have some precedent. There are a few small businesses strewn into the old homes in that part of town." Sam fixed Jake with a steely eye. "You'd know all this if you read the *Arrow Bay Examiner*."

"Or listened to KABW," Caleb said. "Randy Burrows is always going on about it. He's on the council, you know."

"I know, I voted for him, and I *do* listen to KABW," said Jake, thinking about how they'd ended up with a council as a governing body in the first place.

Twenty years prior, Mayor Alderbrook absconded with the town treasury and fled to Brazil. In a backlash, the citizens of Arrow Bay voted to dissolve the office of mayor in favor of a six-person city council, figuring that not everyone could have their fingers in the pie all at one time. Jake wasn't sure that move had been successful with the conservatives on the council, whom he and many others suspected of conspiring together to supplant their agenda on the town. Reed Longhoffer, Verna Monger, and their neighbor Leona Weinberg didn't have their collective digits in some scheme to steal city funds, but they did seem bent on trying to make Arrow Bay as stuffily conservative and uptight as they were.

Until recently, they had been able to bowl over the liberals on the council, but notoriously wishy-washy Jerome Beaverton had dropped a small anvil on his foot at work and had been forced to move to a drier climate when arthritis set in. In his stead, Emma Kennedy, owner of the Illahee Inn and a staunch liberal, had been elected, causing a three-three deadlock more and more over the last several months. That very deadlock and the seemingly glacial pace at which things moved in Arrow Bay had caused Jake to quit paying much attention to any of the issues that had faced the town in the last two years. And after the problems he'd faced last fall...

He took another drink of his Jameson and Pepsi and decided on fish and chips for dinner while Sam opted for the roast beef pepper dip.

"I wish you wouldn't put it quite like that," said Jake.

"Hmm?" Sam said, taking his eyes off the large flat-screen TV.

"You know, about the paper."

Sam shrugged. "It's true. We get it dumped on the porch once a week, and you never even take it out of the wrapper."

"The crossword sucks," said Jake.

"You really should, though. I mean, not much goes on in Arrow Bay, but when things like this Wilde Park mess arise, you'll be on top of things, and I won't inadvertently embarrass you in front of the bartender at the Bitter End," said Sam, grinning slyly.

Jake chose to ignore the last part. "Well, all right, I'll start reading it. Meanwhile, what is the scoop with the park?"

"Basically what Caleb said. Longhoffer wants to plow the park under and put up a SuperLoMart on the spot. Or so the rumor goes."

"Well, on the one hand it would be nice to have something like that."

Sam looked as if Jake had doused him with cold water. "You, a union man, are saying you'd like to have a SuperLoMart in town?"

"My point is," continued Jake, "and keep your voice down, Sam. You can't even buy a bloody pair of socks in this town. You have to go clear to Mount Burlington to get anything like that. And no, I don't support either destroying Wilde Park or shopping at SuperLoMart. A nice union store like Inabinett's Market would be great, tastefully done and stuck, say, on that vacant land near Safeway. *Not* Wilde Park."

"I have very fond memories of that park. Feeding the ducks in the pond, taking Barnaby for walks, listening to you cursing a blue streak after you slipped and fell in the creek."

"Har har, a laugh riot that was." Jake stuck his tongue out at his husband. "Still, you know, it is a beautiful little oasis in town. You've got the marsh land which is full of ducks and birds, the creek, that nice stretch of beach…"

"Not to mention it's the centerpiece of the Sky to Sea trail loop," said Sam. "Blow out Wilde Park, and you'll have a trail that begins and ends at a SuperLoMart."

"Maybe that's Longhoffer's plan," said Jake glumly, thinking of the bike and foot trail that was nearly complete after fifteen years in the making. Sky to Sea had been the brainchild of one of the last living town founders, who had left a substantial portion of his estate to the city—including all of McDougal Lake—to be used as a park. The multi-use trail would be an unbroken circle bordering the city, including miles of beach, lake, and mountain land. Bit by bit, the city had been purchasing property to finish the trail, and it was now nearly complete.

"Wouldn't surprise me. Reed doesn't strike me as the naturalist type. Did you know there are over fifty species of birds and well over three hundred examples of native flora and fauna in Wilde Park alone?" Sam asked. "The trails are all maintained on a volunteer basis and there are monthly work groups there to make sure that trash isn't left behind and the park is kept up."

"Are you their spokesman or something?"

"No, but when I read of all their troubles, I joined the Save Our Park Foundation." He paused for a moment as their food arrived. "Er, so did you. In fact we donated fifteen hundred dollars to the cause."

Jake nearly spit out his drink. "Fifteen hund—I don't have that kind of money lying around!"

Sam shrugged. "You don't. *We* do. It was for a good cause."

Money was one of the unspoken things about their relationship. Jake made good money from the state working as an on-call mate or, more often, his usual job of quartermaster on the *Chelan*, but he couldn't compete with Sam's income. As one of the top maritime designers in his field, Sam was in demand and commanded prices accordingly. He no longer had to worry about cash. Sam had made a personal goal of being able to retire by forty, and he was well on his way to making it. Jake had taken a leave of absence from work and wasn't contributing any money at the moment, so it bothered him to be relying on Sam's income.

"He'll never get it through," said Jake, thanking the waitress as the food arrived.

"He might. Longhoffer isn't afraid of bulldozing his own agenda through. I'm not at all convinced going to the town council form of government was entirely a good thing," said Sam, shaking some ketchup onto his plate for his fries.

"Particularly now, split down the middle. Only Walter Lugar is sort of the middle of the road. Verna Monger, Reed Longhoffer, and our happy neighbor Leona Weinberg are all die-hard conservatives, and Emma Kennedy and Randy Burrows are die-hard liberals. Walter definitely votes from his convictions. I've seen him side with Longhoffer and the others a few times, and I've seen him side with Kennedy and Burrows," said Jake.

"He's with Kennedy and Burrows most of the time. He leans toward labor, the environment, and preservation. I think the park issue is a dead split, though," said Sam. "Good fries."

"I suppose we *should* attend more town meetings."

"Non-political you?"

"Oh, I'm plenty political, so much it almost got me expelled in high school, if you'll remember," said Jake. "I was known for my acidic editorials against censorship, pro stances on gay rights, and the environment. Not exactly a popular stance in a mill town."

"You weren't exactly 'out' in high school though. I mean, you never actually hid it…"

"No, I wasn't. Not exactly, anyway. I don't think anyone thought about it one way or the other. If they did, my friendship with the captain of the football team kind of squashed it."

"An unlikely ally, considering he was your first boyfriend."

"Which no one knew," Jake said. "Excellent fish and chips."

"Anyway, I think it'd be good for you to get more involved with our adopted home town. Particularly with lunkheads like Weinberg, Longhoffer, and Monger in there. I dread what'll happen if they get another conservative on the board. I know for a fact Walt Lugar is getting tired of the backstabbing and the partisan politics of it all."

"How so?"

"He told me down at the shipyard the other day. This thing on the park has really exhausted him."

Jake shook his head. "That's too bad. Walter's a good man. I'd hate to see Longhoffer and the others drive him off."

"As would I."

"It would be easier if someone would just bump the conservatives off, Starting with our neighbor. Or is that bordering on being anti-Semitic?"

"You won't get an argument out of me, and no," Sam said. "She isn't Jewish. Her husband was, and he was a peach of a fellow from what I've heard. She made *him* convert. The rumor, according to my mother, was that she married him for his money. So no, it isn't anti-Semitic to want her bumped off."

Jake looked at him, surprised. "You, oh Ghandi-like one, are endorsing violence?"

"Don't be daft, Jacob. I'm just saying that in…a mythic kind of way, it would solve a lot of problems."

"Wouldn't it just?"

They finished their meal in near silence after that, enjoying the food and the ambiance of the Bitter End. Dusk fell quietly, the sky faded to purple while the wind kicked up crimson leaves outside the door of the bar.

They paid their bill and said good-bye to Caleb and were just about out the door when they heard him yell, "Son of a bitch! O'Conner, you—you—"

"Yes?" Sam asked innocently.

"How did you do that?"

"Do what?" Sam said with a wink as he and Jake exited the Bitter End.

Shaking his head as he watched the couple leave, Caleb returned his attention to the chessboard where he was now in check.

Chapter Three

Since they had been discussing it, Jake and Sam stopped by Wilde Park on the way home. They decided to make a quick walk of the main trail, listening to the gentle trickle of water as Enetai Creek gurgled its way to the bay. The air smelled slightly of wood smoke and salt water, with a hint of the coming frost. The stars were burning sharp and clear and a gentle breeze ruffled the cattails and low alders along the gravel path as they walked.

"I can't stand the thought of this park being plowed under," Jake said again.

"Well, hopefully it won't come to that."

"Here's hoping. Jake furrowed his brow and tilted his head slightly, trying to hear something more clearly.

"What is it?"

"I thought I heard something," he said, pointing off the pathway. "Over there in the brush."

Sam pulled out a Maglite from the pocket of one of the waistcoats he always wore. Jake found himself again thinking of them as something along the lines of Mary Poppins's carpetbag—there always seemed to the right tool, appliance, or flashlight appearing from Sam's black vests.

"See anything?"

"No…wait a minute…okay, you, come out!"

A bulky woman dressed in duck boots emerged from a thicket of salal and sword ferns. She wore a heavy green plaid skirt covered by an open wool overcoat the color of bruised plums. Perched on her head was a green bucket hat. Her green eyes seemed slightly out of focus and she had a smudge of dirt on one cheek. Her aged face was wary, but had once been pretty, with very distinctive cheekbones and a strong, noble chin, but now it was pallid and slightly sunken, with deep lines around the eyes.

"You gave us quite a scare, Gladys," said Sam.

"I thought you were Paige Farelley," she said warily. "Have you seen Paige Farelley?"

"No, Gladys."

She pointed a rather battered black umbrella at Jake. "How about you? Have you seen Paige Farelley? Have you?"

"No Gladys, I'm afraid not."

"You'd tell me if you did though, wouldn't you?"

They nodded in unison.

Gladys Nyberg stood up straight, a haughty expression crossing her face. "I thought you'd say that," she said.

"What are you doing in the bushes, Gladys?" asked Sam.

"I'm on my way home. This is a shortcut. I had to make sure you weren't Paige Farelley before I went home. She'd follow me."

"Hmm. Well, you can see we're not Paige Farelley, so you can go on home now. You'll be safe."

She looked suspiciously at Sam. "I know about you two."

"You do?"

"You've got a dog."

"That's right," said Jake, looking to Sam for help.

"He's a nice dog. Is he with you?"

"No, we had dinner out. He's at home where it's warm."

"You take care of him," said Gladys, stepping into the bushes again and disappearing from sight.

Jake let out a deep breath, suddenly realizing he'd been holding it for the last several seconds. "What was *that* about?"

"Paige Farelley? I'm not at all sure anyone really knows. Gladys hasn't ever hurt anyone. Oh, she's smacked people with her umbrella a time or two, but no one who didn't deserve it. Really, she's harmless. Just talk to her kind of slowly but not condescendingly and you'll be fine." He thought for a moment. "And don't lie to her. She seems to know when she's being lied to."

"I can't imagine having a reason to lie to her," said Jake. "She likes Barnaby?"

"Oh yeah, she loves him. And he's quite taken with her."

Jake felt himself relaxing. If their beagle liked Gladys Nyberg, she must be okay.

They continued down the shadowy path, which would eventually lead them back to the parking lot on Ashton Avenue. They walked close together, their breath hanging in pale clouds about them as the temperature continued to drop. The creek gurgled and muttered to itself, and, in a fit of romanticism, Sam stopped in the middle of the path and planted a sloppy kiss on Jake.

"What was that for?"

"Nothing at all. I'm just very thankful to have you as my husband, is all."

Jake knew he was blushing. "Me too. This last year has been great."

"It has at that," said Sam, knowing the feeling sprang from more than the fear from the previous year, when Sam had very nearly lost his life.

"You know what I mean. If anything I feel closer to you than I ever have." He paused, sitting on a damp log on which frost was already forming, looking into the swirling depths of Enetai Creek. "I don't know what I'd do without you, you know," said Jake.

"Hey, I'm not going anywhere, remember?"

Jake smiled. "I know. But after last year, I want you to know I don't ever take you for granted."

Sam shrugged. "I know you don't. I never thought you did." He sighed, exhaling a great cloud of steam into the night sky. "This is getting all too serious."

"I agree. I'm also freezing my ass off."

"And a lovely ass it is too."

"Thank you," he said, chuckling. "Seriously though, what I mean is this, Sam. I love you and want to be with you always."

"I feel the same, Jake. I really do."

They embraced for a moment, slipping off the half-frozen log, quickening their pace back to the parking lot. They were just about to round the corner when they nearly ran smack into a slight, pointed figure in a long green tweed coat with matching hat and purple ascot walking a charcoal grey standard poodle.

"Oh, good heavens!" squeaked the man.

"Professor Mills?" Jake said.

"Mr. Finnigan?" His voice had always reminded Jake of what a hedgehog must sound like were it able to talk—slightly nasal but at the same time cute.

"It's me and Sam, Professor. How are you?"

Professor Mills adjusted his ascot. "Ah, there you are. Hello there! I'm fine, fine. And how are you both?"

"Well, thank you," said Jake.

"How are you adjusting to town?" Sam asked.

"Oh, the house is lovely, just lovely. The greenhouse, alas...so tiny!" Professor Mills lamented. "But the place in the mountains was just too big for me to handle any longer, and I really couldn't afford help. Gretel can only help her old master along so much," said the professor, patting the poodle.

"We'll have to have you up to the house so you can see where some of your stock ended up," said Sam.

"Oh, I'd like that very much, thank you. I'm afraid right now that I must get Gretel through her paces in the park," he said, brandishing a pooper-scooper. "Then it's off to bed for us. It's chilly tonight. I hope she doesn't take too long."

"Good luck," said Jake, as the professor and his dog disappeared down the shadowed path.

A few more yards brought them out into the parking lot where the professor's tidy red Toyota Prius stood parked next to the Electric Blue PT Cruiser.

"Kind of an odd fellow," Jake said once they had gotten into the car.

"He is. I've always attributed that to his intelligence being off the charts. He was a brilliant teacher. And a wizard with plants," said Sam.

"What was he a professor of?" He pulled out of the parking lot and turned onto Ashton Avenue.

"His PhD was in engineering and calculus. I had him for the engineering part. I always thought he had one in botany, but he referred to the greenhouse he had as a hobby so I'm not entirely sure."

"Ugh...poodles," said Jake. "Actually, it's not the dog so much as those stupid haircuts."

"I know it. Gretel is a sweet dog."

"Poor humiliated dog."

"You know what I'm thinking? I was thinking a nice slice of that pie Mom dropped by the other day would be good about now, with a big scoop of ice cream."

"How about we drop the pie and the ice cream in the blender and make a shake out of it?" said Jake.

"Have I ever told you how much I love that wonderful creativity you have?" marveled Sam.

"The mark of a true genius is being able to combine two desserts into one calorie-laden gut bomb."

Sam chuckled. "Home, Jacob. There's pie waiting."

❖

The next morning, Sam drove down to his office at Sutherland Shipyard to do some project oversight. Jake puttered around the house, knowing from old habits that he had a difficult time writing so much as a letter before noon.

He'd only just sat down when the mail flopped through the slot in the door. Among the bills, a package from Tony Graham. Jake tore it open, finding a paperback copy of Tony's book, *Ending Stereotypes: Coming Out, Standing Up, and Being Proud*, and inside that another carefully written letter which he observed with some annoyance was addressed to Jacob again, something only Sam, Rachel or his mother ever dared to call him.

Sighing, Jake tore open the letter, several pages long, all in Tony's florid, exceedingly exact cursive.

Dear Jake,

I'm glad my letter spurred some good. I can see by your reply that there are still some hard feelings. I cannot blame you. I handled things abysmally. Please remember I was scared and not able to handle what I was feeling. I didn't have the capacity to face the truth. Only growing and maturing has helped that, and I hope you can find it in your heart to forgive me for my cowardice at ending our relationship.

You were always light years ahead in adulthood and always more comfortable with yourself, for which I was truly envious. Many, many times I longed to tell the world to go to hell and be who I was, but at that time wasn't ready to face it. As a result, I threw away the best friendship I ever had.

I hope you enjoy the book. Your mother said she found it enlightening and tremendously insightful.

"Mother? What is she, my press agent?" Jake said aloud.

Jake turned his attention back to Tony's letter, which once again handwritten carefully on blue stationery that distinctly smelled of *Acqua di Gio*, as if he'd sprayed the letter directly.

I hope perhaps someday soon when my schedule opens up to visit you and meet Sam. I'd like to see the man you've become and the home you've made for yourself. Again, I am so pleased you're happy and healthy and that you've taken up with your physical health as well. I'm curious as to what your workout routine is like!

My own life since leaving Port Jefferson has been long and complex, of which you know a good deal. I know you're aware of the public circumstances of my coming out and the strife it cost me, even if my career with the NFL was over. I finally found it necessary to cut a lot of ties with my pro-sport friends and pursue my PhD at Evergreen State. I've just finished up my doctoral dissertation. With any luck it'll be accepted, and I'll be Dr. Anthony Graham, PhD in Psychology with an emphasis on Gay and Lesbian Studies.

I've been offered jobs teaching at some of the more progressive universities and have found one I think I can settle into a nice, long teaching career at. I will be sure to keep you posted on that as soon as I know!

My personal life, ah well, there's the rub! Lovers, yes. Husband, alas, no. I'm seeing a man right now who is fun and interesting and a good person. He works as my personal assistant, but he's hardly someone I can picture myself sharing the rest of my life with.

My days of youth after leaving sports behind were consumed with a relentless obsession for physical perfection. While achieving this I was spotted by someone at Stud Studios, that legendary factory of male erotica. I was flat broke and they offered more money than I'd make in six months as a personal trainer, so I worked as a model for them. It wasn't a career choice for me, but it did pay for a great deal of my master's degree.

Stud Studios? Stud Studio *was* legendary for male erotica. Aside from the typical naked men calendars they produced, they also did out-and-out hardcore pornography. Jake wondered what name Tony had used and why *this* particular little fact hadn't come to light before. He suspected Tony of buying up all the copies he could and having the master files destroyed. It would be just like Tony, trying to erase a potentially embarrassing element from his past.

I've had a string of talented, enlightened men wander through my life, but none of them have had the honesty and basic human decency you possess. The world in which I work I find too many simpletons, radicals, phonies and politicos for my taste. You set the bar rather high, Jake, and I thank you for that. No one should settle for second best.
I hope that you can set the past aside and renew our bonds of friendship so that I may once again bask in your honesty. Again, I hope you can forgive me for the terrible mistakes I made and find room in that big heart of yours to give me a second chance at friendship.
As ever yours,
Tony

"What utter bullshit," said Jake, although he already knew his resolve to stay angry was fading. It took much effort, and he found himself not wanting to emulate his mother's legendary ability to remember any slight, no matter how minor, for decades.

He found himself troubled by the tone of Tony's letter. What did he mean by "as ever yours," and was he hinting about something more than friendship? Jake certainly hoped not. The love of his life was *in* his life. He didn't need any complications or anyone trying to horn in.

Jake opened the basement door and patted his thigh to get Barnaby out of his kitchen basket and follow him down, which the dog dutifully did, promptly moving to his basement basket to continue his nap. Jake gave him a pat before going over to his computer to compose a reply. Forgive Tony? Yes, he could do that. However, he'd always have a sliver of titanium skepticism in his heart when it came to Anthony Graham.

Chapter Four

That evening, Sam came home from work exhausted. Alex had ordered another dozen changes to the *Chinook*, including the conversion of the former wheelhouse and officers' quarters into his private suite, figuring it would save money if he lived aboard. Sam had readily agreed to that, but after four hours had come and gone with Alex changing things as arbitrary as coat hooks in the restaurant, Sam had put his foot down and banned his employer from the restoration project until it was done.

"Banned?" Alex had sputtered, amused. "You can't—"

"I can," Sam assured him. "Take a look at your contract."

As a conciliatory act, Alex had taken Sam to lunch, promising not to meddle any further.

Sam had just locked the Subaru into the garage when the autumn quite abruptly shattered with a banshee-like wail emanating from Leona's next door.

"Oooooo nooooo! *Noooo!* Dang dirty no good so-and-sos.... *Nooooooooooo!*" Sam shut the door to the Subaru and walked cautiously toward the front door, glancing over the chain link fence. Leona clutched the remains of shattered crockery to her chest. Sam ignored her and crept toward the front porches as quietly as he could when Leona fixed him with a slit-eyed gaze and brandished an accusing finger at him. "You!" she hissed.

"Drat, so close," he said to himself, staring at his foot which had just missed landing on the first step of the porch.

"You!" Leona hissed again.

Sam cleared his throat. "Me?"

"You dirty sodomite. This is your fault. Your filthy devil dog broke my Bashful."

"Broke your *what?*"

"My Bashful, you nitwit. My dwarf! My limited edition hand-painted Bavarian lawn dwarf!"

"Mrs. Weinberg," Sam started coolly. "I'm sure—"

"Oh shut up, shut up, you…dirty…buggerer!"

Sam couldn't help it. The archaic word sounded so bizarre coming from his buttoned up neighbor he burst out laughing.

"You think this is funny? You just wait. I'll have Animal Control on you. I'll have the law on your sinning behind. They'll shoot that mutt."

The front door banged open and Jake emerged from the foyer, still drying his hands on a dishtowel. "What the hell is going on?"

"Mrs. Weinberg thinks that Barnaby broke her lawn dwarf…er… Belchie."

"That's Bashful, you filthy queer!"

Sam's eyes shot over to Jake, filled with trepidation. His husband's malachite green eyes had gone flinty, his jaw set. "Jake," said Sam warningly. "Be careful."

"Okay, you buck-toothed old mummy, let me tell you something. My dog has been inside. *All day*. He hasn't set so much as a paw outside since two this afternoon when I took him down to Wilde Park for a walk—on his leash, no less! Even if he had been out in the yard, you'll note that the hideous chain link fence you have installed would have completely prevented him from entering your yard. Our yard is likewise fenced, though much more attractively, I'll add, for the express purpose of keeping him in. In short, no way in hell could Barnaby have gotten out and broken any of your gawdawful, garish, cheap looking lawn trash!"

"I—"

"Furthermore, if you utter another threatening word aimed at my husband or myself I will file a formal complaint against you for a hate crime. I'm sure you are aware you cannot hurl epithets like that at people these days, Mrs. Weinberg. It is a crime. I will also document that you threatened to shoot my dog."

"Actually, she said she'd have him shot."

"Don't correct me, Sam, I'm on a roll."

"I said no such thing!" Mrs. Weinberg protested.

There was no deterring Jake at this point. "I will also see to it that the *Arrow Bay Examiner* has a front page story on your threats and slurs, that the ASPCA is informed, and that KABW has gotten a full report on your hate-filled vocabulary. *Verbatim*. Is that the kind of publicity you wish to garner, Mrs. Weinberg, with an election coming up? Perhaps you'd like me to bring everything you've just done up at the city council meeting tonight?"

Leona Weinberg had flushed a deep shade of puce. Her mouth opened once and snapped shut. She seemed about to fly apart at the seams. "I'll get you, you filthy sodomite. You just wait."

"Go home, Mrs. Weinberg, before you do yourself any more harm."

She marched into her house, her heels clacking on the pavement like gunshots.

"I'm not sure you should have done that, Jake," said Sam, once the front door had slammed.

"Hateful old witch. It'd serve her right if something unpleasant happened to her. Like falling into a threshing machine."

Sam laughed. "You're terrible, you know that?"

Jake shrugged, the fury ebbing from his body. "Nah, just focused."

"You know what I love about you?" asked Sam as he shut the door behind them.

"Hmm? No, what?"

"Your uncanny ability to stay perfectly calm, cool, and collected under pressure."

"Oh ho ho, O'Conner. Go and get ready for dinner, you filthy sodomite."

❖

Arrow Bay's City Hall was the largest structure in town, built as part of a WPA project in 1935. The front façade of the art deco building was finished in gray slate, with a center structure of stacked, progressively smaller triangles over the glass and copper double-doors, ending in a pyramid with a copper top. Sam and Jake had always loved the building, and had spent many hours in the courtyard in front of the hall having lunch and admiring it.

"We'll probably be the only ones there," groused Jake. "Us and Gladys Nyberg with her trusty umbrella."

"If that's the case, I hope she gives old Reed Longhoffer a good smack with it," said Sam, watching the octogenarian hoof it into the building, his maroon fedora squashed on his head like a thimbleberry. Longhoffer was hardly alone heading into the hall. Streams of people were trickling in from the north parking lot in twos and threes.

"Something's up," said Sam.

"Hmm?"

"What is that you've got there?" asked Sam, seeing something in Jake's hand. "Is that a crossword puzzle?"

"No, it's not a crossword puzzle."

"Give it here."

"Aw, Sam."

"Give it here, Jacob," Sam insisted, holding out his hand.

Jake handed over a thin paperback book. Sam examined it, noting the brawny, bare-chested man on the cover, shirt ripped open, breeches riding so low that a tuft of public hair was revealed. Behind him, the bear of the animal sort stood roaring behind him, and at his feet a small, though no less hirsute man lay prone, in grave peril. Given the title, *Survival of the Fittest*, Sam had little doubt that not only would the man be saved, but that his gratitude would be shown in various tawdry ways.

"You brought porn to the town meeting?"

"*Erotica*, thank you. Okay, it's porn. But I needed *something* to keep me awake."

"Look around, Jake. You really think that's going to be a problem?"

"Okay, fine, I'll pay attention. You'll give me the book back after the meeting."

"I don't know," said Sam, glancing at the cover again before tucking it into his inside coat pocket. "They say smut ruins your mind."

"Says the man with the collection of Ursine Studios DVDs."

"Art films." Sam sniffed defensively.

"Oh look," said Jake, grinning. "It's Professor Mills. Professor?"

The willowy little man gave a jump, but smiled upon seeing Jake, pushing his glasses up his nose. "I'm so happy to see you here, Jake. Always good to take civic interest in the place you call home, particularly when an issue of this importance comes up."

"Er, yes," said Jake as they crossed the marble floor into the Town Council Chambers.

Sam and Jake's jaws dropped. The room was nearly full. The council members were already seated at their table. On the right, muttering to one another were Reed Longhoffer, editor of the *Examiner*, and Leona Weinberg, wearing an aqua silk dress and turban. Verna Monger, who was about fifteen years younger than Weinberg, was dressed in an eye-watering fuchsia blazer and black blouse. Her hair was teased up in a brown halo around her head, her mouth clamped shut in a tight screw of lipstick that matched her blazer.

On the other side of the long oak table were Walter Lugar, dressed in clean jeans and tweed blazer, Emma Kennedy, her long hair uncharacteristically pulled up, looking sharp in a no-nonsense blue shirt and vest, and Randy Burrows, whose jovial face was deep in concentration as he hooked up the live feed for KABW.

Jake, Sam, and Professor Mills found three seats in the fifth row just as Randy Burrows started testing the microphone. Chief Sanderson of the Arrow Bay Police Department strode over to the microphone and tapped it several times.

"Folks, the room is nearly at capacity and we're not letting any more in. I am sorry, but it's a violation of the fire code. Please take your seats."

Not taking a seat, Jake noted, was Baldo Ludich. A strikingly handsome man in his late fifties, Baldo stood over six feet tall. He had a thick head of iron gray hair and a beard the same color. His sharp dark brown eyes surveyed the room, few people able to meet such an intense gaze. Baldo looked as if he would be more at home commanding submarines or knocking out international criminals. Jake found himself hoping he aged as well as Ludich. Baldo was glaring at Reed Longhoffer, though Longhoffer seemed blissfully unaware.

"There's Marion Burd," said Sam, pointing out the elegant woman in the front row, a steno pad in her hand. She was chatting with Sam's mother Evelyn, who waved at them.

"And your mother," said Jake, waving back. "How's her teaching going?"

"Very well," said Sam, still looking around the room. "Good God, everyone is here but Crazy Gladys."

"Ha, you spoke too soon," said Jake, as Gladys Nyberg strode in with her infamous umbrella just as they closed the door.

"Who's the Rubenesque lady with the nice smile talking to Mom?" Sam asked.

"Oh...I think that's Reverend Crawford. She's the new pastor of the Unitarian Church. There was a small and unflattering photo of her in the paper. She's really much better looking in person."

"It was probably Jonas Brennan who took the photo," said Professor Mills. "He won't retire from the *Examiner,* even though he's eighty-one and has cataracts so badly he can't tell a buffalo from a shopping cart. Poor old man. He's really a sweet person."

"The *Examiner* could use an overhaul," said Sam.

"Particularly ditching its editor," said Jake.

"Reed shouldn't even have the job. After Jasper Longhoffer died, the paper was supposed to go the youngest son, David," wheezed Professor Mills. "But David is in Europe." He leaned in closer to Jake and Sam. "The rumor is Reed hasn't even told his brother their father is dead, though I find that hard to believe. David was always corresponding with Jasper, and I think the letters falling off would be a clue that something is wrong."

"You'd think," said Jake.

"There is going to be hell to pay when David comes back, you can count on it."

"And when might that be?"

Professor Mills shrugged. "Two months? Four? Who can say? Seems every time he's set to come back, something keeps him in Europe."

Jake was about to ask what kept David Longhoffer in Europe when brother Reed banged his gavel with such fierceness, it sounded like gunshots echoing through the chamber; Police Chief Sanderson involuntarily flinched and looked as if he was about to dive under the table.

The meeting was about to begin.

Chapter Five

"Order now! Order!" barked Longhoffer, his glasses sliding down his beaky nose. He continued banging the gavel a few more times even though the room had already become very quiet. He looked around the room with an expression of deepest loathing and cleared his throat. "We're gathered here today at this unnecessary special meeting—"

Emma Kennedy and Walter Lugar both looked as if they were about to say something, but Randy Burrows held up his hand, silencing them. Baldo Ludich smiled very smugly.

"He's up to something," Jake whispered to Sam, noting Ludich. "Just you wait."

"—on the issue of so-called Wilde Park. Now it is already a foregone conclusion that the land is to be developed."

"Only to you, Longhoffer," said Ludich in his booming, commanding voice, which was greeted with hearty applause.

"Now you just wait until you're recognized, Ludich. You've been warned about this type of behavior before!"

"So much for genteel politeness and working together," said Sam in a low voice.

"I'm afraid I agree with Mr. Ludich," said Walter Lugar. "It does seem to be a foregone conclusion *only* to you, Reed, and perhaps the council members to your left. Fully one half of this governing board has not been apprised of this plan for SuperLoMart to be built on Wilde Park, nor has the city attorney, which I confirmed this afternoon."

"And I confirmed this afternoon," said Emma Kennedy, as though she just bitten into a slug, "that preliminary contracts have already been signed with the company, by *you*, Mr. Longhoffer."

"And I might add today that there are now surveyor tags all over the park," said Randy Burrows, fiddling with a microphone.

"This is outrageous!" cried Baldo Ludich. "How dare you circumnavigate not only the city council, but the entire populace of Arrow Bay!"

The audience grew restless, a general discontented murmur rising. Miranda Zimmerman appeared to be looking through a document with great interest while Baldo Ludich had a piece of paper rolled in one fist. Longhoffer began banging the gavel loudly again.

"People, settle down! Be quiet!" he crowed, as the noise died down. "Now before you go off half-cocked, Miss Kennedy, what I signed was a confirmation that I had received a prospectus on SuperLoMart's plans for development. That is all. There has been no effort to deceive anyone—"

"Baloney!" yelled someone from the audience, to general approval.

A skinny man stood up and pointed an accusing finger at Reed Longhoffer. "What have you got to gain from this, Longhoffer?! You've never done a thing in your life unless it has had some personal benefit for you."

The crowd murmured as one again, significantly louder this time.

"Who was that?" Sam asked Jake.

"Milton Bloomquest Junior. His father was in some business dealings with Reed back in the 50s. Ended up getting the bad end of the deal and lost his shirt. Reed came out with a wheelbarrow full of money, and no one is quite sure how he did it," said Professor Mills.

"Professor Mills has done his homework," said Jake to Sam, impressed.

"This whole deal stinks!"

"People! *You must wait to be recognized!*"

A blonde, horse-faced woman with a prominent Adam's apple stood up, raising her hand.

"Uh oh," said Jake under his breath.

"Who is that?"

"Rebecca Windsor. She owns that new age shop on 35th. Thinks flashing colored lights at you can cure you of cancer, among other things. You know, it's got some stupid name…"

"'Heal Thy Self'."

"That's the place. She's totally wacko. I give her about thirty seconds before she mentions the devil."

"The devil? I thought you said she was a new age type?"

"Well, it's complicated."

"I, for one, am *for* the development of that piece of land," she said in a rather reedy voice, as she brushed her hair out of her face.

"This ought to be good," said Jake as several people made discontented noises.

"The council recognizes Miss Windsor," said Reed, seemingly happy to have found an ally.

"I have been to Wilde Park," she said. "It is a place of deceptive beauty. Many times have I felt an evil presence in that park. I have been stalked by it. I have seen the shadows that move, and I have looked at the tortured trees that grow there."

The room had become very quiet. The citizens, as a whole, had become mesmerized by the sheer absurdity of what they were hearing.

"It is my feeling—no—my *belief* that Wilde Park is inhabited by the devil."

"You owe me a nickel," whispered Jake.

"I don't actually recall betting."

"Miss Windsor," said Longhoffer, unable to hide the irritation in his voice. "Please—"

"It is my belief," she continued, cutting him off, "that this land would best be utilized for commercial purposes, so that people will not be harmed by the negative influence of the land and be driven to commit sordid acts of an unspeakable nature."

"What the hell does she mean by that?" whispered Longhoffer to Leona Weinberg, but the mic picked it up.

"Clearing the land will wipe the slate clean. It will purify it. It will make it whole again once I perform the cleansing ritual, which can be done quickly, efficiently, and relatively inexpensively."

Windsor's last statement was met with groans of disgust from the audience and several shouts for her to shut up. One man finally was able to get her to sit down when he shouted, "Pipe down, Moon Unit, we've got real problems here!" which was greeted with gales of laughter. Red-faced, Rebecca Windsor sat down.

"People!" shouted Leona Weinberg, standing up. "Let us not be intimidated by the far left that would have us believe that this land is anything other than worthless swamp. It is filled with the stench of decay and attracts drug abusers, alcoholics and," she said, looking directly at Sam and Jake, "perverts."

"Now that was uncalled for, truly that was," said Professor Mills to Jake, clearly flustered. "There was no doubt she was directing that at you two."

Longhoffer and Monger seemed oblivious, but Burrows, Kennedy, and Lugar were all staring at her open-mouthed. Kennedy looked furious and for a moment, Jake thought he saw the Reverend Crawford holding Evelyn O'Conner in her seat.

"Commerce," continued Leona, "is the cornerstone of our economy. It is the very foundation of which this nation is...founded...upon."

"How's that for articulate?" said Jake, not lowering his voice.

"Our Christian forefathers," Weinberg continued, glaring at Jake. "Used commerce to build the base on which our country now stands. Progress has always been the American way, from the expansion westward to the founding of our great industries that continue to employ us, feed us, make our families strong and independent, and keep us steadfast in our ongoing struggle to vanquish communism."

"You're joking, right?" said Walter Lugar, his bright green eyes incredulous. "SuperLoMart? Ninety-nine percent of their stock comes from China."

"And it is through the use of industry that America will topple communism, Mr. Lugar," replied Leona acidly.

"Our forefathers were deists, and furthermore, every example you gave came at the expense of the native populations and the environment. Dinosaurs like you are ruining this planet and choking us off with your greenhouse gasses," yelled a familiar voice from the back of the room.

Sam and Jake looked at each other and said in unison, "Alex."

"That's fine coming from you, Mr. Blackburn, given what you've done with *your* property," said Leona Weinberg.

Alex strode into the aisle and instantly all eyes were upon him. He was wearing a black leather car coat, maroon sweater, and very tight fitting jeans. Jake figured Alex could have been reciting the phone book and elicited the same rapt attention of the audience.

"Well, Madam Council, that is part of the answer there. *My* property. Wilde Park is not privately held property, It is entrusted to the city. Secondly, the development of my land has actually restored five acres of wetland and salmon habitat. The *Chinook* is a non-invasive addition to the environment and the area reserved for parking has added fifty trees and cleaned up some of the most contaminated ground in Arrow Bay."

There were murmurs of approval all around. Miranda Zimmerman giving Alex a somewhat bemused look before returning to her note taking.

"I'd be a hypocrite if I said I wasn't for commerce," said Alex, once again taking command over the audience. "But exercised correctly, with the proper permitting, public input," he paused, looking at Jake and Alex, winking, "and of course submitting to the State and County environmental review process. And on that note, I'll let Mr. Ludich take over."

"He isn't recognized!" shouted Reed Longhoffer. "And neither were you!"

"I recognize Baldo Ludich," said Emma Kennedy, her voice booming over the hall.

Jake was once again in awe that such a powerful voice could come from a woman of such slight stature and build. "This ought to be good, if Alex had a hand in it," said Jake to Sam.

"Thank you, Madam Council," said Baldo, bowing toward Emma. "I have here in my hand an injunction filed this afternoon against the half of the city council that has tried to bulldoze—er—if you'll pardon the expression—this illicit land transfer through improper channels."

"You can't do that!" shouted Reed, turning crimson.

"I can, Longhoffer. It's been done."

"You conniving fat wop!" Reed shouted.

Pandemonium broke out in the hall. Ludich's grandmother, Angela Donatello, had been one of the town founders. Angry shouts began filling the air as Alex rushed forward to hold Baldo back. Reed Longhoffer sat back looking pale. In addition to Ludich, a good portion of Arrow Bay's population were of Italian descent. The gravity of his racist outburst seemed to have suddenly dawned on him.

"He's going to get tarred and feathered," said Jake, as Professor Mills stood up and moved toward the front of the room.

Alex had subdued Ludich, and Longhoffer had begun banging his gavel on the table to quell the muted roar that was echoing through the chamber. Tiny Professor Mills made his way through the uneasy crowd to the front of the room and demurely raised his hand. At first, no one recognized him, then Randy Burrows's deep and sultry DJ's voice thundered over the room, "The Council recognizes Professor Grover Mills!"

Suddenly the room had become quiet. The crowd has turned its attention to the balding, diminutive man holding his green tweed hat.

"Good citizens of Arrow Bay," he began. "I have only been among your ranks for just over a year, yet I feel very entrenched in this community. I know many of you from the classes I teach at the senior center, the lectures at the library, or the readings on Wednesday nights at the Arrow Bay Book Club. Many of you I now have the honor of calling 'friend.'

"I came to Arrow Bay, not out of need or necessity, but by *choice*. And I chose this city because it still represented to me the ideal things an American city should be—a close-knit, tidy, beautiful community with a rich and vibrant downtown core, unsullied by the soulless face of corporate America," he said, pausing for a moment.

"Laying it on bit thick, isn't he?" whispered Jake to Sam.

"Don't be such a cynic," said Sam.

"In this town, you can still get fresh baked, homemade pastries and chocolates. You can still shop in bookstores that stock the shelves with local authors. You can go into stores where people know your name and will help you with your special needs.

"I'm not against commerce. I am against *faceless* commerce. Moreover, I am against changing the character of a city that still *embraces* nature rather than shuns it. We are surrounded by and have incorporated into our city greenbelts, hiking trails, bike paths, waterfront parks, streams, lakes, estuaries, and marshes. We have created a symbiotic relationship with nature and wildlife, constructed a unique city, unlike anything else in this part of the state. We have become a model for other communities in Washington, the envy of many other cities who are now scrambling to try to make their neighborhood as lush and verdant as ours. Yet here we stand on the threshold of throwing it all away, for the sake of being able to save ten cents on a can of beans."

Jake appreciated what it must have been like to having studied under Professor Mills or to have sat in on one of his lectures. The entire hall seemed mesmerized by his words. Everything the professor was saying was undeniably true, and Jake regretted complaining about not being able to pick up a pair of socks when he needed them.

"Wilde Park is much more than a strip of land. It is a teeming, vibrant marshland, filled with over thirty species of birds and innumerable aquatic life. It provides a place to walk our pets, rest our minds and just appreciate the world we live in. It provides fields for our children to play sports in, at a time when there is a growing obesity epidemic in this country—and all a stone's throw away from downtown," he said, taking out a blue handkerchief and dabbing his nose before turning and looking around the room. "To lose it to SuperLoMart would be to cut the very heart of this city out and throw it to uncaring, impersonal capitalist mongrel dogs. We must not let our city become yet another faceless strip mall on the way to somewhere else. Let us not forget the fact that the Sky to Sea Trail is nearing completion. This magnificent network of trails for bicyclists, runners, walkers, nature enthusiasts, bird watchers, fishermen, and even in certain areas hunters will soon circle our city like a golden ring. The trail begins—and ends—in Wilde Park. Have we not worked for a decade to get this trail system complete for the benefit of all? And yet here we stand, about to make sure that the trail—which you have fought for, worked and sweated on for ten years—is about to end. After all this will it terminate at a SuperLoMart parking lot? Is that the legacy this city wants to leave its citizens? I humbly submit that it is not." Professor Mills sighed and took a small bow. "Thank you."

The applause was thunderous. Kennedy, Burrows, and Lugar were all beaming at Professor Mills but Longhoffer, Monger, and Weinberg were all scowling. Reed Longhoffer began banging his gavel down until the head snapped off. Grunting in disgust, he threw it on the floor, picked up his hat, smashed it on his head and started to get up to leave. Leona Weinberg grabbed him by the shoulder and started gesturing at him to sit down.

Then, over his microphone, which was still on, Reed said, "Oh, just shut it, Leona. That dirty dago bastard has us over a barrel and these slack-jawed yokels are too stupid to realize they're ruining everything. It's over."

The applause had died down, and now there were several murmurs of outrage. Walter Lugar shouted, "Longhoffer, you're out of line!"

"Stuff it, Walter," snapped Reed, this time storming out the door, the crowd still muttering loudly.

Randy Burrows took the opportunity to seize command of the meeting by leaning into the microphone and belting out, "Quiet, please!"

The crowd, still restless, finally quieted down.

"I move we table the proposal indefinitely in light of public opposition and dubious legality," said Walter Lugar.

"Second," said Emma Kennedy.

"You can't do that without the full council!" yelled Leona Weinberg.

"We certainly can. Reed has cast his vote already," said Walter.

"He has not!"

"Miranda, could you please read back what Mr. Longhoffer had to say about the situation just prior to his leaving. Er, the very last bit. I don't think we need to go over the other."

"'It's over?'" replied Miranda Zimmerman with a wry smile.

"That sounds like he conceded defeat to me. In light of the injunction and the fact that you have no clear title to the land, I'd say tabling the idea is the least of your worries right now."

"What is that, some sort of threat?" snapped Leona.

"I'd say so, as I fully intend to file corruption charges against you and Reed Longhoffer for trying to develop land that is in the public trust," said Walter.

"You goat-herding pot-licker!"

This time the crowd genuinely gasped.

"Now see here, Leona, we don't need that kind of talk here," said Chief Sanderson.

"What do I care what you think? You," she hissed, pointing at Sanderson, then stabbing her finger at the crowd, then directly at Reverend Crawford, "and you and you. Letting this town be overrun by disgusting perverts. I've seen that flag you fly in front of your church. I know what it means. You're condoning sodomy, and I won't stand for it. I'll see you're all run out of town." She wheeled around on Chief Sanderson. "And you too. You're allowing this town to become the next Sodom and Gomorrah. I will not stand for it. I will not!"

Sanderson, completely bewildered said, "What in God's name are you talking about?"

"As if you didn't know!" bellowed Leona, rounding on Crawford, about to spout something else, but the good reverend cut her off.

"I wouldn't be casting stones if I were you, Leona. You're liable to find yourself under a whole rock pile," warned Reverend Crawford.

"To hell with you all," she shouted, and with that, she was gone.

"Someone ought to drop a house on her," remarked Randy Burrows under his breath. "Ladies, gentleman, please, some order? Thank you. Okay then we have it settled…er, any objection, Verna?"

The last town council Republican shook her head.

"Good, good. Okay, we hereby officially close the book on Wilde Park. No bulldozers will be getting near it. That said, I would like to please enlist the help of our intrepid librarian to find out what *exactly* is the legal scoop on the park so something like this can't happen again. Agreed?" asked Burrows.

All council members all agreed.

"Well," said Jake with a satisfied smile. "So much for that."

Chapter Six

"Now, before we adjourn for the night, I believe you had an announcement, Chief Sanderson?"

"There you go, jumping the gun again," Sam said to Jake.

"I didn't think it could get any better than that," Jake replied. "How do you cap knocking Reed Longhoffer from his little pedestal at the top of the dung heap?"

"Shh," said Sam.

"Er, yes, thank you, Councilman Burrows," said Chief Sanderson.

Chief Sanderson, a handsome man in his late fifties with slate gray hair and a burly moustache, took Reed Longhoffer's empty chair. His moustache twitched for a moment or two as he pulled a small piece of paper out from the front pocket of his starched blue uniform. He looked at it and frowned, pawing at the front of his jacket. "Forgot my damn reading glasses," he muttered to himself. He sighed and said, "I am here tonight to inform you that a convicted felon is moving into the city."

Muted gasps of astonishment came from the crowd, and the dismay was palpable.

"I was wrong. This night just gets better and better," Jake said.

"Thirty years ago there was…an unhappy circumstance leading to the conviction of one Misty Snipes. She's been released after serving her twenty-five year sentence."

More murmurs from the crowd.

"Normally we don't inform the general public when a person is released. You serve your time, you pay your debt to society, and you're square with the law. Miss Snipes is a bit of an exception, and the State

Department of Corrections has asked us to relate the information to the population of Arrow Bay."

"Why?" asked Rebecca Windsor. "What has she done that required the Department of Corrections to notify us?"

"I'm not at liberty to give any details..." started Chief Sanderson.

The crowd erupted into a chorus of groans. Even Jake shook his head at the remark.

"You mean to tell me that you have to inform us that we have a felon moving into the area but you can't say *what* she was convicted of? What kind of crock of BS is that?" shouted George Mayhew, owner of Arrow Bay Antiques.

"Yeah!" shouted Marilyn Sandy. "How are we supposed to know what to look for or protect ourselves from if we don't know what she did?"

"Did she kill someone? Did she blow things up? Was she one of those crazy dames who kill their kids because she's got post-modern depression?" asked fisherman Clint Shimmell.

"That's post*partum* depression, you idiot!" barked Trudy Mundy, one of the customs agents Jake recognized from the Arrow Bay ferry dock.

"I remember that name!" yelled Rebecca Windsor. "She was a devil-worshipping cannibal in Seattle. She cooked and ate kids from the local elementary school!"

Pandemonium. Randy Burrows engineered an eardrum-bursting bit of feedback on the speakers to get people to calm down. Finally, when some semblance of order regained, Chief Sanderson said abruptly, "She did not cook or eat any children. She was involved in a crime that left her—"

"Child molester," cried Marilyn Sandy. "You've let a child molester into our midst. That's the only reason they inform the public. She's some sick, twisted, child-molesting monster."

A handsome young man Jake recognized as a detective with the Arrow Bay Police Department from the incident on the *Elwha* the previous year leaned in and said just audibly saying by those close enough to the stage, "You're losing 'em, boss."

"Who's that?" asked Sam, also taking note of the dark haired, dark-eyed, powerfully built man on the stage.

"He's a detective with Arrow Bay," Jake replied. "I spoke to him briefly on the *Elwha* last year when the whole Susan Crane thing happened," Jake said, not wanting to remember it. He pulled up the mental file cabinet of his eidetic memory and came up with the name. "Haggerty was his name."

"Folks," said Chief Sanderson in desperation, "All I can tell you is she is not a danger."

"Then *why* are you telling us about her?" demanded George Mayhew.

"That seems to be a valid question," remarked Sam, thoughtfully stroking his beard.

Chief Sanderson was not able to control his temper. "Listen, people. Miss Snipes has been paroled. She is currently under surveillance and is wearing an ankle bracelet to track her movements at all times—"

"Oh, let's get out of here. If I hear Rebecca Windsor say one more thing about the devil, I'm going to shove a crystal up her nose."

Sam pretended to be appalled at such a remark as they got up to leave. They stepped into the cool October air, the wind swirling around them. Behind them, the meeting was breaking up, as people were filing out of City Hall behind them.

❖

"I wonder what she *did* do?" asked Jake.

"Hmm? Oh. Snipes?"

"Well, why *would* they bring her up unless she *is* a child molester? Seems somewhat odd. I can't remember any other time they've ever mentioned anyone *else* being paroled in Arrow Bay."

"It is weird," Sam replied. "I can't either. Kind of a waste of time. I mean, it looks like the Wilde Park issue has been settled."

"It was worth it to see old Longhoffer's face when Baldo Ludich waved that injunction at him," remarked Jake. "What a nice shade of crimson. Just about matched that stupid hat he always wears."

"Did you see the way Leona singled us out when she said 'perverts'?"

"Hard not to," Jake noted gravely.

"I didn't like that."

"Neither did I. I'm not going to worry about it. I meant everything I said this afternoon."

"I know you did," said Sam. "She might consider that threatening her."

"It was a threat, Sam. I'm not going to have my character impugned by some dried up, conservative Christian prune," said Jake. "That old bat deserves everything that happens to her. Like being run over by an armored truck, for example," said Jake a little too loudly as they got back to his PT Cruiser. He noticed the handsome, goateed Detective Haggerty and nodded to him. The man nodded back.

"I don't *really* wish any harm to the old battle axe," said Jake as he started up the Cruiser and pulled out of the parking lot. "I'm just venting here."

"I know that, Tiger," said Sam, tousling Jake's hair. "You're not in the habit of punching out old ladies no matter how nasty they are."

"I just don't appreciate her antics. We've lived in that house for nearly ten years and for her to get outraged by a gay couple living there is seems a bit like…"

"Politics," finished Sam.

"Precisely."

A silence fell between them as Jake turned onto High Street. The first fat drops of rain slapped the windshield, and as a shower of the Crenshaw's maple leaves drifted past them in the wind, they pulled into their driveway. Jake glanced over Leona's, which was still dark. She wasn't home from the meeting yet.

"Going to work a little before bed?" Jake asked.

"Well, I should try to get the office a little more useable. I'm still not sure about using the mother-in-law apartment for an office. It seems such a waste of space."

"Okay. I have a few things I can catch up on," said Jake, thinking he might go downstairs and try to write for a while.

Sam smiled. "Okay. Make it an hour and a half. Meet you in bed at say 10:30."

"You're on."

Jake watched Sam cross the garage to the door that opened onto the stairs leading up to the office. While Sam clunked up the stairs, Jake shut the garage door, slipping out the side door of the garage and down the small path to the back stoop and kitchen door. He stopped for a moment to admire the Japanese maple growing next to the stoop that Professor

Mills had given him as a homecoming present for Sam the year before. Mills had hauled it out to the car himself, surprising both Jake and Alex.

Jake popped the door open and Barnaby trotted out as soon as he came in. Frowning, Jake stepped through the kitchen and into the dining room, listening for the television. Hearing nothing, he crossed the foyer into the living room, which had one lamp lit. His brother was not there. Jake wondered where Jason was for a moment before heading down to the basement. He was a little concerned about his brother. It wasn't Jason's lack of employment that was bugging him—it was that Jason seemed so depressed lately. He wondered how much the debacle around Jennifer, Jason's ex, had to do with it. Everything, he suspected.

He brought up a blank document in Word but found he was unable to write anything. Instead, he put Moby's *Hotel* into the CD player and turned it up. He didn't even hear Sam come down into the basement. When Sam tapped Jake on the shoulder, Jake nearly jumped through the floorboards above his head.

"Sweet zombie Jesus!"

"I'm sorry, Jake."

"It's okay, it's okay. You took maybe one, two years off my life, tops."

"I wish you wouldn't say that," said Sam.

"Huh? Zombie Jesus. I got that from *Futurama*," said Jake.

"Not that," said Sam, slumping into the chair opposite of Jake. "Although it is a bit disrespectful. I suspect that's the lapsed Catholic in me talking."

"You still miss it, don't you?"

"I miss the ritual. The smell of the incense, lighting candles. Christmas mass." Sam shrugged. "I *don't* miss the confessional."

"And what you had to confess, having it off with the school custodian who was ten years older than you."

"And hot, I might add," Sam said. "I never did confess that. Old Father Malone would have castrated me."

"I guess that's why I don't understand why you miss it. Given it is a religion that wants no part of you. I understand following the teachings of Christ—zombie Jesus comment aside—but look at what so many people do in his name. Our happy neighbor for instance. Leona Weinberg would joyfully have the two of us roasting on a spit all in the name of Jesus Christ."

"It's hard for me to explain," Sam acknowledged. "No one should feel more resentful of it than I. All the times…all the times my father beat me with that belt until my skin was raw—bleeding sometimes—telling me to keep my eyes on that damn crucifix and know I was being punished for my sins. That Jesus ordered him to punish me."

"Your father was a drunken, sadistic bastard. And probably nuts."

Sam gave Jake a wry smile. "Only on days ending with 'y,' as the saying goes. I remember with utter joy the day Mom renounced the faith she'd married into, burning Pop's rosary, his Bible and that hideous crucifix. I stared at them until they turned to ash." He shook his head. "What's bugging you?"

"What makes you think something is bugging me?"

"For one, your gaze went right to the floor, which means you're trying to conceal the truth and, as usual, failing miserably. Also, your hair, which needs trimming by the way, is brushed back from your forehead, meaning you've been nervously running your hands through it since you've been down here. What's wrong?" he asked gently.

"Oh, I'm just worried about Jason. And then there is this," he said handing the letter from Tony to Sam.

"So he'd like to come and visit," Sam said.

"You don't sound thrilled."

"Well, he *is* an ex-boyfriend."

"Gavin Ashworth is an ex as well, and you two are best friends," Jake pointed out. "He's stayed with us—both when he was single and after he and Jeff met."

"Gavin's an exception. He's a stellar human being, he and Jeff both. Besides, you weren't in love with Gavin. You just were great friends who happened to click in a sexual way, too. The classic 'friends with benefits.'"

"And what benefits," sighed Jake, feigning a wistful expression.

"Can it, Norma Desmond, this is not your close up," Sam said with a chuckle and ruffling Jake's hair again. "The point remains the same. You weren't in love with Gavin."

"True. Although I do love Gavin—and Jeff, too—but I wasn't *in* love with him. God knows I wasn't in love with Tony," Jake said.

"So why are you still angry with him?"

"Because!" Jake exclaimed. "Because the one person who should have been there to give me some support ditched me right when I needed him the most."

"Rachel was there," Sam pointed out.

"It wasn't the same," Jake said. "Rachel had her own grief to go through...and she..."

"She wasn't a young gay man."

"You needed the love and support of...well, family for lack of a better word. Because you *did* love Chris."

Jake nodded, blinking back tears. "He was my best friend, Sam. Of course I did."

Sam sighed. "Let's go upstairs."

"Kitchen?"

"Upstairs. Bed. Now."

Sam led Jake upstairs. They closed the door and in the semi-darkness gently undressed one another, then slid into bed.

Chapter Seven

An hour later, freshly showered and wearing pajama bottoms, Jake sat on the edge of the bed, looking distraught. Sam watched with appreciation at the way Jake's six-pack abs bulged prominently as he hunched over.

"Brr. Budge up," Jake said, sliding under the covers and curling up next to Sam. "You're nice and warm."

"I believe they call that afterglow."

"Well, it's nice. This house is bloody cold tonight."

"Wind has shifted. Something's in the air out there," said Sam distantly. He looked out the window at the shifting branches of the Crenshaws' maple trees illuminated in the streetlight as the wind unburdened them of another bucket of golden leaves. Sam would have been annoyed with the trees as well, were it not for the fact that the leaves made for such great mulch.

"What are you thinking of?"

"Mulch," replied Sam. "But you said you were worried about Jason earlier. And I can see you still are. Is it because of the unemployment thing?"

"Nah, I don't care about that," Jake said. "Jason's been keeping the house neat as a pin and throwing in money when he can. He just seems depressed. Finnigans and depression are not a good combination."

"What else?"

"Even though it has been a year I'm still having a hard time reconciling the New Improved Action-Adventure-Jason with the Old-Stick-in-the-Mud version I grew up with."

"Having the rug yanked out from under you by your ex will do that," Sam said. "Especially one who's a sociopath. I know firsthand. I wasn't the same person after Tom."

"Yeah, but…Tom…"

"Beat the shit out of me," finished Sam, uncharacteristically cursing. "While I don't know what it was Jennifer did to J.D., the psychic damage seems to be similar. Abuse is abuse. I recognize that haunted look."

"Which is why I haven't pressed him on the issue."

"I went through a tremendous amount of depression after Tom finally got sent to prison. I felt guilty because I hadn't been able to stop him from killing that man," Sam said. "Survivor's guilt, I guess."

"It wasn't your fault. You'd been gone all of what? Three days when he got into that bar fight? I'm very sorry for the guy he killed even though, according to everything you told me, he was a low-life scum much as Tom was, but I'm happy you didn't have to testify against him. The hell that would have put you through."

"I'd have happily done it to see him sent away."

"Point being, Jason is having to totally refurbish his life. It's not something that happens overnight," said Sam sagely. "You could try *talking* to him."

"I know. I should. I've been distracted myself lately," he said. "Not to mention things have been going so well between us after the Jennifer debacle, that I'm a little afraid if I jump right in and say what the fu—"

"Ahem."

"—heck, it might screw things up again."

"Understandable, but probably unwarranted."

"And then Fathead Tony's letter shows up." He shifted in bed. "You noted the repeated reference to my mother, didn't you?"

"As typical, Ingrid is closer with someone else's children other than her own," Sam said, shaking his head. "I suspect you're not too keen on her telegraphing the details of your life to the illustrious Doctor Graham, either."

"You took the words right out of my mouth. It's not as if I even tell *her* that much, anyway, but I'm intending to bring that up to her when she arrives in two weeks."

"Oh, God," said Sam. "I'd totally forgotten about that. Old Lady Weinberg's hissy fit pushed that bit of unpleasantness out of my mind."

"Sorry," Jake said. "I just wish I knew what the hell was going on."

"With Jason?"

"With my mother. Well, both. Mostly Mom, though. You know how she is. For her to come up here means somewhere in the family there is a full-fledged disaster going on."

"On the plus side it doesn't involve you or Jason," said Sam. "Especially after that...how did she put it? 'Embarrassing incident on Jacob's ferry?'"

"Leave it to my mother to be embarrassed by me finding a corpse in the trunk of a car on the boat I was working on. As if I had mooned her bridge club."

"She has a bridge club?"

"You know what I mean."

"Have I ever mentioned how much I appreciate the fact that both you and Jason take after your father?"

"Repeatedly. Trust me, so do I."

"Back to Tony."

"Ugh. Must we?"

"You have to admit, it's interesting reading, particularly about the Stud Studios stuff," Sam said with a dry chuckle.

"Yes, I thought that might intrigue you."

"Did you look up the website to see if you could find him?"

"Come on, wouldn't you have?"

"Well...yes, I admit I would."

"In any event, I couldn't find a thing. He must have paid them to pull the stuff after he became the big spokesman for gay rights. Harder to be taken seriously when you've done porn, I expect, although that really shouldn't matter, should it?"

"You're opening a large can of political worms with that, kiddo. *Should* it matter? In my book, no. Would it be fodder for the religious right in this country? Absolutely."

"As usual with him, it's jump in with both feet first and think of the consequences later," said Jake. "That's how he blew his knee out on the football field, after all."

"You don't sound surprised he did porn. Or at least posed for some erotic photos."

"I'd be surprised if that was *all* he did. And, no, I'm not surprised. He *is* handsome. You've seen him. He's also vain, narcissistic, arrogant, and self-centered. Chris's nickname for him was the 'Fathead Adonis.'

Doing photos or films for Stud Studios would appeal to his ego." Jake thought for a moment. "He probably bought up the stock and watches himself."

Sam laughed and said, "Oh come on! He can't be that bad."

"Just you wait," Jake replied, and after a moment, laughed as well. "Hmm?"

"Oh, if only Chris were around to hear that. My God, what a field day he would have had."

Sam grinned at Jake. "I don't doubt it."

In tandem, they closed their eyes and listened to the rain outside.

"I love that sound. Rain on the roof when you're all snuggled up and safe," said Sam.

"Especially since it no longer leaks."

"You are familiar with the term wet blanket, Tiger?"

"Sorry, sorry."

"That's better."

"Speaking of safe," Jake said, "do you really think Wilde Park is going to be safe from Reed and Leona and company?"

"Odds are pretty good, with that injunction. And Verna Monger buckled. I didn't see *that* coming. Maybe she has half a brain after all."

"Only half, if that."

He heard the front door bang open as Jason let himself in. Footsteps crossed into the kitchen where they stopped.

"Jason's home," said Sam.

"I'm too tired to talk to him now. And too comfortable."

"Not to mention naked and pink with afterglow," said Sam through a yawn. "And Jake?"

"Yes, Sam?"

"Shut up and go to sleep, will you? Oh, and I love you."

"I love you too, but you might have said that first."

"It's been a decade. I like to keep you guessing."

"G'night, Sam."

"G'night, Jake."

Midnight faded into the witching hour, and Jake finally drifted to sleep. Only the slight rumblings from his brother moving around in his bedroom below disturbed the silence.

❖

October wound its way down toward November languidly, with an uncharacteristic stretch of sunny, warm weather in the mid-sixties. The wind remained light, but just strong enough to continue the shower of leaves from the Crenshaw maples over the Finnigan-O'Conner yard as well as Leona Weinberg's.

Neither Jake nor Sam had spotted Weinberg in the days following the dramatic showdown at the town meeting. The next edition of the *Examiner*, had not only failed to note the spate of racist remarks from two of the council members, but didn't mention the meeting at all. Jake was flabbergasted until Sam had pointed out that as editor, Reed Longhoffer could kill any story he wished, which was what had happened. Sam had made some calls and had a lengthy discussion with Marion Burd. Longhoffer had gone in just before press time with a completely new front page and story of his own, which he'd attributed to Burd. Burd, furious, had walked out—taking the rest of the staff with her. For the moment, Arrow Bay was without a newspaper, as the *Examiner* had shut down. Reed Longhoffer was investigating his legal options to see if he could force his staff back to work.

No one, to Jake's knowledge, had been able to dig up anything on Misty Snipes or her alleged crimes. Jake's searches on the Internet had turned up nothing more than volleyball scores from a high school back east and mention of a Misty Snipes as a bridesmaid in the *Fayetteville Observer*. Jake quickly lost interest, his concern more focused on his brother and the plans he and Sam were drawing up for the backyard, now that the Sky to Sea trail was nearly completed.

The long used, but never officially named trail to Smith's Pond had been behind their fence for decades. Now part of the Sky to Sea Trail, over the summer the path had been widened, repaired and graveled to be ready for use by both walkers and bicyclists alike. After their section of the trail had been refurbished, both Sam and Jake had noticed the traffic beyond the fence had dramatically increased. Neither one objected to it, but they both treasured their privacy.

Sam called Ayer's Fencing mid-week and had them construct a new fence with a stone foundation and cedar top that cut off any view of the trail. They had also run the new fence along Leona's backyard, blocking it from view. Curiously, the old woman hadn't come out to raise fresh hell about the installation of the fence. This had surprised Jake and rendered him deeply suspicious. He suspected Leona Weinberg was plotting something.

Jake and Sam had debated about rebuilding the fence between their house and the Simonton's as the existing fence wasn't high enough to block out the Simontons' nude hot tub sessions, which took place at any time of the day or night year round. Jake and Sam genuinely liked Mr. and Mrs. Simonton despite their proclivity for nudism and did not want to offend them by suddenly building a new high fence. They had almost gotten used to seeing the elderly couple in the buff.

The new fence highlighted the fact that the backyard was woefully in need of landscaping. After making some sketches, the pair had resolved to put in the rhododendron garden as soon as spring arrived.

Jake found himself doodling at his desk instead of writing. His notebook was filling up with sketches and plant names instead of prose. He was happy he had something else to channel his energy into so as not to bulk up with the weight lifting and end up resembling a short, peach-colored Incredible Hulk.

Jake still had not talked to Jason, although he would try to make an effort to do as soon. Jason was suddenly acting furtive and up to something. Jake didn't think it was anything bad. His brother's mood had elevated suddenly, which Jake was happy to see, so he knew something had changed. As soon as the time was right, he'd ask.

❖

As the weekend approached, Jake noticed Sam suddenly became accident-prone. Tuesday, he'd found Sam with a bandage around his hand. Sam said he'd burned himself on the electric kettle while making tea. Wednesday found him with a cut over his eye where he'd clubbed himself on an overhanging cupboard door in the kitchen of his office. Thursday, Sam scared the hell out of Jake when he'd fallen down the porch steps.

"What's with you, anyway?" Jake had asked once he'd made sure he was all right.

Sam had muttered something incomprehensible, then wandered back to his office.

Friday morning, while Jake was eating a raisin cinnamon English muffin and chatting with his brother over coffee, an unholy crash echoed down from Sam's office. Jake and Jason ran out the kitchen door and up the back steps to the office where they found Sam partially under his file cabinet.

"Are you okay?" Jake asked, exasperated. He could tell by looking at Sam that he'd suffered no damage.

Jason scratched his bearded chin. "You've had your share of accidents this week."

A light went on in Jake's head. "I know what it is," he said, snapping his fingers. "It's Mom, isn't it?"

Sam looked sheepishly at the Finnigan brothers. "No, of course not."

"Samuel Patrick O'Conner, you're a lousy liar," said Jake, yanking Sam to his feet.

"It's not your mother *per se*."

"It's the way she delivers news," agreed Jason, looking out the window of Sam's office. An unusual number of crows had gathered around the side kitchen door. "Like Castle Bravo test at Bikini Atoll."

"Exactly. Your mother hasn't been up here in months. The last time she was here, she dropped the bomb about your Aunt Hattie."

"Aunt Harriet," said Jake uneasily, a building sense of dread developing in the pit of his stomach. He knew Sam was right.

"Whatever. The result was the same. Aunt Harriet was hauled away to the local basket weaving academy."

"It was a rest home."

"Yes, the kind with bars on the windows and padded cells," cracked Jason.

"She needed a rest," said Jake.

"I would too if I had attacked Uncle George with a pair of pruning shears," Jason replied. He began counting the crows next door. "What do you call a big group of crows? It's not a flock, I know that…"

"The time before that, she came up here to let you know your aunt's house burned down," Sam said.

"I know, I know. At least they were insured."

"A clutch?" Jason said. "No, that's chickens, I think."

"And before that, it was to let you know that no fewer than five of your cousins in California had died at Easter dinner having consumed a lethal pot of clam chowder," Sam reminded him. He turned to Jason and said, "It's a murder of crows, Jason."

"Bad clams can happen to anyone. And they were second cousins. Not that it makes it any better."

"Admit it, Jake, when it comes to news our mother is a one woman broadcast network of gloom and despair. You should have seen some of the emails I got when I was in San Francisco. 'Your father cut his toe off with the lawnmower, your cat got run over by the mailman, the transmission fell out of my car, Grandma put too much nutmeg in the muffins and ended up in the hospital, Amy thinks she's pregnant, your brother found a dead body on the ferry...'"

"Why doesn't she ever give any warning over the phone?" Jake grumbled.

"She likes giving the personal touch," replied Jason. "What's with all the crows at Weinberg's house anyway?"

"So you see why I am dreading Sunday's brunch," said Sam.

Jake hugged him. "There's no need to beat yourself up about it, goofus."

"If I was still a Catholic, I'd be down at Saint Sebastian's lighting candles and saying a few prayers."

"How about a rite of exorcism?"

"Jason," Jake chided, but he was happy to hear a comment that sounded more like the old Jason. "I don't know what she could possibly impart this time, save that Amy really is pregnant."

"Maybe she and Dad have finally decided to get a divorce," said Jason hopefully.

"That's cheerful," said Sam, massaging his elbow.

"It would be," agreed Jake, knowing that his parent's marriage was like something out of a David Lynch film. "Or Grace Metalious," he said aloud.

"You've lost me, Tiger," said Sam.

Jake rolled his eyes and said, "Amy. You know the backstory there. That happy Thanksgiving when Mom's little...indiscretion came to light."

"You mean when we kamikazed her with the truth," said Jason. "I don't care if there were financial considerations—it's been damned unfair to Dad."

"Dad's been a fully participating member of the little charade," Jake pointed out. "Still, with the other party dead, maybe they *can* get a divorce finally." He considered a moment. "Or maybe Amy *is* pregnant.

If she's as capricious with her birth control methods as she is picking a subject to major in, anything's possible."

"Ugh, what a thought," said Jason, turning away from the window. "Little Hector Suggs clones everywhere, writing odes to Galileo thermometers."

"Gruesome," Jake agreed, and all three laughed.

"We'll just have to handle whatever Hurricane Ingrid throws our way. We've managed before. At least we know *we're* okay, other than our accident prone lug here. And that there is solidarity in numbers. When you get done with work tonight I'd like to go over some ideas for the garden."

"I'll be unscathed, I assure you. And that sounds good. I'd like to go over them too."

"Can I trust you not to kill yourself for the next few hours?" asked Jake.

Sam blew a raspberry at Jake, making Jason laugh. "No. Let's go back to the house."

"Well," said Jason as they stepped out of the garage apartment. "We've also got a formidable weapon against dear old Mum. I've actually got good news."

Chapter Eight

"Well, don't just keep us in suspense, J.D.," said Sam. "Spill it!"

"The photographer at the *Examiner* is about to retire. Well, being forced to retire, more like. Apparently, he took some photos of what he thought were people but were actually a few fence posts."

"Professor Mills did mention something about their photographer being elderly with thick cataracts," Jake acknowledged.

"And he's a little around the bend too, poor old guy. He's nearly ninety, though, so he's entitled," Jason said. "Anyway, the *Examiner* is finally making the jump over to digital and they need someone who knows the ins and outs, so to speak. Derek told me about it. 'Course I'll have to wait until the staff comes back first, but I've got the job."

"That's great!" said Jake.

"The *Examiner* can use your talent, Jason."

"Thanks, Sam." I'll be out of your hair in no time—though with a bit of a caveat. Local newspapers are in trouble these days, and the *Examiner* is no different. It might be a short gig."

"You're not in our hair," Jake said. "It's been great having you here, and I'll remain cautiously optimistic that the *Examiner* can survive. Even with its pedestrian crossword."

"He's all heart, your brother," Sam said, rolling his eyes. "But he is right about you being here. Especially since you clean the bathroom better than he does."

"He who doesn't like the way I clean the bathroom can clean it himself."

"I appreciate it, I really do. I'm just happy I was picking up enough freelance work to keep things going…I was also, well…testing the waters, you might say," said Jason.

• 63 •

"How?" Jake said.

"You've both displayed the patience of a saint, you two. I haven't been exactly forthcoming on what happened in San Francisco."

"We both kind of figured a bad break-up," said Sam.

Jason sighed heavily. He stared at the ground for a moment, then took a deep breath and looked his brother in the eye. "Can we sit down?"

"Sure," said Jake, motioning to the porch steps. Sam sat in front of the two brothers, leaning back on Jake's legs.

They sat down, the crows once again taking flight at the sudden movement. Jason ran his hand through his black, loose curly hair and scratched his bearded chin. "I've been laying kind of low…sorry, Jake," he said, seeing his brother wince at the cliché. "I can't put it any other way. I've been laying kind of low because I was a little uncertain of how getting my name out there would go."

"I don't understand," said Jake.

"I know you don't," Jason said with a sigh. "Let me back up a bit. First, no one likes to admit they've been made a fool. I'm no exception."

"Ah, So it *was* a bad break up with Jennifer."

Jason nodded. "Oh, you could say that. I apologize for being thick headed about it. It wasn't a matter of trust. You know I've always confided in you, especially since we're the only two sane people in our family."

"Well, that's what all my other personalities tell me."

"Yeah, I know. Mom's a modern Alakshmi, Dad's goes through his bouts of melancholia, Amy's…Amy." He smiled at Jake. "I know we'll always agree about that."

"Yeah, that about covers—Mom's a what?"

"Alakshmi is the Hindu god of misfortune."

"Huh," mused Jake. "You think I would have picked that up somewhere along the way." He shook his head. "Back to the point, J.D. What happened? You've done a complete one-eighty."

"Part of it is the growth that comes from a lot of realization about yourself," he started, hesitating as he gathered his thoughts. "Especially when you've had the flooring ripped right out from under you, and you've been dropped into a long, dark abyss."

"I'm sensing this was more than your average break-up," Sam ventured.

"A mild understatement," Jason said. "It was always a dysfunctional relationship. And after it was all over, I guess I had a breakdown."

"Why didn't you tell me, Jason? You didn't honestly think I'd make fun of you or something, did you?" Jake asked. "God, not how after I was when Chris died."

"No...no, I knew better than that. I just didn't want to talk about it. I couldn't—not after the way I defended Jennifer, after what happened at Thanksgiving that time." He shrugged. "It's bad enough being wrong when it comes to you, Jake, but when Mom tells you you're wrong and she's right..."

"Ouch," Jake said with a wince.

"I just didn't want to talk about any of it. And I didn't want to lie to you."

"Jason," said Sam, "We know what you've been through. Trust me, it's no big deal. Everyone heals in their own time."

Jason smiled. "You know, I'd have come to you guys straight away except we'd had that stupid fight. I couldn't just pop in and face you and say I was sorry."

"Well, you could have, actually," said Jake.

"And I am. I'm very sorry I let my stupid infatuation get in the way of our relationship. I can't tell you how much I regret that."

"It's okay, Jason," Jake reassured him. "Water under the bridge."

"It *isn't* okay," Jason said, slamming his fist down on the stair. "I threw my entire life over for that woman. I shattered friendships. I severed ties with people I loved and for what?"

"Take it easy, J.D." He let his brother simmer down for a moment before questioning him again.

"I found her so fascinating. I was enthralled," he said, his voice tinged with humiliation. "She was good, that one. She was mysterious because she made herself that way. I found out she'd been lying to me from the beginning."

"You told me at one point last year that Jennifer wasn't even her real name," Jake said.

"It wasn't. I'm not sure I know what her real name was. The one I found out about—the one that was most traceable, anyway, was Amelia Darrow." He snorted. "If you've got some time to kill some snowy night, I'll give you the rap sheet on Amelia Darrow. It makes for some interesting bedtime reading."

"That name...that name is familiar..." Sam said. "Was she involved in—"

"Hang on, Sammy. I'll get there," said Jason.

"She was what, a con artist?" Jake asked.

"One of her many hats. Con artist, thief, liar. Maybe worse. I don't like to think about that."

"When did you start realizing something was wrong?"

"Not long after the fight you and I had and Jennifer and I left for San Francisco." He shook his head. "I had a good life there. I was building up a reputation both as a news photographer and as a serious artistic photographer. I even had a showing of my work." He looked up at his brother, his eyes etched with pain. "I wanted to share that with you and Sam so much. By that time, though, it was near the end of it, and she had her hooks into everything."

"Jesus, Jason, you're creeping me out a little. What all did she do?"

"I'm not sure I know everything," he confessed. "Other than lying all day long, I know she was a thief. Possibly a blackmailer. Possibly an extortionist."

"How'd you find out about this?"

Jason laughed heartily. "What you meant to ask, brother dearest, was how the hell was I so stupid and why didn't I see this?" He ruffled Jake's hair. "Thanks for being kind."

Jake shrugged. "Go on."

"I had warning signs for over a year. Little things that didn't add up. Secretiveness, phone calls to people that I had no idea of who she was talking to or what about. She was working as a copy editor for some crappy little magazine no one ever heard of, but started bringing home expensive clothing and jewelry." Jason shook his head. "I overlooked it all. I kept telling myself they were just quirks." He shrugged. "The capper, though, was the file cabinet."

"Not your average piece of office equipment?" Sam asked.

"It was a basic two drawer affair, only this one was fire proof and came with a combination lock. It was constantly locked, and she even stowed her laptop in there." He looked at Jake and said, "You know that horrible old story Grandma Devenworth told us as kids? The one with the woman who wore the velvet ribbon around her neck?"

"Oh yeah," Jake said. "The beautiful young woman marries the man, and she's always wearing that ribbon. Gradually, the man grows to hate it and keeps telling her to take it off—"

"And she replying, eerily, 'You'll be sorry if I do. So I won't.'" He shrugged. "It was like that. That cabinet. I watched her get into it, I watched her lock it. I kept telling myself it didn't matter, that I trusted her, that I had to trust her."

"Otherwise, you didn't have much to build a relationship on."

"How abysmally she treated you and Sam should have been enough," said Jason, his voice tight with regret.

"People can do incredibly odd things when they're in love," Jake said. "I even sent a singing telegram to Sam once on his birthday."

"You've never told me that," Jason said, grinning.

"I've only just lived it down."

"That's what you think," said Sam under his breath.

"Go on."

"Well, she never treated me badly—not at first, anyway. It was always good with her. She was always able to explain things away, stuff that in cold reality sounds completely ludicrous, now. In that haze of being in love, when you're only seeing the best in people, it all sounded perfectly rational. " He shrugged again. "I realize now none of what she said was sincere. It was all an act to keep me unaware."

"How'd it end?"

"Just like that story with the velvet ribbon."

"You pried open the cabinet," Sam said.

"It became too much. The designer clothes, the expensive jewelry, the rumors about stuff going missing from the office, the phone calls. I had to know."

"And that's when you found out she wasn't who she said she was."

"Yeah, and quite a bit of other stuff," Jason said, beginning to pace.

"Go on."

"The first thing I found were the Social Security cards. About a half dozen, all in different names. A few different driver's licenses in different names."

"Oh boy," Jake said under his breath. "Right out of Hitchcock."

"Hitchcock?"

"Don't tell me you haven't seen *Marnie*?" Jake asked, astounded.

"I haven't," Jason confessed.

"You were living it. Marnie Edgar, played by the lovely Tippi Hedren, is a career thief. In one scene it shows her opening a compact with a false back that hides her Social Security cards, all with different names."

"Well I'd never say Jennifer was particularly creative, so you can add plagiarist to her list of offenses."

"What else did you find?"

"Weird stuff. File upon file of information on different religious leaders. Well known people, like Paul Carlson, the head of the Seven Thousand Society, that dolt who ran for president a decade ago. Jerry Falwell. People like that." He sighed. "To what purpose, I don't know. I have some suspicions, but I couldn't say for certain. She also had a lot of files on coworkers. Lists upon lists of little indiscretions. Nothing earth-shattering, but enough to be embarrassing," Jason said.

"And if I'm reading her character right, she had one on you. Maybe me, maybe Sam?"

"The folders for you and Sam were empty, but they were there. And yes, one on me."

"What'd you do?"

"I burned it all in the fireplace. I packed up her stuff, and waited for her to get home. We had a great, blazing, screaming fight. Someone called the police. They separated us to cool us off. I kept trying to tell them to run her name so they'd find out. I talked until I was blue in face until finally a detective happened to overhear me. He knew who Amelia Darrow was, and was very interested in finding her."

"I have a feeling this is where it ends badly," Jake said, knowing Jason's destitute condition when he had arrived in Arrow Bay the previous winter.

"By the time the detective brought me back, the place had been stripped, and she had vanished. Everything I'd owned was gone except my clothes." He shook his head. "I was lucky my laptop and camera equipment were locked in my car, which I had loaned to Derek."

"Did you find out what happened to your stuff?" Sam asked.

"Sold, mostly, I've since found out. Not that it matters. It wasn't personal stuff. Televisions, stereos, CDs. All stuff that could be replaced. My profound ability to procrastinate paid off for once. Anything I really valued are all in storage at Mom and Dad's. I hadn't gotten around to sending for them yet."

"Well, that's good."

"I immediately put out that I had been a victim of identity theft. She had managed to get my Social Security number. I cut that off just in time. I didn't get to my bank in time, however. We had a joint account, which she drained. Luckily, my savings was still in my name, and she couldn't touch that."

"So you just left?" Jake asked.

"I left. I couldn't stand the atmosphere at work. Oh, no one blamed me—they all let me know that right up front. No one ever admitted she'd been victimizing them, but I suspect it was going on." He shook his head. "No one blamed me, but I was a pariah for having brought this pall upon the office. Guilt by association."

"And you didn't tell us this...?" Jake asked

"Because I felt such a goddamn idiot. Everything you'd warned me about was true. It was too raw, it was too fresh. I just couldn't." Jason's blue eyes shimmered. "I'm sorry. I should have realized you'd never judge me, but I couldn't bring myself to talk about it."

"It's okay, J.D. I understand," Jake said, standing up and giving his brother a hug.

"Can you forgive me for being such a jackass?"

"I forgave you a long time ago," Jake said, sitting back down on the step. "As usual, you've been harder on yourself than I could have ever imagined."

Sam let out the breath he had been holding. "Does this have anything to do with Derek Brauer taking a job at the *Examiner*?"

"Yeah. Everything, Sammy."

"Alex and I talked about that the other day," Sam said. "Comparing notes about our respective interviews with him. He had a pretty prestigious career with the *Chronicle*, didn't he?"

"Oh yeah," said Jason. "Derek was a rising star there. This is where it gets creepy. At least for Derek."

"What happened?" Jake asked.

"Two or three months after I left, I got an email from Derek that was somewhat cryptic. He tells me he's working on a story and then out of the blue asks me about something I'd gotten Jennifer—or Amelia or whatever—for Christmas the prior year."

"Which was?" Jake asked.

"A little gold four leaf clover."

"And he was asking about this...why?"

"It was at a crime scene." Jason said carefully.

"What kind of crime scene?"

"The very strange murder of one of the people I found files on in that file cabinet. One of the folders I'd burned. A mucky-muck in the evangelical Christian movement."

"David Donner," said Sam. "I remember that case very well. One of the most rabid homophobes on the planet."

"I remember that too," Jake said. He hadn't been particularly sad that the former Klan member turned born-again Christian had been found murdered. Jake had figured it was approximately two hundred twenty pounds less of crap polluting the earth. Sam had chastised him for his language and disregard for human life, but only half-heartedly.

"Right. Derek emails me a crime scene photo that shows of a little four leaf clover found in a pool of the victim's blood."

"Well, that doesn't mean much," Jake said with a shrug. "I imagine there are all sorts of those things out there."

Jason shook his head. "Not this one. I had it custom made for her. It was my own design."

Chapter Nine

"Oh shit," Jake breathed.

"Yeah," Jason agreed. "Pretty much."

"So what happened after that?"

"Derek broke the story, of course. After I uh…persuaded him to leave *me* out of it. Well, now Amelia Darrow is now wanted for questioning in the murder of David Donner. And not long after, Derek starts getting death threats."

"Death threats?"

"They started as threats, but it escalated. Someone took a few shots at Derek. The next letter told him to back off or the next time they wouldn't miss."

"Nothing happened to you?" Jake asked.

"Oddly, no. She could probably find me if she wanted to, but nothing ever came of it." He guffawed. "It almost makes sense. At least in the way she could twist things around. I wasn't to blame. I'd left San Francisco, after all. Even though I confirmed the identification of her necklace, she was the one that left it behind and *Derek* was the one who wrote the story."

"Still," said Sam, "this is why you were laying low like you said."

"Exactly. I didn't want to kick the wasp's nest."

"And Derek—he followed you?" Jake asked. "Why?"

"The threats continued. Derek went to the police. They had no idea where she was or if she was even responsible for the violence toward him. Derek had written a series of stories about gangs in the area, naming some of the leaders, and they could have been responsible as well."

"You don't think so though, do you?"

"I don't. The way things played out, it just seems to have her personal touch."

"I take it things got worse," Jake said.

"Markedly. They *officially* can't be linked to Amelia Darrow, but I'd be willing to bet on it. Derek seemed to think so, too."

"God, what else happened?" Sam asked.

"Two days after Derek went to the police, someone ran his mother off the road and nearly killed her. Two days after that, his nephew was almost picked up by a kidnapper. A week later his sister was attacked and beaten while jogging."

"Jesus," Jake said.

"Again, it could all be a coincidence…or not. Taken as a whole, it is awfully weird."

"So Derek left to wait for things to cool down?" Jake said, shaking his head. "I can't believe I used that cliché."

"You did. I'm a witness," Jason snickered. "Essentially yes, that was why he left. The stress on him, on his family just was too much. I was sending him emails by then about how quiet and peaceful it is up here, and how much better I felt, and he agreed it was time he got out of San Francisco." Jason shook his head. "Truthfully, I was not happy he landed in Arrow Bay. Trouble has a habit of finding Derek. Now that his name is in print again, with a clear location, it could bring her right back to me."

Sam shrugged. "She probably knows already, J.D. She had to figure you'd head back to your family. Unlike Derek, though, you got the hint and left her alone."

"That's what I am hoping, anyway, which probably sounds selfish. Maybe if Derek sticks to covering local politics and the latest drug bust in Kulshan County, he'll not make her any madder. It's been a year now, so I'm thinking it is increasingly unlikely she'll show up. She'd have done something by now if she intended to."

Jake shot his brother a hard glance. While Jason was usually hard to read, he wasn't at the moment. Jason didn't believe what he was saying. He expected Amelia Darrow to turn up again. For now, it seemed better to let the matter rest.

"Well if she does," said Sam, feeling his husband's leg up, "we can sic Jake on her. He's good at taking out homicidal women. Aren't you, Tiger?"

"Sorry, I'm fresh out of out-of-the-way locations to dispatch them. And besides, that never happened, remember? Our names aren't anywhere near Little Susie Sunshine's unhappy demise."

"Amen to that."

"I hope Derek doesn't regret moving to Arrow Bay," Jake said. "Nothing much ever happens around here."

"I think that's what he wants, or so he says. I know Derek too well, though. In a short time, that's going to wear thin. I worry about that." He looked at Jake and Sam and said, "So that's it in a nutshell, dear little brother and brother-in-law. You are not looking at the brightest light in the harbor when it comes to women."

"Everyone is allowed to make a mistake, J.D.," Jake said.

"I made two big ones, then. Jennifer aka Amelia and going home."

"How so?"

He paused. "Well, I stayed with Mom and Dad for a week. You and I always knew the score between Mom and Dad."

"Too well."

"Well, it's worse now," Jason said with a shrug. "They hardly talk to one another anymore. Their guise of keeping things civil seems to have gone by the wayside." He shook his head. "It wasn't that, though. I was used to that. It was being back in my 'creepy' room, as you put it, surrounded by all my old things. You know how Mom keeps our rooms just like they were when we left."

"Now *that* is creepy," Jake said. "Creepy squared."

"You had the sense to clean yours out when you left. I was laying in the same bed I'd been in at eighteen, surrounded by all the crap from high school—photos of me as the All American guy, in my football uniform, holding up my report cards with the straight A's, the levelheaded one who always thought things through," he said with a grin. "Unlike his little brother who went off half-cocked and said exactly what was on his mind at any given time."

"Hey!"

"Oh, don't pretend to be offended by that, Jacob," Sam said, rolling his eyes. "That's perfectly true, and you know it."

"So I'm looking at all this stuff," said Jason, "and I think about the huge lapse in judgment I've made, and I start wondering who the hell am I and what have I become."

"Typical mid-thirties angst," Sam said.

"A lot of truth to that," Jason replied. "That and the sudden realization I've forever been living up to some perceived expectation of how I'm supposed to live my life."

"Ah," Jake said, getting it at last. "Trying to get Mom's approval."

"Yeah."

"Give that one up, J.D. You're a Finnigan male. You'll never get it."

"Would you believe it has taken me some thirty-five years to figure that out?"

"Well, don't be too hard on yourself, Jason. Just your adult life, so only seventeen," Jake said.

"Thanks awfully."

"And so what? You have to live for yourself, Jason."

"I know that now."

"Then not everything that happened was bad," Sam said.

"No. Bad as it was, no. It's left me distrustful of people, though. Okay, women."

"Not everyone you're going to meet is going to be a sociopath, Jason. You had bad luck, that's all," Jake said.

"Don't give up, J.D. I mean, I went from an abusive, sociopathic man-slaughterer to the most wonderful man on the face of the planet. If I'd given up, I'd have never met Raul," said Sam, trying to lighten the mood.

"You start with that Raul stuff again, you're going to be sleeping on the couch."

Jason laughed and said, "You two really do give me hope, you know. Sam's right. I don't know about the most wonderful man on the planet thing, but...I'm just not ready yet. Until I can meet someone without thinking what are you up to really, I've got no business being with anyone."

"Jason, there's no shame in having loved the person you *thought* she was," Jake said. "If you still loved her after you found out she was a psychotic harpy, then we'd be working on the paperwork to have you committed to a nice long stay at Northern State."

"All sympathy, that one," said Sam, jerking his thumb at Jake. He turned to Jason and said, "Give yourself plenty of time. It was a few years before I met your brother."

"I know, I know...," said Jason. "I've been doing a lot of soul searching. I've come to the conclusion I'm not such a bad guy."

"Well duh," Jake said, rolling his eyes.

"You *are* a Finnigan, after all," said Sam. "You're pretty special."

"Except for Amy," the trio said in unison, all laughing.

"You know the job. I didn't want to take it. I've been doing well selling my freelance stuff. I made a lot of contacts in San Francisco, and that's really helped continue to sell my work in different publications. Thank God for the Internet," he said.

"How's it going locally?" asked Sam.

"The art prints Evelyn has been letting me display in her shop have been selling respectably. I wasn't sure I wanted to get back into newspapers. I'm not that person anymore, you know what I mean?"

"We know what you're getting at."

"This is really going to be a fantastic opportunity. I will not only be working for the paper as a photographer, but doing all the technology conversions. I'll be changing all the archives over to digital format and working with an archivist from the Kulshan County Museum to make sure all the prints and negatives are properly preserved. That's a whole other field I've always wanted to get into. Even if the paper collapses, that work will probably take years to complete."

"It sounds perfect, Jason. Not only do you still get to exercise your creativity, but you can feed the tech geek you've always been," said Jake.

"Tech geek, the man says. Who do you and Sammy always come crawling to when your hard drive crashes?"

"Who's complaining? It's nice having a tech geek so close by."

"Thanks, little brother. I'll take that as a compliment."

"It was intended as one."

"I admit it was that part of the job that really appealed to me. And the history that must be in those photo archives…you know they have hundreds of glass plates down there?"

"You'll have to make prints of the more interesting ones," Jake said.

"I never leave any job without having a backup of what I've worked on or found interesting on my hard drive."

"Be sure and tell Mom that. It'll give her something else to disapprove of."

Jason's expression darkened. "Did she give any indication of why she's coming up on Sunday?"

"You know Ingrid. She likes a sneak attack, so no. Has Dad said anything to you?"

"No. And I've been talking to him a lot. He's been very supportive of everything I've decided to do."

"Dad's always been in our corner."

"He has. He was the one who encouraged me to come to you."

"Proving once again our old man is smarter than either of us."

"Amen to that."

"It does make me a little nervous. Sam's right. She's going to drop a bomb on us. Nothing unexpected there, we just don't know—"

"How much TNT is involved. We could call Amy," he suggested. "You know she always tells things to Amy before she gets to either of us."

"Yeah, but that would involve—"

"—talking to Amy," Jason added.

"I'd rather go to the dentist."

"Especially since you run the risk of getting Hector Suggs on the phone."

"For a root canal," Sam agreed.

Jason glanced at his watch. "I need to get going. I told Derek I'd meet him for lunch and then I need to finalize some paperwork. Doris Woolsey, the receptionist at the *Examiner,* said I can still do that even though they're technically on strike." He looked at Jake, resting a hand on his shoulder. "I'm glad we talked."

"Me too, J.D. Don't ever feel you can't, okay?"

"To either of us," Sam said.

"Never again," Jason replied, giving his brother and then Sam a hug. Turning to go, he stopped at the foot of the porch steps and said, "A thought."

"Hmm?"

"A round of Irish coffee on Sunday before Mom blows in?"

"I was thinking of the same thing," Jake said with a grin.

"Well, I guess that proves we're related. I'll quit referring to you as my bastard half-brother from now on."

"And I'll quit telling everyone you're a registered sex offender." Jake said.

"Later, little brother. Stay out of trouble." Jason said.

Jake watched his brother get into his Toyota 4runner and pull out of the driveway, the sound of the car scattering the crows on Leona Weinberg's lawn.

Chapter Ten

Jake climbed the steps to the spare bedroom on the second floor to change the sheets on the bed. He pulled up the blind and jumped in surprise when one of the crows that had been hanging around Leona's suddenly flew past, nearly smacking into the glass. Even more crows had gathered near the kitchen door. He wondered what was going on. Leona was famous for chasing off every kind of critter that dared get near her prize apple trees. She even harassed chipmunks. Why would she suddenly start feeding the crows?

Soon, though, he was lost in thought over the things his brother had told him. Neither Jake nor Sam had ever liked Jennifer O'Hara or Amelia Darrow or whatever her real name might have been. It wasn't the homophobic litany she had launched into in their kitchen nearly three years ago, either. It was the way she had smiled. Her smiles had been robotic, barren of any feeling and had never touched her eyes.

He sighed and went about changing the sheets. At least it brought Jason back.

A cloud passed over the sun, dropping the temperature in the room. Jake shivered, a chill shooting up his spine. The hackneyed platitude about gooses and graves came to him before he could stop it. He shook his head and looked out the window at the darkening sky. He smiled as he watched another cartload of maple leaves scatter over Leona Weinberg's yard. Down the road, a car door slammed shut, and the crows took flight again.

"Maybe it should be a crow walked over the grave, instead of a goose," he said aloud to himself when the shiver had returned. He shook his head and left the room, not watching as one by one, the crows gathered around the back kitchen door to the Weinberg house.

❖

Throughout the night, the wind had howled. Jake slept restlessly, unable to catch hold of any deep, curative slumber. Instead, he listened to Sam's deep snores mingle with the wailing tempest until the gusts abated and the storm blew itself out about two.

At six, he pretended to be asleep while Sam crept out of the room. He then lay in the bed until the first tendrils of light crept across the ceiling from the gap in the blinds. Finally, he gave up. He dressed in sweats and bypassed the coffee, heading down to the basement to work out. It was his day off from the weights, so he opted for a good run on the treadmill.

While running, he glanced at the rain outside. It had been a fitting ending for a weekend involving their mother. Only the bomb she dropped had landed with a fizzle.

"Your father and I have been separated since last Christmas. I've decided to divorce him."

"Gee Mom, try and temper the blow a little bit, why don't you?" Jason said.

Jake said nothing and continued eating his salad. Ingrid Finnigan stared expectantly at her son. "Well? Don't you have anything to say?"

"Well, honestly Mother, it's about damn time. We all know about your little financial arrangement with a certain member of the Graham family—"

"I'm sure I don't know what you're talking about," huffed Ingrid Finnigan, arching an auburn eyebrow. "Your sister fell apart at the news."

"Of course she did," Jake and Jason said in unison.

"So, who's the other guy?"

"Jason, you have always had a vulgar imagination," Ingrid said.

"Come off it, Ma. New hairdo, new color for that matter—and I have to say the red suits you."

"Thank you. And do not call me 'Ma.' You know how much I hate that."

"—new dress, nails done up perfectly. You're not putting on the dog for us."

"If you must know, I have been seeing someone," Ingrid said. "Fred Stanley. And before you give me that judgmental look, Jason David, your father and I have been living separate lives for years. He's been having a relationship with someone else for quite some time, for the record."

"That's not a judgmental look, Ma. It's shock and horror at your choice. Fred Stanley? He's a car salesman."

"Who looks like a porn star gone to seed," Jake added, also aghast at his mother's choice in companions.

Sam snorted and erupted into a coughing fit reaching for his water and chugging some down quickly to soothe his throat.

"Fred Stanley," Ingrid Finnigan continued, acid dripping from each word, "is the most successful Mercedes-Benz dealer in the entire western United States. In fact—"

"Oh, come on, Ma!" Jason cried.

It had gone downhill from there. Ingrid complained about the meal, berated Jason's choice of career, and intimated both Jake and Jason were freeloading on Sam's income.

"Nothing could be farther from the truth, Ingrid," Sam had said, his voice icy. "And furthermore, it's none of your business."

Jake had enjoyed seeing the stricken look on his mother's face. When Ingrid had met Sam ten years ago, she'd been less than kind, but since then, Ingrid Finnigan had never crossed him. She had quickly grown to like him—better than she liked her sons, Jake figured—and had an annoying habit of taking Sam's side, even when he was wrong. They hadn't exchanged sharp words in a decade. She quickly changed the subject, unloading another bomb on them.

"I've decided to sell the business."

"You've *what*?" Jake said.

"I'm going to sell the bookstore. If I can't get someone to buy the business, I'll sell out the inventory and just get rid of the building. You'll need to come and get the books you've been putting aside for years in that steamer trunk in the attic."

"But you can't."

"It's my business. Of course I can."

It was *that* news that had struck him hard, not the news of the pending split of his parents.

As he ran on the treadmill, sweat pouring down his face, he wondered why the idea of selling the bookstore bothered him so much when it finally dawned on him that it was one of the last connections he had to Chris Aponte. They had worked there together, spent a lot of time talking, joking, laughing. Jake realized it wasn't the store itself that meant so much as the memories it represented.

He finished his workout and went upstairs. After his shower, he slipped down to the kitchen to find Sam and Jason talking away, Jason putting a plate of ham and eggs in front of Sam. Jake filled his coffee cup and joined Sam at the butcher's block kitchen table as Jason placed a plate of steaming eggs and ham in front of him. Jake picked a small piece of ham off the plate and patted his leg, where Barnaby had already arrived. He handed the dog the ham, skritched his ears and then returned to his breakfast, digging into the eggs.

They ate in the stillness of the kitchen for quite a while, not wanting to bring up the events of the day before. Jake looked out the window as the rain clouds continued to break up, leaving patches of dark blue sky behind the gray clouds. The sun flickered through and hit the wet pavement of High Street, which began to steam.

"Huh?" Jake asked, having heard Jason direct something at him.

"I asked how you were."

"Fine," Jake said, returning to his eggs. "Should I not be?"

"Well, you did just find out your parents are getting divorced," Sam pointed out.

"Oh, that's nothing, Sammy, you know that. We've been making bets for years, actually," Jason said.

"I've always wondered why they continued with it," Jake said. "I figured once Amy was out of the house..."

"Me too."

"Well, none of us were privy to the exacting details of the agreement around Amy," Sam pointed out.

"Thank God for that," said Jason, shaking his head. "Do you think she meant it?"

"Which part?"

"About not knowing what you were talking about in reference to the Amy agreement."

"Part of having borderline personality disorder is the ability to revise history to the point where you actually *believe* the revised history. It becomes the truth. Oh, she knows about it, but it'd be..." He shrugged. "I don't know. Like something she read in a book a long time ago."

"When I hear your mother say things like that, knowing they're not true, I'm always amazed you two turned out so well adjusted."

"That's because of Dad's influence," Jake said. "Speaking of, what'd Dad say?"

"That in typical fashion, Mom was making it all about her. He was the one that finally filed the paperwork."

"I'm not surprised."

"He also confirmed they've both been seeing other people for years, but we knew that."

"Did Madge finally decide she wanted to be more than the other woman?"

"You know Madge. She doesn't give a rat's ass about that kind of thing," Jason pointed out. "Dad said with it being a community property state, he didn't want Ma interfering with the Finnigan family things."

"Would she do that?" asked Sam, slightly aghast.

Jake and Jason merely looked at him.

"Sorry, sorry. My mistake. There's me thinking Ingrid might have her lucid, human moments."

"She does, but not when it comes to personal property," said Jake. "Which is why it floors me she's selling the store."

"Frankly, I'm far more upset to hear Mom's selling the bookstore than hearing she's shacking up with Fred Stanley."

"Me too," Jake said. "So much of our lives were there."

"I think the happiest parts of our childhood were spent in that bookstore," Jason said, with a sigh. "I'll miss it, but it isn't as if I'll ever be going back to live in Port Jefferson again. You?"

"Let's see, pigs would have to take to the air, hell would have to turn arctic and I'd have to start voting Republican first," said Jake.

"You know, you could have just said 'no,'" said Jason, getting up from the table to rinse off his plate and place it in the dishwasher. "I'm off. The staff is still unofficially on strike after the stunt Reed Longhoffer pulled with Marion's story last week. We're meeting to see what our next move is. As far as I know, Longhoffer is still trying to run the thing single-handedly and not having much luck with it."

"Good," said Sam and Jake together.

"They're putting together their own paper. Derek said they're going to the printers today and will have it out by tomorrow, a day ahead of the *Examiner*. They're calling it the *Arrow Bay Protester* and plan to run some not-too-nice things about Reed."

"What about the brother, the one who's really supposed to be running the thing?" asked Sam.

"David," replied Jake.

"Leave it to Mr. Photographic Memory," said Jason. "I wish I'd inherited that from Dad instead of the large—"

"J.D.," Jake said, cocking an eyebrow at his brother.

"—feet," said Jason. "What exactly did you think I was going to say, Jake?"

"Nothing, nothing," said Jake, blushing furiously.

"Anyway," said Jason, "David Longhoffer has had a flurry of emails sent to him and the *Examiner*'s lawyer has also been attempting to get a hold of him, basically insisting he come back to run things. Reed is on his way out for good at this point, I think."

"He's lucky he doesn't get sued for libel. Did you read that article?"

"I don't think anyone in town missed that," said Sam. "Randy Burrows read it over KABW."

"It could get very interesting," said Jason, clearing the plates off the table.

"Indeed it could. Another town meeting like that one, and they'll hang him from the nearest pole," said Jake.

Jason grunted, lighting his pipe and blowing out a few smoke rings. "Just so long as I get to keep my job, I'll be happy."

"Ready to go back to work, eh?"

"And then some. Not that cleaning your toilets hasn't been delightful," Jason said with a wink. "Anyway I best be off. See you this evening sometime," he said, and with a puff of cherry-scented tobacco, he was gone.

"Amazing what a little confession can do for the soul."

"Spoken like a Catholic."

"Ex-Catholic, and argue with me that he seems greatly relieved in just a few days since getting that off his chest."

"I can't, and you know it," said Jake. "Now, how about we sketch out the backyard and take advantage of the weather while we've got it?"

Chapter Eleven

"Okay, so we've got the boulder area covered," said Jake, while Sam marked some things down on a sketchpad. "And we can bulk up this side of the house." The clematis was starting to die back and look ragged, the only thing about it that he didn't like. "We'll cut this back and let it thicken up next spring," said Jake, making a notation on his steno pad as he wrinkled his nose. "Ugh, did I step in something? Has Barnaby been out here?"

"He never goes outside of his sand pit," said Sam. "What the heck is that?"

"Smells like gone-over meat," said Jake absently. He looked over at the Weinberg house, where the crows fluttered restlessly near the side door to the kitchen. "Oh shit!"

"Jake," said Sam disapprovingly. "As a writer—what are you doing?"

Jake handed Sam his steno pad, heading over to the fence. Jake held on to the top of the chain link, vaulting himself over. "Jesus, Mary and Joseph," he murmured, covering his mouth and crossing himself with his left hand.

Jake shooed away the crows, heading for Leona's back door. He peered through the panes of glass into the kitchen, where the lights were ablaze, illuminating pale pine tile and an island. Several apples lay scattered on the floor. Looking just beyond the island, Jake spotted a hand clutching an apple, a large, half-eaten section already brown. The fingers were purple and swollen, but the nail polish was just as shiny and perfectly done as always, and the same Jungle Red that Leona Weinberg always wore.

Jake didn't bother trying the door. He called over the fence to Sam, "Call the police. Mrs. Weinberg's dead."

❖

Two hours later, the police finally pulled the body out of the house covered with a sheet. The wind kicked up long enough to unfurl it from one end, revealing a set of purple, swollen ankles in iron-gray pumps. A corner of Leona's fuchsia dress fluttered in the wind like a waving hand. Jake turned away, not wanting to remember the image, but knowing undoubtedly he would for a long time. Why in the hell they hadn't loaded her into one of the black body bags that appeared on every crime show he'd ever seen?

Jake and Sam remained on their side of the fence, talking to officers periodically as the police tromped in and out of the house. The couple drifted back to the bench on the porch where they waited to be formally questioned.

After the body was pulled out, activity died down a bit. Jake and Sam had been sitting quietly with Barnaby between them when the tall, goateed detective Jake had remembered from the *Elwha* walked up their driveway.

"Mr. Finnigan and Mr. O'Conner? I'm Detective Adam Haggerty. I was wondering if I could get your statement."

It was not a question. Jake looked Haggerty up and down. He stood about six feet, four inches tall and had a lithe swimmer's build. Jake could tell Haggerty was no stranger to a gym, with ample biceps and well-defined pectoral muscles under his black dress shirt. His dark blue suit appeared tailored very carefully, though he was wearing a pair of practical black Doc Marten boots instead of regular dress shoes. Despite the cold, his suit jacket was slung over one arm. His dark brown hair was slightly shaggy, parted down the middle, and swept back carelessly. His goatee was a shade lighter thanks to some reddish undertones, and neatly trimmed. Haggerty was clearly younger than Jake, but not much. The goatee, he suspected, was to combat a rather goofy grin and very boyish face. Detective Haggerty was a handsome man, but his dark eyes were very probing and sharp. Jake knew instinctively this was not a man to trifle with.

"Have we met before, Mr. Finnigan?" he asked, his brow creased.

"A little over a year ago. You responded to the corpse found on the *Elwha* before Kulshan County responded. If bulldozing their way in can be referred to as 'responded.'"

"Ah, that," replied Haggerty, as if wanting to avoid a particularly unpleasant memory.

"Do we need to come downtown?" Sam asked.

"Later to sign your statements, but it's not necessary right now," he said, still standing over them.

Jake motioned to the chair. "Please sit down, Detective."

Barnaby leapt up from in between them, letting out a low growl as he approached the man, who sat down carefully.

"Pipe down, Barnaby," scolded Sam. "He's one of the good guys."

Adam Haggerty held out his hand for the dog to sniff, which he did vigorously. He wagged his tail, and let Haggerty pat him on the head. Haggerty scratched his ears for a moment and, apparently satisfied, Barnaby trotted off the porch for back door and his food dish.

"I must have passed inspection."

"He doesn't trust just anyone," Sam said. "He has an antagonistic relationship with a cocker spaniel in the park. And he's not too fond of that kid with the unibrow down the road."

"Can I get you something to drink, Detective?"

"Glass of water would be nice, thanks," said Haggerty, producing a pad from his jacket while Jake got his water and rejoined them on the porch.

"There are how many people in the household?" Haggerty asked.

"Sam and I and my brother, Jason."

"Okay. How long have you lived here?"

Jake blinked. "What's that—"

"Nearly ten years," Sam said.

"Were you on friendly terms with Mrs. Weinberg?"

"We spent most of the time ignoring one another," Jake said. "It was a matter of pretending one or the other didn't exist."

"From what I gathered, she was not exactly popular with *any* of her neighbors," said Haggerty.

"You saw her at the meeting," Jake said. "She could be very unpleasant."

"I gathered that. Not *exactly* the most open minded of individuals. She has a call record several miles long on the Jacoby family."

"The fence dispute," Sam said. "I remember that. She tore into poor Leanne one day nine years ago. April 27th. It rained that morning. I don't think anyone in the neighborhood missed that one."

"Uh…right," said Haggerty. "Then there's the ongoing fight with Mr. and Mrs. Crenshaw over the maple trees."

"They can be a pain—the leaves, not Al and Phyllis. And the leaves make excellent mulch. I don't know why the old bat—"

Sam cleared his throat loudly.

"Oh, knock it off, Sam," he said, exasperated. "Why beat about the bush? The old crone loathed us because we're a couple of homos and made no bones about it. Everyone on High Street knows that. And I might add the feeling was mutual," Jake said emphatically. "She was a mean-spirited old biddy with horrible taste. You saw the collection of dwarfs on the front lawn and the topiary out back. Imagine having to live with that next door for ten years. That and all those clucks of the tongue every time I stepped outside to so much as get the mail."

"Oh, just tell the nice detective how you really feel," said Sam, covering his eyes with his hand.

"*And* she was always after Barnaby. Never mind the dog is always fenced in or on a leash. If something horrible happened, it was Barnaby's fault. When that stupid dwarf Baleful got smashed last week—"

"Bashful," said Sam, still holding his head in his hand.

"Did she think it might have been one of her klutzy yard workers? Nope, it was the gay guy's dog."

"Our relationship with our neighbor was strained at best," Sam said simply.

"Well, like I say, it seems it was with everyone on the block, except maybe the Fujiokas, but it seems they're snow birds and aren't around much." He jotted a few notes down. "When did you last see Mrs. Weinberg?"

"At home, or in general?" asked Jake.

"I can't remember," said Sam. "I think it was—"

"Wednesday. Before the meeting. I can't recall seeing her home after that."

"No, me either. How long had she been…"

"Dead?" Haggerty asked. "Oh, I'd just be guessing at this point."

"A week at least," said Jake, grimacing. "Based on the smell, and the fact that her fingers had already bloated, meaning gases were breaking down the body. The ring on her hand looked like it had been squeezed around a Ball Park hot dog."

"Well, that's me off hot dogs for a while," Sam said, looking green. "I could have done without that, thank you, Tiger."

"You have some training in the field?" asked Haggerty, an eyebrow shooting up.

"Jake's a writer," Sam said. "And we're both avid mystery fans. You name any mystery writer worth two cents in the last fifty years, we've probably read them," Sam said. "Not to mention *CSI, Bones*…all the forensic shows…"

"Bit of an amateur sleuth then, eh?"

Jake caught a flicker in Haggerty's eye that he took to mean he was being relegated to the "trouble" file.

"Absolutely not," said Jake, the thought of last year's events with Susan Crane fresh on his mind. "I leave the detecting to the detectives, er, um, detective. I have zero interest in being involved in any kind of investigation."

"I'm confused," Sam said. "Mrs. Weinberg died of natural causes, right? I mean, she probably sent her blood pressure through the roof after the meeting last Wednesday and gave herself a stroke or heart attack or something, right?"

"It's possible. The autopsy will tell us more. We've got no reason to believe anything suspicious is going on. There were no signs of a struggle, and the house was locked when we arrived, but we treat situations like this as a crime scene until we know more," Haggerty said absently.

"The pool," Jake said, apropos of nothing.

Haggerty gave him a crooked grin. "I beg your pardon?"

"I've seen you down at the pool before when I've gone swimming. You've got a tattoo of a phoenix on your left shoulder."

"You're very observant, Mr. Finnigan."

"To the point of being annoying," said Sam under his breath.

"It's not my fault. I've got a memory that's nearly photographic. It's a blessing and a curse. It's not always fun remembering that your second grade teacher had two rather large moles that sprouted gray hair like a smoke tree in bloom."

This time Haggerty did laugh. "Do you recall what happened on Wednesday when you last saw her?"

"My second grade teacher?"

"Mrs. Weinberg, you dope," Sam said, shaking his head.

"Oh! Yes. Vividly," said Jake. "She was threatening to shoot Barnaby."

"Why?"

"She thought that he had broken one of her hideous dwarfs."

"The aforementioned Bashful," Haggerty said, making another note.

"Right. Then she used some derogatory words toward us," said Jake slowly.

Haggerty looked up from his notepad. "Oh?"

"Nothing terrible, I suppose. The 'f' word did not rear its head, but archaic or not, the words she used would still be considered a slur."

"Sodomite and buggerer," Sam filled in cheerfully.

"And what did you say?"

Jake shrugged. "I told her to pipe down or I'd file a report on her with the police, that she was harassing us. Jeez, I feel bad about that now."

"Why is that?"

"Well, if her blood pressure *did* do her in, I probably raised it up a few levels with that speech," Jake said. "I may not have liked her, but certainly didn't wish any ill will on her." He considered. "Not any *serious* ill will. At least, not that wasn't done for comic effect like a Warner Brothers cartoon. You know, anvils falling from the sky."

"Or that something might run her over, like say an armored truck," said Haggerty with a smile.

Jake found himself blushing under Haggerty's direct stare. "Oh, that. I wondered if you heard me. Well, I didn't mean that. Not really," he said. He then shook his head. "Nope, I can't say that honestly, Detective. Had she been run over by an armored truck at that particular moment in time, I probably wouldn't have been too upset. She'd just spat the word 'pervert' at the two of us in a public forum, something I found pretty damn reprehensible. If an armored truck ran her over at that moment in time I'd have probably tipped the driver."

"Is he always this candid?" Haggerty asked Sam.

"Jake's incapable of lying."

"It's not a bad quality," Haggerty pointed out. "Okay, so after your argument on Wednesday, that was the last time you saw her?"

"No," Jake and Sam said at once.

"But you just said..."

"You asked when the last time we saw her at *home* was," stated Sam. "We *all* saw her later that evening at the town meeting. I can't remember seeing her after that."

"Neither can I, which is weird upon reflection. I should have realized something was up over there. The crows should have been a big giveaway."

"Crows?"

"Yeah, yesterday Jason noticed a whole flock of crows outside of the back door and window over there."

"Murder, Jake, they're a...murder...of...we'll stick with flock," said Sam.

"It was the crows that brought you over to her house?"

"No," said Jake, looking over there. Six police cars were parked in front of the house, lights flashing. The coroner's van had left, leaving a group of uniformed officers still milling about the place. Inside the kitchen came pops of light from camera flashes. "It was the smell. Sam and I were going over plans to revamp the side and backyards and well, once we got parallel to the back door at her house..." Jake shuddered.

"Yeah it was pretty pungent," said Haggerty. "It seems Mrs. Weinberg ran cold. Her house was cranked up to seventy-eight degrees."

"That explains why she was always yelling at the gas guy," said Sam, shaking his head. "She constantly accused the meter reader of reading her meter wrong."

"Say that ten times fast," said Jake under his breath. "That's true, though, she did. Got be a regular monthly row," he said, something occurring to him. "Although seventy-eight degrees seems a little warm even for her."

Haggerty looked at Jake and asked, "Meaning?"

"Well, I read this book. *The Teacup Assassin*. The body of this particular acid-tongued gossip columnist was stuck in a very warm room by the murderer to speed up the decay and obscure the time of death," said Jake.

"That wasn't *The Teacup Assassin*, was it? I thought that happened in *Knifey Wifey*?" asked Sam.

"Nope, *Knifey Wifey* had the actress that got pushed down the lighthouse stairs. Remember, it took like fifteen pages for the body to get to the bottom of the stairs."

"Which you bitched about probably defying the laws of physics."

"Right," said Jake, thinking. "I can't believe it took over a week for someone to miss her."

"The actress in the lighthouse?" Haggerty asked.

"No, Leona."

"How so?"

"Well, she was so buddy-buddy with Longhoffer, for example. It seems *he* would have missed her at the very least."

"Except," Sam pointed out, "She had a tiff with Longhoffer at the end of that meeting. Not to mention the whole staff of the *Examiner* has walked out."

"I guess with writing and Jason and my mother visiting I know I didn't even think of Mrs. Weinberg."

"No, me either. I've been getting my quarterly taxes done with my accountant all week. She was about the last thing on my mind."

"You know, that's pretty sad," said Jake. "Here she is dead on her floor for probably a week, and no one missed her." He looked at Sam, then at Haggerty. "Just doesn't seem right, does it?"

Chapter Twelve

Later, as Haggerty drove away, he had an uneasy feeling in his stomach. Something wasn't right about the death of the old woman, and he knew the autopsy results would reveal that. He'd worked too many homicide cases not to know when something was amiss. And Finnigan had been right, cranking up the heat *was* a way to speed decay and obscure the time of death.

He wasn't sure what to make of those two. Sam O'Conner was about as threatening as a butterfly, and it wasn't only his outward teddy bear-like appearance that made Haggerty draw that conclusion. O'Conner radiated a gentleness not common to many men. It made Haggerty think of how soft-spoken and kind his grandfather had been. Haggerty felt in his gut that O'Conner was very much like him in that regard.

Finnigan, he couldn't really place. He still remembered the haunted look of horror on Finnigan's face when he had been on the *Elwha* the previous year, after the body of Susan Crane had been found. Finnigan was holding something back, and Haggerty wondered what it was.

One thing he was certain about: everything Finnigan told him was the absolute truth. He was as straightforward as his husband claimed him to be. Haggerty found that refreshing, but Finnigan's laser-like perception was a bit disconcerting.

He began to wonder more about Mr. Finnigan and Mr. O'Conner. It would probably be wise of him to check their backgrounds out thoroughly. And that of the brother, whom he would talk to later as time allowed.

Adam Haggerty didn't feel they were responsible for their neighbor's death, but the way Jake Finnigan had so vehemently denied any attempt to insert himself into the investigation struck him as being a bit off, particularly after his husband had told him what an avid mystery fan he was. Those types of people did put themselves in the investigation, always thinking they were smarter than the police.

Haggerty picked up his cell phone and dialed the number of his partner, Detective Sharon Trumbo. She picked up on the first ring.

"Trumbo."

"Hi Sharon, I'm on my way back in."

"Next time you get to go with the body," Sharon groused. "Particularly if we're out of body bags. Not only do I dislike not being with you when you question people, I don't have to witness the ooze factor."

"Sorry," Haggerty said. "We're not the only ones short staffed right now. After the whole Crane affair last year, the coroner's office is still in a bit of turmoil."

"How do you forget to order body bags? Sorry. Sorry. Forget it," Sharon said. "What's it look like?"

"I'm not sure at this point. Looks like the old lady was eating an apple. Possibly she choked or had a stroke or coronary. No obvious signs of foul play."

"But…?"

"Why do you assume there's a 'but'?"

"You're calling me. I'm willing to bet something about this doesn't sit right with you. What gives?"

"I'm not sure just yet. One of the neighbors pointed out to me that the house being so warm is a classic attempt to speed decay and obfuscate the time of death."

"Helpful neighbor. Homicidal neighbor?"

"Nah, I don't think so. But I'd like you to run some background checks."

"Okay. What names do you have?"

"First is an Albert Allen Crenshaw. DOB 7 January 1952. And the wife, Phyllis Benson Crenshaw, DOB 9 October 1958. Located at 99 High Street."

"Got it. Next?"

"Jason David Finnigan. DOB 30 April," he said, giving the year. "And his brother, Jacob Allen Finnigan, 31 October, a year later. 100 High Street."

"Okay, any others?"

"Samuel Patrick O'Conner. DOB August 2, 19—"

"Hang on," said Sharon, fumbling with a pen.

Haggerty gave her the year and said, "Also at 100 High."

"That last one sounds familiar."

"It does?"

"Yes..." He heard a rustle of papers in the background. "Ah, that's why. I was just reading about him. He was in the *Examiner* a week or so ago. He's a maritime architect in charge of the new ferries they're building at Sutherland Shipyard in town here, and he's project manager on that old boat they're turning into a hotel."

Haggerty nodded to himself, remembering the article. He knew Sam O'Conner's name had sounded familiar. "That's right, I read that too."

"So what, these guys live next door to the old lady?"

"Yes. Two are brothers."

"I gathered that. What's the relationship with O'Conner and the other two?"

"Jacob Finnigan and O'Conner are a couple."

"Ah, got you. Hmm."

"Hmm?"

"Oh, nothing, nothing at all. I just know Leona Weinberg was a Class A bigot. I can't imagine the idea of living next to a gay couple thrilled her tremendously."

"Living next to *anyone* didn't thrill her tremendously. I have ten statements here on what a spiteful old bitch she was. If this turns out to be a homicide, it's a miracle no one did her in sooner."

"You think it might be a homicide?"

"I don't know. Something wasn't right there. I could feel it. So could the neighbor, actually."

"The neighbors thought something was wrong?"

"Neighbor. One to be specific. Jacob Finnigan. Same one who noted the thing with the heat. I'd like to find out if we're both right."

❖

"Quit staring at it," said Jake irritably, flipping back to the Discovery Channel. Sam was perched near the living room blind, ostensibly to lower it, but he had paused, locked in thought while looking over at Leona's.

"I can't help it. I feel..."

"Guilty?" Jake shook his head. "You can take the boy out of the Catholic church…"

"Come on, Jake, don't have a go at me over that again." He lowered the blind and plunked into the couch next to Jake. Jake casually wrapped his arm around him, holding him closer.

"I'm sorry, Sam. You know I don't normally go after religion just for the sake of it. I guess I've just had my share of hypocrisy this week."

"I know. I just wish you took my spiritual beliefs a little more seriously."

"It's not that I don't. I just can't understand how you can still feel so attached to a church that wants no part of you and works very hard to exclude you. And in the past would happily have burned you alive."

"I know, I know," said Sam glumly. He stared at the television, where a soothing female voice was calmly describing the eruption of Mount Pelée in 1902 that had incinerated some thirty thousand people.

"Maybe you should try Evelyn's church," said Jake.

"Hmm?"

"Your mother's church. I've heard some good things about the Reverend Crawford. Not to mention the way she stuck up for us at the meeting."

"But they're Unitarians."

"Oh, clutch the pearls, Samuel," said Jake, rolling his eyes. "And I'm surprised at you. That sounded an awful lot like something dear departed Leona Weinberg would say—would have said."

"You're right. I'm sorry."

"It was just a thought," said Jake, rising to turn up the heat. "Or you can talk to Gavin about Buddhism. They're more in line with your way of thinking anyway."

"I'll mull it over."

"I'm off to bed."

"I'll be up in a minute."

Jake left the room, but paused on the stairs. He stepped back down, and turned around the corner and said to Sam, "Have you thought, Sam, that maybe what you miss is the church and not the religion?"

"What do you mean?"

"I mean it's the ritual you miss. If the teachings of Christ are truly what you believe in, then it really shouldn't matter what wrapper they're delivered in, should it?" He smiled and said, "I love you. Don't stay up too late."

Sam pondered for a moment, then picked up the phone and dialed his mother's number. "Hi Mom," he said, hesitantly. "No, everything is all right," he reassured.

"Hey, I've got a question for you. Uh huh. Yeah. Um, can I go to church with you next Sunday?"

❖

News of Leona Weinberg's demise spread through the town like a midsummer conflagration. KABW heralded the news with a ten minute back-to-back playing of "Ding Dong, the Witch is Dead," Randy Burrows dancing around the radio station while it was playing. The local ABC affiliate was up to cover the story, so Jake, Sam, and Jason had to duck behind the curtains and pretend no one was home when reporters came knocking. Thus far it had not made it to the press that they had been the ones to find the body. Jake sorely hoped to keep it that way, going so far as to put the thumbscrews into Jason.

"Not a word to anyone."

"Who would I tell, little brother?"

"J.D., you do work for a newspaper, don't you?"

"Yeah, but I'm not a reporter."

"Your old friend Derek Brauer is, isn't he?"

"Well..."

"Not so much as an uttered syllable, okay? I know I don't need to remind you about last year's trip down a similar darkened pathway."

"I'll just employ my usual diversionary tactic," said Jason, with a grin.

"Which is what?"

"I start talking about fishing."

"That usually works?"

"It has always worked on you," said Jason, scratching his bearded chin. "It's a subject that bores him senseless."

"Nice to know we have something in common. Start telling him about all the good fishing holes on Boulder Creek."

"What good fishing holes?" Jason asked, frowning slight. "You haven't mentioned—"

"J.D., if you've not discovered any fishing holes on Boulder Creek it isn't my fault."

"Well, I've been spending most of my free time looking for work. Now that I'm employed again..." he trailed off, a gleam in his eye. He shook his head. "Anyway, fishing should do it, unless it is a really interesting story. Derek is very tenacious."

It was all Jake could do to keep from cursing aloud. Unhappily, Derek was also the reporter Alex had given all the pertinent materials on the entire Susan Crane affair to, judiciously excising everything involving Jake and Sam.

"Ugh," said Jake, his head starting to throb mildly. "Well, if fishing doesn't steer the conversation from our dear departed neighbor, try bird hunting," said Jake, peering out the kitchen window at Sam's office. He could see Sam pacing in the garage apartment. "How long has Sam been up there?"

"Since before I got up at six."

Jake frowned again. Tuesday morning, and Sam was already pacing. It was not a good sign. Either something was going wrong with the *Chinook* project again or someone at the Department of Transportation was haranguing him over the new ferries. Jake knew Sam was pushing to have at least one of them finished to Safety of Life at Sea certification and the DOT was resisting. He suspected it would only be a matter of time before the feds required SOLAS standards for all the boats, but the DOT was not going to go that route unless they absolutely had to.

He clomped his way down the basement steps to the workout room. Today, unlike most days, he really didn't feel like exercising. While certainly not depressed over the death of Leona Weinberg or even remotely upset, he was a little gloomy over the whole incident. He wondered how he'd ever be able to look over without seeing the bloated purple hand clinging to the apple on the white tile of the kitchen floor, or the gray pumps attached to the thick, purple ankles.

He shook his head and got on the treadmill, walking at first and then working up to a run. He generally didn't run, preferring a fast-paced walk, but some days he liked the feel of running. After sufficiently warming up, he did his usual hour on the weights, focusing on the upper body, his heart still not in it, but pressing ahead nonetheless.

He couldn't place what was bothering him. The revelation about his parents' dissolving marriage was niggling at him, but not in a serious way. Jake found himself in the unenviable position of loving his mother dearly but not liking her very much. He'd discovered that at the age of twelve, and the relationship had been downhill pretty much from that point on. The knowledge that she suffered from a genuine psychological affliction had only tempered it so much. He realized someone could be mentally ill and *still* be an asshole. It was hard to take any comfort in that.

As he finished his butterfly presses, he realized what was clanging around in the back of his mind—it *was* Leona Weinberg.

It wasn't exactly that she was dead, though that was part of it. Pausing for a moment to search his feelings, he eventually came around to what it was. *It felt unfinished.* And worse yet, he felt a familiar sense of entanglement in it, as if he were a spool that was slowly turning as the thread wrapped around and around him, gradually covering him. It was a sensation he'd had the year before in dealing with Susan Crane.

Jake shook his head, trying to get the image out of his mind. He finished working out, showered and dressed, sitting down at the kitchen table for a cup of coffee and the *Times* crossword to take his mind off things. He finished it up leisurely, contemplating what he was going to do with his afternoon. Whatever it was, it was going to be something indoors as the idea of working outside anywhere near the empty Weinberg house gave him a case of what he could only think of as the "heebie-jeebies."

Chapter Thirteen

Jake was about to head upstairs when the phone rang. Without thinking he picked it up, neglecting to read the caller I.D. He said, "Hello?" into the receiver only to be greeted with an odd snuffling sound. He looked at the receiver for a moment. "Hello?"

"J-j-j-jake?"

Oh no, he thought. *It's Amy.*

"Amy, is that you?"

"J-j-ake! Isn't it just awful!" moaned Amy, erupting into a spate of fresh sobbing.

The throbbing in his head picked up. He began massaging his temple. "Let me guess. You just found out about Mom and Dad."

"Y-y—yes. Mom just called twenty minutes ago."

"She told me she had already talked to you. Sunday," said Jake, angrily.

"Well, she left a message on the machine. Hector and I were away getting boxes for the move."

"Move?"

"Yes. Hector's been offered a job at that liberal arts college near Mount Burlington. Considine University. Isn't that near you and Sam?"

Only too damn close, thought Jake. *Jason's going to be thrilled.*

"Fairly close," said Jake, deliberately ambiguous.

"Jake, what are we going to do?"

"We? Do?" Jake asked, picturing his lithe sister with the ash-blonde hair, looking quite like a younger version of their mother, only with brown eyes. "I don't see how we're involved."

"But Jake, we can't let them do this."

"Why not? They're adults. They can do whatever they want."

"But it'll break up the family. I mean, look at what it's done to you and Jason."

"Amy, where have you been the last year? Jason's *here*. He's been living with Sam and me."

"He has?"

"Do you not read your email? I sent that to you months ago."

"I've been busy," Amy sniffed. "I've had so much to do with my degree."

"Oh? In what this time?"

"Applied arts," said Amy, the sniff leaving her voice. "And don't you use that condescending tone of voice with me, Jake. I have the paperwork in and will be awarded the degree at the December graduation. And I've got a job already lined up at the new college. I'll actually be *using* my degree."

"Touché, Amy. I didn't think you had it in you," said Jake. He knew he was working up to a full-fledged migraine. "And as it happens, I'm writing full time now."

"Jake," Amy implored. "Come on now, let's not do this."

"You're right. Congratulations."

"Thanks," said Amy with sincerity. "I'm sorry if I've been out of touch. There has really just been so much going on. Jason is well?"

"Um, yes." He wouldn't be discussing the Jennifer O'Hara/Amelia Darrow ordeal with his sister. "He's got a job lined up here in town and is doing a lot of freelance work."

"That's good."

Jake felt his anger starting to build again. "Listen, Amy, what is it I can do for you?"

"I don't know," she said, the quiver returning to her voice. "I just am so upset."

"Come on. You didn't see this coming? Don't you remember what it was like the whole time we were growing up?"

"Well, I always thought..." She paused. "I guess if I really think about it, they argued a lot. They never seemed particularly close. I just thought maybe after we left things got better."

"I expect with us gone, they only had each other to face," said Jake, still rubbing his temple, happy Amy wasn't there to see him staring at his shoes. "I think sometimes we acted like a buffer."

"It has gotten strange over the last few years. Look, Jake, I've really got to go, but...well, thank you. And let's not let that happen to us, okay?

I mean, falling apart. We're the only family we've got, you know," said Amy, ringing off.

Jake groaned, replacing the receiver. Typical of his sister. Once she felt all right, it was time to go. He shook his head, got up, and began rummaging around in the pantry for the Excedrin. He knew Amy was correct, however. There was the family he had made for himself as well—Sam, Rachel, Caleb Rivers, Gavin and Jeff, Alex... They were certainly every bit as close to him as anyone he was related to.

There's the family you're born to and the family you make, he thought. Where had he read that? Armistead Maupin, most likely.

That made him think about Rachel again. In the last three weeks, she'd sent only one email, and all it had said was that she was "busy" and would write more soon. He debated about sending her an old-fashioned telegram inquiring if she had lapsed into a coma, but wasn't even sure if anyone even did telegrams anymore. Stroking his chin, he thought maybe he'd send her something goofy in the mail she'd have to sign for.

He swallowed two Excedrin with a gulp of orange juice, pondering whether or not he wanted to go lie down for a while and let the pills take effect. He knew he wouldn't get any writing done with a headache and thought of some mindless tasks he might do instead. Given the events of the previous day, he felt he was due a little down time before delving back into the murder of his best friend.

❖

Jake lay down on the living room couch and put a pillow over his eyes for a while in an effort to rid himself of his migraine. Dorothy and Sophia had parked on the couch and were not happy being displaced, but they resettled almost immediately at his feet. He let the sounds of the house flood into the darkness. The furnace had just kicked on, the blower whooshing as it circulated warm air throughout the bungalow.

He didn't realize he'd fallen asleep until the phone rang. Jake picked up the receiver from behind his head.

"Hello."

"Jake, I just got the strangest goddamned letter," said Rachel Parker.

"I was just about to send you something embarrassing in the mail to sign for, Sadie McKee," Jake said, calling his best friend by her old nickname.

"I knew I should have waited another day before calling you," said Rachel in mock lament.

"Excuse me, darling, but where the hell have you been? And don't tell me busy or I'll place your photo in the *Outsider* personals under diva seeking man into high heels and having radishes thrown at him."

"Didn't you do that to Amy once?"

"How do you think she met Hector Suggs?"

"Oh, you have no idea how good it is to hear your voice," she said. "And it is true, though. I have been busy. How are you doing?"

"Oh peachy, but—"

"And that handsome husband of yours?"

"Sam is good, but Rachel—"

"I know, I know. I've behaved horribly, and I owe you an explanation. Let me just apologize and say I know I've been a terrible, terrible bitch. I did the one thing I said I'd never do."

"You ate human flesh?"

"I'd forgotten about that one," said Rachel. "I fell in love."

"Oh. Well, if that is all…"

"No, Jake. For real this time."

"Oh," said Jake, taken aback. "Well, let's hear all about him."

Rachel sighed. "There isn't much to tell. It's over."

"Oh Sadie, I'm sorry."

"Yet again, I picked the wrong one. He was a big, burly blonde Swedish god with a penchant for black turtlenecks and jackets with patches on the elbows. He knew all about cooking, classical music, and old MGM films. He had a body that wouldn't quit and a libido to match. We spent hours making love on a bearskin rug at a lodge in Vermont and eating petit fours and drinking expensive cabernet. It was heaven, sheer heaven."

"What happened?"

"I found out the son of a bitch was married."

"Ouch. When did that happen?"

"Six weeks ago. I had a little nervous breakdown. I told my boss to go perform a sexual act on himself with both hands and an umbrella and walked out."

"At least you were creative."

"After that, I figured I needed some help and got on some antidepressants and anxiety meds."

"I'm sorry, sweetie."

"It doesn't end there. My Swedish god still wants to keep things going."

"Without getting a divorce."

"Naturally. It's a 'marriage in name only' and 'she knows all about it' and 'we just stay together for the sake of the kids.'"

"Ha, where have I heard that lately?"

"Pardon?"

"Nothing," said Jake. "Where are you now?"

"Well, you'll be happy to know the condo sold, and I've left D.C. for good."

"I'd say I was bitterly disappointed, but since you said you'd be coming home last year, I can't say I'm upset about that particular development," said Jake.

"I'm currently staying with my sister in San Francisco."

"Sadie," said Jake, "Are you okay?"

"I just take it day by day, Jake. Some days I think I'm perfectly fine, and some days I fall apart completely. I guess I'm having my midlife crisis a bit early."

"It'll be okay. You're one of the strongest people I know. You'll get through it."

"Oh, I know I will," said Rachel, drawing in a shuddery breath. "It just royally sucks. Here I am thirty-three and starting all over again."

"Sadie, you're more than welcome to come here. We're a little full at the moment, but we can make room."

"Jason still there?"

"He is, but he's doing a lot better," said Jake. He told her what prompted Jason to leave San Francisco and his new job at the *Examiner*. He followed up with the recent events with his mother, but skipped over the recently deceased Leona Weinberg.

"You know, J.D. and I have that in common," she said.

"What's that?"

"We have lousy taste in prospective spouses. I should just give up. Find myself a nice nunnery. Do they even have nunneries anymore?"

"I'm not sure, outside of Shakespeare. You'd be better off with a houseful of cats. You're more the crazy cat woman who mutters to herself and throws oatmeal cookies at children when they walk by."

"Your writing must be going well, given that description. Maybe I should come up and we can have an all-night booze and bad TV fest like we used to."

"I'd love that."

"Love what?" asked Sam as he entered the living room.

"Is that Sam? Tell him hello from the Magic Sweater."

"The Magic Sweater says hello."

"Rachel? Let me talk to her!"

And because he knew he'd not be able to avoid it, Jake handed over the receiver to Sam and let the two chat for a while. Jake replaced the pillow over his head, enjoying the sound of Sam's deep, melodic voice as he talked and laughed. After a few minutes, Sam handed the phone back to Jake.

"You okay?" Sam asked.

"Headache," replied Jake, taking the phone back.

"So it's settled. I'll be up for Thanksgiving."

"That would be fantastic," said Jake as Sam sauntered out of the room.

"Oh my God, I nearly forgot what prompted me to call. Other than a huge sense of guilt, of course," she added hastily. "I got this bizarre letter from Tony, although it's apparently Doctor Anthony Graham now."

"Oh really? What did he say?"

"It was a very wordy apology for being a creep in high school. He seems to be trying to make amends. I'm wondering if he's not in some sort of twelve step program."

"Twelve steps won't be enough for Tony."

"I tend to agree. I'm still not happy with him for how he treated you after Chris's death."

"My mother thinks I should just let it go." Jake said.

"When did you ever listen to her? Although I suppose she has a point. It's probably more effort to be upset with him than just let it go." She exhaled heavily. "Did you see the photo of him on his last book? Pretty hunky. Age may not have improved his personality, but it *has* improved his looks. Why wasn't I born a gay man?"

"You were. You're just in a woman's body is all. You know, you could always get a sex change."

"Not on your life. I'd still end up spending money on vintage Chanel, only I'd be a drag queen. It's cheaper to keep things the way they are."

"You've got me there."

"Anyway, our lovely god-like one is making serious amends and wants to 'renew our friendship.' He glossed over the fact that the last words I spoke to him were something about how I hoped he met up with someone with a scorching case of herpes."

"He may have chosen not to remember that, yes. The cynical side of me wants to know what the hell he wants." He considered for a moment. "Although I have my suspicions."

"What's cynical about that? I mean, when did Tony Graham ever do something that wasn't for the sole and total benefit of Tony Graham?" She paused for a moment. "What do you suspect?"

"You read his latest tome?"

"It took me a while to get through it," she confessed. "It kept putting me to sleep."

"Given his transformation into the political beast he has become, did he mention Chris to you in any of your letters?"

"No," she said, catching on. "You don't think he's writing about Chris, do you?"

"Chris is a ready-made icon for him to exploit."

Rachel let out a slow breath. "I hope not. I really, really hope not. Think of what that would do to Chris's parents."

"I could be totally off base. I suppose people can change," said Jake carefully. "I mean, do you think you're the same person you were in high school?"

"Hmm, no, that's true. I'm much more of a bitch now than I ever was then."

Jake laughed, feeling an overwhelming sense of warmth flood over him. He wished she could come before Thanksgiving and told her so.

"I'd love to, Jake, and I will if I can manage to tie up everything. I've still got to get my things settled in D.C. and I think I can face that now. Just talking to you has made me feel so much better. I am really, really sorry I let things slip so much."

"Doesn't matter."

"It does, Jake."

"Then don't dwell on it, okay? Just get your butt in gear and get up here. Besides, if you've been with your sister as long as you say you have, I know she's probably close to driving you nuts by now."

"She's such a neat freak. I don't know how Mark puts up with her. I left my shoes under the coffee table and she about came unglued."

"Well, give her a hug for me, okay? And call me soon. And hey—if you're in San Francisco and haven't stopped by Gavin and Jeff's, you better or you'll never hear the end of it."

"I haven't had time, but I will," she promised. "And you're right. I never will hear the end of it. Last time I came here without checking in on them Gavin mailed me a hideous armoire from his parent's store. Took me ages to get rid of that damn thing."

"That's our Gavin, using furniture from the Ashworth storeroom as a form of retribution. Speaking of, I better get in touch with him myself. I haven't emailed in a few days and when that happens, he has the police do a wellness check."

"He doesn't."

"He does," said Jake, remembering the last time it had happened. "I think the police were a bit surprised to find out I wasn't an eighty-year-old man."

"I'll see the boys and I'll call you at the end of the week while I'm wrapping my crapola up in D.C. I'll need the positive reinforcement so I don't do something stupid like rent a male escort."

"Just make sure he's cute and play safe if you do."

"Of course, darling. I don't think I've had anything near me without a layer of latex since that sad little virgin Andrew Smith," she said wistfully. "Hey, I wonder if he's free?"

"Married, six kids."

"Six! My gods, his poor wife."

"She had three to start with. They've since had three more. I saw him about two or three months ago. He looks like he's fifty, but claims he's happy."

"I'm sure he did. Okay love, gotta go. Give Sam a big hug for me, and I'll call you soon."

They rang off, leaving Jake to slump back down on the couch and cover his eyes with the pillow. The silence of the house descended all at once, the dripping of the tap in the bathroom once again filling his ears. He heard a heavy sigh from across the room and lifted the pillow from his eyes, observing Barnaby shift in his basket and continue with his nap. Jake smiled and replaced the pillow watching the swirls of colors behind his eyes as the migraine continued to pound in his head. He mentally wished it away, wanting to be on his best form for meeting Derek Brauer in the evening.

Chapter Fourteen

Rachel in love, he thought. His tough-as-leather best friend had always claimed she was immune. One failed relationship after another had left her nearly completely jaded; Jake knew that her claims of immunity were to shield the fact that she fell in love all too much. Because of that she had steadfastly refused to let herself get too emotionally involved with anyone the last several years, fearing that she would lose sight of her career as a federal prosecutor. Rachel was demanding of her experts and agents, but her giving nature and genuine caring made her highly respected. Her awards had stacked up, and she was considered among the best in her field.

All because of Chris, Jake thought. Their murdered friend had spurred a change in Rachel's career, from environmental law to criminal. She and Chris had been close, and the unsolved murder had lit a fire in her as strong as the one that had burned in Jake.

Sleep was slowly creeping in. Jake felt as if he was suspended in midair, the warm currents of a desert wind flowing over his body. He opened his eyes and saw himself standing on the sparsely wooded slope of a cinder cone, the layers of iron-rich ash rusted into a palate of sunset hues. Slowly turning to his right he saw the lumbering, slumped shape of Mount Adams, its cool glacier-clad surface indifferent to his presence. He raised his hand in greeting to the mountain then started to run down the slope of the cinder cone, bouncing into the air slow and weightlessly, as if he were on the moon.

He could see people in the thicket of Lodge Pole pines at the bottom, and recognized Reverend Crawford and Randy Burrows. They were speaking silently into a microphone stand but waved at him as he passed by. Walter Lugar was standing just behind them, replacing the wheel of his red Mini Cooper, and just beyond him, Emma Kennedy was applying a coat of frosting to the boughs of one of the pine trees.

"I don't think I like the look of this, do you?" she asked him.

Jake reached up and tasted the frosting, which was cool and vaguely lemony. He glanced up at the tree, which he realized was made of graham crackers and mint chocolate. He snapped a piece of branch off and ate it, smiling brightly at Emma. He nodded without saying a word and continued down the path of the ever-thickening forest. The foliage was changing to that of the high northern Cascades—salal, Oregon grape, maple and tall Douglas firs. He had the distinct feeling something was following him, but not in a threatening way. He felt no fear even as the forest grew thicker with every step.

Leona Weinberg suddenly stepped out from behind a tree, brandishing an apple and shaking her fist at him. Her face was purple and bloated, her skin covered with an oily sheen. She opened her mouth and screeched, "Sodomite! You did this to me!"

Jake woke with a start, the pillow falling off his head. Barnaby stirred and stretched, getting up to sniff the pillow and trotting away toward the pantry and a snack. Jake picked up the cushion and shook his head, happily free of the migraine. A quick glance at his watch revealed he'd been asleep nearly two hours.

Groggily, he arose and stretched, heading through the kitchen and out the side door. He went up the outside steps to Sam's office and let himself in, yawning loudly. Sam was over at his computer and didn't look up.

"Feeling better?" he asked Jake.

"Yeah, I think so." Jake slumped onto the couch. "I had the strangest dream though."

"That's hardly new, is it? You've had weird dreams for the record books." Sam turned around in his chair. "I mean, there was that one about the giant squid attacking the submarine while you were on the beach watching with Queen Elizabeth. I mean, what was that all about?"

"Probably something deeply disturbing and sexual."

"I'm not introducing a squid into our relationship. Unless of course the squid was symbolic for a guy in the navy, in which case…"

Jake chucked a cushion at Sam, and Sam laughed and tossed it back to him, glancing at the clock. "Lunch?"

"I had breakfast a little while ago," said Jake. "But I'm feeling a little hungry, so sure."

Sam went into the kitchenette in the office, looking through the fridge for something appetizing. He pulled out some sandwich meat and cheese and turned on the stove to grill a sandwich. Retrieving the butter he asked, "So what gave you the headache?"

"Come on," complained Jake. "The weekend we've had? Mother, Leona Weinberg—"

"Ugh, you can stop right there." Sam buttered two slices of bread and tossed them into the pan, adding cheese.

"I feel a bit bad over that."

"I thought you said you didn't," Sam asked, adding slices of turkey.

"I didn't at first. She was such a hateful old bigot, it's hard to have sympathy for her."

"I sense a 'but' about to be spoken. You want some soup?"

"I'm souped out."

"Likewise. We need to expand our menu a bit." Sam expertly flipped the side of bread with the melted cheese onto the bread with the turkey. "So?"

"So? Oh, the 'but.' Yeah," he shook his head. "I keep thinking of her dying alone over there. Choking on the apple or having a heart attack," he said, keeping his voice steady. "It's just sad, is all."

"Leona Weinberg chose her path a long, long time ago, Jake. People as mean as she was choose to be that way," Sam said, flipping the grilled turkey and cheese onto a plate. "You want it cut in half?"

Jake shook his head. "Not necessary."

"Why don't you tell me what is really bugging you," Sam said, buttering two more slices of bread and dropping them into the pan.

"What do you mean?"

"Ah ha! Don't give me that with the big eyes 'what do you mean.' You're staring at the floor. I don't even have to turn around to know that."

"Oh, can it, you big ape."

"Am I wrong?"

"Fine, but admit, you've been thinking about it too."

"Quit talking with your mouth full, you uncouth heathen." He finished making his sandwich. After consuming half his sandwich, he said, "Okay, I admit it. I've been thinking about it."

"You don't think she died of natural causes either, do you?"

"I'm not sure what to think."

"It's the thing with the thermostat I keep coming back to," said Jake. "Yeah, we know Leona did jack up the heat, but she was also a world-class cheapskate."

"It was why she kept arguing with the gas guy." Sam agreed.

"You really think *she* would have turned up the heat to seventy-eight?"

Sam looked into his husband's malachite green eyes, shrugging. "I don't know. My gut is telling me it's no coincidence, but I really, really hope it is."

Jake returned Sam's gaze and nodded. He too was hoping it was merely a coincidence that Leona Weinberg had dropped dead when she had, but he couldn't shake the feeling that someone had murdered their odious neighbor.

❖

Hours later, Jake glowered at his brother whom, he observed, at least had the decency to look chagrined. Sitting opposite of Jake was the strikingly handsome Derek Brauer, who had just "tagged along for dinner" as Jason had said. Aside from the fact that he had nothing prepared for dinner, Jake didn't like the idea of being interrogated about the demise of their neighbor. In the end, they had gone to the Illahee Inn.

"How's your roast?" Sam asked Jake.

"Fine, fine."

Jason cleared his throat and took a sip of water.

"The wine is excellent," said Derek, taking another swig.

"Not much of a wine connoisseur," Jake said.

"Oh? What's your poison of preference?"

Jake looked at him again. Derek had a sparkling smile full of very white teeth. He had dimples to die for, and dark brown eyes that were sharp and unflinching, taking note of everything. His hair was cut and spiked in every direction—the rough and tumble look that likely took some time to perfect—and his heavy, black-framed glasses fit his face in a stylish *GQ* manner. His lack of shaving for several days also seemed to be a calculated part of his look, along with the maroon shirt that was ever so slightly too tight.

"Jameson," Jason answered. "Favorite of the Finnigans."

"Indeed," Jake agreed. "Usually with some Pepsi, as I like my alcohol sweet, though straight up is fine."

"How about you, Sam?" Derek asked.

"Well, I don't drink often, but when I do it's usually something Caleb makes over at the Bitter End. Lemon drop or appletini or something like that."

Derek looked at Jake and flashed the white teeth again. "Wine, like whiskey, has a lot of elements to it. It takes time to develop an appreciation for the subtleties, same as with whiskey. Though I always say the best wine is the one you like. I don't go for the snobbery of saying it has to be expensive. One of my favorites is a local Skagit Valley wine that retails for about fifteen bucks. The best wild huckleberry wine I've ever tasted."

Jake studied Brauer for a moment and judged the comment sincere. He still couldn't make up his mind about the man. He wasn't unlikable—far from it. He *seemed* very genuine, not at all guarded, and very warm and engaging. He had a good sense of humor, was quick to laugh, and appeared very upbeat.

Seemed was the operative word, and Jake wasn't quite buying it. Underneath it all was a flat note, a hint of insincerity. Derek was not at all acting like a reporter. He hadn't asked anything the least bit pointed, and nothing about the town meeting. Jake wondered if Jason had duly warned Derek not to bring anything up, or if Derek was attempting to lull him into a false sense of security before starting a cross-examination.

"The Inn has a good cellar, even if it is haunted," said Jason with a wink to his brother, referring to the stores of the Inn.

The Illahee Inn Bed and Breakfast was known for its elegant accommodations and the fact that it didn't serve breakfast, contrary to the title. There was a continental brunch served at about ten in the morning, but Emma Kennedy was not a morning person, and the hours of the Inn reflected it.

"Have you seen Emma tonight?" Jake asked.

"She must be around here somewhere," said Sam, looking around. "There's Professor Mills, Verna Monger and that dishrag husband of hers, the Reverend Crawford, and that creepy guy from the police department…"

"Nelson Dorval," Derek said. "One of the most unfriendly people I've ever met."

"Who's he with?" asked Jake, noticing the startlingly attractive woman. She had black, shoulder-length hair casually styled in loose curls, and distinctly Asian features, but pale white skin and green eyes. She was wearing loose slacks and a blazer and looked bored beyond belief.

"Detective Sharon Trumbo," Derek answered as the pair rose to leave. "Very nice woman. Sharp as an X-Acto and a great sense of humor. I wonder what she's doing with *him*? Are you friends with Ms. Kennedy, Jake?"

"Pull your eyes back in your head, Jason," said Jake. We're not close, no. I got to know her a bit through the ferry advisory meetings. Tough as nails but a heart of gold. I voted for her."

"So did I," said Sam. "Excellent business sense, and she single-handedly revitalized a part of Old Town that was going to get plowed under for some ugly condos."

"The houses that are near Sutherland Shipyard?"

Sam nodded. "Those cute little Victorians. She bought the whole row, fixed them up, and turned them into rentals. I guess she's selling them off a bit at a time now."

"She is," agreed Derek. "She's taken some of the money and invested into the *Chinook*."

Jake dropped his fork with a clatter. Sam looking at him, one eyebrow raised.

"Mr. Blackburn told me," Derek said, shrugging.

"I understand that," said Jake. "He didn't tell me."

"Well, you've haven't hardly seen him in the last six months," said Sam.

"I know, I know. It's my fault. I've been preoccupied lately."

"You mean you've been busy," Sam reassured.

"You really need to come up for air from that manuscript," Jason said, patting his pocket. Jake suspected Jason was longing for his pipe, but smoking indoors was prohibited.

"There are days when I think it is writing me," Jake said. He shook his head. "That makes no sense whatsoever."

"Jason didn't mention you were a writer. Actually he's told me very little about either one of you, to be honest," Derek said, giving Jason a sideways glance.

"That's because we're painfully boring," Sam said cheerfully.

"I guess I should have mentioned Jake's a writer. He's published a few stories and articles, but has been working on this book for...how long?"

"A decade. I've only just been able to dedicate myself to it full time, thanks to the generosity of my husband here."

"Just be glad I charge my clients so much."

"So you write mainly fiction then?"

"Mainly," said Jake, being purposefully cryptic. He did not intend to get into what his book was about. It looked as if Derek was about to ask when the oak and leaded glass doors to the dining room opened up and Alex walked in with Emma Kennedy and Miranda Zimmerman.

"Speak of the devil," said Derek.

Alex and Emma Kennedy were involved in a deep conversation as the trio crossed the room and sat down at a far table on the opposite side of the main dining hall.

"Wonder what that is about?" Derek asked.

"Don't know," Jake said, making a mental note to see Alex soon.

They resumed eating, Derek ordering another bottle of wine while they finished the meal. The Victorian willow china was cleared away and they ogled the dessert menu before ordering cheesecake.

"When you have time, Jake, I'd like to ask you about your workout routine. Jason tells me you're a walking junk-food garbage can, and yet you look incredible."

"Thanks. I'm actually cutting back on the weights a little bit. I'm starting to look a little too bulky," Jake lamented.

"If only I had that problem," said Jason.

"You and me both. Problem is I loathe working out. I'm fine with walking but all that banging of metal and running till you're ready to drop doesn't do it for me."

"I think you look fine," said Derek.

"So do I," said Jake, squeezing Sam's thigh under the table. "I only worry about your family's penchant for diabetes."

"Which is why I walk. And diabetes be damned, this is excellent cheesecake."

"I feel like I'm in an episode of the *Golden Girls*," said Derek.

Laughter erupted from the table where Alex, Emma, and Miranda were sitting. Alex glanced across the room, caught sight of Jake and Sam, and immediately came over to their table.

"You've been avoiding me," he said solemnly to Jake.

"I've done nothing of the kind, Alex. You've got yourself all wrapped up in that old boat of yours."

"Which you haven't even seen yet."

"And I've had things going on, which I'm sure Sam has filled you in on."

"Not lately. He banned me from my own boat," said Alex, winking at Sam.

"You didn't tell me that."

"I'm sure I told you. Didn't I tell you?"

"You always think you tell me things, and then you forget."

"No, that's you."

"Be that as it may," said Alex. "I'm going to call you, and we're going to have lunch next week, okay?"

"Absolutely," said Jake, smiling.

"Good. Now Sam, I had an idea about the boat..."

"No, no, no!" said Sam, burying his face in his hands.

Alex broke into a hearty chuckle. "Oh, you're so easy. Well, I've got to get back to my guests. Emma wants a financial report and Miranda's updating me on what she's dug up on Wilde Park, since it seems Longhoffer isn't going to give up as easily as we all thought."

"What do you mean?" asked Sam.

"You'll have to wait for the town meeting next week, but I can say I believe I found his backer."

"I wondered about that," Jake said. "Reed has never struck me as being loaded with cash."

"He isn't. That's why he's pulled my father into this, though I'm sure if I confronted him with it, he'd deny it."

"Your *father*?" said Derek.

"Just one in a long line of sins," said Alex with a sigh. "He's also trying to plow under most of his neighborhood and prevent the eastern half of the Sky to Sea trail from being done. A real peach, my father."

"You going to be bringing this up at the next town meeting?" asked Jake.

He patted Jake on the shoulder and before turning and walking back to his table said, "You'll just have to wait and see."

"Boy, there's a mystery there," Derek said.

Jake smiled to himself, remembering Sam had told him Alex said the same thing about Derek. He was about to say something when his eyes caught who had just strode into the Illahee Inn.

"Oh, shit," said Jake.

"What is it?" asked Sam.

"Look who just walked in," said Jake.

Chapter Fifteen

All four of them turned toward the dining room's two tall mahogany doors to see Alex's parents standing in the doorframe. His slate gray hair appeared glued to his head with hair cream, in a style that had gone out with the Eisenhower administration. Bright blue, red-rimmed eyes burned from his chiseled, weathered face, his expression haughty. His broad-shouldered presence commanded space, and although he seemingly took up the entire doorframe, his shoulders looked slightly hunched. She was an elegant woman in her early sixties, her graying hair pulled up in a tight bun. She wore a pale blue suit complete with gloves. Her burgundy handbag was large enough to conceal a machine gun. She had kind features, soft blue eyes, and a round, firm mouth that been turned down slightly by time.

All four of them turned to see if he had spotted his parents in the doorway.

"Oh shit," said Sam.

"He hasn't seen them yet," whispered Jake.

"Talk about speaking of the devil…" Jason trailed off.

"Those two despise one another, don't they?" asked Derek. "I've seen Blackburn the Second in the office. I *wondered* what the hell he and Reed were doing. I knew he couldn't be there just to rant about how Alex ousted him from the family business."

Just at that moment, Alexander Blackburn II spotted his son sitting at the table. He marched stalwartly across the room, nearly colliding with Jake's chair. The room had gotten deathly quiet since he had entered. One woman had frozen with her fork halfway to her mouth; another was chewing her breadsticks with such ferocity Jake wondered if her jaw would be able to take the force of it.

Alexander Blackburn shattered the silence by barking, "Well, I see they let anyone in here."

Alex looked up from the table at his father towering above him, and he managed a thin smile. "Hello, Pop."

"Don't you call me that." Blackburn hissed. "I have no son. My son died the day he stuck a knife in my back."

"Oh come now, Dad," said Alex quietly. "What a boring dig. You can do better than that."

"Alex," said Vivian Blackburn, looking between her husband and son, a pained expression on her face. "Please, A.J., not here."

"Shut up, Vivian. I'm having a word here with the son of a bitch who threw me out of my own company like I was yesterday's trash. How kind of him to leave me with my savings and investments, even though that is nearly gone because of all the lawyers I've had to hire trying to break down his illegal takeover."

"It wasn't illegal, Dad. And that's why you've gone broke paying lawyers, because there is nothing you can do."

"But the ungrateful little bastard didn't stop there, did he, Vivian?" Blackburn ranted, his voice growing louder. "Not only did he throw my ass out on the street, he tossed out every one of my board of directors. Freddy Thompson killed himself, you know. I hope you're happy about that."

Alex's expression became stony. "Just good business, isn't it, Dad?" he asked, his voice like sharpened steel. "Isn't that what you said about Maureen Barnham? Just good business?"

The sound of A.J. Blackburn's fist hitting his son's face was flat and somehow not dramatic. Alex's head flew backward, blood pouring from his nose. Jake and Sam were instantly on their feet, as was Emma Kennedy.

"Now you listen to me, old man," Alex said, turning to face his father, his voice filled with barely controlled fury. "That is the last time you hit me, do you understand? The next time you try will be the last time you draw a breath on this earth."

Blackburn stared his son in the face, his nostrils flared, breath coming in heaves. His fist was still balled at his side, his face a mask of hatred. Next to him, Vivian Blackburn wept silently, her hands covering her mouth.

"I think you had better leave, Mr. Blackburn," Emma Kennedy said.

"That's a swell idea," said Jake, moving in next to Blackburn.

He returned his gaze to his son, unclenching his fist. "You just wait. All of you. You just wait until I'm done with this crop of bumpkins you call a town. Wilde Park is just the beginning. You mark my words. Come on, Vivian, let's get out of here."

"And I will thank you to never set foot on the premises again," said Emma.

Blackburn turned and looked as if he was about to say something, but again eyed Jake, whose arms were crossed in front of him, and decided better of it. He stomped out of the dining room, Vivian Blackburn trailing after him like a wraith.

Jake turned to Alex, who was dabbing at his nose with one of the cloth napkins. "I'm sorry, Emma. I'll pay for everyone's dinner," said Alex.

"What are you, nuts? That was the best piece of dinner theater this town has ever seen," she said, as patrons slowly began talking and resuming their meals. "I should charge double."

Alex laughed as he stemmed the flow of blood from his nose. "Ah, I knew there was a reason I went into business with you."

"That old Irish sense of humor," Kennedy agreed.

"Alex, are you okay?" Miranda asked.

"Yeah, it's not broken or anything. The old man can still pack a wallop though."

"What the hell was that all about?" Jake asked, kneeling next to Alex.

"A very old wound that I rubbed some salt in. I shouldn't be too surprised that he flipped out like that," he said, taking notice of Jake's arched left eyebrow. "Ah, you want an explanation."

"No, he doesn't," said Sam, tugging Jake up. "Come on, Nosy, show's over."

Jake gave Sam an insolent look and turned back to Alex. "You sure you're okay?"

"Yeah, Jake. I'm fine. I'm sorry if I spoiled your dinner."

"We were on dessert anyway," said Jason.

"Jason," Jake said, exasperated. He turned his attention back to Alex. "Call me tomorrow, okay?"

"Will do," said Alex, dabbing his nose. "And Jake? Thanks for coming to my defense."

"Any time, Alex. Any time."

❖

They had said their good-byes to Jason and Derek and headed for Wilde Park. It was another flawless, clear night, with the sliver of a waning moon slowly rising over Mount Baker. Frost had started to form on the grass by the time they arrived, and Jake was happy he'd decided on his heavier coat. They took the path that led down to the water, and on the beach they found the trunk of an old Douglas fir, long polished smooth by the waves, and sat down, listening to the gentle lap of the waves on the shore and the gurgle of the creek beside them.

Sam glanced around for a moment, and then passionately kissed his husband.

"Yowsa," said Jake, feeling the blood rush to various parts of his body. "What was that for?"

"For being gallant."

"Oh, knock it off."

"Well, you were. You jumped right to your feet ready to pound that old bastard were he to try something again."

"I would have, you know. I don't know how anyone—a father in particular—could hit someone like that."

"Well, Alex did mention rubbing salt in an old wound."

"Yeah, but hitting Alex would be like kicking a puppy, you know?"

"You have a point. Although when he told his father if he ever hit him again it would be the last thing he did, that was a tone I'd never heard before. I could see Alex pulling the trigger on someone."

"Sam, that's an awful thing to say." Jake shrugged, moving in closer to Sam to share the body heat. "You're right, though. I mean, it was just…"

"Icy?"

"Yes," said Jake. "Like this log. My bum's going numb."

"Yeah, mine too. But it's such a pretty night."

Jake closed his eyes, listening to the comforting gurgle of the creek as it emptied into the Bay. He took a deep breath and opened his eyes, looking across Ferryboat Channel over to Rosario Island. The lights of the tiny village near the ferry dock glimmered in the clear air, the rest of the island a dark mass behind it. The small ferry *Rosario Islander* cut across the channel, its navigation lights shining brightly in the darkness. To his right, the lights of Arrow Bay blazed in a steady orange glow.

"What'd you think of Derek?" Jake asked Sam.

"I like him well enough."

"But?"

"Even though I'm glad he didn't start quizzing us about Leona, I can't say I entirely trust him."

"Jason probably warned him not to. I wish he'd deterred him with more hunting stories. Dinner was kind of awkward." He paused. "I don't trust him either."

"The Weinberg thing was hanging over everything the entire time," said Sam.

"Like the drunk uncle at Christmas no one likes to talk about. Something I didn't understand about what Derek said about the *Examiner*. Was Reed Longhoffer actually relieved of his post?"

"From what I gather, the younger brother, David, is en route to Arrow Bay as we speak. Marion sent out the S.O.S. and included the copy of last week's *Examiner* to him as evidence. Reed is probably going to be replaced on his post as soon as the younger brother comes back, but right now they're playing it cool and letting him think he's won."

"I also wonder what Alex meant about Longhoffer not giving up on the park here."

Sam sighed heavily. "That worries me too. Reed Longhoffer is a slippery one. If he can force the sale of this land by some odd loophole, he'll do it. And knowing he's in league with Blackburn Junior doesn't exactly fill my heart with joy and mirth."

"A match made in hell. Two times the oily deviousness for the price of one. And then there was the somewhat cryptic statement he made."

"'Wilde Park is just the beginning.' Doesn't sound like anything pleasant to me."

What I can't figure out is why those two are so determined to stop the Sky to Sea Trail from being completed."

"Don't kid yourself, Jake. While you know I support it, and love the unique character this town has with the greenbelts Professor Mills spoke so eloquently about, it locks up a *lot* of real estate. The town's nearly reached its building cap. Unless they expand the city limits again, the Sky to Sea is going to basically shut off any more commercial development in town."

"Those two old bastards—"

"Jacob."

"They're old bastards, Samuel, you'll have to deal with the obscenity. In any event, those two sons of bitches—"

"Now you're doing it to goad me."

"—could do more for expanding commerce in this town by rehabilitating some of the buildings in Old Town."

"I agree in principle, and certainly something should be done, particularly with the old hotel, but none of the buildings in Old Town could house a SuperLoMart. Arrow Bay is such a tourist draw and is such a pretty little town. I don't understand why anyone would want to destroy that."

"Me either," said Jake. "But I assume that's why Alex has the intrepid Ms. Zimmerman on the case?"

"No one knows this town better than our lovely librarian. I don't think there's a skeleton in this town's ample supply of closets that she doesn't know about," said Sam, shivering. "Okay, beautiful out here or not, I'm freezing my butt off."

"Well, we can go home and warm up your butt."

"I was thinking of a long soak in a hot bath."

"Yes, I'm sure you are."

"I didn't say I'd be in the tub alone," said Sam.

"Ah, lovely old claw foot tubs. I knew there was a reason we kept it in the house."

"You mean aside from the fact it weighs a bloody ton and could only have gone out of the house via a hole cut into the roof," said Sam, rising.

They started back up the hillside and into the park proper. The cold had chased most of the day users of the park away hours ago, and the trails were empty. They decided to loop the long way around to the parking lot to get a bit of a walk in. Bracing as it was and despite the temperature of Sam's posterior, neither of them wanted to let the cold, quiet night flit away without being fully appreciated.

"How's your headache?" asked Sam.

"Gone, finally. Must have started to go when I was talking to Rachel. It was good to hear from her finally."

"She's such a wonderful person. I just wish she could find someone equally as wonderful for her."

"I'm sorry things are going so badly for her, but I'm happy she's finally getting out of D.C."

Sam stopped suddenly. He turned to his right, peering into the thicket of wild roses bordering the creek.

"What is it?"

"I thought I saw something."

"Maybe it's Misty Snipes, come to cook your children and eat them," said Jake with a yawn.

"Oh har har. Don't you ever catch something out of the corner of your eye and can't tell what it is, but you're sure you saw something there?"

Jake gave Sam an appraising look and said, "How long has it been since you had your prescription updated?"

"Oh, quit being Mr. Clever." Sam stopped suddenly. "Did you see that?"

"See what?"

"I just thought I saw somebody go into the bushes."

"Probably Gladys. She scared the hell out of us the last time we were here, remember?"

"I don't think it was Gladys."

"Where about?" Jake asked.

Sam pointed to a thicket of huckleberry and sword ferns enveloped in a swath of shadow. The streetlamp nearest them cast the far edge of the path into deep gloom, and it was nearly impossible to see between the branches.

"In there?" Jake asked, picking up a large rounded chunk of granite from the edge of the path.

"About there, yes."

"Okay Gladys Nyberg, you've got until the count of three, and I'm throwing this rock in. One, two, three." Jake hurled the rock into the thicket with a quick rocket launch of his muscular arm.

"Ouch! Son of a bitch!" Detective Adam Haggerty leapt up from the brush.

"What the hell are you doing creeping around in the bushes?"

Haggerty was rubbing the back of his head. "That's assaulting a police officer, I'll have you know," he said.

"No it isn't," said Jake. "I thought you were Gladys Nyberg and threw the rock about five feet away from where I *thought* someone might be. No jury would convict me."

Haggerty gingerly massaged where a lump was rising like bread baking in an oven. "I still don't appreciate being pelted by large stones, Mr. Finnigan."

"I'm sure you don't. If you hadn't been hiding in the bushes, it wouldn't have happened."

"Had it crossed your mind I might be hiding out in these bushes on work related matters?"

Jake appraised the detective, clad in blue sweats and New Balance tennis shoes. On the front of his sweatshirt were the words ARROW BAY POLICE DEPARTMENT and the city seal. "Undercover, I'm sure."

"Of course," said Haggerty irritably. He followed Jake's eyes to his sweatshirt and scowled.

"I think, Sam, that Detective Haggerty was out for his evening jog when he heard our voices. And he dove into the bushes to *spy* on us. Maybe he was hoping to hear us give away some sort of incriminating sort of statement, like 'Oh dear, I wish we'd dumped Leona Weinberg's body in the ravine instead' or 'Gosh, weren't those bloodstains hard to wash off.'"

"Oh, drama, drama, drama, Jacob," said Sam, massaging his temple with his left hand. "Really, Detective, my husband is a very nice fellow when he's had enough sleep and hasn't been fighting a headache all day. Sometimes the author just creeps through a little too much."

"Either that or he was hoping to catch us snogging as some sort of cheap thrill," said Jake, eyeing the detective again.

"Snogging?" said Haggerty.

"He picked that one up from *Harry Potter*. Jacob, you're being an ass. Leave the nice detective alone before he tosses your well-meaning butt into the cooler overnight for being a melodramatic snoop."

"I am not being a snoop," protested Jake. "Don't you want to know why he was in the bushes?"

"Well, frankly Detective Haggerty, it *is* a fair enough question. You about scared the hell out of us."

"I apologize," said Haggerty, scratching his goatee. "I *was* jogging. I do it when the weather's reasonably good. I heard your voices, and I honestly didn't know who it was so I ducked into the bushes. Despite what was said at the meeting, drug deals have been taking place in this park, so I thought I'd see what was going on."

"And once you realized it was us, why didn't you come out?"

"I couldn't be sure you weren't dealing drugs."

"What, to each other?" asked Sam, incredulous.

"And had it been a drug dealer, what would you have done? Slapped them and told them to knock it off?"

"The waist pouch contains my cell phone and badge."

"And you would have asked them politely not to shoot you?"

Haggerty unzipped his sweatshirt, revealing a shoulder holster.

Jake looked skeptical, shrugging.

"We'll just leave you alone now, Detective," said Sam.

"Look, I'm sorry if I startled you."

"I think I'll recover," said Sam. "Now if you'll excuse us, we'll just head home."

Jake opened his mouth to protest, but one warning look from Sam made him close it. He glowered and gave Haggerty a nod before heading back up the trail toward the parking lot.

❖

Adam Haggerty watched the pair, a grin spreading on his face. The two of them reminded him of some 1930s comedy pairing, like Myrna Loy and William Powell, which he found fascinating. Haggerty also thought that if circumstances were different, he might like to know them in life. But he had a case to work on.

He stepped back on the gravel path and resumed jogging, which he had been doing before hearing their voice. He hadn't wanted to tell them he had also seen someone *else* in the park, which was why he was in the bushes.

He thought the figure he'd seen had a weapon, possibly a knife, but he couldn't be sure. He didn't want to alarm them unduly, so he hadn't mentioned it.

The cold night deepened, the temperature dropping even lower. Haggerty had finally had enough and jogged back to his car. Once inside, despite his freely sweating body, he quickly turned on the heat, watching the strange depths of Wilde Park disappear in his review mirror as he pulled out onto Enetai Avenue.

Chapter Sixteen

Derek Brauer stepped from his car Tuesday morning, October the 16th, feeling a steady rush of happiness surge through his veins. He was working on a good story, and finally felt his life was falling into place after the derailing it had taken in San Francisco.

Entering the *Examiner* office, Derek bid hello to Doris Woolsey, the paper's receptionist, before stepping into the newsroom. He had been surprised by the new desks and computer terminals, figuring a small outfit like the *Examiner* would have last been decorated around the year of his birth. The wooden file cabinets against the pale sage painted walls remained, but they were officially antiques and added an air of class to the newsroom. Above the file cabinets, the walls were lined with historic photos taken by the *Examiner*'s photographers over the years. The latest one, a color shot of the ferry *Kulshan* arriving in the fog, had been Jason's contribution.

No, for a chicken shit weekly rag, it wasn't a bad gig, all things considered. He could file the stories for the weekly in his sleep, knocking them out in two hours tops, and then focus his energies elsewhere. His fuel bill was becoming exorbitant until he found out a commuter train ran from Mount Burlington to Seattle. That had made life—and his continued digging into stories that he knew would not please his editor *or* Jason—much easier.

Reed's door was shut and the blind drawn. The thought of Jason drew his attention to the red light burning over the basement door. Jason was downstairs developing some black and white photos. He sighed at that. Jason was actually working on making prints of the old negatives to use up the last of the chemicals. The transition to digital and a modern operation was underway, though the paper was bleeding money.

He shoved these thoughts aside, waving at Marion Burd, who was busy typing away furiously at her computer while talking on the phone. She waved back while he crossed over to his own desk in a cubbyhole between a stanchion and the filing cabinets. He liked the desk as it gave him some privacy from the rest of the newsroom, which held the desks of advertising manager Duane Mollet, "Northwest Life" writer Joyce Eckhart and senior reporter Marion Burd. He could buckle down and sort of shut off the rest of the newsroom from where he sat, and more importantly, kept everyone else from knowing what he was working on.

Derek might—*might*—have settled into the quiet life, had it not been for the Susan Crane murder story being dumped into his lap. He was still unsure *why* Alexander Blackburn III had given him the information that had broken the case. Derek didn't like McAvoy, Blackburn's stooge, and he didn't like being manipulated. After the story faded from the public conscience, Derek began poking around into his "patron's" background and had found a less-than-snowy past. Derek felt in his bones there was much more than the man was letting on, and to reaffirm to himself that Blackburn couldn't be trusted, he'd snuck into the crime scene where Crane's killer had been caught after the police had left it. Derek had nearly killed himself in the process, but he'd uncovered one thing: there had been more people involved than McEvoy or the police had let on, he was sure of it.

While he felt free to poke around Blackburn's background, McEvoy was not someone Derek Brauer wanted to cross. The man had a face like a pit bull carved in granite and eyes that glittered unpleasantly. They missed nothing, Derek could tell. McEvoy had eyeballed him with the stare of someone who has had a long distrust of not only the press, but humanity in general before he tossed over the documents without a word. Derek had thanked him and watched him go, making a note to check into his background as soon as he had a chance.

What he had turned up scared him more than anything he had so far: nothing. McEvoy's past was as blank as white paper, his Internet profile virtually non-existent. This development left Derek with a queasy feeling about black ops, CIA spooks, and a litany of other deep cover government operations. Derek had little doubt McEvoy had a long trail of corpses behind him, and for the moment, he had backed off delving into Alex Blackburn's history.

Derek was able to get the feel of the town and its people. It was nothing like the pace of San Francisco but was compelling in ways he had not expected. Derek found the town more and more unnerving. For all its bucolic setting with Mount Baker looming over the town, the San Juans, the sprawling, beautiful vistas imbued him with a hallucinogenic sense of abnormality. Arrow Bay was *odd*, unsettling to him. Having been at the *Examiner* for a year, Derek now knew that all-American façade presented and promoted by the town had a huge crack in it. Scandal and deceit bubbled right below the veneer. He'd found evidence of that dating back to practically the moment Arrow Bay had been founded up to the present day. He'd combed countless back issues of the *Examiner* and found story after story.

This course of inquiry had led him to Miranda Zimmerman, the lovely blonde librarian who had also taken a keen interest in her hometown. Talking with her, Derek found out even more of the sordid bits of Arrow Bay's history. Miranda had documented some of the weirder events in a thick scrapbook which she kept locked in a large safe at her home.

He didn't like her, though. He hadn't been able to charm her, and even though he had no interest in women, he prided himself on being able to charm *anyone*. Zimmerman was having none of it, and that first meeting had been his last. Zimmerman was suddenly unavailable. In retrospect, he knew he'd made his mistake when he turned the conversation toward the Blackburn family.

Jason strode over to his desk with a plate of pastry. "So tell me what you're working on," he asked, taking a bite of a raspberry Danish.

"Still waiting for the cause of death of Leona Weinberg. Marion's been kind enough to hand me that since—" He looked over at the closed office door that had REED LONGHOFFER, EDITOR on it in gilt letters. "Is he in?"

"Not this morning. I gather he's gone down to the police department to harangue them over something or other."

"Anyway, she's let me take that since she's bound and determined to hunt down everything Reed's been trying to hide on the whole Wilde Park fiasco."

"Marion's a trooper. And she's plenty pissed at him for calling her an 'old fossil' the other day."

"I thought you were downstairs," Derek said, motioning to the red light.

"I was. I was about to go grab some photos for Marion. Jonas is down there cleaning out his stuff."

"Why's he got the light on?"

"Haven't the foggiest. He may very well have turned on the wrong switch," he said, grabbing Derek's phone and pushing the number for the extension for the basement. "Jonas, this is Jason. *Jason.* Yes. I'm fine. Jonas, why have you got the development light on? Yes, it is. I can see it from here, Jonas. Yes. No, shut it off. Well if it's dark in there now, try the other switch. Well, turn the lights on and then turn the other switch off," he said, shaking his head and covering the mouth piece. "They didn't retire him a moment too soon."

"What's he doing after he leaves here?"

"Daughter is coming from Arizona to collect him. She's been after him for years to move down there to be closer to the grandkids—Hi, Jonas. No, no. It's Jason. *Jason.* Yes, okay, I'll be right down," he said, hanging up. "He turned off the light and now can't find the switch. I better watch him to make sure he's not making off with our photo archives," he said, walking away from Derek's desk and clomping down the cellar stairs.

Derek chuckled and flipped through his mail—letters from the usual two or three old cranks in town who complained about his stories. They never left their names, but he recognized the handwriting after a while.

The third envelope was different. Plain manila with no return address. The front looked as if it were standard Times New Roman font, with just his name and the address for the *Examiner*. Derek slit the envelope and shook a single sheet of paper out.

Unfolding it, he wasn't sure whether or not to take it seriously. It was a letter made up of cut outs from newspapers, a message spelling out a chilling warning:

Weinberg was no accident. She won't be the last, either.
From a Concirned Citisen

He looked around to see if anyone else had seen the letter, or his opening it. Everyone seemed thoroughly engrossed in their own work. Still glancing around, Derek carefully opened his bottom desk drawer and pulled out an empty zip-lock bag he kept for paperclips. Using a pen he neatly slipped the note and the envelope into the bag, sealing it tightly. He shut the letter up in the bottom drawer and pondered what to do next.

❖

In his office at the Arrow Bay police station, Detective Adam Haggerty listened carefully to the argument Chief Sanderson was having across the hall with veteran detective Nelson Dorval. He was carefully folding a piece of blue *kami* paper into a butterfly. He had already finished the hummingbird he'd started when Dorval had entered Sanderson's office, but this tirade was lasting longer than he had anticipated, forcing him to start another piece of origami.

Haggerty found origami soothing. It kept his mind clear and helped him focus his thoughts. The difficulty of his cases could be judged by the amount of origami flooding his office. On the last case he'd worked, the top of the filing cabinet turned into a small zoo of brightly colored paper animals. The case before that one had resulted in only five different creatures. He speculated the Weinberg case would end up occupying most of his file cabinet top again.

Dorval was, as usual, making no effort to keep his voice down. Most of the squad on the second floor was able to hear his outburst. Sanderson had responded in his usual soft-spoken manner, but over the last few minutes his voice had raised enough so that Haggerty could hear him.

"He comes in here looking like a goddamn bum," Dorval said. "Always playing that goddamn music in his office and never dressing to code."

"I'll admit his methods are a little unorthodox, but they are effective. His cases are watertight and if you've not noticed, the conviction rate on his cases is well over ninety per cent!"

Haggerty made another careful fold, smiling to himself. Both he and the chief knew that *all* his cases had resulted in convictions. Sanderson was superstitious and didn't want to ruin Haggerty's winning streak. Haggerty would be the first to admit his success was due in great part to his partner, Sharon Trumbo, who was as fanatical about details as he was. Kulshan County's brand new crime lab and their highly efficient, overworked team also contributed to his overall success. Haggerty was always one to give credit where it was due.

Steve Pickens

"Is anything wrong with his reports, Dorval?"

"No."

"Is there anything wrong with the quality of his work?"

"It isn't that, George, it's—"

"Let me remind you, Nelson, you're only *acting* captain. As soon as Montgomery is back from maternity leave, you're back to being detective. This is the third unprovoked rant you've had about Haggerty in the last month, and I've damn well had it. Haggerty has put his time in and he earned that goddamn promotion. The next time you come in here to have a bitch fest I suggest you damn well have something to back it up or I'll put you back on traffic duty again. Now get out!"

Chapter Seventeen

Adam watched Dorval storm out of the office and down the hallway. There was the slam of the Chief's door, then silence as people got back to work.

He sat back in his chair, looking at the empty side of the desk where Sharon Trumbo usually sat. She was out at lunch, probably picking up her usual salad and soup combo from the Bitter End. He hoped she would get back soon.

Part of him knew Dorval was absolutely correct. He often went for long stretches without speaking to anyone and quite often did have low jazz music playing in his office. It helped clear his head. They were not conscious forms of rebellion in any way. He had the goatee because he felt he looked too young without it and knew from experience suspects didn't take him seriously when questioning them. One had made a cutting remarking about Doogie Howser, and the Van Dyke had started growing the next day. He didn't follow the dress code to the letter, as he was always tramping through Arrow Bay's pastures and creeks and got tired of shelling out for new shoes.

Adam made the final fold on the butterfly and held it in the palm of his hand, his long, narrow fingers cradling the pale blue figure that had moments before been a square of flat paper. He placed it softly on Sharon's desk, which was set back-to-back against his.

The contrast between the two desks was noticeable. Sharon's was a clutter of things, including an ailing jade plant, photos of her family and friends, and a huge stack of papers. Her screensaver was always set to the scene of a river with leaves gently floating across the silver surface.

His desk was completely bereft of anything personal, save for a copy of *The Portable Blake,* which he always had with him. Pens were all in their cup, papers neatly stacked, and everything was right within reach. The only anomalies were the stack of *kami* paper and a box of Junior Mints, which he tended to eat obsessively when concentrating.

The walls of their office were a blend of their tastes, however. Together they had decided they weren't going to have the same sterile, boring offices as their coworkers and had decided to put photos up—something else that probably irked Dorval. The Trumbo/Haggerty office was the only place outside of the lobby that actually had photographs. He and Sharon had mutually decided to have scenic photographs of Arrow Bay and Kulshan County. Their last purchase, ironically enough, was a silver gel photo of Wilde Park in the fog, with the sun just bursting out. The photo had been taken by Jason Finnigan.

Sharon Trumbo poked her head in the office, as if to make sure there wasn't a new crime scene in the space, stepping cautiously in before sitting at her desk, setting the bag with her soup and salad down. She caught sight of the blue butterfly on her desk and said, "Ah."

"Ah?"

"Well, this," she said, picking up the butterfly, "explains why I nearly collided with Dorval on my way in."

"Our acting captain has a bee in his bonnet," said Haggerty.

"He's still pissed at Nancy for putting us on the Weinberg thing," said Sharon dismissively, referring to the other captain in the police force, Nancy Flowers. "He always waits until she's gone to go to George."

"I have noticed that," he said.

"How was your dinner with him the other night?" he asked.

"Don't remind me," Sharon said, rolling her eyes. "That's why he's in a bad mood. I thoroughly rained on his parade. I told him never to cross the line like that again."

"Was he inappropriate?"

"No," Sharon said. "Just…sneaky. It wasn't a date. He is married after all and he really *did* go over some department policies, but it just *felt* creepy. I just wish I'd been a little more patient: I could have seen Blackburn Junior punch out Blackburn the Third."

"Probably best you didn't," Haggerty said. "You know Dorval would have wanted to throw them both in the tank."

"I hadn't thought of that. You're right," she said, fishing out her plastic soupspoon.

"Chicken noodle?"

"Chicken and dumpling."

"It smells good," he said wistfully.

Shaking her head, Sharon pulled out a second container of soup and set it before him. Grinning, he opened the soup and inhaled deeply. "You're a treasure," he said.

"And you are a pain. One of these days when I say I'm going to get lunch I wish you'd just let me get it for you too, since I do that anyway. And you owe me $4.50."

Haggerty dug out his wallet and handed her a five-dollar bill. "Keep the extra for me being a pain."

"That I can do," she said, taking a bite out of her salad. "So what's new?"

"Leona Weinberg did have apple in her throat, but that wasn't what caused her death."

"What did?"

"Poison."

"Poison?"

"Digitalis," Haggerty replied. "Organic, not from any pharmaceutical company."

"I knew that was too much to hope for. Where'd it come from?"

"All over, I expect. Foxglove grows wild all over the place around here. Highway 22 is lined with the stuff."

"In the spring and summer."

"It's still deadly when it has died back," Adam replied.

"Was it in the apple?" Trumbo asked.

"Yep. It was in *all* the apples. Small puncture mark on the uneaten ones, hidden skillfully in the calyx."

"The what?" asked Sharon, several years out of a biology class.

"That bit at the bottom that used to be the flower," said Adam. Continuing, he said, "And it's a damn good thing she was a loner. Anyone grabbing one for a snack would have keeled over dead. Every apple in that bowl had a lethal dose in it, three times the amount required to kill an adult human," said Haggerty. "Not that it takes much to be lethal."

"She didn't taste it?"

"Digitalis is sweet. It would have been easily masked by the apple."

"Okay, so where did the apples come from? You're acting awfully calm about this when there's a potential product tampering case here," said Sharon doubtfully.

"Nope, not a product tampering case. The apples came from her own backyard. It's a good thing Leona was greedy and didn't share any with the other members of the council."

"You're sure about that?" Sharon joked. "Well, with two others on the council…"

"Sharon," Haggerty chided gently.

"Sorry, sorry. So how'd the apples get poisoned?"

"There was no evidence of a break-in. At first glance anyway. Take a look at this," said Haggerty, opening his desk drawer and tossing a crime scene photo over to Sharon.

She picked it up and studied it. It was a color photo of the walk leading up to the front door. Flanking either side of the path spaced at regular intervals was a collection of ugly ceramic dwarves.

"I saw these while I was there. What am I looking for?"

"Keep looking at the dwarves," said Haggerty gently. "Notice anything about them?"

"Other than they're all hideous? No."

"Keep looking. It's not readily apparent."

"The figure closest to the door is different. The colors are too bright. It's a hide-a-key, right?"

"I had it dusted for prints. Nothing, of course, totally wiped clean."

"But it was there, right? In a compartment in the bottom?"

"World's ugliest one I've ever seen, but yes. Which leads me to wonder what that broken one looked like."

"Broken one?"

"Finnigan and O'Conner told me that about two weeks back Weinberg arrived home madder than hell. She accused their dog…" He pulled the report out and began flipping through it. Finally, he found what he wanted. "…Barnaby, a beagle, of breaking her dwarf Bashful."

"But the dog didn't do it," said Trumbo. "The yard is completely fenced in, and I get the feeling the O'Conner-Finnigan boys keep an eye on their little guy."

"He's a very well-behaved animal. The neighbors across the street and next door said they've never seen the dog loose in the neighborhood. O'Conner said he sometimes lets him run around at the park, but never lets him out of sight."

"You trust him on that?"

"I've got no reason not to. Your report indicate otherwise?"

"No. Nothing so much as a traffic ticket, although there was a car accident last year. O'Conner was not at fault. Sister works for the ferry system, mother teaches art at the college and has her studio in town, as you know. Both of them are clean as well. Sam O'Conner has won several design awards for his ships, done some major contracts in this country and abroad and has a sterling reputation. Files his taxes on time, no problems there either. Two things did crop up."

"They were?"

"Domestic violence in his early twenties. Seems a previous boyfriend beat him up pretty badly. Said individual, a…Thomas White, is currently having an extended stay at the pen in Walla Walla courtesy of the state for manslaughter."

"Poor guy," Haggerty said, shaking his head. "O'Conner, that is. He seems like a very gentle soul. Hitting him would be akin to torturing defenseless animals."

"Second incident predates that, back when he was just a kid. A little odd…"

"What was that?"

"The death of his father. Police found him at the bottom of the Harbor Steps in Seattle. No one came forward to having witnessed the fall, and he had a blood alcohol level well above the legal limit for being intoxicated even back then. It was ruled accidental."

"Why is that so odd?"

"Well, for one thing O'Conner is the mother's maiden name. She had all their names legally changed two months after the death of the father, one Philip Baker."

"Did you run him?"

"Oh yeah. Rap sheet quite long there—domestic stuff, drunk and disorderly, bar room brawls. Philip Baker was one mean guy, it seems," said Sharon. "The officer at the scene is retired now but I called him on a hunch. Something in that report just seemed a little off."

"This soup is incredible," said Haggerty, closing his eyes and taking a spoonful, enjoying every flavorful nuance as it spread over his tongue. "What'd the guy say?"

"Nothing, really, just that something felt a little wrong."

"Like?"

"Like the kid had a black eye and so did the mother, for one. Allegedly the kid—Sam O'Conner—had a schoolyard fight. Evelyn

O'Conner said she had tripped in the garden. She and the kids were living with her brother and sister-in-law at the time. They hadn't even seen Phil Baker in three or four years, so they said. They claim not to have seen him the night in question, either."

"Okay, that is a little weird," Haggerty admitted. "You don't think the kid had anything to do with it, do you?"

"No, and neither did the guy I spoke to. He wasn't certain about Evelyn O'Conner or the brother either, but let it go because the brother was good friends with the police chief, the mayor and the county prosecutor to name a few. And, in any event, he said he knew the world was better off without a bastard like Phil Baker in it so he dropped it."

"I'm inclined to agree," said Haggerty. "What about the Finnigan brothers?"

"The elder, Jason, has a lead foot. Several speeding tickets, all paid on time. Former photojournalist for the San Francisco *Chronicle*. Was known as professional and polite by the SFPD. Covered a few of the more gruesome cases down there. Editor at the *Chronicle* feels he didn't really have the stomach for what he was doing so he left."

"That happens," said Haggerty, thinking of the first murder he'd ever seen. It had nearly been his last. He glanced up at the photo Jason had taken now adorning their wall. "I would say his talents certainly lie elsewhere anyway."

"I'd agree. I love that photo. He's got a great eye, and that would be wasted on crime scenes. I know what you're thinking."

"Emerson's attic."

"That was a rough one."

He smiled at her, nodding. There was a reason Sharon Trumbo was his partner. They simply worked well together, each bringing their own unique perspective to a case. Sharon's laser-like perceptions had been off-putting to most of her partners in the past, just as Haggerty's eccentricities had alienated him from most of the other detectives in the force. For some reason, his and Trumbo's styles just melded, and the results were truly remarkable.

"What else on the older brother?"

"That's about it. He was the victim of identity theft in San Francisco and had a heck of a time repairing his credit. Other than that, he's just been hired on at the *Examiner* as photographer and archivist."

"And the brutally honest younger brother?"

"Well, you remember the Susan Crane case. He was one of the folks on board the ferry *Elwha* who found her body."

"All too well," said Haggerty, considering. "Maybe that is why he so keenly denied poking his nose into the investigation. He looked really shaken by that."

"I think I know why."

"Oh? What else?"

"I'll get to it. The background check didn't reveal anything in the last several years. Works for the ferry system and has for about eight years. Currently on a leave of absence. Prior to that, went to school at Western Washington University in Bellingham. Grew up in Port Jefferson across Admiralty Inlet. No criminal background at all."

"In short, not likely to have snuck over to Leona Weinberg's house with a syringe full of distilled foxglove," said Haggerty. "What prompted the other comment?"

"Well, he had no criminal background, but the Port Jefferson PD remembers him very well."

"Oh?" Haggerty said.

"Yeah. Back when he was in high school, his best friend was murdered. It seems Mr. Finnigan wrote a scathing letter and published it in the school paper. The local newspaper picked it up, and then the Seattle affiliates. Caused a bit of trouble."

"From a high school kid's letter?"

"Finnigan does his research. It was a blistering accusation of homophobia. He accused the police of ignoring the case because his friend was gay. Most of the police took it for what it was—the emotional outpouring of someone who'd just lost their best friend since early childhood, but it triggered an investigation into the department by the state."

"Hmm, what'd they find?"

She sighed and said, "You want my gut feeling?"

He arched an eyebrow at her.

"I think his accusations had some merit. It was big good ol' boys club at the Port Jefferson PD back then. Other than the one detective who spent a good deal of time on the case, it was shoved under the rug. There was basically nothing to go on, but I got the impression they didn't do as much as they could have."

"And the state?" asked Haggerty.

"It's between the lines. You know how stuff like that goes. They found they could have probably done more, but that they'd really done nothing wrong. Finnigan didn't file a complaint."

"Well, you were right," Haggerty said. "That explains some things."

"What exactly were you thinking?"

"Do you remember seeing him on the ferry last year?" Haggerty asked.

"No. I was so mad when that idiot Danvers came on board and ordered us all off, I hardly remember anything else about that day."

"When I first saw him, he was shaking, and not just from the cold. I'd guess borderline shock. His face had a very haunted look to it, and I couldn't place what it was. I knew he was upset. Who wouldn't be after seeing that? But I could tell it ran deeper with him."

"With what happened to his friend, it would be hard not to flash back on that," Sharon said.

"Exactly. Who killed his friend?"

She shrugged. "No one knows. The case is still open. Ice cold, but still open."

"Well, that explains a little too," he said. He looked at Sharon. "You think any of them had anything to do with Leona's demise?"

"I can't see it. I suppose people have done it for less, but I trust your instincts. When you say O'Conner is about as threatening as a butterfly, you're right. He didn't even defend himself when his ex-boyfriend was beating him. Neither Finnigan brother has what I'd call a predisposition to violence. What did you think of their assessment of the argument they had with her?"

"Pretty tame stuff," said Haggerty, picking up a piece of *kami* paper and making two quick folds on it. "Leona Weinberg was an established bigot, as was well demonstrated at the town hall meeting two weeks ago. However, they'd both been living in a well-preserved state of ignoring one another, which all the neighbors agreed upon as well."

"Any of the other neighbors suspects?"

"No. And now that we've got approximate time of death, we've got to find out what Mrs. Weinberg was doing in the hours leading up to her eating that poisoned apple."

"And how someone could have snuck in there and poisoned them," said Sharon. "High Street is lighted pretty well. Even with the key, you'd think someone would have seen something suspicious."

"All working families in that area. Even if Finnigan and O'Conner were home, you can't see Weinberg's house that well from theirs, the way it is set into that lot. The backyard has a high fence. And right behind that fence..."

"Part of the Sky to Sea Trail," said Sharon.

"Currently it runs out at the park at McDougal Lake. There are plenty of places to park, walk up the trail, and hop that pathetic fence Weinberg has there. Right in the corner, next to—"

"The apple tree. Yeah, I see that. You can't see into the backyard easily from either of the neighbors. You could take your time. Pick some apples off the tree or even some good ones off the ground, poison them right there, then—"

"Use the key to open the back door, since it's the same lock."

"The key which had already been procured in the dark some time before."

"Slip in, exchange the apples, slip out. Then it is only a matter of time before Leona picks up one of them and takes a bite."

"There's a lot of ifs there, Adam."

He handed her the origami crane. "I know it. But we know one thing. Poisoning someone takes patience. It takes planning and care," he said, suddenly laughing.

"What's funny?"

"Well, that more than anything clears Mr. Finnigan in my mind. If Leona Weinberg had been shot dead in her tracks, I'd be more suspicious of him. He just doesn't strike me as the patient type," said Haggerty, massaging the lump still on the back of his head.

"You're right. Which means we've got one scary killer out there."

"More than we might realize."

"The thermostat?"

Haggerty nodded. "Finnigan's right. *Someone* turned that up, and I'm willing to bet it wasn't Leona, a well-known cheapskate."

"Which means whoever killed her..."

"Was watching and waiting."

"And willing to risk going back in there again even after he'd accomplished his goal," said Sharon with a shiver.

"Yeah. Clever, observant, patient, and willing to take risks."

"A deadly combination."

Chapter Eighteen

The blinking cursor seemed to mock him. He picked up a pen, and drummed it on his lips, glancing out the small half-window of the basement at the leaves drifting past. Jake shut the computer down and went up the stairs to the second floor and looked around the spare bedroom, his eyes drawn to the window facing Leona Weinberg's house. He deliberately looked away, turning to the far window at the Crenshaw house across the street. The recent winds had taken down most of the leaves, but some were still coming down in the breeze currently swirling outside.

Jake had heard from Phyllis Crenshaw that a distant nephew was coming out to settle the estate. Jake assumed the place would be sold and wondered how hard it would be to sell it with a death having occurred in the home.

Again, he found himself wracked with a sudden sadness for his bigoted neighbor. She had died alone with no one who cared near her. He wondered what it had been that had finally done her in. Perhaps it had been a sudden attack of acute bigotry and she had flopped over like a fish out of a net. He had a sudden image of Leona Weinberg with a fish body floundering around on the floor and had to stifle a laugh, feeling instantly guilty.

"Oh knock it off," he said aloud. "She was a horrible old bat, and if she died alone and friendless, that's her own damn fault."

Once the words were spoken aloud, he instantly felt better. He knew it to be true and as a believer in karma, Leona Weinberg was responsible for whatever happened to come back and bite her. He was amazed it had taken as long as it had.

He glanced at his watch and knew he'd better start dinner. He went downstairs and walked into the kitchen and began pulling items out of the fridge, pausing long enough to turn on the radio to KABW before he started dicing an onion.

"Randy Burrows here coming to you on this fine October afternoon on Radio KABW, the voice of Arrow Bay. We've got forty-eight degrees on the temperature gauge outside my window and sunny conditions with a light wind out of the south-southwest. You were just listening to Dave Brubeck's classic 'Take Five' and we'll have another bit of the magical Mr. Brubeck after this brief message."

Jake tuned out the message for Arrow Bay Mufflers and Exhaust, adding the onions to the frying beef that would eventually end up as Shepherd's Pie. He was just about to dig out the carrots when the grating voice of Roxy Eggans came hurtling over the radio.

"This is a news bulletin from Roxy Eggans, your KABW radio and cable news reporter. The coroner of Kulshan County has determined that the death of Arrow Bay City Councilwoman Leona Weinberg is officially a homicide. Repeat, Councilwoman Leona Weinberg was murdered by person or persons unknown."

Jake felt a chill suddenly overtake him as if the blood in his veins turned into arctic water. The word kept repeating over and over in his head, murdered, murdered, murdered, *murdered*.

"The Arrow Bay Police Department has not released any details," Roxy continued, "nor do they have any suspects at this time. Chief Sanderson says the murder of Leona Weinberg will be discussed at the town meeting tomorrow night."

Jake sat down at the table, feeling as if someone had sucker-punched him. Roxy continued to drone on for several more minutes before being replaced by the mellow jazz of Dave Brubeck. Jake felt his stomach clenching like a fist, the same thought in his head: another murder in Arrow Bay.

He held his head in his hands, unsure of what to do. After ignoring the affairs of Arrow Bay for nearly a decade, Jake found himself rapidly and inexorably drawn in, like light into a black hole.

❖

"The atmosphere in here is very jovial and light," said Sam, glancing around at the murmuring crowd currently packed into the city hall auditorium.

"Yeah, like *Macbeth*," said Jake cynically.

"Shouldn't you say *the Scottish play*?"

"Why? We're not performing it," said Jake looking around the crammed City Hall, "Besides, in the context of what is happening around us, tell me I'm wrong."

"I can't. Although I'm not sure if it's *Macbeth* or something not quite as dark—like, say, Thanksgiving with your mother."

"C'mon, Sam. You know it's not *that* bad. I mean, we don't have to eat my mother's cooking for starts."

"Touché, touché."

The city council, as usual, was seated with of those of the left on the left, and Reed Longhoffer and Verna Monger on the right. Verna was looking pale and drawn, and her make-up appeared to have been applied hastily, as one eye was missing its usual blue shadow, giving the impression that she was constantly winking. Reed sat at her left, his red hat still firmly on his head and his gloves on. The furnace had conked out, and it was nearly as cold inside as it was out. Emma Kennedy, Randy Burrows, and Walter Lugar were all clad in heavy coats, as was Police Chief Sanderson.

"You really think they'll talk about the murder?" Sam asked.

"You think they have any choice?" Rebecca Windsor walked in and Jake let out an audible groan.

"Budge up for a couple of old ladies," said Evelyn O'Conner, sitting down next to the two men. She was accompanied by the Reverend Milly Crawford. They took the last two seats at the end of the aisle next to Sam and Jake.

"Speak for yourself, Evelyn. I'm not *that* old."

"There are less years ahead than behind."

"Mom!" said Sam, horrified. "Have a little respect."

"Listen to your son, Evelyn," said Milly. "I don't believe we've met. I'm Milly Crawford."

Sam reached over Jake to shake her hand. "Sam O'Conner. And this is my better half, Jake," said Sam, nudging Jake, who was watching Baldo Ludich and Alex Blackburn come in the door right behind Gladys Nyberg and Professor Mills.

"Huh? Oh, yeah, nice to meet you," he said distractedly as Adam Haggerty walked through the door, his leather trench coat firmly tied around him. Sharon Trumbo, bundled up in a long wool coat the color of plum Fiestaware, accompanied Haggerty. Jake caught his brother taking several photos of her as she came in.

Taking the steps up to the stage, Sharon sat down next to Chief Sanderson, while Haggerty leaned down next to Randy Burrows and said something in his ear. Burrows nodded, getting up to check the equipment. A professional video camera was set up at one end of the stage. It seemed the meeting was going to be broadcast at some point on the KABW public access channel.

"He's a bit distracted, you'll have to forgive him," said Sam, poking Jake in the ribs.

"That's okay, we all are," agreed the Reverend Crawford. "News of that old biddy getting bumped off 'ran all through town like spilled mercury'."

Jake raised one eyebrow. "*Lady in the Icebox*," said Jake.

"One of my favorites. I loved the part where Claypoole discovers the diary inside the frozen side of beef."

"Oh, that's a classic scene. How about later when the housekeeper's head ends up in the bowl of punch at Lady Cashmeyer's party?"

"Now that was good, I'll admit. But nothing beats the Long-Haired Stranger being done in by the drawer of rusty knives being emptied from the second floor of Cashmeyer Manor," she said with a chuckle.

"Is this conversation entirely in good taste?" Sam whispered to Jake.

"No, I suppose not."

"We'll have to talk later," said Reverend Crawford. "Maybe at church on Sunday?"

"Ooo, nice try Reverend," said Jake. "Maybe my husband here, but I'm afraid if you wait for me to show up to Sunday services, you'll be waiting until—"

"Jacob."

"A long time, I get the drift," said Reverend Crawford, smiling. "Nonetheless, our doors are always open, Jake. Stop by any time."

Randy Burrows started testing the mic, the low rumble of the crowd dying down. Reed Longhoffer still looked like he sucked lemons for sport, his frown deepening when Miranda Zimmerman snapped on the camera. He continued scowling, staring right down into the front row where Derek Brauer and Marion Burd were both scribbling on steno pads. He didn't even look up when Jason snapped several photos of him.

Walter Lugar leaned into his microphone. "We'd like to thank everyone for coming tonight. After we make a few announcements, we'd like to turn things over to Chief Sanderson, who I am sure will try to answer all your questions." There was some general muttering from the crowd. "We'd ask you to please hold your questions until Chief Sanderson takes the mike," he said, glancing back at the two detectives and Chief Sanderson.

"Our topic of discussion tonight is, once again, Wilde Park," continued Randy Burrows, arching one eyebrow as he looked down the table at Reed Longhoffer. "We bring this issue up again as diligent efforts of the press and some concerned citizens have turned up documents that prove our esteemed councilman Mr. Reed Longhoffer lied to everyone in this town hall two weeks ago and continues to spread lies through Arrow Bay's only newspaper, the *Examiner*!" boomed Burrows, pointing an accusatory finger at Longhoffer.

As expected, the audience erupted into chaos. Reed Longhoffer jumped to his feet, jabbing his finger back at Burrows, shouting obscenities, which Jake assumed would be drowned out on the camera by the roar of the audience. Emma Kennedy began to bang the gavel loudly, which had little effect. Sanderson and the two detectives looked at one another uneasily as the din in the audience grew before Baldo Ludich stood up and shouted, "SIIIILLLLLEEEENNNNCCEEEE!"

It had the desired effect. The audience fell silent and with a few more bangs of the gavel, things were quiet as Reed, still standing and breathing heavily, slowly sank to his seat.

"May I approach the council?"

"Council recognizes Baldo Ludich."

Ludich approached the table with a manila folder. He stood directly in front of Reed Longhoffer, opening a folder. He produced a hefty document and slammed it down on the table. Longhoffer looked at Ludich with utmost loathing.

"I have here a copy of the letter of understanding signed by Mr. Longhoffer to SuperLo Corporation promising exclusive rights to develop the plot of land known as Wilde Park. Care to comment on that?"

"Why don't you go screw yourself, Ludich?" spat Longhoffer, to the collective gasp of the auditorium.

"I am recommending that based on this information, the council vote on removing Mr. Longhoffer," Ludich shouted.

"You can't do that without the full council," said Longhoffer with a smirk. "And since one of the council can't attend tonight's meeting, you can't vote me off."

"Ms. Zimmerman?" Baldo asked, looking up at Miranda.

"This ought to be good," said Reverend Crawford. "Makes me wish I'd brought some popcorn."

Miranda Zimmerman stood up and walked to the nearest microphone, clearing her throat. "The town charter specifically outlines that if a member dies or becomes incapacitated, the remaining council can vote in a replacement member until the next full election can be held. As you know, that will be in November of next year."

"That's ridiculous." Longhoffer shouted. "Any yahoo can't just be sworn in."

"Actually, as long as they are a registered voter and over the age of twenty-five, they can, according to the town charter," Miranda Zimmerman said stiffly.

"Excellent. In that case I nominate Alexander Blackburn," and when there were some dismayed mutterers in the background, he quickly added, "the third, that is."

"Motion seconded," said Walter Lugar.

"Any other nominations?" Miranda Zimmerman asked.

The townspeople of Arrow Bay were no fools; they knew the job of city councilman was thankless and cumbersome, with a limited amount of recognition and heaps of scorn. A few brave souls put their hands up, but before anyone could be recognized, they quickly lowered them again.

"Mr. Blackburn?" Miranda asked.

"I accept," Alex said, bowing.

"Fine then. With no one else wanting to jump into the fray, all those for appointing Alexander Blackburn the third as interim councilman raise their hands."

Walter Lugar, Emma Kennedy and Randy Burrows raised their hands. Verna Monger and Reed Longhoffer did not.

"Motion carried," said Miranda. "Now if you'd please step up, Mr. Blackburn."

Alex strode nonchalantly up to the table and stood next to Walter Lugar. After a few words were exchanged, Alex raised his right hand and was sworn in by Chief Sanderson. He sat down in the empty seat next to Walter Lugar, then after checking his mic, he said, "I want to assure the residents of Arrow Bay that I will work for the benefit of the town and its people."

Longhoffer sat with his arms crossed, livid. "Like you did with your father," he spat.

"The internal business dealings of Blackburn Enterprises are none of your concern, Mr. Longhoffer. And don't think I don't know dear old Dad is in cahoots with you regarding your attempt to plow Wilde Park under, even if he does want to remain in the shadows."

It was meant to be heard only by Reed, but everyone in the audience caught it. Everyone attending the meeting now knew the fact that Alexander Blackburn Junior was involved in the plot to destroy Wilde Park. The blood drained out of Longhoffer's face.

"With respect to Wilde Park, Ms. Zimmerman and I have spent a great deal of time combing through the city records. After finding Logan Wilde's will was *not* in the city archives, we checked with the county and found Logan Wilde had no will."

"See, what did I tell you?" Longhoffer erupted.

"*However*," continued Alex, "That meant that upon his death, the property would pass to his closest relative, whom in this case happened to be one Jasper Wilde of Denver, Colorado. We spoke at length to Mr. Wilde, who remembers his cousin fondly and his trips out to Arrow Bay in the 1970's. He said it was his cousin's wish that the parcel of land be turned into a park, and that he simply hadn't had time to make out a will before being backed over by a Wonder Bread truck in the fall of 1974."

Jake couldn't help but laugh. He covered it as best he could in a coughing fit, and he was sure Alex was trying not to laugh himself.

"Mr. Wilde has since started a search for the title to the property, which is in his possession, and has assured me once it is found, he will sign the property over to the Arrow Bay Parks Department, thus settling any future controversy about the park or its future use," said Alex emphatically.

"I move we close the matter," said Randy Burrows.

"Second," chimed Emma Kennedy.

There were general cheers and applause around the audience. Even Gladys Nyberg looked pleased. Professor Mills clapped and hopped back and forth gleefully, looking like a garden gnome.

"Now, as to the business of Mr. Longhoffer's obvious attempt to circumvent the law—"

"Can it, Burrows, I resign!" he spat, whirling on Chief Sanderson. "And if you've got the balls to arrest me, it'll be a cold day in hell. You're so damn dumb you can't even figure out who killed poor Leona. Why haven't you arrested those two perverts living next door to her? They killed her."

Jake and Sam looked at one another, then up at Longhoffer, who had whirled around to face the audience, trying to pick them out. Milly Crawford was on her feet at once. "How dare you, Mr. Longhoffer. How dare you throw out such irresponsible accusations and defame the character of two citizens of this town! Not only do you have no right, it is reckless to the extreme."

More than one loud "yeah" and "right on" rose through the crowd. Somebody said, "Shut up, Longhoffer!" which was greeted with more shouts of agreement.

"We'll leave the matter of charging you with anything up to the city attorney, Mr. Longhoffer," said Alex. "Meanwhile, all those in favor of accepting Mr. Longhoffer's resignation?"

All the hands along the table went up, including Verna Monger's. Reed Longhoffer rounded on her like a startled snake, but Verna only looked at him and shook her head.

Just then, the door banged open. Rushing down the aisle in a long camel hair coat was a tall man with salt and pepper hair and a thick goatee. Reed Longhoffer looked up and went noticeably pale. "David!"

"Boy, this isn't Reed's night, is it?" said Sam.

"Return of the prodigal son," noted Reverend Crawford.

David Longhoffer made his way up to the council table then hesitated a moment, looking for a familiar face. He knelt down to Emma Kennedy and whispered to her. David Longhoffer made a few animated gestures and nodded, casting glances at Reed, who was, preparing to leave. Finally, after a few more muttered words, David Longhoffer went to the center of the table and picked up Alex's microphone.

"Uh, hello. I'm David Longhoffer. I—uh—that is to say, uh—well, um..."

"Not much of a public speaker, is he?" noted Reverend Crawford.

"Just tell them what you told me, David," Emma said.

"I just wanted to tell you that as of midnight tonight your town's newspaper is under new leadership. I've finished up my business in Luxembourg and, well, I've come home to stay."

The audience roared with approval, Jake and Sam standing up and clapping, while the members of the city council applauded.

"As you know, it was my father's vision that the *Examiner* remain as evenly balanced as possible, examining all sides of every issue in as non-partisan a way as possible. I'm sorry to have read some of the things recently printed in your town's paper," he said, looking at his older brother with a deep amount of hurt. "Dad would be so disappointed in you, Reed."

It was the last straw for Reed Longhoffer. He stood up abruptly, knocking his chair over backward. He stormed past the members of the Arrow Bay police department, heading for the back door, his coat whirling around him. With a flash of his red hat, he was gone, the door slowly closing behind him.

For the next several minutes, the council spoke among themselves while the crowd in the auditorium murmured. The show generally being considered over for the day, several people left. There was a muted sigh of relief when the furnace abruptly kicked on, sending warm air into the hall, and within a few moments, Jake was able to take his coat off and sit comfortably. He was about to mention to Sam that maybe they should consider heading out when Walter Lugar asked for quiet again.

"It's been decided unanimously by the council that we will wait until the next scheduled meeting before deciding on a replacement for Reed Longhoffer. Interested parties should submit their names to one of the council members no later than two days before the next meeting. We will make a decision at that point. Remember, the appointment will only last a year until the citywide elections next November.

"Now at this point I'd like to turn things over to Chief Sanderson," said Walter, taking his seat.

Chapter Nineteen

"Thank you, Councilman Lugar," said Sanderson, seating himself in Reed Longhoffer's vacant chair. "As everyone is well aware, the autopsy report regarding Mrs. Leona Weinberg was made public today," said Sanderson, casting an unhappy glance at Randy Burrows. "While I cannot discuss the details of the investigation, the evidence collected at the scene does indicate Mrs. Weinberg was the victim of homicide."

The room filled with conversation again, this time at a more frenzied pitch. People shook their heads in general disbelief, some of them pointing to Sanderson.

"We have no reason to believe anyone else is in danger. This appears to have been a *very* targeted event. We would ask anyone having knowledge of Mrs. Weinberg's movements after the town meeting two weeks ago up until Sunday, the 16th of October to please report it to detectives Sharon Trumbo or Adam Haggerty, who are sitting behind me. You do not have to identify yourself, and we will be taking tips by phone on the department's tip line. The phone number is in the book."

George Mayhew, the owner of Arrow Bay Antiques, waved his hand around until Chief Sanderson acknowledged him.

"Do you have any suspects at this time?"

"I'll let the lead detectives handle the specific questions," said Sanderson, leaving a surprised Sharon Trumbo and Adam Haggerty to approach the table and take a seat while he inexplicably left through the same door Reed Longhoffer just used. This caused another stir in the crowd. Jake watched Alex give up his seat for Sharon Trumbo, then take the seat she had just vacated, an inscrutable look on his face. He glanced toward Miranda Zimmerman who stared at the door that had closed behind Chief Sanderson.

"At the present time we have no suspects," confirmed Adam Haggerty, looking directly at Jake. "We've questioned the neighbors of Mrs. Weinberg extensively, and no one remembers seeing anything out of the ordinary in the days leading up to her death."

"Are any of the neighbors suspects?" asked Rebecca Windsor, standing up suddenly.

"None of the neighbors are suspects, Ms. Windsor. While I am unable to give you specifics on the cause of death, I can say it appears that someone specifically targeted Mrs. Weinberg. This was not a random act."

This was also greeted with another general rise in voices from the crowd. People began to look around uncomfortably, as if trying to spy out the killer among them. Jake closed his eyes and reluctantly called up the scene in Leona Weinberg's kitchen. He could see the yellow tile and matching stove and fridge, the sunflower curtains and the black granite top of the kitchen island, he could see Leona's feet sticking out from behind the island, gray shoes pointed upward, her purple hand still clutching the desiccated apple. Around her were several more apples that had been spilled from the bowl, probably clutched at as she fell....

No broken glass. Nothing else out of place. No sign of a struggle.

Murder, he thought. *Murder and an apple. It can only be one thing.* Jake turned to Sam. "She was poisoned," he said, a little too loudly. He sunk down in his seat as soon as the word began spreading its way across the auditorium. Adam Haggerty shot Jake an icy stare.

"Well here's another fine mess," Sam said, smiling crookedly. "I warned you that all that mystery reading was going to harm you one of these days."

"What are you doing about the Mad Poisoner?" someone shouted.

"Why aren't you telling us the truth!?" demanded Marilyn Sandy.

"We are telling you the truth," said Sharon Trumbo, exasperated. "We are doing everything we can to apprehend the person or persons responsible."

The plural caused the audience to erupt in a fresh burble of loud conversation, all the while looking more suspicious and accusatory of one another.

"I know you've got poison in your basement, Milton Sandy." shouted gray-haired spinster Norma Middlebrook, the second grade teacher at Arrow Bay Elementary.

"Well, of course I have poison in my basement," retorted the balding Milton Sandy. "I'm an exterminator, for crying out loud."

"Yeah, and a bad one, I've *still* got rats in my house," yelled Paul Driggers, owner of Hidden Treasures, Arrow Bay's junk shop.

"I'm surprised that's all you've got," rejoined Sandy, which was greeted by gales of laughter.

"Selma McKinney's got poison in her basement. I've seen her giving it to the squirrels." yelled Sheila Doyle.

"You're just saying that because I won the blue ribbon for my quilt at the fair this year, Sheila," shouted Selma McKinney. "And as for having poison around, I seem to recall you saying you could just kill Leona Weinberg not more than three months ago!"

"She was against my quilt because I used unconventional fabrics in my construction."

"You mean you used her cashmere coat when she left it behind at the guild meeting, is what you mean."

"People, please," implored Sharon Trumbo.

"If you ask me whoever killed that old bag did the town a favor," said Clint Shimmel. "She was a vicious old battle axe. I saw her push a kid into a snow drift last winter when the little girl didn't get out of her way fast enough."

"Was that before or after you left the Bitter End?" asked Trudy Mundy, the Customs officer, and again the crowd laughed.

"We all know who killed her!" yelled Rebecca Windsor breathlessly.

"Don't you dare say it was the devil, Rebecca."

"Of course it wasn't the devil!" screeched Rebecca. "It was Misty Snipes! The Plaid Scarf Strangler!"

The crowd now erupted into general confusion. Sam looked at Jake and said, "The *what* strangler?"

Jake shrugged. Trumbo and Haggerty were looking as perplexed as everyone else. Miranda Zimmerman shrugged while looking at Alex.

"Thirty years ago Misty Snipes murdered at least six people. All of them were strangled with plaid scarves!" Rebecca shouted.

"Aw, come off it lady, you're off your rocker!" bawled Clint Shimmel.

"I have copies of the articles at home. She was acquitted of the murders due to lack of evidence and later spent time in a mental institution in Danvers, Massachusetts. Now she has come here to finish out her terrible work."

"Where on earth did she dig that up?" Sam asked Jake.

"No idea. I couldn't find anything on her on the web." Jake thought of the insane asylum at Danvers and shivered. It had supposedly been the inspiration for H.P. Lovecraft's Arkham Asylum, and Jake couldn't think of a more sinister-looking building.

"People, please. There was no plaid material found at the crime scene," Sharon Trumbo said.

"Like we're supposed to believe you? You let a dangerous murderess into our midst without telling us, then withhold information on a murder in our town and we are supposed to find you credible?" Rebecca said.

"Well, actually they did tell us about Misty Snipes," replied George Mayhew. "And how do you know that the reported Ms. Snipes is…uh… *the* Ms. Snipes, the Plaid Cravat Killer?"

"*Plaid Scarf Strangler*," corrected Rebecca Windsor. "If you were paying attention, you'd know that, you oaf!"

"I'm kinda impressed he pulled out the word 'cravat'," said Jake.

"Me too," Sam agreed.

"Why should anyone pay attention to the likes of you, anyway?" said Sheila Doyle. "No one knows exactly when the shuttle is going to land with you, do they Rebecca?"

"Ignore her, Rebecca, she's just mad you placed second in the fair with your quilt and she didn't even get honorable mention," said Selma McKinney.

"I'd look out if I were you, Rebecca. McKinney has a lot of plaid in her collection. You may find yourself at the end of Misty Snipes' handiwork."

"At least I can recognize plaid," said Selma icily.

The Reverend Crawford was watching this exchange with rapt attention. Detectives Trumbo and Haggerty looked as if someone had recently poured sugar in their gas tanks, and Miranda Zimmerman was trying not to laugh.

"People, we're getting off topic here," said Sam.

"Oh what do you know about it?" said Sheila Doyle. "You don't even quilt!"

"He'd probably still be better at than you, Sheila," said Selma McKinney.

"Both of you shut up!" cried Rebecca.

The two women rounded on Rebecca. The color had drained from her face as she realized what she had just said.

"Why don't you go out and try to find the devil in Wilde Park, *dear*," said Selma McKinney.

"Yes, do let us know if you find him," agreed Sheila Doyle.

"I've got a better idea," said Milton Sandy. "Why don't the three of you shut up!"

"Hear hear," agreed Trudy Mundy.

"That's the last time I ever call you for your services!" shouted Selma McKinney. She turned her gaze on to Marilyn Sandy. "And the last time I ever let you see me at the doctor's office, Marilyn. When I have blood taken, I like it for the nurse to find the vein within the first two tries instead of filling me full of holes like I was a pincushion!"

Marilyn Sandy flushed crimson. "Next time come in after your feeding time, you black-hearted vampire! Maybe then I wouldn't have to go prospecting!"

Selma launched herself at Marilyn Sandy's head. The two began pulling each other's hair and cursing a blue streak, then spilled out into the aisle, flailing and screaming at one another. Marilyn slapped Selma across the face, and Selma banged Marilyn's head into the carpeted aisle. Milton Sandy hadn't lifted a finger and seemed to be enjoying the fight, and Derek Brauer and Marion Burd took notes furiously while Jason Finnigan snapped photos. Sharon Trumbo and Adam Haggerty leapt to their feet to break the two women apart; however, Sharon slipped on her way down the stage and landed in the front row, knocking Derek and Marion Burd to the ground. Walter Lugar was instantly on his feet to assist Sharon, while someone threw an orange wedge at Rebecca Windsor. It clocked her in the head, and she dropped like a lead weight, and then suddenly the air was filled with flying fruit from the snack table at the back of the room.

Evelyn O'Conner was pulling at the Reverend Crawford's coat trying to get her to the exit, but Milly Crawford was laughing too hard to move, tears running down her face. Emma Kennedy and Randy Burrows made a hasty exit out the same door Reed Longhoffer had escaped from not long before, and Baldo Ludich was escorting the frail looking Professor Mills out the side door as rapidly as he could. Trudy

Mundy was now at the back of the room launching more fruit at Rebecca Windsor's head, while Verna Monger, Miranda Zimmerman, and Alex Blackburn slipped quietly away from the stage and out the side door on the right hand side of the auditorium.

Jake was watching with bemused interest until a piece of melon flew close to his head. He grabbed Sam, who was ducking for cover and pulled him down the aisle, the Reverend Crawford and Evelyn O'Conner right behind them. They piled out the door and into the hallway, spotting the lights of the Arrow Bay police cars outside the front door. Sam quickly led them up to the second floor, down a hallway and then out the fire exit that lead into the back parking lot.

❖

Reverend Crawford was still laughing when they found her car parked along Central Avenue. Evelyn O'Conner scolded her, and then climbed into the driver's side of the Reverend's car, shrugging at Sam and Jake as she pulled away. Alex's Jaguar cruised past and he and Miranda Zimmerman waved, and right behind them was Baldo Ludich with a harried Professor Mills in Ludich's mint-green Ford Explorer. Professor Mills waved weakly at Jake and Sam as they drove past.

"And you said these meetings were boring," said Sam as they walked slowly down Central Avenue.

"Remind me not to get too close to the Arrow Bay Quilters Society again," said Jake.

"Vicious lot, aren't they? They've been feuding like that for decades, according to Mom."

Jake stopped in his tracks and turned toward Sam. Sam looked him in the eye, and they both burst out laughing.

"Did you see who pelted Rebecca Windsor with that orange?"

"No. Whoever it was has a hell of an arm."

"It was Gladys!" said Sam as they sat down on a bench just off the city hall parking lot. "Never seen a truer aim in my life."

"Me either. I—"

Jake quickly quieted down when he heard some voices approaching from the other side of the hedge that bordered the length of Brooks Street. He didn't recognize who was speaking at first, but quickly realized it was Emma Kennedy and Randy Burrows.

"You've got some melon in your hair," said Emma Kennedy.

"That would have been that weasel Chad Rudd. You can bet dimes for dollars he'll put in for Longhoffer's vacant seat."

"Yeah, I know. I'm surprised he didn't jump in tonight."

"Baldo got Alex's name in too quick. Here's my car. I'm all for Blackburn staying on if he can maintain focus. He's got a lot on his plate but he'd be good on the council."

"Can't be any worse than Weinberg. Wish we'd done something about her sooner," said Kennedy.

Jake looked at Sam, startled. Had he heard right?

"Well, you know, some things can't be rushed. The end result was better than expected though."

"Got that right. Two down, one to go."

"Take it easy Emma. See you Saturday night."

"You bet."

Jake watched and waited until both cars turned left onto Central Avenue. Jake rose with Sam right behind him, and they walked stiffly around the hedge and up Brooks Avenue to where Sam's Outback was parked.

"Sam."

"Don't jump to conclusions, Jake. We don't know what it was they were talking about."

"'Wish we had done something sooner? Two down, one to go?'"

"There, you see, now Reed Longhoffer isn't dead," said Sam.

"No, he's not," agreed Jake. "He's blocked in by your car," said Jake, wincing.

Sam had parked the blue Outback correctly, but Longhoffer had not parked his car in the slot. He had parked his Cadillac to take up two spots on Brooks Avenue and in retaliation, someone in a green Malibu had boxed him in. The only way he could get out was if the Malibu or Sam's Outback were moved out of the way. Jake and Sam approached cautiously, as Reed was leaning up against his car. Sam slid around quickly to open the passenger side for Jake before coming around to get in on the driver's side.

"Bet you enjoyed that, didn't you?" Longhoffer said.

Jake ignored him and opened his door, preparing to get in and get away before he could utter another syllable. Unfortunately, he was too slow.

"Cat got your tongue, faggot?"

Jake slowly closed his door, turning around to face him. Longhoffer caught a look at Jake's expression, then eyed his physique and took a step backward. Clearing his throat he said, "You don't scare me!"

"And you don't scare me, Mr. Longhoffer. And any attempt you might make at trying to belittle me or my husband to bolster your pathetic, insecure little existence will have absolutely zero effect on me. Good night," said Jake, opening the door of the Subaru.

"I don't care what the stupid shit detective said, I know you killed Leona. You faggots hated her, and you decided to get rid of her."

Jake slammed the door shut and was on Longhoffer before Sam had a chance to get out of the car. Longhoffer cringed against the side of his Cadillac when Jake cornered him, his face flushed with fury.

"One more word out of you, Longhoffer, and you'll wish you were right alongside that withered old prune." He jabbed Reed Longhoffer in the chest with his index finger. "If I hear of you uttering another epithet or accusation at either one of us one more time I'll have a team of lawyers down on your ass like black on coffee. Do I make myself clear?!"

Jake smelled Longhoffer's stale breath. Seeing the fear in Longhoffer's eyes, Jake returned to the Outback, glaring at him as Sam guided the car out of the parking lot and onto Brooks Street. Longhoffer seemed to shrink back into his car, deflated.

"Jake," said Sam.

"Please, Sam, not now. I've got a pounding headache."

"Let's go downtown, then. I'm sure Caleb can whip us up something for a headache," said Sam. He took his husband's hand and gave it a squeeze. "It'll be okay, Tiger. I hate that word, too."

"I know, Sam. Especially spewed from the lips of someone like Longhoffer," he said, slamming his fist onto the dashboard. "Dammit, I hate it when I lose control like that."

Sam shook his head, chuckling. He negotiated the turn with his left hand, not wanting to release Jake's hand. He sighed and said, "I think you were remarkably controlled, really, having just been accused of being a murderer."

"I know I can be a hot head, Sam. It's part of my charm."

Sam snorted, but said nothing.

"When I lose it like that, it's just..." he sighed. "It makes me think about your father. And your ex."

"You're not remotely like either one of them, Jake. You didn't hit Reed."

"Yeah, but I wanted to, Sam. I wanted to pound his hateful little heart into the ground."

"I think Mother Teresa would like to pop Reed Longhoffer one, Tiger. And no matter how much you *wanted* to hit him, you didn't. *That* makes all the difference."

"If you say so."

"It does, Jake," said Sam, parking outside the Bitter End. "You may be built like a gorilla, but the resemblance ends there."

"Thanks awfully."

"Anytime," said Sam, kissing Jake on the cheek. "There is one thing I have to tell you, though."

"What's that?"

"'A team of lawyers on your ass like black on coffee?'"

"Hey, now, that was spur of the moment."

"I know, but really, Jake..."

Jake laughed as they got out of the car, his heart lightened. They stepped into the Bitter End and sat down at the end of the counter, where Caleb Rivers, just ending his shift, joined them for a round of drinks.

Chapter Twenty

Reed Longhoffer knew something was wrong when he stepped in from the garage. He felt an instant sharp pain in his leg, and the kitchen light didn't come on though he repeatedly snapped the switch up and down.

Cursing, he stepped back from the door and saw a razor blade jammed into the side of doorframe. When he had yanked the door open and rushed in, his leg had brushed up against it, neatly slicing through his pants and into his leg. He reached down and felt his thigh, bringing his hand up to his eyes. In the muted light filtering in from the street lamp outside, his fingers came up wet with blood.

"Son of a bitch!" He looked back at the doorframe, where the blade glittered evilly. What the hell was going on? How had the razor blade come to be stuck in the door?

Someone had to be in the house. He turned back around, intending to go back into the garage and leave. He grabbed the doorknob, but the assembly fell apart in his hand. Exasperated, he threw the knob aside and made his way into the living room, light from the mercury vapor streetlamp filtering through the windows. He went to the study, knowing his gun was in the top drawer of his desk. He flung open the drawer, but it was gone. He began pawing through the other drawers.

Then he heard the growling.

Reed Longhoffer froze in place, slowly turning around to the source of the deep-throated growl. Looking through the study door and out into the shadows of the vast living room, he could see nothing, save for the lump of the sofa and the hulking mass of the television set. In the pit of shadows leading from the living room into the dining room, he thought he saw something shifting in the darkness.

"Who's there?" he called out, angry with himself at the quiver in his voice. "I'm not afraid of you! I—I have a gun!"

The growl deepened, and this time Reed caught sight of glaring yellow eyes. He suddenly realized that his home had not been invaded by a human—or at least none that was still around. Whoever had been in here had left him a very unhappy present, which was now homing in on the smell of the blood running down his leg.

But he was wrong on that score. As he turned to move into the living room, he heard a single word breathed out in a harsh whisper:

"*Kill!*"

Even as he turned and ran he knew he'd never make it. The beast darted from the darkness and knocked him flat. The animal began attacking Reed Longhoffer, its jaws tearing into his flesh. Reed screamed, trying to claw his way to the front door, but the heavy animal kept biting.

All at once, the heavy beast was gone. Reed pushed himself up, looking for the nearest available weapon. He grabbed the spike on his desk he kept for paid bills. He was just able to grasp it when the animal was back, tearing at his neck. Finally the jaws clamped on his throat, and Longhoffer knew he was done for. With the last ounce of his strength, he began stabbing the animal with the spike. The beast leapt away, yelping, watching warily as the life flowed out of Reed Longhoffer.

The last thing Reed saw were the yellow eyes closing in on him again. With one last ounce of strength, he lashed out with the spike and landed a lucky blow, jamming the spike up through the ribs of the animal and into its heart.

The beast died seconds before Longhoffer, whose last thought on earth was, *I'll get the son of a bitch who did this...*

❖

"Where does one start with a story like this?" asked Jason, flipping through the images he had taken from the meeting the two days before.

"I don't know," said Derek, leaning back against the couch.

Jake set aside the crossword puzzle he was doing, and went to get something to drink out of the kitchen. He was feeling tired and not particularly social, and all Derek and Jason had done over the last three hours was look through the photos of the last town meeting and discuss how they were going to cover the story. It had all become very wearing.

In the kitchen, he poured himself a tall glass of cranberry juice and decided against putting a shot of vodka in it. He then clomped down the basement steps to check his email and mindlessly surf the Internet.

Jake booted up his computer, and brought up his email flipping through the junk or things he didn't intend to answer right away, smiling at once when he saw an email from Rachel was in the box.

Hi Handsome!

Finishing up here in D.C. What a mess! Condo sold and all the furniture with it. I've packed up the electronics and photos and am having them shipped to Mom and Dad's in Port Jefferson for easy access. You would not believe the amount of junk from high school I still have. We'll have to go through it and have some laughs.

Tony managed to get my phone number. Has left three messages but I've not called him back yet. Not sure I will. Arrogant S.O.B. Swedish God has also left messages, which I've also ignored. He and his rabbit-faced wife can both go to hell.

Love you—R.

Jake laughed at the last line, quickly hitting reply, telling her the upstairs guest room would be ready for her when she arrived and updating her on the events that had been happening in town.

He sent the reply off and noticed an email labeled P.S. from Rachel a few emails more down. He jumped to that and opened the two-line message.

Gavin says you had better call him as you are pulling a 'me' on you. I told him what he could do with that assessment.

Jake smiled, but realized Gavin was right. He hadn't talked to his old friend in quite a while with the recent events happening in the town. He picked the phone up and dialed the San Francisco number from memory, Gavin answering on the second ring.

"Ashworth-Gilmore Burlesque House."

"You've cleaned the place up then. Last time you were a house of sin and opium den."

"Turns out we weren't zoned for that," said Gavin. "Rachel tells me you're into bumping off the neighbors now."

"I really must have a talk with that woman about her choice of words. Particularly when there's an active murder investigation going on."

"So someone murdered the old bat, eh? Wow. I bet property values have jumped by thirty or forty percent."

Jake shook his head, Gavin's face looming in his mind's eye. Of Portuguese decent, Gavin Ashworth stood six feet in height and had wavy black hair squashed under a baseball cap, a thick, black beard he kept neatly trimmed, and soulful, nearly black eyes. He was a grad student when they had met in college, and they'd become lovers, then exes, both pairing off with different mates over the years. Gavin and his husband, Jeff, had often gone on vacations with Jake and Sam and made a point of getting together with them twice a year.

"I don't think such a statement does much for your karma as a practicing Buddhist."

"Ha! Whaddya think whacked the old lady? *Her* karma came back around and got her, mark my words."

"Yeah, well, pity it hasn't rounded out on Jeff's mother," said Jake.

"No shit," said Gavin. "Wait until I tell you what she did this week."

"Oh? What?"

"Oh, no you don't, Gobo. You're not derailing me *that* easily. C'mon, give me the details about the old bat that once charmingly referred to me as 'a degenerate Hell's Angel.'"

"You *were* on your Harley. You're covered in tattoos, and you and Jeff were in full biker leathers, I might add."

"I'm an English professor and poet. I'm about as close to a Hell's Angel as Bob Dole."

"You *look* the part. At least until you get close and see all your tats are all literature related," said Jake.

"You're trying to derail me again."

Jake wished for about the hundredth time his friends lived closer. "There's no mystery. Someone poisoned her."

"Oh," said Gavin. There was a crash on the other end of the line, followed by Gavin giggling. Jake heard Jeff cursing a blue streak.

"What happened to Salt?" asked Jake, referring to Jeff by his old nickname. He may have sported the same look as Gavin, minus the tattoos, but he was Gavin's polar opposite in appearance—blonde hair, blonde beard, and pale blue eyes. Not long after they'd gotten together, Rachel had remarked that they'd looked like salt and pepper shakers together, and the nickname had stuck.

"He's trying to put together some IKEA shelving. He may be a brilliant landscaper, but when it comes to building stuff…"

"You can get over here and put *your* shelf together any time, Mr. I'm-Heir-to-a-Furniture-Store-Empire," Jeff called out to him. "And one more word and I'm telling your mother you bought furniture at IKEA."

"Carry on, you're doing great, sweetie," said Gavin.

"That's a fair point—why are you buying shelving from IKEA?"

"It's simple and functional, and we don't carry anything like it, though Dad tells me that will be changing. And you're doing it again."

"*Jeff* did it that time," Jake pointed out. "And that's all I know. She was dead for about three days when we found her."

"*You* found her? Oh, Jake, are you okay?"

"It wasn't as bad as last year," said Jake, trying to dismiss images of the corpse of Susan Crane from his head. "Although I did see one purple, bloated hand," he said. "With fake red fingernails. They looked like Chiclets jammed into plums."

"Ugh. That was…vivid. Seriously, that's scary shit, Jacob. You know that poisoning someone requires a lot of thought. It's deliberate and calculating."

"After last year I'm not so hot on the true crime, but you're right, and, believe me, it's the first thing I thought of. We're not dealing with someone stupid. From what I've been able to read between the hieroglyphics the police are throwing out, there's not a trace of evidence, either."

"Wonder what kind of poison?"

"I don't know, and you'll forgive me if I don't run right out and ask Detective Hides-in-a-Bush what it was."

"Repeat that last bit?"

Jake brought Gavin up to speed on all the latest events.

"Jesus, I thought you moving out of Seattle was a good thing. I didn't realize you were going to move into Twin Peaks."

"I have to admit I'm worried. If this is all somehow tied up with the SuperLoMart controversy…well, then it has an unfinished feel to it, Prof."

"You think it'll happen again?"

"I hope not. The town's on the edge of panic, what with this alleged convicted criminal coming here to roost."

"You left out that bit."

"For your benefit, I'm telling you I'm rolling my eyes so you can get that in your head before I regale you with the tale of Misty Snipes and the last town meeting."

It took Gavin nearly five minutes to stop laughing.

"I really hope you took notes, Tiger, I really do," said Gavin. "Or better yet, filmed it."

"The cable access channel cameras were there, but someone cut them off early."

"Oh, too bad!"

"All kidding aside, Gav, I'm worried."

"I have an easy solution for that."

"What's that?"

"Stay the hell out of it. Don't make me come up there and tie you to a chair. After last year and the two of you nearly getting killed... You scared us half to death, Jake. Don't stick your neck out again."

"He's not getting involved in police investigations again, is he?" Jeff called out from across the room. "Tell him to knock that shit off."

"I'm not, I'm not! I swear. It's just unfortunate proximity, is all. Sam and I have no interest in getting involved with the police on this one," said Jake, knowing it wasn't quite the truth.

"I'm gonna hold you to that," said Gavin. "And I will come up there, though it won't be for Christmas."

"Huh? You're missing Christmas?"

"That's courtesy of Queen Gilmore," said Gavin. "Who's dragging us all to some family house in Carmel. Or I should say dragging Jeff. She doesn't want me to come, which is of course why—"

"—you're going. Well, you've attended enough Finnigan family gatherings. You've had plenty of training in the Art of Uncomfortable Holidays."

"Jeff knew you'd say that," said Gavin. "Jesus, I'd rather be anywhere on *Earth* but there, but goddamn it, I'm *not* going to let her win on this one."

"Stick to your Colts, Prof."

"On a lighter note, it was delightful to see Rachel. She's tired, too thin, and she needs you, Jake. I'm glad she's leaving D.C."

"I've missed her. And every time I work on the book, I miss her more."

"How's that going?"

"Pretty well, now that I have the time. I may finish it before I turn fifty."

"I'm glad you're writing full time again. Your voice needs to be out in the world, Jake. I mean that."

"I know you do."

"And I mean it about Rachel. She needs you right now."

"I know. We've got a lot to talk about," said Jake, wincing, as there was a thump and some laughter from upstairs.

"What was that?"

"J.D. and his friend, Derek Brauer."

"The reporter?"

"Yep. You got my email on that whole thing."

"Yeah, well, watch your back around Brauer. I have a few friends down here with his size twelve prints on their spine. He may be lying low for now, but don't expect that to last."

"Duly noted, Prof," said Jake, as another unholy crash on the other end of the line was followed by Gavin's uproarious laughter.

"Look, hot stuff, I gotta go before Jeff takes the whole damn house down. Keep me posted, will you? And I mean email me or call me daily, kid. If you don't, I'm gonna call your esteemed Detective…Uh…Hardy?"

"Haggerty."

"I'll call him up and have him do a wellness check on you, got it?"

"Got it, Prof."

He paused for a moment before saying, "If you *do* turn up anything, let me know that, too."

"I thought you said stay out of it?"

"I did. And I mean it."

"However…"

"Yeah, yeah, you know I want to find out who topped the old cow too. Just be fucking careful, okay? *Both* of you. And keep your eye on Brauer."

"I'm gonna miss you guys at Christmas."

"We'll come up for New Year's. Promise."

"Love you, Prof."

"You too. And give that handsome man of yours a big, sloppy wet kiss from us both," said Gavin, ringing off.

Chapter Twenty-one

Jake replaced the receiver back on the cradle, a small ache in his heart. Christmas without Gavin and Jeff was not going to be the same. Sighing, he turned back to his computer and brought up the latest chapter to the novel he'd been hammering on for nearly a decade.

Soon, however, Jake flipped over to the Internet, idly looking over the *Seattle Times* online, thinking about Rachel's arrival and how Jason's room/his future office needed painting. Jake thought that something blue-green would be nice, something that inspired tying a rock to his legs and jumping off the end of the Central Avenue dock.

Huh? Jake shook his head. He looked up at Sam. "What?"

"I said I could continue talking to you and not having you hear a word I say or I could tie a boulder to my legs and jump off the dock on Central Avenue."

"You wouldn't get far. You'd end up on the deck of the *Chinook*," said Jake, sticking his tongue out at Sam. "What's up?"

"I was just seeing if you'd like some dinner at some point or would you rather continue hiding from Woodward and Bernstein upstairs."

"Neither one of them was a photographer."

"I couldn't think of an appropriate photographer-reporter combo."

"The only combos I know of are all literate. And nearly all of them tragedies. Romeo and Juliet, Tristan and Isolde. I can't think of any that don't come to a horrible end."

"How about Newman and Woodward?" Sam asked, kissing Jake with passion.

"That's good for a start. Oh, and before I forget," he said, kissing Sam deeply and wetly, "that's from the Boys from the Bay."

"Salt and Pepper? Aww, how are they?"

"Not coming for Christmas. Jeff's mother is being a diva and Gavin is crashing the family gathering she doesn't want him to come to."

"Well, he's been to enough of *your* family's holiday gatherings to steel his courage."

"Funny, that's *exactly* what I told him," said Jake, kissing Sam and patting his lap. "Sit down."

"No, no. Too late. Work to do, work to do…"

"You're a cad, Samuel O'Conner."

"Insulting me archaically will earn you no points, man. And to think I was going to massage your sore shoulders."

"They wouldn't have been so sore if you hadn't…" Jake stopped, watching Sam laugh loudly. "What's so funny?"

"You're blushing. It's really endearing."

Jake stared at his boots, scowling.

"Oh, knock it off. Come on, let's go to the Bitter End. I don't feel like cooking tonight."

When they got upstairs, Derek was jamming his arms into his jacket while Jason was frantically replacing camera equipment into the scuffed brown camera bag. Derek began tugging on his boots, cursing the laces, which were laced too tightly to slip the boot over his ankle.

"Where's the fire?" asked Jake.

"Probably not the best thing to ask a reporter," said Sam. "There may *be* a fire."

"Not a fire," said Derek. "Another body."

"What?" asked Jake breathlessly.

"Sky Heights Road."

"Boulevard. Whose body?"

"Marion didn't know. It just came over the scanner. What's the quickest way to get there?"

"Sky Heights is just on the other side of the hill here," said Sam. "Well, down the ravine, at any rate. But to get there by car, you'll have to go clear down Dawson, then up Enetai Avenue."

"Damn."

In another flurry of movement and a slam of the front door, they were gone, Barnaby standing in the foyer letting out several woofs of dissent in their wake. Jake looked at Sam, grimacing.

"We're not even going to think about it. We're going to the Bitter End and having a nice quiet meal."

❖

All hope of a quiet meal was dashed the minute they set foot in the bar. Tuned to the local access channel, the huge flat screen on the wall showed the live feed from the camera held by Randy Burrows, whose booming voice was giving a commentary along with repeated questions shouted at the police whenever an officer was within earshot.

"I regret the day KABW ever got that local access channel," said Jake glumly.

"At least Randy and Walter have built a studio for it at the station," Caleb said. "Although the entertainment value of walls falling down and lights constantly going out before they got the studio built shouldn't be overlooked."

"It gave it a very David Lynch-like feel," Sam agreed.

"Huh, that's the second allusion to *Twin Peaks* in one day," said Jake.

"I always felt it was more like *Peyton Place*," said Sam, looking at the chessboard. Caleb had captured his rook.

"You'll have to find a more hip, up-to-date reference," Jake said. "How many people even know what *Peyton Place* was about?"

"He's right, you know," Caleb said. "Not to mention we've gone from creepy mothers giving their kids enemas to multiple homicides in this town. Maybe *Twin Peaks* isn't so far off."

"Even *Twin Peaks* is getting to be in the dim past these days," Sam said.

"You're in check, incidentally," Caleb informed Sam.

"Blast."

"Where's Roxy?" Jake asked, watching Randy Burrows gently escorted away from the scene by an Arrow Bay police officer.

"Who knows?" Caleb said. "At least this way we're actually getting some news, other than the color of the walls of the home and the charming décor."

"Just whose house is it anyway?" asked Sam.

"They haven't said yet, but it looks familiar," said Caleb, pausing long enough to grab Paul Driggers a bottle of Arrow Bay Amber.

"Big old place off the road like that could be any number of houses," said Sam, smiling as his cheeseburger arrived.

Trudy Mundy had just arrived, still in her Customs uniform but sans firearm, as Caleb had repeatedly told her it was not allowed on the premises. She was with a tall man with short-cropped hair and thick eyebrows whom Jake assumed was Mr. Mundy when she stopped next to them, staring up at the flat screen television.

"What's up?" she asked Caleb, who was already handing her a Naughty Shirley Temple, her usual.

"Found a body," said Caleb, looking to the presumed Mr. Mundy with raised eyebrows.

"Just a beer," he said.

"We have over thirty."

"Give him an amber, Caleb, he'll like that," said Trudy, not looking away from the screen. "That looks familiar, where is it?"

"Somewhere on Sky Heights," said Jake.

"You know you could end the mystery if you called Jason. He must know who it is by now," said Sam, who was fuming at the loss of his rook and being back in check.

"He's busy," said Jake. "I've seen him in the background there a half dozen times already snapping photos."

"You don't need to call him," said Trudy Mundy, turning to face them. "I know whose house that is. It's Reed Longhoffer's."

❖

"Jake, are you okay?" Sam asked for the hundredth time.

They had left the bar shortly after they found out whose house it was. Jake had suddenly lost his appetite and wanted to come home. Sam had asked for to go boxes and wrapped things up quickly.

"Everything okay, Sam?" Caleb had asked.

"Not sure," Sam said, eyeing Jake, who was looking like a deer in the headlights of an oncoming Ford Excursion.

"If there's anything I can do, let me know, okay?" he said as they left.

Now at home, Jake was just sitting mutely on the couch, staring at the wall.

"Jake?"

"I'm fine, Sam. I'm just…" he looked into Sam's expressive brown eyes. "I was just talking to Gav about this, about how it had the feel of an unfinished thought. Now Longhoffer... It's just kind of a bad déjà vu, you know? Like a repeat of last year."

Sam smiled gently at Jake. "Upstairs."

Jake walked up the steps and into their bedroom, allowing Sam to place him on the bed, lay him flat, and take off his shoes. Sam pulled the comforter up around him, telling him he'd be right back. Sam returned with a hot toddy. He propped Jake up on the pillow, narrowly avoiding stepping on Sophia before joining Jake on the other side of the bed. Barnaby joined them a few moments later, curling into a ball at Jake's feet.

"You want to tell me all about it, or do I have to tie you down and force it out of you?"

"You can always tie me down," said Jake.

"Stow it, Mr. Emboldened-by-Alcohol. What's up?"

"You mean other than the murder of Reed Longhoffer?"

"We don't know that. Dead yes, murdered no. And what does that really have to do with us, anyway?"

"A pervading sense of dread and déjà-vu."

"So you said," said Sam, sliding under the comforter. "Brr." He looked at Jake again, taking his hand. "Big difference this time, kiddo. We are *not* involved in it."

"I know it, I know, it just seems like it's following us, somehow."

"What is?" asked Sam, perplexed.

"Death."

Sam burst out laughing.

"I fail to see what's so funny about it."

"It's hysterical. You make it sound like Death is stalking us at every turn."

"Come on, Sam. We have a fight with Leona Weinberg, and she turns up murdered. We have a run in with Reed Longhoffer, and he turns up dead."

"Jake, be serious. I know I'm the left-brained one, but even you can see logically that A has nothing to do with B."

"I feel like I've got a curse on me, a killing power."

Sam erupted into a fit of giggles again. "Better watch out. Seriously dangerous brain powers here. You might be dead within minutes."

"Samuel Patrick O'Conner, you are one insensitive S.O.B."

Sam stopped laughing. "Oh Tiger, I'm sorry. But come on, you have to see how ridiculous that sounds. If one had anything to do with the other, there would be bodies littered all over the highway every time you drove into Mount Burlington. I don't think I've ever been with you once where a driver hasn't pissed you off in some way or other."

Jake gave a grudging smile. "Well, okay. Maybe I was being a little melodramatic."

"You were being a drama queen, Macbeth," said Sam, snuggling closer to Jake. "Now come on, what's really bugging you?"

"It's a lot of little things. Gavin and Jeff not being able to come up for Christmas, the specter of Tony Graham, and…well…your sister."

"Nora? I wasn't aware you had talked to her."

"I haven't. It was something Amy said to me on the phone the other day, after the news about Mom and Dad. About being the only family we have. I just got to thinking. I feel a little responsible for the blow-out you two had."

"You aren't responsible for Nora acting like a nuclear reactor reaching the China syndrome."

"Intellectually I know that," said Jake. "It's just she's your only sister."

"And because you've patched things up with Jason, naturally you're feeling a little bad for me." Sam ruffled Jake's hair. "I love that about you, you know. Your consideration."

"What if I don't make it, Sam? What if I don't get published? I'm not even sure I *want* this manuscript published."

Sam shrugged. "Then you'll write another."

"What if that one comes to nothing? What if Nora was right, and I end up just working for years and it never amounts to anything?"

"Nora said this to you?"

"No, not exactly."

"Jake, first of all, Nora's never been completely rational when things don't go the way she wants them to."

"I realize that, but—"

"Second, Nora needs to mind her own business."

"I suppose, but—"

"And third, Jacob, I have every confidence in you. If it takes until you're eighty to get published, it doesn't make one damn bit of difference to me. My God, Jake, you worked your ass off to get me established, and because of your earnings, your hours and hours of overtime, particularly the six months I was out of the country, the house is paid off twenty years early. Remember, we are husbands after all. Equals. What's mine is mine and what's yours is mine," Sam said, winking.

"A paragon of generosity, you are."

Sam laughed. "If it makes you feel any better, the fight I had with Nora over your taking time off to write was only part of it. It was about a lot of things, Jake. Money, mostly. Mine. Nora seems to think I shouldn't be doing with my money what I am."

Jake took a sip of his toddy. "This is really good," he said, enjoying the warmth that spread not only from the toddy itself, but from the whiskey. "In what way? Other than with me, which I knew about."

"Helping Mom out."

"I don't understand that."

"Neither do I. Nora still blames Mom for the way things happened in Seattle. That we did without for so many years. She doesn't seem to remember the fact that Mom took a whole hell of a lot to keep us from getting hurt. "I just wish Nora would let it go, you know? Phil Baker has been dead a long time. It's just time she moved on."

"What else?" said Jake, feeling something wasn't being said.

"Nothing, Jake, really," said Sam.

Jake let it pass, but he knew there was more to it. Jake could sense Sam was not ready to go over whatever was bothering him now, and he snuggled closer to him and reveled in his warmth, his love, and the feeling of connectedness.

Chapter Twenty-two

Their blissful solace abruptly shattered when the front door banged open, Jason presumably having arrived home.

Jake sighed heavily. "Jason's home. Alone, I wonder?"

"Sounds like," said Sam.

A secondary bang caused Barnaby to look up and let out a woof, only to lower his head a second later and go back to sleep. Jake sighed again and burrowed down in the comforter, still unable to get completely warm despite the whiskey in the toddy. He wondered if he wasn't coming down with something.

"We could go down and find out what's going on," said Sam.

Jake shook his head. "I don't want to know that badly. You go if you want to."

"You done with your toddy?"

Jake nodded.

"Then I'll take it downstairs." He took Jake's cup and walked out of the room, Dorothy and Sophia trailing after him. He realized their food dish must have been empty. Entering the kitchen, he found Jason and Derek sitting at the table, looking somewhat shell-shocked.

"Was it bad?" Sam asked.

"I've seen some weird stuff," Derek said. "In a city the size of San Francisco, you *expect* to see weird stuff. But this—" He glanced at Jason and shook his head.

"This takes the cake," said Jason. He got up and went to the cupboard, pouring himself a shot of Jameson.

Sam's eyebrow shot upward again. "What exactly *did* happen to Reed Longhoffer?"

"I'm not supposed to tell this to anyone, you realize. The police were furious when they found out the two of us had gotten in there. More so when they found out I'd taken photos."

"Detective Haggerty threatened to arrest us," Derek said. "And he confiscated the memory cards from Jason's camera."

"He thought he did," said Jason, grinning for the first time. "When have you ever known me not to back up my cards, D?"

"You sly son of a bitch. You finally took a page out of my book."

Jason rolled his eyes and said, "You can only hear 'back up everything twice' so many times before you take it to heart—if only to shut you up."

"And?" Sam prompted.

"The place was torn apart. There was blood everywhere..." said Jason.

"The smell was horrible," Derek continued. "Reed must have been cold-blooded as the heat had been cranked up."

Sam felt an unpleasant plummeting sensation in his stomach but remained mute. He'd be sure to mention the heat being turned up to Jake.

"And Reed was in the study and that *thing* was still on top of him, jaws clamped on his throat."

"Dear God," said Sam, horrified. "What thing?"

"A timber wolf," said Derek.

"It was *not* a wolf. It just *looked* like a wolf."

"What was it then?"

"A big dog," said Jason. "A really damn big dog. It might have been a wolfhound, but wasn't a wolf. It was definitely a very, very *big* dog."

"Was? It was dead too?"

"Reed managed to kill it with a spike—you know, the kind you put receipts on. I didn't even know people still used things like that."

"Like lawn darts, they've gone the way of the dodo in most homes due to the penchant for young children to end up on the pointy end of them," said Sam. "But knowing Longhoffer, does it really surprise you he had one?"

"No," said Jason. "He jammed it up its ribs. Killed it, but it was too late. The thing had torn into his throat by that time. Right through the jugular would be my guess. Reed bled out pretty fast."

"I don't think I realized how much blood the human body holds until tonight," said Derek grimly.

Sam shook his head again. It was bizarre; it was unbelievable. Who would plan such a gruesome way to kill someone? And why? Why go to the trouble to do something like that?

The three men sat in the quiet of the kitchen until Derek bid Jason and Sam good night, leaving them in the silence.

"I can't believe it," Sam said, trying still to get his mind around Reed Longhoffer's demise.

"You're not the only one. The police are baffled as well. And freaked out. You could tell. Detective Haggerty and Sharon both looked very upset."

"Sharon?"

"Uh, yeah...Sharon Trumbo."

"I understand why," Sam said. "Something like that takes a lot of planning...patience..."

"And clearly not a sound mind," said Jason. He sighed, swigging the last of his drink down. "Something else I need to talk to you about."

"Oh?"

"Derek's having some troubles financially. He was wondering now that I'm working if I could move into the second bedroom in his place to help him with the rent."

"Oh," said Sam, surprised. "And it wouldn't bug you? You know, having a gay guy for a roommate?"

"Yeah, because that would be so different from now."

Sam pinched the bridge of his nose, wincing. "Right, right. Sorry. I must be more tired than I thought."

"Well, I know you don't see it that way because Jake and I are brothers."

"I guess that's it. And I'm tired. Will you be moving soon?"

"Yeah, fairly," said Jason. He looked at Sam. "I thank you guys for putting up with me. You've always made me feel welcome, but I feel like I've been invading your space."

"J.D., it's been no trouble."

"I know, but I've been infringing on your hospitality for nearly a year now. You've never once asked me to help with the bills or anything. I've kept the house clean as best I could, more so I could contribute—"

"Which we've really appreciated. It's been no bother, Jason."

"It's time for me to get out on my own," he said, looking directly at Sam again. "Well, sort of. And I'll be helping Derek out."

"You're welcome here any time. And if Derek drives you nuts, you know you can always come back."

"Thanks Sam, I appreciate it," said Jason, rising to go. "I better get to bed. It is going to be a long day at the office tomorrow."

"I bet. Sleep well."

"I'll try. After seeing that..." he shrugged. "The Jamesons will help. G'night, Sammy."

Sam put Jason's glass and his cup into the dishwasher. After a moment of thinking about Reed Longhoffer, he bolted the dog door shut and checked all the doors and windows on the ground floor before going upstairs. He walked slowly up the stairs and into their bedroom, looking closely at Jake who was fast asleep, Barnaby still at his feet.

"What is going on, Jake?" he said quietly. "What is going on?"

❖

Sam frowned at the thermometer and looked at Jake. "You're not getting out of that bed. Your temperature is at one hundred now and has gone up half a degree every hour."

Jake was not about to argue. His head felt like it was packed full of cotton, and he ached from head to foot. With his birthday only three days away, he was perfectly content to stay in bed until he began to feel somewhat human again.

"Is there any of that cough syrup left from last year that Doctor Masuoka gave me?"

"You mean the stuff with the codeine in it?"

"Uh huh."

"Half a bottle at least, but I don't think—"

Jake erupted into a coughing and sneezing fit that caused both Dorothy and Sophia to flee the bedroom.

"I'll just go get it for you, shall I?" said Sam, who had taken cover behind the door until the fit had passed.

An hour later, the sheets seemed to irritate Jake's skin so he got up, pulling the comforter off the bed, and slunk downstairs, plopping unceremoniously on the couch. He propped his head up with the cushions and pulled the coffee table closer so all remotes and the box of tissues were close. He pulled the comforter up to his chin and snapped on the fireplace. He flipped the television on and went over to the Discovery

Channel, which was airing a program about ghosts. He left it there, finding the idea of an afterlife, even in ghost form, somewhat comforting in his current state.

Glancing at the bedroom door, he thought about what Sam had told him this morning. He wasn't entirely sure how he felt about Jason moving out. While it had been nearly a year, it certainly hadn't been an inconvenience to have Jason about. He'd miss him.

Jake sneezed again, which brought on a coughing fit that lasted over a minute. He was just finishing when Sam came in from the kitchen, having just returned from Walgreens with a full supply of cold medication for his stricken husband.

"That sounds bloody awful," he said, setting a glass of orange juice next to Jake, along with Dayquil capsules, which Jake downed immediately. He felt Jake's forehead and frowned, then went back into the pantry to retrieve the thermometer.

"Thag you for de oradge juice."

"You're welcome." He clicked the button on the thermometer and then stuck it under Jake's tongue. "I ran into Mom when I was down at the drug store."

"Dith you pick her up?"

"You're not feeling that bad if you can drag that old chestnut out. She'll be bringing you some chicken soup up later."

"Thad's nice of 'er."

Sam pulled it out of his mouth. "One hundred one. Take the comforter off."

"But I'b freezingth."

"I know you're freezing, but you're too hot. Come on now," said Sam, gently tugging the comforter away.

Jake shivered. "Meany."

"Just for a bit until that Dayquil has a chance to take hold and lower your temperature a bit. Have some more juice." He walked over to the hearth and turned up the gas fire. "That should help any chills you might have."

"Easy for youb to say. Where's Jason?"

"Work, I would imagine. They're running a special edition today. He promised to bring one home later."

"Poor Davibth Longhoffer. Just gets back and his brother is eaten by a wooth."

Sam burst out laughing.

"Thangs a lot. I'm dyingth and you're laughing at me."

"You're hardly on death's doorstep, kiddo," said Sam, feeling Jake's forehead again. "I don't like that fever though. And it wasn't a wolf, for the record. Jason was right, it was a wolfhound."

"Can I have the comfrobter back, please?"

"All right, but just cover your legs. And incidentally, you're falling out of your boxers."

"I know," said Jake with a wicked grin. "Thab's why you bought 'em, remember?"

Sam kissed Jake on the forehead. "I remember. Try to get some rest, okay? If you need anything, use your cell phone," he said, placing it on the coffee table next to the tissue.

"Okay."

"I'll check on you in a half hour, okay? I've got a few things I have to take care of, but then I'll be in here with you the rest of the afternoon."

"Sam, you don't hab to—"

"Have has nothing to do with it, Jake. I want to be here for you. You know as well as I do you've taken care of me a dozen times with colds and my back and yet you've hardly ever given me a chance to reciprocate," he said, tousling Jake's hair. "You're annoyingly healthy."

"I don't feel so healthy right dow."

"I know. Just relax and try to get some rest, okay? Barnaby's in with me, do you want him in here?"

"No, the cats are keeping be combany."

"Okay then. I'll be back in a half hour to check on you."

Jake nodded as Sam left, stealing the comforter back over himself and shivering. He hadn't had a cold so severe in many years, and wasn't enjoying it. He wasn't sure if Sam came back in a half hour or not, as he drifted off to sleep. When he opened his eyes again, he was sitting on an overstuffed couch of plum velvet in a room he did not know. The walls were painted emerald green with black crown molding. On the wall beside him was a reproduction of William Blake's *The Web of Religion*. To his left was an end table with a lamp that looked like the planet Saturn; feeling that all this was vaguely familiar, Jake looked at the floor to make sure it wasn't the stitched pattern that had appeared in *Twin Peaks*. Finding nothing but highly polished floorboards, he sighed and sat back up, only to find Reed Longhoffer and Leona Weinberg sitting across from him in two straight-backed chairs. They were both white as sheets with huge black circles under their eyes and remained stock-still, their hands resting in their lap.

Jake eyed them suspiciously. "If either one of you starts talking backward, things will go very hard on you."

The two remained motionless, like dolls. Not wanting the pleasure of their company any longer, Jake went through a set of French doors into a dining room, where nearly everyone who had attended the town meeting was seated, all in formal dress. The maître d' moved stiffly forward and asked his name. Jake gave it and was surprised to see the maître d' was Walter Lugar. He smiled at Jake, his blue eyes bright, and led him to a table that was set for four.

"The other guests will be arriving soon," said Walter, bowing and leaving Jake by himself to survey the room.

Rebecca Windsor was eating a large orange with Gladys Nyberg, who looked completely bored as Rebecca yammered on. In between bites a devil, or perhaps *the* devil, only eleven inches high, kept grinding pepper onto her orange, causing her to sneeze with nearly every bite. On her left, the Reverend Crawford was chatting with Evelyn O'Conner, while Nora O'Conner in a red dress sat grumpily to her mother's right playing with a breadstick. Trudy Mundy walked by with a loaf of French bread, smacking Nora in the head as she passed. Jake burst out laughing as Nora looked around, bewildered.

"I'm sorry, Mr. Finnigan, your guests have not arrived yet," said Walter Lugar, having materialized from nowhere. 'Would you care for a drink?"

"I'll have a Burning Bourbon," said Jake, not knowing what he just ordered.

Walter nodded, bowed again, and left Jake to continue looking over the room. Milton Sandy was busy spraying Sheila Doyle in the face with his exterminator canister while his wife, Marilyn, kept poking her in the arm with a hypodermic needle. At the table next to them were Randy Burrows and Emma Kennedy, both holding plaid scarves in one hand and large red apples in the other; Verna Monger, wearing a long red sequined dress, was singing "Fever."

"Have I ever told you," said Sam, taking a seat next to him. "You have the strangest dreams?"

Jake turned to look at his husband, who was dressed in a tuxedo with a forest green tie and cummerbund. He smiled, giving Sam a kiss on the cheek. "You look wonderful."

"Well, don't get used to it. I only wear tuxes for dreams and theatrical dance numbers. And don't think you're getting one of those tonight either," said Sam warningly, taking a sip of a scarlet drink that was bubbling and hissing.

"What is that?"

"Burning Bourbon," said Caleb Rivers, holding a rather phallic looking pepper grinder. "Pepper?"

"Caleb, is that a salmon costume?"

"Overt symbolism. You know I like to fish," said Caleb, grinding a mound of pepper into Jake's drink. "Pay no attention. The real drama is out there," he said, motioning with the grinder to the crowd. "And don't worry about that pepper. It's organic and grown in a local greenhouse."

"Not bad," said Sam, raising his glass to Caleb's retreating fish fins.

Jake nodded in agreement, but followed Caleb's advice of looking out into the dining room. The wax-like Leona and Reed had moved to a table slightly apart from everyone else. A third man was sitting at the table, but his back was to Jake. Meanwhile the main course arrived, large steaming turkeys on silver platters. Jake's mouth watered at the thought of a succulent slice of turkey, when Rebecca Windsor suddenly rose and shouted, "It's Misty Snipes! The Plaid Porcupine Killer!"

"I thought it was the 'Plaid Scarf Strangler?'" Jake asked Sam, who, engrossed in a book, merely shrugged and turned a page.

Something large, spiny, and multicolored knocked Rebecca Windsor down. Jake turned to the entrance of the dining room where a skeletal woman dressed in a black overcoat let out a maniacal laugh and hurled plaid porcupines out at the dining room.

Jake looked over at Sam, who looked over the top of his book with mild interest and said, "Well, it beats flying monkeys."

Jake was horrified as people in the town began falling over left and right, plaid porcupines stuck like Velcro to their clothing while Misty Snipes continued to pelt the dining room with them. Finally Walter Lugar returned, hitting a buzzer that he held in his hand and insisting that she stop at once. She had taken to throwing around the dessert when Jake's eyes snapped open to the sound of the front door buzzer bleating in his ear.

He whipped the comforter aside, having sweat through it, and slowly rose, every joint in his body aching. He held his head, groaning as he approached the front door, walking through the small foyer and flinging the door back with a bang.

Adam Haggerty stood outside on the porch, looking somber.

Chapter Twenty-three

"Funny," said Jake, his decongestant finally working. "Of all the people in the world, I didn't expect it to be you." The codeine was also working—he was completely stoned, his head feeling like it resided about six feet above his neck and was filled with sunny, April freshness.

"I'm sorry...April what?" Haggerty asked.

"Did I say that out loud?"

Haggerty nodded, looking utterly confused.

"Never mind."

"May I come in, Mr. Finnigan? I have some questions I'd like to ask you."

"Sure, why not," said Jake, leaving the door open and walking away from it, heading back to the couch and flopping down. "What brings you here on this lovely day?" He grabbed a handful of tissue and blew his nose loudly, dropping the tissue in the paper sack Sam had left him.

"Ah, um, er, um, could you adjust your boxer shorts, please?"

"Oops," said Jake, pulling the comforter over his exposed genitalia. "Sorry. They do that."

"Quite."

"What can I do for you?"

"I'd like to know where you were after the last town meeting."

"Why? I thought I wasn't a suspect."

"We have another body now."

"And that makes me a suspect?" he asked, blinking away the cartoon bluebirds that had settled on Haggerty's shoulders.

• 185 •

"I understand that you had some sort of altercation with Mr. Longhoffer after you left the meeting."

"Who said that?"

"That's not important. Do you deny it?"

"No, I don't. Reed was being a prick," he said, wanting some juice but not wanting to get up. He wondered when Sam would check on him again. He also wondered when Sam would notice Haggerty's car in the driveway. He looked out the living room window and toward the driveway, only spotting Sam's Outback. Haggerty had evidently parked on the street and walked up.

"What was the dispute about?" asked Haggerty.

"Parking arrangements," said Jake, resting his hand on his chin. "Did you know that in China, they don't use forks?"

Haggerty frowned, scratching his chin. "Um, Mr. Finnigan, maybe you see this as some sort of joke, but I assure you I do not. Two people are dead. Coincidentally, these two people are known to have had confrontations with you and your husband less than twenty-four hours before their deaths. Now, as a fan of mysteries you can see why that would lead the police to think the situation somewhat suspicious. I need to get the facts, even to just rule you and Sam out."

"I'm sorry, detective, I'm not being flip. It *was* about parking. Reed had parked too close to our car and he couldn't get out." He thought a moment. "Did I say something about forks?"

"You did," Haggerty confirmed. "That was the extent of your conversation with Mr. Longhoffer?"

"Hmm. You know better or you wouldn't be asking. And that little bluebird next to your ear knows too." He blinked. "Forget I said that."

Haggerty suppressed a smile. "Please continue."

"Reed got insulting. Abusive, even."

"About?"

"The old battle-axe next door, the *late* Mrs. Weinberg," he said, sneezing.

"Bless you."

"Tank you," said Jake, blowing his nose again.

"Mr. Longhoffer was abusive? What did he say?" Haggerty asked, taking notes.

"He accused us of doing the old biddy in," Jake said. "Saying we should be arrested, we were perverts. The usual diatribe, you know…

you know...you have the most amazing dark brown eyes, Detective? They remind me of Sam's. Yours are a shade lighter, though, like antique walnut."

"Uh...ooh, kay...Did he...Did he use any words of a derogatory or denigrating nature?"

Jake laughed, which caused him to erupt in another coughing fit. Once it had subsided, he took another swig off the bottle, lying back against the pillows. "What a nice way of putting it. You're asking if the word 'faggot' was trotted out. The answer is yes. Funny word, that. It means 'bundle of sticks.' I've never been sure how a bundle of sticks got confused with two men who liked to shag one another. I'll have to look that up," he said, wagging a finger. "These things are important."

"Yes...um...and then what happened?"

"Then..." Jake wondered if he should mention that one of the cartoon bluebirds on Haggerty's shoulder had just relieved itself. He sighed wheezily and said, "I told him to back off or he'd have lawyers on him like black on coffee."

"Like what?"

"Black on coffee. It wasn't one of my finer moments in creative writing, Detective Haggerty, but I get a bit shirty when people trot out the 'f' word at me." His head swimming, he sat back and closed his eyes. "Where do you suppose the wolfhound came from?"

Adam Haggerty nearly dropped his pen. "How did you know about that?"

"J.D., Detective. Don't forget, my brother is now working for the *Examiner*." He thought for a moment. "You can probably get that out with a little hot water. Though I'm not sure if it's ink or paint or actual birdshit."

"Of course. I told both of them not to say anything," said Haggerty, annoyed. He looked up, blinking. "What birdshit?"

"Jason and I don't have secrets, Detective. Won't go any farther than me. I am wondering about the butterflies in the room though. Is it warm enough for them, you think?"

"Butterflies? Are you all right, Mr. Finnigan?"

"After the meeting we went to the Bitter End," said Jake, ignoring the butterflies and returning to reality.

"Can anyone verify that?"

"You mean someone *other* than Sam?"

"Yes."

"Caleb Rivers, the bartender, who played chess with Sam until well after 11:30. They've been playing this particular game over the last month."

"And what did you do while they were playing?"

"Ate. I talked to several people who came in, including my former captain, Rhoda Trelawney."

"When did you leave?"

"About twelve thirty, after we helped escort a drunk into a police car. One of your finest should be able to verify that, I should think," said Jake, yawning.

"Do you remember the officer's name?"

"He didn't give it," said Jake. "But the license plate on the patrol car was WA779AB. It was an unmarked car, but there was a scratch along the trunk lid."

"You can remember all that?"

"Yep. I told you I have a near photographic memory. For instance, the first time I met you, you were wearing that same trench coat, no tie, a blue shirt and socks with the Tasmanian Devil on them," said Jake, feeling exhausted.

"Uh, what's going on here?" Sam asked from the archway.

"Detective Maggoty was asking some questions," Jake said, yawning. "Haggoty."

"How much of that cough syrup have you had?"

"Just a pinch," Jake said. "Makes my chest not hurt."

"I'll just bet," Sam said, eyeing the bottle. He turned to Haggerty. "I'm not sure anything he told you would stand up, Detective. He's running on codeinated cough syrup."

Jake burst out laughing at the mention of "codeinated" until he erupted into another coughing fit. Sam waited until it had subsided, checking on Jake's temperature again before ushering Adam Haggerty into the kitchen.

"I'm sorry," Haggerty said. "I should have realized he was ill."

"It's just a cold, but when Jake gets sick, he does it with flourish. It'll be bronchitis by the end of the week, no doubt. And as you might have noticed, codeine affects Jake rather strongly. Coffee?"

"Thanks," Haggerty said, accepting a cup from Sam. "I was asking him about the events after the town meeting."

"Longhoffer was killed right after the meeting, then?"

"As near as we can tell. Mr. Finnigan says he had a minor altercation with the deceased, then proceeded to the Bitter End where you both remained until well after midnight."

"That's about it. You can verify that with Caleb Rivers, the bartender. And Officer Tallmadge, who we handed off the drunken fisherman to at about twelve thirty that night."

"Tallmadge," said Haggerty, making a note of it. "Mr. Finnigan said Mr. Longhoffer accused you of having a hand in Mrs. Weinberg's death?"

"Actually, I think it was along the lines of, 'I know you faggots killed her.'"

"Mr. Longhoffer was not a nice man," Haggerty agreed, making another note. "I've yet to come across anyone who had anything nice to say about him." He thought a moment. "One person."

"Likely Alexander Blackburn Junior," Sam said, thinking of what Alex had let slip at the town meeting.

"I can neither confirm nor deny that."

"Slippery, that," Sam said with a grin. "Look, there's no point in beating about the mulberry bush. Reed got accusatory, and, well, my husband is not a violent man, Detective Haggerty, but he *is* a bit of a hothead. Considering Jake's physical characteristics and being known for having a hell of a right hook, he showed remarkable restraint."

"I probably would have punched Longhoffer," Haggerty said.

"Jake and I don't believe in violence, Detective, although Reed Longhoffer was the type of person to even push *me* to the edge." He shook his head. "And even though Jake grabbed him by the collar, he verbally hit Reed with one of the few things he'd actually understand—threat of a lawsuit and a team of high-priced lawyers."

Haggerty again suppressed a smile. He was beginning to like Sam O'Conner. Both of them were obviously innocent, but Haggerty also followed his gut. It had never led him astray, but he also left no rock unturned. He scribbled a few more notes, wanting to rule the couple out for good. "Again, I'm sorry about Mr. Finnigan. I really didn't realize he was quite as ill as he is." He thanked Sam for the coffee and got up to leave.

"I'll be watching it, trust me. Like I said, Jake has this nasty habit of turning colds into bronchitis or pneumonia practically overnight," Sam said as they crossed over to the foyer. "Last year after that business with…" Sam checked himself. "He fell into the river and within a week was laid flat with bronchitis. "

"How did he—"

Just then, the front door banged open and Evelyn O'Conner swept into the room carrying a crock-pot and the smell of hot chicken soup.

"Sam, I've got some bread in the car if you can grab…" She caught sight of Adam Haggerty. "Well, Detective Haggerty. I can't say I'm at all surprised to see you here. You have a murder committed in this town and naturally you seek out a minority to pin the crime onto."

"Cool it, Mom. He just came here to ask some questions."

"That's what Hoover used to do as well, *just ask questions*. Did you check to see if he planted a bug anywhere?"

"This isn't *Mission Impossible*, Ma."

"No, but with those Republican cretins in Congress eroding all our personal freedoms and turning this country into a police state…"

"Kitchen, Ma, please. Go plug the soup in."

"I have my eye on you, Detective," she said as she went into the kitchen.

"You'll have to forgive her. She's kind of a conspiracy theory nut."

"Well, actually I agree with her, but you can rest assured I didn't plant any bugs in your home."

"Well, if you had, that's what you'd say, isn't it?"

Haggerty held up his hands, his trench coat flapping like wings. "No bugs, I swear."

"Fine, I believe you." Sam walked out the door with him to retrieve the bread from his mother's car.

"Well, thank you for your time," said Haggerty.

"Not at all, Detective. I hope you catch the guy soon."

"So do I, Mr. O'Conner. So do I."

Chapter Twenty-four

"Evelyn, quit fussing over me," said Jake, taking a spoonful of soup.

"You don't look good at all, Jacob."

"I'm fine. Well, okay, not fine, but I'm feeling better," he said, enjoying another spoonful of Evelyn O'Conner's famous chicken soup. It was about the only thing he could tolerate eating when he was sick.

Sam came in with the bread a few seconds later. "Cup of tea, Mom?"

"And a slice of the pumpkin bread would be wonderful, Sam, thank you," she said.

Sam nodded and left the room. Jake ate another spoonful of soup, feeling much warmer and more relaxed, even though he still was achy and uncomfortable. He took another spoonful then sat back, aware Evelyn's eyes were still on him.

"What?"

"Sam told me that Jason is moving out. How do you feel about that?"

"I'm fine with it."

"Jacob, this is me you're talking to."

"Well, I'll miss him," said Jake, after a moment's consideration, adding, "And I think it is a disaster in the works."

"Ah ha. I thought you might say something like that," she said, twisting her emerald ring round and round on her right ring finger. "Do you not approve of Mr. Brauer?"

Jake tried to decide how best to answer that question. He remembered Gavin's warning, and Jake was unwilling to trust him despite the fact that Derek Brauer was certainly likeable, handsome and very intelligent.

"I think he bears watching," he said. "I just think he was part of the problems J.D. had in San Francisco, and I'm not at all sure it's a good thing. I know Jason wants to help Derek with expenses. They are old friends and all, but it just seems to me Jason was trying to make a clean break of it, make a completely fresh start. But it is Jason's life, and I've got no right to butt my nose into it."

"Very wise. There's something you're not telling me."

"San Francisco, for a very big city, is still rather insular."

"Ah, Doctor Ashworth, I presume?"

"Says he knows of many people with the imprint of Brauer's rather large shoes on their back," Jake confirmed.

"Hmm."

Evelyn respected and was quite fond of Gavin and Jeff, having shared many a holiday meal with them in discussion of everything from multiple realities to meditation to Bigfoot.

"I would say then, Jacob, that your assessment of the situation is probably correct and exercising caution when it comes to Mr. Brauer might be well advised," she said as Sam approached. "Ah, thank you, Sam." She took her cup of tea as he set a small plate of pumpkin bread next to her. "I wish my darling daughter would live by those words. Sam tells me she's made your life somewhat difficult. Planting a little seed of doubt, as it were."

Jake nodded as he took another sip of soup. "Nora never took my plans very seriously. I know Nora's very career oriented, but she never seemed to take into account that it might not be the kind of career I want."

"We all knew you weren't cut out to be a career employee with the ferry system, Jacob. You've always been far too creative for it. I'm glad you are writing full time again. You've got too much talent to let it lie dormant. I think it is fantastic that you and Sam are in a position to be able to let you follow your passion," she said, taking a bite of bread.

"Thanks, Evelyn," Jake said, finishing his soup. "And thank you for the soup. It is, as always, wonderful."

Evelyn beamed. "Anything for my boys," she said, sipping her tea again. "And let me guess, Sam. Nora busted you over the financial situation with Jake."

"Ma," said Sam.

"We have no secrets here, Samuel," said Evelyn with a wag of her finger. She retrieved another piece of buttered pumpkin bread. "Secrets are dangerous things. They end up getting revealed at a horrible price."

"She's right, you know."

"Yes, she did. What business of hers it is I don't know."

"Your sister, progressive as she is, still doesn't get that your relationship with Jake is just as any marriage would be."

"Nora doesn't see things quite that simply," said Sam.

"No, I know it."

"That's because Nora sees things in Noravision, and that doesn't include subtlety, nuance, or acknowledging other people exist," said Jake.

"Would it help if I pretended I was insulted to sound like a good mother?"

"You *are* a good mother," Jake assured her.

"Maybe it would help your sister if you had a *proper* ceremony," said Evelyn. "I mean, vows exchanged in your living room hardly is what a mother dreams about for her son."

"We've thought about it," said Sam.

"We can't agree on what colors to have."

"Or where to honeymoon, since no-fly-boy over here won't step foot on an airplane."

"You can see a lot of this country by rail."

"Can't get to Europe by train."

"There's always the *Queen Mary 2*," said Evelyn. "If he doesn't want to fly, don't try to talk him into it, dear. When you've had a premonition about dying in a plane crash, it's wise not to ignore it."

"Thank you, Evelyn. She does have a point, Sam. Maybe going through a ceremony would get Nora off your back."

"I am not going to go through a ceremony just because my sister doesn't have an accurate handle on our relationship," said Sam sharply. "When and if we do it is because *we* choose to, and not for any other reason. I need to get back to work. See you tomorrow." He kissed his mother on the top of the head and stalked out.

"Hmm, guess I'll have to remember not to bring that one up again," said Evelyn, rising. "You get some rest, Jake. Would you like some more soup?"

"Not right now, thanks."

He watched her go then settled back into the depths of the sofa, pulling the comforter back over himself. He wasn't cold any longer, just aching and wishing he felt better. Jake hated being sick, not only for the general discomfort, but for the helpless feeling it always gave him. He disliked anyone having to take care of him, which was another reason the money issue still bothered him...and another reason he was angry with Nora. If she really had argued with Sam about their financial arrangements, not only was it truly none of her business, it showed that she didn't take their relationship seriously. That, more than anything, annoyed Jake greatly.

His thoughts turned to Reed Longhoffer. What kind of twisted individual set a wolfhound on someone? It was certainly possible to train a dog to kill, but he didn't want to imagine what kind of training it would be, or what it would do to the poor animal.

The next thing he knew, he felt Sam's hand pressed against his forehead. His eyes fluttered open, and he saw Sam's face etched with concern.

"Your fever is up. Time for another dose."

"Yes, sir," said Jake, swallowing more Dayquil capsules. "What time is it?"

"A little after three," said Sam. He sat in the chair his mother had occupied earlier, sighing. He began to fidget, playing with the coaster on the end table.

"Spill it, Sam. What's bugging you?"

"Nothing."

Jake looked at him, arching an eyebrow, but not saying anything.

"All right. Nora's bugging me."

"Thought as much. I imagine we're irked by the same thing."

"That my dear liberal sister doesn't seem to equate our relationship as being equal to hers with Ben?"

"Something like that. What *did* she say to you?"

Sam shook his head. "It was nasty, Jake. She said I should be protecting my assets, that things had a way of changing."

"Ah," said Jake. "She didn't throw in the word 'statistically' did she?"

"She did."

"Okay, I'm really no longer upset that she isn't a part of our lives. As of this moment, I'd really like nothing more than to grind a grapefruit in her unappreciative face."

"Take a number."

"I don't get it. I mean, just because she can't manage a relationship for more than two years, why does she expect ours to deflate after ten?"

"Because Nora's about as insightful as your average teaspoon. I suppose I shouldn't be terribly surprised. She's never once sent us an anniversary card."

"Sam," said Jake dramatically. "Will you marry me?"

Sam whipped his head over to Jake like a shot. He looked his husband in the eyes and said, "Jake, will you marry me?" with the same amount of drama.

"I asked you first," Jake pointed out.

"Well, we'll both answer at the count of three. One…two…three…"

"Yes," they said in unison, erupting in giggles.

Jake smiled. "I had little doubt."

"Neither did I. I suppose we shouldn't joke about it though. Some of our brethren take weddings very seriously."

"I know. You know how I *hate* weddings. Funerals, too."

"I think I was aware of that when I said 'I do' standing next to the fireplace over there with all of three people in the room. Five, including us."

"It was kind of obvious, wasn't it?"

"And I'd rather skip the funeral, Tiger."

"You know what I mean."

"I do. It might be nice to have proper rings, though."

"I told you, I don't need a fancy ring. The titanium band is just ducky in my book."

"Show the depth of your commitment, I know. However, did it ever occur to you in that feverish little brain that I might like to get you something nicer than a titanium band?" said Sam.

"Well no." He couldn't think of a single reason to object. "All right. But not yellow gold. And no diamonds. I've never cared for them."

"Me either," said Sam, giving his husband a long hug and a kiss on the forehead.

"Sam?"

"Yes, handsome?"

"How long would it take to train a dog to kill someone?"

❖

Derek Brauer's head still felt like it was coming off his shoulders. He stared at his copy on the computer, completely and utterly dissatisfied, but he would have to send it in soon enough if he wanted to make deadline. The rest of the paper had been set except for the lead story. He sat back and ran his fingers nervously through his hair, then shook his head and hit the SEND button. For better or worse, the story was going to press.

He sat back in his chair, wishing he had a cigarette. He hadn't smoked in two years, but still the cravings crept back like unwanted relatives whenever he was under stress. And this case was stressing him out.

Something was decidedly foul in Arrow Bay. It had everything to do with the murders, of course, but something more sinister was going on. Whoever had engineered the two crimes was very cunning, very patient, and very bizarre. Poisoning was fairly mundane, but the killer had gone to extraordinary methods of delivery. Using a half-starved wolfhound as a weapon was something else entirely. It was preposterously symbolic. He'd looked up the symbolism of wolves on the Internet in regard to people and came up with wolves standing in for "a cruelly rapacious person" which, of course, was his ex-boss to the letter. It just seemed like an astonishingly arduous way to make a point.

Derek glanced over at the editor's door. Reed's name had been scraped off and David's painted in gold letters the day before. He'd been locked in there all day, refusing to see anyone. No one was quite sure if it was grief or what. Marion and Joyce both agreed the two brothers had loathed one another, though Derek supposed David had to have some residual guilt. It was simply bad timing. Undoubtedly, the killer had previously set the date of murder. David arriving back in town was more than likely a coincidence.

Bizarre, he thought again.

He'd checked with the local kennels. No wolfhounds were missing from any dog breeder in Washington State, and Customs didn't have any record of anyone bringing a wolfhound across the border. All that was good and well, but if you had the money and the resources, you could get anything over the Canadian border. It was too wide open and too understaffed.

Guilt, he thought again, looking at David Longhoffer's door.

"What's up," said Jason, handing him the mail.

"Ah, well. Not much to tell."

"Somehow I doubt that. Got your story in?"

"Off and running."

"Good man," he said, glancing over at Marion's desk. "Marion said she'd have some more word on the case late this afternoon. She was going to bug the coroner on the autopsy of the wolfhound."

"Necropsy. That's what you call it on an animal."

"Well, in that case that's what's being done on both of them as far as I'm concerned. Only I wish the poor dog hadn't died," he said with a snort, wandering off.

There was little grief over the death of Reed Longhoffer in the offices of the Arrow Bay *Examiner*. People felt shock and abject horror over the way he had been killed, but Derek also sensed a great deal of relief that there was not going to be the prolonged fight over the ownership of the paper they had all feared.

Derek sifted through his mail, tossing away the junk until he came across an envelope that looked familiar. With a sense of mounting dread, he carefully slit open the envelope. Derek shook it until the letter dropped out, and then unfolded it using the opener and a pair of scissors.

Sickness swept over him. He backed away from the note, knocking over his coffee mug. It fell to the floor and shattered like a bomb, spraying the office with coffee and ceramic shrapnel, causing everyone to look up.

Marion Burd looked over the top of her desk, catching Derek's ashen face. "Derek, what is it?"

He couldn't answer. He kept staring at the blood-soaked piece of cloth. He was sure it was the same type of pinstriped Oxford shirt Reed Longhoffer had worn daily.

"Call the police, Marion," he said. "Get Detective Haggerty. Tell him it's urgent."

Above where the cloth had been taped, another message was spelled out in clipped-out pieces of the Examiner:

Two down, many to go!
Watch your back!
Enemies of Arrow Bay, a grim fate awaits you!
A Concirned Citisen.

Chapter Twenty-Five

The first heavy frost came to Arrow Bay in the pre-dawn hours of Sunday, October 29th. Clint Shimmel was heading into Arrow Bay toward his landing craft, the *Sea Eagle*. Shimmel hauled gasoline trucks out to Orcas and the other islands in the San Juan archipelago. He normally didn't work Sundays, but he could use the extra cash with the holidays approaching. Unfortunately, he was the first to realize just how slick the frost was. His '88 GMC pickup hit a patch of ice on SR 22 and slid right into the ditch. He was furious because his wife, Marietta, had warned him against working on the Sabbath, and knew she'd tell him he got just what he deserved.

At the same time, Alexander Blackburn Junior got out of bed, not caring if he woke his wife up or not. He stomped down to the office of his home. Like all the others on the street, was part of a gated community. Their goal of driving up prices and taking out the eclectic collection of farmhouses and 1950's ramblers that surrounded them had largely been thwarted by Clint Shimmel and several holdouts preventing gentrification of the area. Shimmel's ramshackle old farmhouse was across the fence on Bay View Road. Thinking of this irritation, Blackburn called his lawyer. As he bellowed orders at the man, he noticed a battered car driving slowly down the street, right headlight flickering as it went. Blackburn looked out past the faux gingerbread trim on their retro Victorian, scowling. *Who the hell let that riff-raff into the neighborhood?* He'd be talking to the security people about that, soon as he finished berating his attorney.

Across town, his son was coming to complete alertness after a deep meditative chant. His left foot was asleep from sitting in a cross-legged position for too long, but he didn't mind. Unlike his father, he felt content and happy. The reorganized company was doing better than he'd expected, and the final layers of paint were being applied to the *Chinook*. Move day was scheduled for November 7th. He was looking forward to moving day not merely for the change of scenery, but for the symbolic act of renewal. He had taken great strides to remove the darkness from his life, and now he had a real chance at making a clean break of it. The interim job on the city council would be yet another opportunity to make amends.

He was deeply disturbed over the deaths of Leona Weinberg and Reed Longhoffer. Arrow Bay hadn't had a homicide in nearly twenty years, excluding the incident with Susan Crane, which had technically not happened in Arrow Bay. Now they were facing two very bizarre unsolved crimes. He would have to talk to Adam Haggerty about how the case was going, assuming Haggerty would talk to him. He might still be holding a grudge.

The frost thickened, coating windshields and glazing leaves. Reverend Milly Crawford left her bungalow on the far side of the churchyard, walking slowly past the roses that lined the walkway to the white and blue-trimmed rectory. Some of them still had blossoms, now iced with a glittering layer of frost. She marveled at their beauty for a moment before heading into the church, hoping the frost hadn't killed the roses but making plans for other plants if it had.

As she stepped into the church, she abruptly stopped short. The air was sweet with the scent of stargazer lily. She looked up at the altar and there were four enormous bouquets of them, arranged with sprigs of cedar boughs. She looked behind her for a moment, then closed and locked the door, approaching the altar cautiously.

Nothing else was out of the ordinary. They were in simple glass vases, their fragrance nearly overwhelming when so close. She didn't see a card or any indication of who had left them. Smiling, she rearranged them so as not to interfere with services. She wondered who had left them, stopping in her tracks when she realized whoever had left them would have had to force their way into the church. Making a swift examination of the building, she saw nothing amiss. No broken glass, no forced locks, no broken down doors. All the windows were closed and locked. She had used her key to get into the church, so whoever had left the flowers had locked up when they left. Curious.

Deciding that one of her parishioners or her assistant Milo had brought them in, she shrugged it off, completely missing the note taped to the podium that read:
For fighting the goode fight!

❖

On the other side of town, Jason Finnigan watched the sun rise from the kitchen window of Derek's house.

It had not been a good night.

They had come home at two in the morning, right after last call and the bartender at the Bitter End had called them a cab to take them home. Jason wasn't drunk, but Derek was close to passing out. It had taken all his strength to haul him up the stairs and get him into bed. Derek had been mumbling and had burst into tears more than once before finally nodding off a mere two hours ago. Jason was exhausted but not able to sleep.

Everything had crashed down on Derek after he had reported the note.

Adam Haggerty had been furious he when he discovered Derek had received a *first* note. Haggerty had lectured Derek for a full twenty minutes, pointing out that Derek could face charges of impeding the investigation. Derek told him he couldn't be sure if the first letter was a joke or not.

Haggerty blinked, incredulous. "So that's why you made sure not to handle it and put it carefully in a plastic bag?"

Haggerty told him he would like to speak to him alone. They went into one of the conference rooms and did not come out for ten minutes. Meanwhile, Detective Trumbo went over the note carefully but couldn't find any prints to lift.

"Is it his shirt?" Jason said. "You know, Longhoffer?"

Sharon Trumbo eyed Jason for a moment, then nodded. She opened her mouth to say something else when the conference room door opened up and a very haggard looking Derek Brauer emerged.

"You better go rescue your friend," she said sadly.

"He's on his own for this one," Jason said, furious at Derek.

"Does anyone recall seeing this letter delivered?" Adam Haggerty asked the room in general.

"I handle all the mail," receptionist Doris Woolsey said. "It came in with the others. As I was busy, I handed the mail to Jason when he said he'd be happy to distribute the mail."

"There's no postmark on this letter," Haggerty said.

"No, there is not," said Doris. "When Dolly Flagler, the postmistress, catches a local letter from Arrow Bay to Arrow Bay she often just puts a black line through the stamp and moves it along. I suspect it's not strictly protocol, but it does the trick."

"And this came in today?"

"It was not in yesterday's mail, nor was it on the floor when I arrived. Sometimes letters to the editor come through the slot on the door. Some people like, say, Clayton Leeks will drop a letter by after we've closed because they're too cheap to mail it. Clayton did that yesterday."

Haggerty sighed. "If you recognize another letter like this, do not open it. Call for me at once, please. Don't even touch it, okay?"

Everyone nodded and watched as Haggerty and Trumbo left muttering to one another. Derek grabbed his pea coat and fled the building, Jason right behind him. They went out to the top of Cultus Mountain, where Derek stared out over the city of Arrow Bay sprawled below, the glacier-clad peak of Mount Baker rising in the east.

"You okay?" Jason asked.

"Yeah, I'm okay. Haggerty wasn't very happy with me."

Jason lighted up his pipe and puffed out a few rings of vanilla-scented tobacco. "Well, it was a pretty bone-headed thing to do, Derek. You've worked around the police long enough to know when you should be handing over evidence."

"The police don't always need to know *everything*."

"Don't start that bullshit again," Jason said. "You were thinking you could break a big story. I've seen you pull stuff like this before."

"This isn't San Francisco, J.D. I've really got to prove myself here, and there isn't a lot of opportunity to do it."

"What a load of crap. You cemented your reputation breaking the whole mess with Susan Crane last year. You were hoping to do a one-up."

"I—okay, so you're right."

"I know I am. And you had better watch it or whatever bridges you've started to build here will burn right up. With you on them."

"You don't think withholding that note… You don't think it contributed to his death, do you? I mean if the police had known…if they'd had it…"

"There was no way of knowing from what you got who might have been a target. And I doubt it matters. Someone wanted that miserable son of a bitch dead. They were going to kill him no matter what."

"We're all suspects now, you know. Marion, Joyce, you, me. Everyone at the paper. Even David, though I don't see how."

"That's pretty natural until he can pin down our whereabouts. I suppose David could have paid to have it done," Jason pondered. "But then why wait all that time? And why do it right when he comes back? Why not do it when you're out of the country?"

"I think you're smarter than our illustrious detective."

"I doubt that very much. Detective Trumbo and Haggerty have to rule out *everyone*. God knows plenty of people at the paper had motive to do him in."

"How can you say that?"

"Easy," said Jason. "It's the truth. Marion could have killed him for the hatchet job Reed had done on her reputation by printing up that story he wrote with her name on it. Joyce and Doris both hated him."

Derek looked down at the ground. "I couldn't live with myself, you know, thinking that I had…in some way contributed to someone's death. Even someone as hateful as Reed Longhoffer."

"This is me you're talking to, Derek. You put your own goddamn family in danger covering that story in San Francisco. You really expect me to believe that you'd feel some remorse over that old homophobe getting offed? Don't even try that on me."

Staring out the window, bathed in the cold light of the frosty morning, Jason still wasn't entirely sure if Derek's actions had had any direct effect or not. It didn't matter if Derek had thought it was a hoax or not. He should have taken the note to the police. Perhaps then, they could have assigned protection to Reed Longhoffer…but on the other hand, as Jason had pointed out, the note hadn't said anything about Reed Longhoffer. One victim does not constitute a pattern.

Jason resisted the urge to call Jake and bounce his thoughts off him, but it was only six in the morning. Jason sighed and put on a pot of coffee, knowing there was going to be no sleep for him that day. Better get on with the day and try to put things into perspective.

Jason went into the living room and snapped on the television, stretching out on the couch. He would wait until it was a little more daylight, then sneak up to his brother's house and pick up the last of his things. Glancing around at the living room, he wondered if he wasn't making a mistake in moving in. He hoped Derek wouldn't start to lean on him as he'd done in San Francisco when things had gotten bad for him before.

Jason snapped off the television. Getting up, he went to his room, stripped down to his underwear, pulled on long johns and his fishing clothes. Grabbing his hip waders and pole and tackle box, he decided to head down to the river and fish for a while to clear his thoughts.

❖

An hour after Clint Shimmel's vehicle had been pulled from the ditch, the first of Arrow Bay's sanding trucks got underway, passing through High Street just after the sun rose. Jake's eyes flitted open. Sam was clinging to him, and Barnaby and the two cats crowded on the bed. One of the cats was actually under the covers.

Feeling his throat completely dry, he sat up in bed, sniffing heavily. He felt no better than the day before, but no worse, save for the dawning realization that the furnace had gone out. Groaning, he struggled to get up, waking Sam in the process.

"Whazza?"

"Furnace went out. Again. I thought you were going to have that damn thing looked at."

"Ugh," said Sam, sitting up. "It's cold."

"Yes, we've established that," said Jake, putting on his slippers. "Haven't you got church or something today?"

"Not until nine. What's wrong with the furnace?"

"It's out."

"I'll go get it. You're sick."

"You look too cute in your flannel boxers. I'll get it," said Jake, stomping down the stairs. He paused at the foot to read the thermostat. Fifty-two degrees. Shivering, he continued down to the basement, when suddenly he stopped stock-still. Something wasn't right. He couldn't place a finger on what it was, but something was amiss. He looked the room over very carefully, from the exercise equipment to his desk, but nothing seemed out of place.

Irritated, he clomped over to the furnace and pulled the grate off it, bending down to reignite the pilot light. At once, the pilot ignited. Jake closed up the grate and watched for a moment with a satisfied smile as the furnace blustered into life.

It was then it hit him: there was something on his desk.

Jake thudded over and found a thick, green leather-bound journal leaning against the keyboard. It had one of his post-it notes attached, which simply said FOR NOTES in block letters. He picked it up and gave it a cursory glance, flipping it open. His name was embossed on the front inside cover. The pages were lined but blank. Sam could be very thoughtful.

He set the journal next to the keyboard and resisted the urge to fire up the computer. That could wait until the afternoon. All he wanted was a glass of orange juice, a piece of toast, and more cold meds. His sinuses felt less congested, and he felt considerably less achy as he trudged up the basement steps. He made sure the cats and Barnaby had plenty of food and water before pouring himself a glass of orange juice and dropping two pieces of buttermilk bread into the toaster. Sitting at the table, he cinched his robe around himself tighter, waiting for the house to warm as the furnace caught up. He'd have to call the repairman tomorrow.

Barnaby trotted through the room *en route* to his food dish as Sam came trundling in behind him, his hair sticking up in random directions like ruffled goose feathers. He walked over to the coffee pot and emptied the basket, adding fresh coffee and water. With a snap of the switch, he sat down at the table and rested his head on his hands, still only half awake.

"What time are you picking up your mother?" asked Jake.

"Eight thirty. What time is it now?"

"Almost seven thirty," said Jake, rising as his toast popped up. "Toast?"

"Uh uh. Not hungry."

"You're not getting sick, are you?"

"Probably. You know how it is. We like to share everything," he said with a yawn. "On second thought, toast sounds good."

Jake dropped two pieces of bread in while adding butter and blackberry jam to his toast. He sat back at the table, bit into a piece of toast, and frowned. "Can't taste anything," he said.

"That'll take a day or two," said Sam, tilting his head as he heard the front door open up. Barnaby instantly looked up from his food dish in the pantry and took off for the door, skidding through the kitchen as he went.

"Jason?" Jake called out.

His brother entered the kitchen, still in his hip waders, looking exhausted. He gave Jake and Sam a hug and then sat down, sighing.

"You're not sick too, are you?" asked Jake.

"No. Do I look that bad?"

"Like you haven't slept all night," Sam said.

"I haven't. Had a bit of a rough night last night."

"Everything okay?" asked Jake suspiciously.

"Oh, everything is fine. I think. Derek just pulled a boneheaded maneuver." He launched into the story of everything that had happened, starting with the first note and ending with Haggerty lecturing Derek.

Jake listened very carefully, pausing long enough to swallow his first dose of Dayquil for the day. He sipped his orange juice and asked, "What did the note say? Exactly?"

"It said, 'Two down, many to go. Watch your back enemies of Arrow Bay. A grim fate awaits you.' And it was signed 'A concerned citizen,' although both words were misspelled. Included in the note was a piece of Reed Longhoffer's blood-soaked shirt."

"Zodiac," said Jake, lost in thought.

"What?"

Jake shook his head. "Sorry. The Zodiac killer in San Francisco did the same thing in the late 1960's. He killed a cab driver and cut a piece out of the guy's blood soaked shirt. He then sent swatches of it in with certain letters to prove they were really from him."

"God, I'd forgotten all about that. They still talk about it at the *Chronicle*. This guy is really sick."

"I won't argue with that," said Jake. "But I have to give him an *F* on creativity. At least as far as the notes go. That's a copycat method, and even the way of making the notes is horribly clichéd. Any idea of what papers they were from?"

"The police are looking into that, but Derek felt certain they were from the *Examiner*."

"They probably are. This guy is no idiot. These crimes have been thought out. Yet he is going to the trouble to make himself look less intelligent by the spelling mistakes. He can't possibly be fooling anyone. Haggerty must see…that…" said Jake, his voice trailing off, his eyes glazing over.

He got up and rushed out of the room, opening the front door. He stared over at Leona Weinberg's house in complete disbelief. "Oh...no! I *knew* something had been bothering me about all of this, but I couldn't put my finger on it. How could I have been so blind?"

"Jake, what is it?" Sam asked, his voice etched with concern.

Jake spun around to face Sam and Jason. "What do you see?"

"What? Leona Weinberg's house."

"Right. But what do you see?"

Sam shrugged. "It's empty. You can tell no one has been in there in a while. Has a feeling of abandonment."

Jake shook his head. "No, you're not being literal enough. Look at the house again and tell me what you see."

"A white house with red shutters with little hearts cut in them," Jason answered. "And a whole bunch of dwarves in the yard."

"Bingo."

"I don't follow," said Sam.

"How did Snow White die?"

"Well, she didn't, not really," said Jason.

"I've got it," Sam said.

"I'm still not following."

"Snow White. When the witch was trying to get her, what did she give her?"

"A poisoned apple," said Jason, grinning.

"And Reed?" asked Sam.

"Eaten by a wolfhound, more or less," said Jake. "You remember what Reed always wore?"

"That damn red hat!" Sam nearly yelled.

"Exactly. No one goes around with a red *hood* on anymore, unless you're talking a sweatshirt, and Reed wasn't the sweatshirt-wearing type," said Jake. "It's a bit of a stretch, but it's not completely out of range."

"Red Riding Hood?" Jason said uncertainly.

"I suspect the killer had to fudge a bit, as who the hell could lay their hands on a real wolf these days, but it's no mistake it was a wolf*hound*."

"Right out of *Grimm's Fairy Tales*," said Sam.

"Grimm's were all terribly moralistic. They had a real sense of justice to a lot of their stories," said Jake. "That's what this guy is doing. 'Enemies of Arrow Bay, a *grim* fate awaits you,' the note said."

"A very sinister justice," said Sam, staring at Leona Weinberg's house. "And I would argue there wasn't as much a sense of justice in Grimm as there was revenge. That's not exactly my idea of justice."

"You're right," said Jake.

"You're forgetting something, though," said Jason.

"What?"

"Well, the common thread between Reed Longhoffer and Leona Weinberg was the city council and Wilde Park. Doesn't that put a third member at risk?"

Jake and Sam looked at each other, dread in their eyes. Both wondered exactly what Verna Monger was doing, or if she was even still alive.

Chapter Twenty-six

When Jake tried to call Verna Monger, he found out she had left the state on some emergency family business overnight. Jake had thanked the housekeeper, a woman with a thick German accent, wondering if there was an emergency or if Verna had astutely gathered her life might be in danger. She wasn't a stupid woman.

Jake showered, dressed, and saw Sam off to church while helping Jason pack up a few more of his belongings. By the time Jason left, Jake was feeling completely exhausted again and had to lie down. With Verna Monger out of the state, the next target was undoubtedly out of harm's way, so Haggerty could wait. Jake wasn't entirely sure that Haggerty was even in his office on a Sunday.

Barnaby joined him on the couch and for the next hour he drifted in and out of sleep, dreaming of Leona Weinberg dressed as Snow White spinning around her yard with bluebirds fluttering about her head, her lawn dwarves leaping up to defend her from a dark, faceless shape that cackled and held out a glowing red apple in one hand. He awoke with a start, groaning at the aches that had returned, and got up to blow his nose. He took another swig of the cough syrup with codeine and gulped another cup of hot coffee before heading downtown.

He parked his PT Cruiser in front of the Public Safety building just after ten, sneezing and hacking all the way into the lobby, where the policewoman on door duty gave Jake a look as if he might be some form of biological weapon. When he asked to see Detective Haggerty, she waved him through the metal detector then asked him to wait for Haggerty.

"What was your name?"

"Shackleford," said Jake, unable to help himself. "Achoo! Rusty Shackleford."

"He's says his name is Rusty Shackleford," said the guard into the phone. "What's he look like? I don't know, about five feet five—"

"Six and three-quarters."

"Five foot six and three-quarters, kind of shaggy hair, goatee. Looks and sounds like he's got a cold."

"You got that right," said Jake, sneezing again.

The guard replaced the phone on the cradle and nodded to Jake, handing him a badge that said VISITOR in big red letters. "Go on in. Take the elevator to the second floor; take your first left, go down the hallway about halfway. He's expecting you."

Jake wandered down to the elevator and waited for it to take him up to the gray cube farm on the second floor. It was mostly empty now, save for a man in a suit. Jake had seen him before. The man eyed him for an uncomfortably long period, but Jake did not look down or break his gaze. He wouldn't have in any case, but the cold meds and cough syrup were making him feel slightly fuzzyheaded. He had to fight the urge to blow the man a kiss just to irritate him. Finally, the man looked away when the phone at his desk began to ring.

Jake counted doors before he realized the guard hadn't given him an exact number. Halfway down, he looked into an open office and found Adam Haggerty, looking glum behind a big desk, surrounded by an array of colorful origami cranes, frogs, stars, and assorted creatures.

"What do I owe the pleasure, Mr. Shackleford?" asked a smiling Haggerty, beginning to fold another piece of paper.

"Sorry about that," said Jake, entering the office.

"Not at all. When someone from the front desk calls up and says someone downstairs is here to see me and gives me Dale Gribble's alias I knew it could only be one person."

"I wasn't counting on you being a *King of the Hill* fan," said Jake, feeling dizzy. He placed his hand on the doorframe to steady himself.

"Please sit down, Mr. Finnigan. You look as though you're about to pass out."

"I'll try not to," said Jake, taking the seat to the left of the two desks.

"Please tell me you didn't drive down here."

"Felt fine when I left. It just keeps coming back on me."

"Sharon's gone to get some coffee," said Haggerty. "Would you prefer some juice or something else?"

"Maybe a glass of water."

Haggerty rose and stepped out of the office, leaving Jake to sit back and feel his head spin. He sneezed loudly twice, sitting for several minutes holding the bridge of his nose. The pressure behind it was unbearable, but the codeine was rapidly working on the pain.

"You don't look so good," said Sharon Trumbo, placing three cups of coffee on the desk.

"Just a cold. Thanks for the coffee. I'm not sure I'm up to it."

"You should have some hot lemon water or maybe some tea."

"Detective Haggerty is getting me some water," said Jake.

Sharon stood up abruptly and shut the door to the office. Sitting back down, she said, "He's under a lot of stress and sometimes he gets to the breaking point. I know he was a little hard on your brother's friend, but he should have come forward with the note."

"I wholeheartedly agree. He probably wasn't hard enough on Brauer," said Jake with a sneeze. "Do you have your gun?"

"Erm, well, yes," said Sharon.

"I may ask you to shoot me at some point," he said, blinking. The butterflies had returned.

"You really should be in bed—" she stopped as Jake held up a hand.

"Believe me, I wouldn't have come down here if I'd not felt it was important. After my brother told me the contents of the second note, I felt I had better get down here," said Jake, leaning back in the chair. He eyed the steaming cup of coffee. "Sugar?"

"I've some packets in my desk," said Sharon, opening a drawer. "How many?"

"Four. I normally don't put that many in, but I can't taste anything. Hopefully this will help," said Jake taking the sugar packets from her and stirring them into the coffee.

"What is so important that you felt you had to come down here?"

Jake sighed and took a sip of his coffee as Detective Haggerty entered the room and handed Jake a bottle of water.

"Sorry," he said, closing the door behind him. "I ran into someone on the way back," he said, taking his place behind his desk, and giving Sharon a *we'll-talk-later* look. "What's up, Mr. Finnigan?"

"Have you noticed anything similar about the crimes?" Jake asked.

"We can't discuss open cases, Mr. Finnigan, even if one of the victims was your next door neighbor," said Haggerty slowly.

"Okay, don't discuss, just…listen."

"Mr. Finnigan—" Haggerty began.

"Adam, hear him out, okay? He wouldn't have dragged himself down here half dead if he didn't think it was important."

Haggerty sighed, picking up a piece of bright blue paper. He folded it in half very carefully. "Okay. But if anyone asks, you're here because you had some more information about Leona Weinberg's movements the day she died."

"Agreed," Jake said with a deep breath. "I don't know why I didn't see it sooner. Maybe because I've been trying to purposefully keep myself out of this whole thing," said Jake, ignoring Haggerty's raised eyebrows. "I know serial killers usually choose the same M.O., which of course isn't the case here."

"We're not even sure we are talking about the same perpetrator, Mr. Finnigan."

"Oh, come on. Both were members of the city council. Duh. Even Rebecca Windsor can put that two and two together and get four. Or the devil," said Jake, watching Haggerty fold the paper. "I really wish you could see these butterflies. You'd like them with all the other colorful animals you have there."

"Butterflies?" Sharon asked.

"Mr. Finnigan, have you been imbibing your codeine cough syrup again?"

"Doctor prescribed. Just got a top off, in fact. Only thing that kills the pain in the lungs."

"I think you'd be better served by some antibiotics."

"It may come to that." Jake watched the iridescent butterflies swoop around Haggerty's head. "The butterflies are really cool, though." He charged on. "The modus operandi was the same for both victims."

"I don't see how," said Sharon.

Haggerty stopped folding paper and looked at Jake carefully for a moment. "Go on."

"Leona Weinberg was a meddling, bigoted old bat with horrible taste. She did have a passion for Disney memorabilia, though. You had to have noticed it. The shutters are red with little hearts cut out in them and those horrible, horrible lawn dwarves in the yard."

"Right," said Sharon.

"How was she killed?"

"Poisoned apple," said Adam Haggerty, resuming his folding.

"Right, just like—"

"Snow White," said Sharon. "And Longhoffer…"

"Always wore the maroon hat," said Adam. "Which, fudging a bit, is red, as in—"

"Riding Hood." Sharon looked up at Adam, cross. "You've thought about this."

"I was mulling it over," said Haggerty sheepishly. "I was going to run it past you later."

"It seems logical then, given the contents of the second note, that whoever is doing this is targeting the dissenting members of the city council. Which would mean Verna Monger is likely the next target," said Jake. "Except for she's out of town now and luckily out of harm's way."

"Which is why you called the house at approximately 8:35 this morning," said Haggerty, making another fold.

"How'd you know…Ah? Tap."

"Yes. We could see which way the wind was blowing. When two of three members of the city council are murdered, it isn't too illogical to assume the third who shares their beliefs might be the next in line."

"Except I don't think she is," said Jake.

Haggerty sat up, setting down a nearly completed origami turtle. "Why not?"

"Because she redeemed herself. Grimm's fairytales are all about the evildoer getting it in the shorts by the end of the story."

"Well, wait, Snow White wasn't the evildoer in the story," said Sharon.

"I know, I know, but let's face it, kids, whoever is doing this isn't playing with a full deck of cards," said Jake, wincing at the cliché. "Look…I know it's unorthodox, but can I see the crime scene photos of Leona Weinberg?"

Haggerty eyed Jake carefully for a moment, then opened his desk drawer and handed a packet to Jake.

"Photographic memory or not, when I'm sick and on cold meds, the file cabinets in the old noggin sometimes don't open. The butterflies get in the way, too," said Jake, thumbing through the photos until he found the one he was looking for. It was a long shot of Leona Weinberg on the floor, her arms outstretched, one still holding the apple, her feet askew. Her eyes were open and her face horribly purple. Jake concentrated on the position of the body itself. He held the photo up for Trumbo and Haggerty to look at. "Notice anything?"

"It's how the body was found," said Sharon.

"Look at her position. Think of a body falling to the floor. Would it really have fallen in such a way?"

"It's possible," said Haggerty.

"I don't think so. I think she's been posed this way."

"Why?"

"Because the wicked stepmother in Grimm's was put to death by placing her feet in hot iron shoes then forcing her to dance until she fell down dead," said Jake, looking at the photo again. "I noted it at the time but didn't really think much about it. Take a look at the shoes with regard to what else she was wearing," said Jake, showing the photo once again to Trumbo and Haggerty.

"I don't see anything…" said Haggerty.

"You do, don't you Detective Trumbo?"

"Yes, I do," she said with a grin.

"While I hate anything that resembles a stereotype, Detective Haggerty, you've just given valuable evidence of your heterosexuality."

"I… What are you talking about?"

"Her shoes, Adam, are gray. Steel gray, I might add. Which do *not* go with her blouse or her skirt."

"Leona's taste in lawn decoration may have been awful, and she may have been outfitted by *Old Lady USA*, but she would not have worn gray pumps with that outfit. I can't remember her wearing anything but black patent leather Oxford pumps. Always sounded like gunshots going up the sidewalk to her front door."

"I think you might have something, Mr. Finnigan," said Adam Haggerty, looking over the photo.

"But he's mixing stories," Sharon pointed out. "Or she."

"*Snow White* and *Cinderella*." Jake nodded. "Yeah, but really, do you think he—or she—would have been able to lay his hands on some real iron shoes and make Leona do the Charleston until she dropped dead? I mean, I'm not even sure that'd kill you."

"I'm thinking it wouldn't do you any good," said Sharon.

Jake shrugged. "The butterflies—which are iridescent purple around you, by the way—seem to agree. So you must be right. And that being said, whoever is doing this is fuckin' nuts, don't you think? I'm pretty sure getting the fairytale aspect to it was what he was after and maybe he kinda winged it. The poison apple is certainly straight out of Fimm." He shook his head. *"Grimm!* Damn cough syrup."

"How much of that have you had?" asked Haggerty.

"A wig or three. Swig. Four. Four exactly. And I think the point was the symbolism, not the method."

"With Weinberg?" asked Adam.

"Yep. She may have *lived* in Snow White's cottage, but she was *really* the wicked stepmother. Hence, the gray pumps."

"Long way to go to make a point," Sharon said.

"Again," said Jake, swirling his index finger around his temple in circles. "Fuckin' crackers."

Sharon stifled a laugh, but was not able to contain her smile. Jake grinned right back at her.

"As for Reed Longhoffer, I think it's a case of wolf-eating-wolf, ho ho. Although I have to admit I feel more for the furry one than Longhoffer," said Jake, sneezing again.

Adam looked at him with a raised eyebrow, but said nothing.

"And why do you think Verna Monger is no longer at risk?" she asked.

"I can't explain it. A hunch, I guess. She voted for kicking Longhoffer off the council. This guy might consider that an act of redemption and not do whatever he's got planned."

"Which means someone else in town we don't know about might be targeted," said Sharon.

Haggerty shrugged, arching his long, narrow fingers into a steeple in front of him thoughtfully. "We may not know in any case. I thought Monger might be an obvious choice for the next victim. That's why I put her phone and house under surveillance," he said with a sigh. "Then I thought that this person surely would have realized we figured out, at the very least, the connection between Longhoffer and Weinberg, making Verna Monger far too obvious a choice for his or her next victim."

"If he's using those against Wilde Park as his criteria for bumping people off, he's got a pretty narrow list. There were only a few at the meeting who spoke in favor of demolishing it for the sake of a big box store. I don't think he'd consider Rebecca Windsor a serious target," said Jake with a sniff.

"No, neither do I," Haggerty said. "Besides if anything happened to her, I'd look at Trudy Mundy," said Haggerty, grinning crookedly.

"I guess the next question would be who had dealings with Reed Longhoffer in regard to the SuperLoMart deal," said Jake, thinking aloud more than anything else. He snapped his fingers and said, "Oh, for fuck's sake. I know!"

Adam arched an eyebrow and said, "Who?"

Jake blinked. "Who what?"

"You just said...oh, never mind. You've professed no interest in being involved in a murder investigation, so we'll take it from here," said Haggerty.

"Too bloody right," said Jake, rising unsteadily to his feet. "If you'll pardon the expression."

"No worries, Mr. Finnigan," said Haggerty. "And thank you for coming down. It's been most illuminating."

"You're welcome."

"Are you absolutely sure you can get yourself home okay?" Sharon asked.

"Yes, I'm fine, thank you. It's a very short distance, and I'll be okay. If I don't feel well enough by the time I get down to my car I'll call someone. Actually, I think I'll just sleep there for a while."

"Nah, I don't think so," said Adam, picking up the phone. "I'll have one of the patrol officers take you home."

"If you'll forgive me, I'd rather not arrive back at my house in a patrol car. The neighbors have been...well, *curious* to say the least given the recent circumstances. I'll call Sam to come get me. Church should be out by now."

"You're absolutely certain? I don't want you getting behind the wheel, Mr. Finnigan. Especially if you've been taking that codeine cough syrup."

"Relax, Detective, I promise I won't get behind the wheel. I've never driven impaired in my life, and I don't intend to start now. I'll call Sam as soon as I get to the car," said Jake, wishing now he'd just called in his information. He stopped at the door, closed his eyes and said, "C'mon, you gotta know who's next. I mean, there's only one other person besides Verna Monger."

"Mr. Finnigan, are you sure..."

"I'm fine," said Jake. "But you might want to check up on Alexander Blackburn Junior."

Before Haggerty or Trumbo could say anything, Jake left the room.

Chapter Twenty-seven

Jake stepped outside the office and made his way down to the elevator, nodding to the guard as he left the Public Safety Building.

Back in the Cruiser, he felt a bit better, but kept his word and called Sam. Sam picked up on the second ring.

"Hello?"

"Service done?"

"Yep. Mom and I were just having a chat with the Reverend Crawford."

"Can you come and get me?"

"Wait, aren't you at home?"

"No, I went down to talk to Haggerty like I told you. I'm feeling a bit light-headed and promised him I wouldn't drive."

"I thought I asked you to wait. Full of that cough syrup, no doubt. What were you thinking, Jacob?"

"I thought I could get down here and back before it started affecting me."

"I'm tying you to the bed when I get you home. You're not leaving the house until you're feeling one hundred per cent better. Have you forgotten your bout with Mr. Pneumonia the last time you pushed yourself too hard?"

"No, sir," said Jake sheepishly. "Just come and get me, okay?"

"All right. I'll bring Mom with me, and she can drive the Cruiser home, you big dope."

"I'll be right here."

❖

"And what was Jake doing out of bed?" Evelyn asked Sam.

"You know Jake, Ma. You can't tell him anything."

"He seems like a very headstrong lad," said Milly Crawford, noticing something stuck to the podium for the first time. She had a habit of not standing still while delivering one of her sermons, preferring to move about. In any event, she would likely have overlooked the white three-by-five note card that was taped to the front of the podium on the altar. She popped the card off and read the message, chuffing.

"What's that, Milly?" Evelyn asked.

"My secret admirer did leave me a card after all," she said, holding out the card. "Though he's not much of a speller."

Sam caught a look at the card and blanched. Reverend Crawford caught his expression at once. "Sam, are you okay?"

"When did you get that?"

"What, this? It must have been left by the person who left me all the flowers," she said motioning to the stargazer lilies. "I assumed Milo must have let them in," said Reverend Crawford. "Sam, what is wrong? You look like you've seen a ghost!"

"That's not just from anybody, Reverend Crawford. That note is from the person who killed Reed Longhoffer and Leona Weinberg."

❖

Jake's trip home had been delayed, as Adam Haggerty had to question everyone involved with the note. Once home, however, he did exactly as Sam instructed and went directly to bed, where he promptly fell asleep. When he awoke several hours later, he felt surprisingly better. He sat up in bed, patting his thigh and calling for Barnaby to join him on the bed. Jake petted the dog for several moments then got up, wanting a glass of juice.

He walked downstairs and found Sam sprawled out on the couch, snoring gently. He'd forgotten to take off his glasses, which were askew, and Jake noticed several white hairs in Sam's beard. Sam was going to be a very distinguished, handsome man into midlife and well beyond.

He crept around him and looked into what had been Jason's room. Sam had indeed been busy. All the furniture had been pulled out of the room, save for the mattress and box spring. The walls were looking particularly dingy, even though the curtains had been removed and daylight was streaming through the window. He stepped into the room and walked to the window, looking out at the side yard, in which they still had not started any work. Leona's death had pretty much curtailed that, neither one of them wanting to be near her house.

Who the hell is doing this? Jake thought angrily. Susan Crane was bad enough, being dumped on the ferry, but someone was targeting his town, the place he had called home for nearly a decade now. He felt personally attacked, even if he did not happen to like either person who had been murdered. Moreover, Leona Weinberg being a neighbor just put it too damn close.

Someone was out there now, he noticed abruptly. The front door was open, and a Jeep Cherokee rental was in the driveway. Jake leaned closer to the glass, realizing anyone could see him blatantly staring out at the house next door. He was wondering who it could be when the doorbell buzzed, making him jump.

He quickly cinched up his robe and headed out for the front door, Sam stirring awake on the couch.

"Wazz? Who's there?"

"Someone is at the door, kiddo," said Jake, going to answer the door. He pulled it open to find a tall man of about thirty-five dressed in a brown bomber jacket, and tight jeans, and biker boots. He flashed Jake a smile that indicated teeth whitening and a very good cosmetic dentist. His coal black, wavy hair was combed back, matched by an equally black beard. He took off a pair of Harley Davidson sunglasses to reveal dark brown eyes. Jake thought he detected Donna Karan's *Be Delicious* cologne on him, but wouldn't trust his nose in the present circumstances.

"Hello, I was wondering if you could help me possibly?" the man asked. He had a deep baritone voice.

"I'd like to," said Jake.

"Pardon?"

"Smooth, Ace," said Sam, coming up behind him as Jake turned a particularly stunning shade of crimson. "Sam O'Conner," said Sam, offering a hand. "How can we help you, Mr...?"

"Kyle O'Brien," the man said, shaking Sam's hand.

"Jake Finnigan," said Jake, recovering long enough to shake the handsome man's hand.

"I'm Aunt Leona's nephew," he said. "I've just gotten in from San Francisco to settle her estate."

"Come in and have a seat," said Sam, gesturing toward the living room.

"Thank you," said O'Brien, entering the house and crossing over to the living room. "Very nice house you have here, Mr. O'Conner, Mr. Finnigan. And a beautiful yard, too." He sat down while Barnaby, recently appeared from upstairs, sniffed his hand and allowed himself to be petted. "I can't imagine why Aunt Leona would find you so objectionable."

"Ah, well," started Jake.

"She didn't approve of our relationship," said Sam simply. "It seems your aunt was a little...erm..."

"I think the word you're looking for is 'bigoted,' Mr. O'Conner," said Kyle O'Brien. "Aunt Leona was not what you'd call open-minded. Had she known that I, her only living relative, had married a woman of Chinese descent, she might have made different arrangements for the settling of her estate, which, I might add, is considerable."

"Ah ha," said Jake.

Kyle O'Brien arched an eyebrow. "Not to give you the wrong impression, Mr. Finnigan, I didn't say anything because I chose to keep my private life private, not because I was afraid of being cut out of her will. I didn't even know I *was* in her will. She had never been close to my father or myself. I *did* come out here for a few summers when I was a kid, so she must have looked back upon them fondly," he said, shrugging. "She was a much kinder woman back then. When her first husband died—Uncle Raymond—she really changed. She withdrew and became very religious. We thought she'd change when she met Uncle Silas—Mr. Weinberg. No such luck. He was a kind man, but a bit of a milquetoast and she bulldozed over him. She quit talking to my father and mother because she believed them to be immoral," he shrugged. "For reasons I'm still not sure of, she kept in contact with me, one letter a week, right up until the time she died."

"And she kept you up to speed with the events of High Street."

Kyle O'Brien nodded. "Her reports about her new neighbors were so disturbing to me I actually ran a background check on you, Mr. O'Conner. You see, she never would say what the nature of her complaint was, but she was so distraught I had to find out." He shrugged again. "She was horrible, but I still saw her though my childhood eyes, I guess. I'd gently try to nudge her in my letters, but…" he finished with a shrug.

"I understand," said Sam. "Can I get you something to drink? Coffee? Tea?" Sam glanced at the clock on the DVD player. "Scotch?"

"I'll take a double of Jameson's," said Jake.

"You're sick," said Sam.

"Can't think of a better way to get rid of a cold," said O'Brien.

"Me, either."

"I can, Mr-Four-Shots-of-Codeine-Cough-Syrup. *You* get a glass of orange juice. Mr. O'Brien?"

"Kyle, please. A double shot of Jameson sounds great."

Sam left and returned a few minutes later with a double and an orange juice, which Jake scowled at.

Kyle took a large swig of his and smiled. "Of course all I found out was that you're a successful maritime designer with a raft of accolades and achievements. I was perplexed to say the least. When she finally got around to mentioning Mr. Finnigan, I put two and two together. I sent her a steady stream of 'live and let live' letters which seemed to work, but over the last month or so, she seemed to be getting more and more upset about it. I don't think it was anything you were doing. Aunt Leona was seventy-eight and not in the best of health. The content of her letters was often erratic and disjointed. Had this not happened, I was going to come at Thanksgiving and see what exactly was going on and see if it might not be time for assisted living."

"We're sorry for your loss," said Jake, suddenly feeling terribly guilty for all the harsh things he'd said to Leona Weinberg. Being in failing health would have explained several things.

"I appreciate that," Kyle said. "Though really I mourned for her long ago."

"Have the police been able to give you any idea who they think might have…" Sam asked.

Jake looked at him, utterly astonished. What had gotten into him? He was forever telling Jake to stay out of the investigation, and here he was asking about it.

O'Brien shook his head. "No. They haven't given me any details other than they have several 'persons of interest' and that it was not a random killing. I gather they really don't have much to go on."

"Did they tell you there has been a second murder?" asked Sam, once again making Jake's jaw drop.

"They did mention that another member of the city council had been murdered, but stressed it might not be related to my aunt's death. The detective mentioned my aunt and this other man were in favor of some sort of land development issue that was very unpopular with most of the population of the city."

"That's putting it mildly," said Jake quietly.

"I assumed it was one of two people—Reed Longhoffer or Alexander Blackburn, though the police didn't say," said O'Brien. "Aunt Leona would often write about them. I never quite got the nature of their friendship. She seemed to actively despise both men, but at the same time considered them allies to some bigger cause."

"Alexander Blackburn?" Sam asked.

"Junior, or the third?"

"She never said."

Jake and Sam glanced at one another, but said nothing.

"Well, I don't mean to take up your time," said O'Brien, rising. "I actually just came over to see if you might know a place I could stay in town. I could stay at the house, but quite honestly the idea gave me the creeps."

"I understand," said Jake. "I'd try the Illahee Inn. Very nice bed and brunch in the old part of town on the water. Excellent food there as well."

Sam headed into the kitchen for the phone book. "I'll get the number for you."

"I'll be doing some improvements to the house," said O'Brien slowly. "I can't sell it the way it's been…"

"Saccharinized?" Jake suggested.

"It is worse on the inside, if you can believe it. She had some valuable antiques in there, but they were all shoved in the back bedroom. The rest of the house is some pretty awful late 1970's colonial style furniture all wrapped in plastic. I'm giving all that away and storing the other pieces until I have time to go through them properly."

"Here's the number," said Sam, handing O'Brien a small slip of paper.

"As for the outside of the house, I'm having the shutters and the trim replaced. The yard has been pretty well maintained, but I'll have a crew clean it up. The topiary in the backyard will be trimmed into just plain bushes. Those damn dwarves are all going to the landfill. I know she loved them, but no one else will. After all that is done, I'll have the place painted. There will be quite a bit of activity over there the next few days. I'll be giving the other neighbors a heads up so they don't think the place is being looted."

"After all is done, will you be placing the house on the market?" asked Jake.

"Yes. I thought of relocating up here, and am very tempted to, but I just couldn't…live there," he said, turning to go. He paused on the door porch. "She was the one who tore down the original house and put that sixties ranch house in there. I understand the house was much more in the flavor of this one. I'm not sure why she did it, other than it disrupted the flow of the rest of the neighborhood." He shrugged. "It was just the kind of thing she did."

Chapter Twenty-eight

Sharon looked up at Adam, who had just hung the phone up again. "Any luck?"

"No answer."

"What'd the patrol car say?"

"Everything looked fine. Nothing out of the ordinary. They don't appear to be home. One of the cars is not parked in the garage, which was left open."

"So maybe Mr. Finnigan was wrong," said Sharon.

Adam glanced up at her from the report he was reading, but said nothing.

"You don't think so," said Sharon.

"I don't know. I know we can't go busting in there without probable cause. We've left messages, we've done our due diligence."

"Isn't there any other way to get a hold of him? What about Alex Blackburn? The son, I mean?"

Adam laughed. "I doubt very much that Alex has any current information on how to get in touch with his father. Very little love lost between them."

"Have you tried?"

"Of course I have," Adam said. "I can't get a hold of Blackburn the Third, either."

"You're afraid, aren't you?"

Adam looked at Sharon and nodded. "Yeah, I am. I'm afraid we're already too late."

❖

Jake and Sam stepped back inside the house, shutting the door tightly behind them. Jake made his way back to the couch, Sam joining him, slipping his arm comfortably around his husband.

"I feel like a bit of a bastard," Jake said.

"I don't know why. How were we to know? We weren't living here to see the *old* Leona. Who knew she had tenderness toward kids?"

"Did you have any idea she was that old?"

"No. I mean, I knew she was up there, but she's held up pretty well. Or had, anyway."

"Do you feel like…I don't know…like something is hovering over Arrow Bay?"

"Like some unseen evil? Well, there have been two murders linked to each other."

"They haven't, you know. Not officially. I think Haggerty thought I was off my rocker. I *felt* off my rocker."

"Detective Haggerty is a very thoughtful person. And I think he likes us. Or respects us at any rate. I doubt he thinks you're off your rocker."

"I can't see Emma Kennedy or Randy Burrows being the type to bump either Weinberg or Longhoffer off," said Jake, thinking aloud.

"I can't either, but you know how divisive things have been on the city council for the last few years. The whole Wilde Park thing brought that to a head."

"If you're going to paint that with the Wilde Park brush, you'll have to add Baldo Ludich to the list. He was really getting in Longhoffer's face over the whole issue."

"Baldo certainly has the strength to wrangle a wolfhound. But killing over the park?"

Jake went into the kitchen, returning a moment later with the phone book. He quickly flipped through the pages in the front until he came up with a generalized map of Arrow Bay.

"I'd say he's got motive," Jake said, pointing to where Ludich lived. "His house backs right up to Wilde Park. Imagine how the property value would have plunged had that SuperLoMart gone in. He'd never have been able to unload the place."

"Okay, by that criterion, you've also got to add in Alex, as the *Chinook* is going to park very near there."

"Ugh. I'd rather not. I still feel bad about thinking him guilty of bumping Susan Crane off last year."

"Well, I'd cross him off for sheer lack of time. He's been so wrapped up in the *Chinook*, I don't think he'd be capable of plotting out such elaborate murders."

"What O'Brien said about an Alex Blackburn in Leona's letters…"

"Oh, that had to be Junior since we know he was financing the whole little scheme," Sam replied.

"I agree. And I also agree that Alex hasn't had the time," said Jake, happy to leave Alex off the list. "What about along here, Chickadee Lane? It overlooks the park. There's that one big house, yellow with the white trim. The only one that is high enough to overlook the park and out onto the water."

"The Burd House?"

"Is it a home for swallows or something?"

"B-u-r-d, you goofball."

"As in Marion?"

"Indeed," said Sam. "Losing your million dollar view, downgrading property values, and editing your story without permission to give it a Republican slant when you're a dyed-in-the-wool member of the Democratic Party sounds like motive to me."

"Marion Burd? Who probably weighs ninety-eight pounds after a dunk in the bay?" asked Jake, incredulous.

"Never underestimate the resourcefulness of intelligent people. Or stupid people, come to that."

"Yeah, but that wolfhound had to have weighed more than she did."

"Have you seen said wolfhound?"

"Well, no."

"Drugged, it would be dead weight but not impossible for someone like Marion to move. Besides, it was probably trained."

Jake tried to picture petite, immaculately dressed Marion Burd dragging an unconscious wolfhound into a cage and then lifting the cage up. "I just don't buy that, Sam," said Jake. "That house is right on the road. Don't you think *someone* would have notice Marion Burd prancing around with a gigantic dog yelling, 'Kill! Kill!' at the top of her lungs?"

"You're letting your prejudices get in the way, Jake. Think of how the murders have worked. They took patience, skill and a lot of planning. These weren't spur-of-the-moment crimes. Given enough time and anger, you'd be surprised at what someone can do," said Sam sadly. "Although when it comes to Marion Burd, I happen to agree with you."

"Thank you very much."

"As for the others…"

"Oh, don't start," said Jake, snapping his fingers. "Emma Kennedy."

"What about her?"

"She's gone in on the *Chinook*. Maybe Alex is too distracted, but Emma would want a return on her investment."

Sam nodded, scratching his beard in deep thought. "Randy Burrows could certainly wrangle a wolfhound."

"So the two of them get together to bump off Leona and Reed, thereby eliminating any threat to Wilde Park, and thusly, their investment," said Jake. "There's only one problem with that though. Baldo found out that the land was in trust already."

"Yeah, but not until just *before* the second town meeting. Remember, Reed was already moving ahead. By the time they found out, it might have been too late to stop."

"Or they didn't want to. In any event, they wouldn't have to bump off Verna Monger because she'd already be so terrified with two of her friends having been murdered, she'd probably vote however the other council members did. And she did, come to that."

Sam tapped the map with his index finger. "Gladys Nyberg lives around there too, but I can't see her as a killer. She's really got no stake in any of it, didn't associate with the other two, and she's always been more direct, like smacking people with her umbrella."

"Agreed. Looking for the crazy person to be the murderer is a cop out. Besides, Gladys isn't known for her subtlety."

"Who else could have wanted them both dead? Reed had no shortage of enemies, but I'm not familiar with Leona Weinberg enough to really come up with another idea."

"Say, what's gotten into you?" asked Jake suspiciously.

"What?"

"What happened to that reading me the riot act over not getting involved with nasty little homicides?"

"Oh, that," said Sam, blushing. "Well, dear Leona was our neighbor. I suppose we owe it to her."

"Dear you-dirty-perverts Leona? What did you put in that iced tea you're drinking, anyway?"

"Never you mind," said Sam, moving his drink away from Jake.

Jake snagged the tea away from Sam and took a big sip. He looked at Sam and raised his eyebrows. "Ah ha! Just as I thought. Nothing."

"You know I'm not much of a drinker."

"I know it," said Jake, looking out the window at the now bare bigleaf maples in front of the Crenshaw house. "What about the neighbors?"

"Other than us, I assume."

"I didn't murder either one of them, did you?"

"I've been meaning to tell you something, Jake."

"Don't even," said Jake, rising to look out the window again. "You're about as violent as your average potted palm."

"Ever seen a triffid?" Sam asked, waggling his eyebrows.

"Those are fictional plants, Samuel."

"Well, on a more serious note, Reed did tend to bring the worst out in a person. I thought Detective Haggerty had cleared all the neighbors?"

"Mr. Origami said so, but what do you think?" Jake motioned for him to rise and join him at the window.

"What do I think?" He looked across the street at the Crenshaw house. "I think Al and Phyllis are about the least likely pair of murderers on the block."

"I would agree with that."

"Now the Jacoby family at number 96…" said Sam. "You know them. Couple in their sixties. Mrs. Jacoby plays organ for St. Stephen's."

"Knock it off, Sam. Churchgoers regularly commit murders. It's been documented."

"I know, I know. What I meant was, Mr. Jacoby is a retired insurance salesman. Do you think either of them have a creative bone in their body to come up with such a bizarre way of killing people off?"

"Ha, no."

"The Millers across from Leona had no cause to interact with her. They're never home."

"Well, damn. I guess Haggerty was right."

"What about Reed's neighbors?" asked Sam.

"I doubt they even knew he was there. That big old house out on Sky Heights is so far off the road and so far from anyone on either side I can't see his neighbors being in too much of a state over anything. On the other hand, there are always property disputes, borders, throughways, that kind of thing. I suppose Haggerty's looked into all that."

"One can hope, anyway."

"I wonder if the notes were genuine, or just meant to throw the police off," said Jake, lost in thought.

"How so?"

"*Enemies of Arrow Bay*...I mean, if you think outside Wilde Park, that throws open the door to a whole lot more people, doesn't it?"

"It certainly does," he said, and without realizing it, moved closer to Jake. They sat down together on the couch, both cogitating the unpleasant prospects of what might lie ahead.

"Uh, you know," said Jake slowly. "I told Haggerty he ought to check on Blackburn Junior."

"The money behind Longhoffer. Surely Haggerty thought of that?"

"I'm sure they both had, but their attention, like ours was tuned on the next likely victim, Verna Monger."

"Well, I haven't heard any sirens, and Jason hasn't come burst into the place, so my guess is, nasty old Alexander Blackburn Junior is probably just fine."

❖

"Junior?" called Vivian Blackburn as she came into the large house on Dormer Window Road. She had been shopping all afternoon, and her arms were loaded with packages. When her husband didn't reply, she set the packages down on the living room sofa.

"Junior? Lord, why have you got the heat on so high?" she asked, examining the thermostat, which was turned up as high as it would go. The furnace continued blowing unabated until she knocked the temperature down. The smell hit her—something was burning.

"Alexander?" She ran upstairs and went through the upper rooms. They were empty, but the pervading smell of something burning wafted through the house. She went back downstairs, hastily checking her husband's den, her sewing room, and the guest room.

At last, she walked into the kitchen, where the burning smell was overwhelming. Vivian Blackburn stopped in the center of the room. The oven was sending up puffs of intermittent smoke. She walked over and snapped it off.

"Lord, Alex, what have you been cooking now?" she said, having been subject to many of her husband's culinary disasters. She threw open the oven door, waiting for the smoke to clear so she could see what unfortunate thing her husband had roasted.

She screamed loud enough for the neighbors to come running. When Deedee Dumont got into the house, she found Vivian Blackburn on the floor in the corner of the kitchen, still screaming and shaking violently. She finally had to slap the woman to knock her out of hysterics.

"Vivian, what is it? What is it?"

Vivian merely pointed.

Deedee Dumont rose slowly, noticing for the first time the horribly charred smell roiling through the kitchen. She followed the direction her friend was pointing, finally seeing the charred, hulking mass in the oven. When she finally realized what it was, she ran over to the sink and vomited, emptying everything in her stomach.

Alexander Blackburn Junior had been roasted in his own oven.

Chapter Twenty-nine

The *nature* of Alexander Blackburn Junior's passing did not appear in the papers. Adam Haggerty was doing his level best to keep the latest Concerned Citizen murder from being reported. He was afraid the case was slipping out of his control. The chief was calling for the FBI to be brought in, but Haggerty had pleaded his case and asked for a little more time, sure that he and Trumbo would be able to crack it.

Blackburn's death had been reported. His obituary was printed dutifully in the *Examiner*. It perplexed many, however, that private services had already been held. Tongues wagged even more when Vivian Blackburn had a complete breakdown and had to be whisked away to a private sanitarium.

Jake was not happy for having made the correct assumption as to who might be next in line—and though he had not seen the official reports of how Alexander Blackburn Junior had died, he knew it was connected to the other two murders. He wondered how Adam Haggerty and Sharon Trumbo felt about it.

Jake reviewed the obituary with great skepticism, particularly knowing about the letters that had been sent and the fact that Alexander Blackburn Junior was considered an "enemy of Arrow Bay" by many. Everyone knew he had close ties with Reed Longhoffer after the second town meeting, when Alex had inadvertently spilled the proverbial beans, and it wouldn't have taken much prodding from any competent researcher to find out just how much.

On the seventh of November, a few days after Blackburn Junior's obituary had appeared in the paper, Sam called Jake to let him know the *Chinook* was about to be towed to her permanent moorage spot just west of Wilde Park.

Jake grabbed Barnaby and hopped into the Cruiser with his camera. He drove down to Sutherland Shipyards on the waterfront where Sam met him at the gate and took him over to the dock where the *Chinook* was positioned with two tugs at her sides.

"Will you look at that," said Jake, looking in awe at the ship.

Sam had resurrected a derelict vessel, turning her into the gleaming, streamlined craft she once had been. Her knife-like prow was accented by a stripe of a dark but brilliant red covering a row of portholes for the hotel's staterooms. The *Chinook*'s stack, once elongated by British Columbia Ferries, had been restored and cropped back to its original squat, shaved down profile, which blended in with the rakish lines of the former ferry. Jake snapped several pictures of her and was not alone. He spotted Jason taking photos for the *Examiner* and recognized the names of all three of Seattle's network affiliates filming the ferry as tugboats moved her out into the channel. Slowly she inched forward, stern first, as she was to be backed into the new mooring spot along the shores of the bay.

"I can't say I'm sorry to see her go," said Sam, with a sigh.

"Alex been bugging you again about changes?"

"Not so much this week, now that he's got all his stuff moved in. It was little things here and there. I don't think he's ever going to be completely satisfied, but that's the way it goes with Mr. Blackburn."

"Where is he, anyway? This is his big day. I thought for sure he'd be around for the photo op at any rate."

"He was here a while ago. He gave his speech and broke a bottle of very expensive champagne over her bow. I saw some noticeable cringes when he did that, by the way."

"Hmm." Jake walked back through the yard and by one of the workshops. He heard raised voices and slowed down, motioning for Sam to catch up.

"What is it?"

"Shh! Quiet," he said, creeping over to the side of the workshop. He thought he had recognized the voices and he hadn't been disappointed. Adam Haggerty and Alex were standing behind the shed eyeing one another.

Alex was standing with his arms crossed, not looking at all happy with Haggerty, who looked disheveled as if he hadn't slept for quite some time.

"I'm telling you again, Adam, back off. I let you know where I was the day Dad was killed. I know you've verified that."

"You left out that you had threatened him," said Adam, a hint of annoyance in his voice.

"He *hit* me in a public place. Of course I threatened him. I certainly didn't *mean* it, as violence goes against everything I believe in."

"Alex, this is me you're talking to. I certainly know what you're capable of."

Alex shook his head. "I'm sorry, Adam. It's my fault we haven't spent much time together. I understand why you'd have that impression of me…but these last several years I've done *everything* I could to shed that. I can't say this without sounding schizophrenic, but that was the old Alex Blackburn. Honestly, Adam."

"I know what you've been trying to do, and I applaud it, Alex, I really do. You'll just have to forgive the skeptical cop in me and give me some more time to wrap my head around it, okay?"

"Fair enough. I'm very happy you have someone you can work with who you trust on this."

"Sharon's one of about three people I trust at Arrow Bay PD," said Adam, sounding sorrowful.

"I know it doesn't come easy, particularly with that jackass Nelson Dorval waiting to plant the knife in your back at every turn. Remember, though, it's Dorval who has the damaged credibility with some in this town—not you."

Haggerty sighed. "I've got to get this one solved, Alex."

"Then let people help you. You already had Jake point out the Grimm's Fairytale angle to you."

"We'd gotten there at about the same time, funnily enough. You know, Alex, I'm under a lot of pressure to haul you in. Dorval in particular thinks you're the one doing this."

"Dorval's lucky I'm not running straight to Derek Brauer to let him know exactly how dear old Dad was killed. I'm goddamned cooperating with the police. You remind that pink-nosed son of a bitch of that when you report back to him. As much as he'd like to pin this whole thing on me and get me neatly out of Arrow Bay, both of you know perfectly well I was in full view of a dozen witnesses when my old man was killed."

"Oh, he's got an answer for that."

"I suspect he does. Something about how people with my kind of money never get their hands dirty."

"It's uncannily like being in the same room with Dorval." Alex shook his head. "So that is what this is all about. It always comes down to money, doesn't it? Dorval resents those who have it. He always has. Even when we were kids. He always failed to realize it never made a damn bit of difference to me."

"Dorval, like more than a few in this town, is still prejudiced by your admittedly wild youth."

"They don't even know the half of it. You don't either, Adam. You and I met when I was at the turning point in my life. You met the…"

"The kinder, gentler Alex?"

"Exactly."

"For the record I don't think you had anything to do with this. But there are still some questions I've got, and you've got to be a little more forthcoming, Alex," said Haggerty.

"I've never lied to you, Adam."

"Maybe not, Alex, but you have left out large chunks of the truth. Last year? Everything that happened with the Crane case? That is all sorts of screwed up. A one-eyed monkey can see that. I don't think anyone but Dorval gives a damn about that case. Everyone else—myself included—was just happy to have it closed."

"You're convinced that the correct perpetrator was caught?" Alex asked.

"Absolutely. There was a raft of forensic evidence eight miles high. I have no doubt as to who was responsible. There were, however, some lingering questions…"

Alex grunted. "The perpetrator was caught. Dorval has it on authority who it was. He's got the county sheriff's reports. All the evidence corroborated what McEvoy reported. The case is closed. Why does he care?"

"Because he feels something isn't right there, and he'd just love to tie you to it somehow. Me? I've got enough work to last me a lifetime, much less go on with a case that was out of jurisdiction *and* closed. I don't suppose you'll tell me what…ah…additional information you might have?"

"Some snowy evening," said Alex slowly. "After you've retired."

Haggerty laughed. "I understand. Though can I tell you of my suspicions sometime?"

"Oh sure. After the *Chinook* is open. Over steaks and a bottle of Johnny Walker. You can deliver a message to Dorval. Tell him to back the hell off on that Crane case."

"That sounded like the old Alex there. The one that used to warn people not to screw with him. You gave me a shiver."

"I'm sorry, but I protect the things I value highly," said Alex. "And the people, Adam. For the record, I count you among them."

"I appreciate that, Alex. As for Dorval…"

"Let it eat the guts out of him. He won't find anything."

"You really do trust the Finnigan brothers, don't you? And Mr. O'Conner?" Haggerty asked.

"I'd trust them with my life, Adam. Jake is like the little brother I never had. Sam, too." He sighed. "I suspect you've drawn the lines together a little? In regard to them?"

"Oh, a little."

"If the Finnigan-O'Conners had anything to do with Susan Crane, I can assure you it was nothing to do with her demise. The correct person was caught."

"Oh, I've no doubt of that. I've just suspected that Mr. Finnigan being so adamant about not getting involved with this case had more to do with the death of his friend from high school."

"And naturally your razor-sharp mind latched onto that. The question is, does Dorval have any idea?"

"Not from me he doesn't. And Sharon thinks he's a complete pig, so no worries there."

"Dorval's got far worse things on his hands than rehashing a closed case."

"Don't I know it? I'm sorry, Alex," Haggerty said.

"You can't apologize for other people. For the record, I had nothing to with my father's death. I had nothing to gain by it. While I indirectly gained from Reed Longhoffer being killed, I had nothing to do with that, either. I did not in any way have anything to do with any of the murders. You've got my word on it."

"That's good enough for me, Alex."

"Besides, you've already checked out my alibis," Alex said with a wink. Haggerty cleared his throat and looked away, Alex braying with laughter. "You're just doing your job, I know. But you can tell that son of a bitch Dorval you're wasting your time by continuing to bother me on this issue. I know you have a list of suspects a mile long."

"You aren't kidding there."

"Dorval really is a coward, isn't he?" said Alex.

"And a bully. One day he'll get his."

A silence fell between the two men. Jake and Sam waited anxiously for one or the other to say something, but only the sounds of horns from the passing tugs shattered the quiet. For a moment, they considered back stepping and clearing out, afraid of one or the other discovering them, but then Alex spoke.

"I have to get going. I'm expected to be there when the *Chinook* arrives. It won't take long for her to get there."

"I realize that. I'm sorry to have stolen the thunder from your day," said Haggerty.

"Nonsense. I don't see how being accused of multiple murders and being a complete psychopath put a damper on the day at all. Take it easy, Adam."

"Won't be any of that for a time, I'm afraid," Haggerty said. Jake could hear how tired he was.

"Keep with it, Adam, you'll get there. And when you do, let me know when you find the man who baked my father like a Duncan Hines cake mix. If it weren't for how badly my mother took it, I think I'd thank him," Alex said, starting to walk directly toward Jake and Sam.

Sam grabbed Jake by the collar and dragged him around the corner so rapidly that his heels cut tracks in the gravel. They ducked behind a large wooden crate just in time for Alex to go stomping past them, heading for his Jaguar.

"That was close," said Jake.

"A bit, yes," Sam breathed. "Let's get out of here."

Chapter Thirty

Sam and Jake went back to Jake's PT Cruiser, joining the procession of cars moving slowly down Enetai Avenue to the spot where the *Chinook* was to be permanently moored. Jake glanced down at Wilde Park as they crossed the bridge over the creek, wondering if such an innocuous piece of land had truly sparked the murders of three people.

It was three, now, as he had suspected all along. Alex had said as much to Haggerty. They were now dealing with *three* homicides in their sleepy little burg. No wonder Haggerty was sounding exhausted.

"...And then I thought we'd take the alligator with us," said Sam.

"What? What are you talking about? What alligator? Oh, I get it. Paraphrasing Pratchett at me. I see how you are. Well, then, what was I missing out on while lost in thought?"

"I suspect you were thinking about what I was talking about," said Sam. "The fact that Daddy Dearest didn't depart this world via natural causes."

"You know, it is scary how much we think alike. I was, indeed, thinking of that. Did I hear correctly when Alex made reference to a Duncan Hines cake?"

"You did," said Sam, stroking his chin thoughtfully. "Hansel and Gretel?"

"If memory serves, the Blackburn home on Dormer Window road is one of those retro Victorian affairs, replete with faux trim, which, in architectural terms, was called gingerbread. I can't decide whether this guy is being creative or just a horrible plagiarist."

"Jacob," Sam scolded. "A man is dead."

"On the other foot," said Jake, turning down the newly cut road named Chinook Place, "I can't also decide if he's doing us a service or not. These have all been horrible, awful people."

"I can hardly find an argument for that. And I feel damn guilty over it."

Scrubby brush gave way to sculptured grounds that had obviously been landscaped. Full-grown Japanese cherry trees flanked the road. Empty of blossoms now, their branches were wrapped in white LED fairy lights. A handsome copper archway stretched over the road, spelling out CHINOOK HOTEL in script, flanked by leaping Salish-styled Chinook salmon. To either side of the letters were stylized depictions of the ship. The arch was lighted in soft pink spotlights. They drove through the arch, following the road down a gentle hill to the parking lot three hundred feet away.

The parking lot looked natural. The back-to-back angled parking lines were broken in the middle by a long median peppered with more Japanese maples, rhododendrons, and ornamental grasses. The parking lot was surrounded by carefully cut lawn leading to a nine-hole golf course and beyond that was a large forested area.

"He's done a hell of a lot of work," Sam said. "This was just a thicket of blackberries before."

"I know," said Jake, pointing to the large breakwater where the *Chinook* was going to call home. "Looks just like the one the *Queen Mary* is in down at Long Beach. She'll be safe from any kind of wave action in there, and impact from the tide will be pretty minimal."

"She'll be floating, but you'll hardly notice it. There's a spot," he said, pointing out an empty spot in the rapidly filling lot.

Hopping out of the car, Jake crossed a small footbridge over a creek that burbled loudly. He snapped some photos of the *Chinook* making her stern-to approach, then stopped to look at the creek below him. He couldn't remember a creek under Enetai Avenue at this location, and made a mental note to ask Alex about it. He snapped more photos of the *Chinook* as Alex stood behind a podium temporarily erected on the gangplank that, for the moment, was attached to nothing. Jake clomped off the footbridge and made his way through the crowd to the front of the audience, where he spotted, among others, Reverend Crawford, Evelyn O'Conner, Police Chief Sanderson, Marion Burd, Professor Mills, Emma Kennedy and Randy Burrows, who was setting up a video camera for KABW.

Alex caught sight of Jake and Sam and flashed his usual million-dollar smile, then began speaking.

"Thank you all for attending the relocation of this historic vessel to its new permanent home. It is my hope that the *Chinook* becomes a tourist draw that will benefit the entire community."

Applause was scattered. Jake watched everyone's reactions carefully to see if he could tell anyone bearing ill will toward Alex and his endeavor. He didn't wish for him to become the next victim of the "Concerned Citizen" of Arrow Bay.

"As you can see there is still much work to be done. The restoration of this area, which was home to the Arrow Bay Cannery before it burned down, contained highly contaminated soil deposits, which have been thoroughly cleaned. The undeveloped area on the other side of Chinook Creek will be restored to the wetlands it once was before the cannery filled in the land there."

Jake ducked behind Sam as Randy Burrows swung the camera around to film the area in question. Jake noted with some irony Alex was not mentioning the copse of trees was going to contain a good-sized lodge at some point.

"The restaurant onboard the *Chinook* will feature locally grown produce, locally raised meats, and seafood caught by Arrow Bay fishermen. I've been lucky enough to entice my good friend Chef Keith Selman and a good number of his staff to take over the Chinook Winds Restaurant."

There were audible gasps at this, followed by a great deal of enthusiastic applause. Jake looked at Sam with one eyebrow raised, unsure of why this was such a big deal, other than the obvious fact that he must have been a well-known chef.

"You never watch the Food Network, do you?" asked Sam.

"No... Well known?"

"Right up there with Emeril Lagasse or Rachael Ray. Whole line of cookbooks and the like. It'll be quite a coup to have him in Arrow Bay."

"The Illahee Inn's incomparable pastry kitchen will be providing all the bread and baked goods served here, as well as trying out some new recipes, thanks to the generous efforts of Emma Kennedy."

"Ah ha," said Jake under his breath.

Alex glanced over his shoulder, where the *Chinook* lay poised to be eased into her new slip. He nodded toward several workers who had been standing aside. "Folks, we all need to step back and give the experts in this plenty of room while they ease her in. I'll close by saying thank you for coming, and there are commemorative ornaments being distributed to all who attended today. I hope you'll join me again in the spring, hopefully sooner, when we open for business. Thank you," he said, with a deep bow, hurrying off the podium as they wheeled the gangplank away. He shook several hands and said something to Marion Burd, who nodded and stepped away.

Jake spotted Jason snapping more photos as the *Chinook* eased back into the slip. Alex watched, turning away with a wince. He spotted Jake and Sam and he worked his way over to meet them. "I can't watch it at this point. I know it'll be okay, but I just don't want to watch in case something happens."

"It'll be fine, Alex," Sam reassured.

"I hope. I hate giving speeches. I'm much happier giving interviews. I told Marion I'd be with her in about twenty minutes."

"Spring before you open?"

"Yep. There's still fitting out to do. None of the furniture or restaurant equipment is in yet. None of the decorating has happened either. There's a lot of bare steel still in there," he said. "A walk through right now would be pretty disappointing."

"He's right, Jake." Sam said, watching closely as the *Chinook* backed into the slip. "Are you closing the front end off?"

"Yes. Same load of boulders as the ones that make up the jetty. The hull paint is good for fifty or more years, so I'll leave it to the next person as to how they're going to get the rocks out of the way," said Alex. "There will be a small electrical current run though the hull to discourage marine growth as well, and of course the creek empties into the holding bay which will keep the salt content down."

"Where does that water come from? I don't remember ever seeing a creek there on Enetai Avenue."

"There isn't one. It comes out of the woods there—it's all run off from the hillside. Every time they cut more trees down up around Sky Heights, the water jumps. It's down to a trickle in the summer, but it keeps on coming. There's a large pond behind the lodge site back there, and it is very deep."

"I notice you left out any mention of said lodge."

"No reason to start off on the wrong foot. Truth is," he whispered, "it's all been pre-zoned and permitted. I can start construction any time, but I want to make sure the old girl is turning a profit before I get into it."

"Nice deal you've struck with Emma."

Alex turned and let out a sigh of relief; the *Chinook* was in. The vessel's white flank was nearly eye watering in the muted November light, thrown into particular relief by the red stripe running the length of the vessel. In the stripe was a long line of portholes, sunlight winking on the glass like eyes. Her regal profile, while not quite towering above them, was certainly a sight to behold.

"Gibbs called her the *'Queen Elizabeth'* of the inland seas," said Alex with a reverent tone in his voice.

"Gibbs thought highly of his own work," said Jake, looking the vessel up and down. "Still, she's lovely, Alex. I'm glad you saved her."

"As am I," agreed Sam.

Jake's patience began to frazzle a bit. As much as he appreciated the *Chinook* and truly admired her, he was determined to get some information out of Alex. Alex and Sam continued to rhapsodize about the ship's lines and her lovely profile and how it was all going to be such a huge success until Jake finally blurted out, "Alex, what really happened to your father?"

Alex looked at Jake then to Sam, and then burst out laughing. "I am again victim of the Finnigan directness. But I'm going to put you on the spot, Jake, what exactly have you found out?"

"I'm sure I don't know what you mean."

"Jake, you know you're incapable of telling a lie."

"Okay, okay, we sort of overheard you," Jake said.

"I know. I saw you. Don't worry, I'm not angry. I know you couldn't exactly help overhearing what Adam and I were talking about."

"I had no idea you knew one another."

"We met at college. The summers I spent up here and in the islands, Adam and I got together for much of it—we share a scuba diving enthusiasm. Quite by accident, we ended up at the UW at the same time. We drifted apart when I left the country to do the genealogy work in Britain. When I came back to Arrow Bay we renewed an acquaintanceship, but it was nothing like the friendship we once had."

"I'm sorry to hear that."

"I am, too. I hope we can get back to where we were, but between his job and mine, it's been difficult to schedule anything. And when Adam isn't working, he's usually wrapped up in some woman or other."

"Does he suspect you of…?" Jake couldn't quite bring himself to finish the sentence.

"Of bashing my father over the head and baking him at four-fifty in an industrial sized oven? No." He looked up into Jake's eyes. "You don't, do you?"

Jake had to think for a fraction of a second. He tried to think of Alex disabling his father by smashing a gold candlestick into his skull, then putting the prone, bleeding man into his own oven, turning it up, and then walking out, knowing that his mother would surely be the one to discover the body.

"No," he said. "No, I don't think you could have done that."

"Ah, but paying someone to do it, that you can see me capable of," he said, grinning. "Adam thought the same thing."

"Well..."

"Don't feel bad about it, Jake. Just think about the situation. Does it make much sense that I'd do that?"

Alex had everything he wanted and had exacted the best revenge on his father by taking the family business away from him. He looked Alex straight in the eye and said, "No, it doesn't."

"And if I was going to pay someone to kill dear old Dad, it would have been to my advantage to do so *before* I took over the company. Would have made my wresting control of it a lot easier," Alex said, running his fingers through his hair. "I've atoned for a lot of my sins in many ways, Jake, and I'm trying to live my life in as much harmony as I can, but killing my old man was too good for him. Getting the company away from him, watching him wriggle and suffer over it—that was getting back for all the rotten things he did to me as a kid. And an adult. Killing him would have deprived me of that." He shook his head. "God that sounds horrible. It's awful and wrong and I'm trying to let it go, but someday I'll tell you everything that bastard did to me and maybe it won't sound so terrible."

"Alex, I think I have a very good idea of what you mean," said Sam. "Trust me, it doesn't sound as horrible as you might think."

"It's still not karmically healthy," Alex said. "Now that the old guy is dead, maybe I can let it go finally."

"I think you'll find it helps a lot. I speak from experience."

Alex gestured to a bench, and the three of them sat down, Alex in the middle. They watched as the crews continued to secure the *Chinook*. A door had opened on what had once been the car deck level, and the gangplank lowered.

"Dad was trying to wrestle control of the company from me. I really should put the emphasis on trying. There's no way he could touch us. There is, refreshingly, too much of the Blackburn family on my side of the issue to go back. We're already turning a healthy profit a full year ahead of schedule, even with all the capital expenditure," he said, motioning to the *Chinook*. "Those that were on the fence were happy to be making more money and figured why mess with something that wasn't broken?"

"What's up with Dorval?" Jake asked. "Isn't he like a manager or something?"

"I don't think they call it that, but he is Adam's superior. As for what is up with him, he's incapable of believing people can change. Dorval knew me from my youth—God that makes me sound like an old fart, doesn't it?"

"A bit," Sam said. "Did you grow up with him?"

"Kind of. My parents owned a summerhouse near where the Dorvals lived. They always resented our money. I think Nelson Dorval feels I'm the apple that didn't fall too far from the tree."

"Then he's an idiot," Jake said. "All he'd have to do is talk to you for five minutes to realize…"

"Thank you for that, Jake. And there, of course, is the problem. I could talk until I was blue in the face. It wouldn't do any good as far as Nelson Dorval is concerned. I'm cut from the same Blackburn cloth as my bastard father."

"We heard Haggerty asking about the Susan Crane thing," said Sam.

"Then you know he is satisfied with how things ended up."

"Could Dorval make an issue of it?"

"No. I'll see to it."

"Alex—" Jake said warningly.

"Ah, there you are, Jake, my conscience at my shoulder. Don't worry," Alex said, ruffling Jake's hair. "Nothing bad or illegal. I will say having money and political connections proves useful from time to time. Is that enough information?"

"Let's just say I don't need any more."

"I know Haggerty doesn't suspect you, but I gathered from his tone that he considers personal issues to be a likely motive," Sam said.

"He did. He does. You have to understand, Adam is under tremendous pressure to bring someone in. The chief is leaning on him to get this solved. There's talk of having the FBI come in, though I admit I'm not completely sure how that works."

"So Dorval suspects you, but had you keep it from the papers as to what happened?"

"No, *Adam* had me keep it from the papers. And I did so as a favor to a friend." he sighed. "Poor Mom. She's had a complete breakdown. She's gone somewhere to rest. She refuses to set foot in that house again. I can't say I blame her much for that."

"Somewhere? You mean like an asylum?"

"They don't call it that when you're wealthy," Alex said. "It's called a 'private hospital' and you go there for 'a rest' which usually means drying out from booze or pills, but in some cases means going there when your mind has gone *boing* from seeing your husband baked in an oven."

"Alex," Sam said. "Your choice of words—"

"Oh, I can't help it Sam. My father was a bastard, and there was something very poetic about it. Totally insane, mind you, but poetic nonetheless."

"Poetic or not, these aren't random killings," Jake said. "He told you that."

"About the *Grimm's Fairy Tales*? Oh, yes. Adam thinks you're quite smart for figuring that one out. Although it puts him in a rather awkward position."

"He likely has to put Jake down on the list of suspects," Sam said.

"*Me?* I just want this creep caught," said Jake a little too loudly. People looked up in surprise.

"Easy, Tiger," said Sam. "You're making the natives restless."

"And be warned, Marion Burd has hearing like a bat."

"Sam figured her for a suspect."

"For Reed and Leona, maybe, but what is the connection to my father?"

"Oh come on, Alex," said Jake. "Everyone heard you at the meeting. You all but named your father as being the one in collusion with Reed on the SuperLoMart deal and Wilde Park."

"Ah, well, yes. There was that. Reed's personal papers will be a sight to behold. A few years back, the old plywood mill burned down, after it had just about been run into the ground. Reed was a major stockholder in that, and so was my father. I always suspected the two of them being in on that. I'm sure there are a lot more skeletons."

"You think that was why he was targeted? Because of his connection to Longhoffer?"

"I suspect that is part of it. Although from the killer's perspective, I'd have thought once Reed Longhoffer was dead, that would have been the end of it. There has to be something else, some other criteria the killer is using to target his victims."

Flummoxed, the three of them sat in the quiet, enjoying the sight of the *Chinook*. Jake was looking forward to seeing the completed ship. Someone had raised the American flag at the stern and the signal flags spelling out "Chinook" behind her mast. At the top of her mast, Jake was pleased to see three flags flying—the Blackburn Transportation house flag, Black Ball flag and the original B.C. Ferries flag with the dogwood blossom in the center. He knew Alex's eye for detail would not have let that particular element slip by. The sun broke out from the clouds at that moment, illuminating the vast white flank of the ship. She sparkled in the light, looking more like a living being than a cold piece of steel.

"Wonderful vessel, Mr. Blackburn!" Professor Mills enthused, sidling up to the three men. "I remember seeing her when I was just a young man down at Colman Dock. Lovely little ship."

"Did you know Gibbs, Professor?" Sam asked.

"Not personally, no," Professor Mills said. "But ah, the man could design ships. In fact…"

A beeping came from Professor Mills' watch. He looked at it, frowning deeply.

"Everything okay, Professor?"

"Oh bah, it's nothing. Just a reminder to take my…well, I certainly don't need to worry about *that* anymore. Gentlemen, if you'll excuse me please?"

Professor Mills drifted away, replaced a moment later by Marion Burd, and Alex politely excused himself. The crowds were beginning to disperse as the main show was over for the day. Jake and Sam decided to head back to Sutherland Shipyards to pick up Sam's car. As Jake drove back to the shipyard, the first fat splats of rain smacked the windshield.

"At least it held off until the ceremony was just about over," said Sam, looking at his commemorative ornament in the shape of the *Chinook*.

"Lunch?"

"How about the Bitter End?"

"Sounds good. We can pick up your car afterward."

Chapter Thirty-one

Tuesday afternoon wasn't busy for the Bitter End, the lunch crowd already having come and gone. Jake and Sam were happy to find their usual table unoccupied. They ordered Pepsis and looked over the menu. Maddy Ferguson, the bartender who worked the shift before Caleb, brought them their sodas.

"What'll it be, fellas?"

"Well," said Jake, looking over the menu. "Nothing with turkey in it since we're just over two weeks away from the usual Thanksgiving turkey glut. In which case, I want something good and loaded with red meat, so I'll take the double bacon cheeseburger with fries, a side salad… what's the soup today?"

"Beef barley."

"And a cup of soup."

"And for Mr. O'Conner today?"

"Grilled chicken and Swiss with a salad please, served with the sandwich if that is okay," said Sam. "And has Caleb made a move yet?"

Maddy nodded. "Just yesterday. Said something about it giving you fits for a while."

"Do you mind?" Sam asked Jake.

"No, go ahead, but you better be back when your meal arrives."

"You'll have to eat your soup and salad long before that," said Sam, moving over to the chessboard.

"Yes, but I hate to eat alone," said Jake, turning to look up at the big screen television. KABW's local cable access channel was still showing the *Chinook*'s arrival, although someone at the studio must have been working a fast edit as they had there was footage taken both down at the yard and as the former ferry moved backward up the channel. It then cut to a live feed of Randy Burrows poking the microphone in Alex's face as he asked a few questions. At some point, they cut back to the new studio where a woman began talking about something unrelated.

"Thanks, Maddy," said Jake as she brought him his soup.

"Oh God, look at her."

"Hmm?"

"Roxy Eggans."

"Oh."

"Arrow Bay's very own celebrity. At least she thinks she is," said Maddy disgustedly. "I swear you run into that woman's ego five feet before you ever get to her."

"How did she end up on KABW? Excellent soup."

"I don't know. I thought Randy had better taste than that."

"Maybe some favors were granted," said Jake, looking at the blonde, buxom woman with too much make-up. She had high cheekbones and sparkling blue eyes her perpetual smile did not touch. She was dressed in a bright blue blazer with a fuchsia scarf and a dove pin on her lapel.

"If you mean what I think you do, not a chance. Randy's been after Kelly Zawiki forever."

"Kelly Zawiki? At the Bluegrass Nursery?"

"That's the one. She's a perfect size six, and I'd hate her if she wasn't so nice."

"Sorry, Maddy, I tend to notice Cody Hunter more when I'm at the nursery," Jake said, thinking of the burly, scruffy man who only shaved about every six days and had arms like two cannons.

"He's a cutie, isn't he?" she agreed. "As for Roxy, I think the deal being struck was more along the lines of the lot behind KABW that Randy expanded onto. He'd been after that piece of property for years and Roxy wouldn't sell it. I think that maybe she arranged for Randy to get the land if Roxy got the job. I may have to kill him for it," she said, walking away to get Jake's salad.

"Damn," said Sam from behind him. "The SOB is trying to stalemate the game."

Jake finished his soup, his eye still on KABW. Roxy was talking about something to do with a problem with Arrow Bay's sewer system. The camera cut to a shot of a city worker, then back to Roxy. She talked for a few more minutes when suddenly the Reverend Crawford's face popped up on the screen.

"Hey, Maddy, turn that up please!"

Maddy pulled a small remote control out of her apron pocket, pointed it at the screen, and the Reverend Crawford's voice echoed over the half-empty bar.

"...times like these it is important to come together as a community. That's why I felt it was important to do something to help the healing begin. It's never too late to start the healing, even if the one responsible for the crimes has not been apprehended yet."

The scene changed to a shot of Bedford Memorial Park, which was located on a hill above town. Roxy Eggans's nasal voice came over the image: "The memorial and healing service will be held at Bedford Memorial Park and is open to all residents of Arrow Bay. Reverend Crawford will hold a short sermon for Reed Longhoffer and Leona Weinberg, then will lead a group prayer. People who knew Reed and Leona are encouraged to share their fond memories of the two notable townspeople."

The camera cut back to Reverend Crawford, who said, "We'll be having the service on Wednesday the fifteenth at two in the afternoon, rain or shine."

The camera was back on a live shot of Roxy Eggans, who was now going on about vandals who had destroyed the record pumpkin at the Kulshan County Harvest Fest. Maddy set down Jake's salad and muted the television again.

"Well that ought to bring out all the head hunters," she said.

"That's kind of what I was thinking," said Jake, knowing who was really behind the plan. He heard Sam *thunk* a chess piece down and then return to the table.

"That ought to give *him* fits for a while," said Sam, looking up at the television for the first time. "My God, what is that?"

"That, I think, is going to be Arrow Bay's answer to Diane Sawyer," said Maddy.

"Is that Roxy Eggans? What has she done to herself?"

"Given the tightness of her face I'd say a little nip, tuck and yank on the back to pull up the slack," said Jake.

"Remind me to go home and cancel our cable. And that was catty of you, Jacob."

"Hey, I still haven't forgiven her for trying to sell us that place with the asbestos tile in it."

"I'd forgotten all about that," said Sam as Maddy returned with their orders. "Although she may not have known it was full of asbestos at the time."

"My ass she didn't. She knew damn well it did. She failed to disclose it. We could have sued."

"Maybe we should have, given where she's turned up," said Sam, shoving Jake's empty salad plate aside to take up his chicken sandwich.

"Did you see what the Reverend is up to?"

"No," said Sam. "I was trying to box Caleb in."

"She's having a memorial service for Reed and Leona the fifteenth."

"You think Haggerty is behind it, don't you?"

"Of course I do. He knows the killer won't be able to resist showing up. He's probably already hopping up and down mad that the death of… you-know-who hasn't been reported."

"You mean Voldemort?"

"That is my joke and you know what I mean."

"Well, it's not a bad idea."

"It's a stupid idea. The killer won't make any mistakes. He or she hasn't so far, and won't at this little gathering. He'll—or she'll—sit back and watch everyone and get a big kick out of it then go and…I don't know. What's left for them to do from *Grimm's Fairy Tales*? Lord knows there's enough violence and gore in there."

"I'd rather not think about it," Sam said. "I think you're right though. Haggerty isn't going to catch this cat by conventional means."

"And according to Alex, he's under a lot of pressure to catch the guy."

Sam attacked his salad while Jake ate his fries. Maddy returned to fill their sodas and then changed the channel after complaining she couldn't stand another second of Roxy Eggans.

"I feel bad for Detective Haggerty," said Sam.

"So do I. It can't be easy. This isn't like last time. Little Susie Sunshine was a little more clear-cut. I don't have a clue about who is doing this," said Jake, annoyed. "I keep thinking I've overlooked something."

"How so?"

"A slip up somehow. I can't think of what."

"Maybe you could use the memorial service to your advantage," said Sam.

"What do you mean?"

"You could take the time to maybe ask a few questions of, say, Randy Burrows or Emma Kennedy and see what they meant by that whole 'two down' comment. Maybe ask Marion Burd what she felt about Alexander Blackburn Junior, or how a SuperLoMart going in across from her house would have affected her…"

"Technically, Sam, that's what is known as 'poking your nose into a murder investigation,' which is something we're not supposed to be doing, remember?"

"You heard Alex talking to Detective Haggerty. He needs the help."

"Samuel Patrick O'Conner. A decade together and you still keep me guessing."

"Good," said Sam, stealing a French fry off Jake's plate. "I like keeping a little mystery in our life."

"As long as it doesn't involve corpses, I'm all for it."

❖

Jake Finnigan was one of those rare and fortunate people who knew exactly what his strengths and weaknesses were. Some qualities, such as his bluntness, were both. He knew he'd never win any awards for treacle coating the truth, but that didn't mean he was without tact. He could, in fact, be very tactful and still be direct. But not when his patience was wearing thin.

"What is it now?" said Sam, who wore suits like a second skin. His dark blue, vested Nautica suit made him look like a movie star from the forties. He adjusted his black silk tie, ran a comb through his hair and beard, and adjusted his round, wire-rimmed glasses before turning to Jake to help him straighten his tie.

"It's hopeless," bemoaned Jake.

"It's your damn muscles. Your additional bulking up has made the suit too tight through the shoulders. I thought you were cutting back?"

"I have," said Jake. "It takes a while for it to play down."

Sam looked at his husband with a critical eye. "Nope, that'll never do. Take it off."

"But—"

"Take it off. Put on your khaki slacks and black dress shirt."

Jake did as he was told. When he returned, Sam was holding out his black sport jacket and maroon tie. Jake slipped the coat on, letting Sam tie his tie for him. When he inspected himself, he had to admit he not only felt more comfortable, but looked it.

"Much better. Throw your Calvin Klein black wool top coat over that, and you'll look great."

"You mean we'll look like twins. You've got an identical coat."

"Big deal, it's a top coat, and your leather pea coat isn't formal enough. It's thirty six degrees out there and no one will notice. Have you worked out what you're going to do?"

"Yep. I'm going to sneak up behind Kennedy and Burrows and slip them a mickey. Once they're drugged, we'll sign them onto a cargo ship headed for Trinidad and ransack their file cabinets."

"You forgot about using the blackjack on Detective Haggerty and selling him on the black market for transplant organs."

"I hadn't got to that part yet. That happens after we lock Marion Burd in the cellar of the Illahee Inn and wall her up alive until she tells us that she bumped Reed Longhoffer off."

"Silly me," said Sam. "I forgot."

"Did you call Jason and tell him to bugger off?"

"I called your brother and asked him to maintain a discreet distance."

"I don't think he knows the meaning of the word," said Jake, straightening his tie. "And I'll have to watch Derek as it is. I'm sure he'll be lurking in the bushes with his notepad, trying to figure out who did what to whom."

"Jason said Derek took himself off the story. After the run in with Haggerty, he didn't want any part of it."

"Have they received any more notes?"

"No. And Haggerty deemed the one sent to Reverend Crawford a hoax."

"He what?"

"You," said Sam, handing a brush to Jake, "need a haircut. And you heard me."

"What the hell is Haggerty playing at? He knows that wasn't any hoax."

"Don't rush to judgment, Jacob. Did you ever think that Haggerty may just be putting that out to fool the killer?"

He had to admit Sam had a point. "Okay, I will give him the benefit of the doubt."

"I saw the note," said Sam. "Given what was reproduced in the *Examiner*, it looked like a match. Not that I'm going to send a letter to the editor proclaiming as much. I don't even like to think of what *Grimm's Fairy Tale* I might end up in."

"I don't think you're an enemy of Arrow Bay, Samuel. It *could* be a hoax. Anyone could get copies of the *Examiner* and clip themselves a note."

"I agree," said Sam, sliding his coat on. "Only thing is, there was a methodic neatness to these letters. They weren't all hodge-podge. They were cut uniformly and pasted on like the guy used a t-square or something."

"Possible that he did. And someone could have noted that when they saw the letter."

"Wait. You just said you didn't think it was a hoax, I thought?"

"I don't. I'm just thinking at it from all angles," said Jake as they walked down the stairs. He called out to Barnaby, who jumped off the couch. Jake put his leash on and opened the front door.

"You think we should take him?"

"I don't see why not. He needs a walk anyway."

"Yeah, but it's a memorial service. What if he…"

"Hmm," said Jake. "I see your point. Well, we'll walk him around a bit first so he doesn't decide this happy gathering is an opportune time to relieve his bladder."

Chapter Thirty-two

Once in the PT Cruiser, Jake drove north up High Street then turned onto Hope Street, cutting over onto the heavily wooded, seldom used Dawson Road. Jake had never liked the road, feeling something wasn't quite right about that area of woods below Cultus Mountain. He always expected to see Bigfoot ambling his way across the road, or something worse.

"You know, if you dislike this road so much, you shouldn't take it," said Sam. "Slow down, the road curves ahead."

Jake did as he was told. "I don't *normally* feel this way about the woods. I grew up in the woods. I love the woods. But there is just something not quite right in here." He glanced in the rear view mirror at Barnaby, who seemed to be unusually intent, looking out the windows. "Even Barnaby doesn't like it."

"That's because there's a lot of wildlife in here. Possibly even bears."

"I've never looked up the history of this part of town. In fact, I've never looked up much of the town's history."

"You should. I think you'd find it interesting. There's a lot of sordid stuff that went on in Arrow Bay, particularly during Prohibition."

"And what makes you think I'd only be interested in the sordid stuff, Samuel O'Conner?"

"Come on. You're a huge fan of true crime. What part of boring ordinary history would really interest you?"

"Well, okay. Perhaps you're right."

"I know I'm right. And there's nothing wrong with that. I mean, who would be interested in the boring history? You should talk to Miranda

Zimmerman. She's the local expert. I've heard she knows where all the bodies are buried in this town."

"The librarian?"

"Yes. Nice blonde lady. We've talked about her before. She's helped me track the history of some long lost boats from this area."

"It's an idea."

The trees fell away, and they emerged on the side of the hill. Once as lushly forested as the valley they had just left, it had been logged sometime in the last century. The trees had never grown back. Jake took a left and drove down the hill past the misnamed Green Mountain, which was a deforested hill of wildflowers and tall grass. At its foot was Bedford Memorial Park, five acres of rolling meadows. The entrance to the park was a large, unattractive wrought iron gate which always reminded Jake of thistles that had grown together. It stretched upward, its black bars locked in agonizing coils, BEDFORD MEMORIAL PARK spelled out across the top in foot-high brass letters.

The road diverged just inside the gate. Jake turned to the right and pulled the PT Cruiser in the first available slot, taking note of Verna Monger's Buick. He let Barnaby out and attached the leash, leading him over to Monger's car.

"Jake!" Sam scolded, as Barnaby urinated happily on the Buick's front tire.

"What? He had to go!"

"And there was something wrong with the tree over there?"

"Oh, he couldn't wait that long. Besides, better Monger's Buick than one of the tombstones of the founding fathers of Arrow Bay, *n'est ce pas?*"

❖

The day was cloudy and cold. The wind was not blowing, and everything was still. Heavy dew had made the grass and bare branches glisten with moisture. The sky was leaden and gloomy, a deep gray that held the threat of rain. Looking down the hill, Jake could see a slice of Lake Palmer and beyond that, Arrow Bay spread out against the barrier of the water. It was nearly monochrome with the gray sky, gray splinter of Lake Palmer, and muted browns and yellows of the meadows around them. Jake found it suddenly depressing to look at and turned away, focusing instead on his feet and Barnaby as they walked toward the gazebo.

The gazebo was all that was left of a turn of the century amusement park that had once been on the land. Large enough for a brass band, the gazebo stood in the center of an amphitheater. Reverend Crawford was already speaking about the passage of life and of the incredible cruelty that people inflict upon one another, but how not to lose sight of God in such circumstances. Jake nodded to Sam and began to slowly move about the crowd.

At least sixty people were there. Jake spotted Professor Mills, Baldo Ludich, Gladys Nyberg, Rebecca Windsor, and Verna Monger. Trudy Mundy, her husband, and Clint Shimmel appeared to be muttering something to each other. The members of the Arrow Bay Quilter's Club were all standing well apart from one another, though Sheila Doyle and Norma Middlebrook were staring daggers at each other. Chad Rudd, the presumed successor to the City Council, was standing near the Reverend Crawford and to the right of Evelyn O'Conner, whom did not at all look pleased that she was near the man. To Evelyn's left was Marilyn Sandy, in scrubs and obviously on her lunch hour from the hospital. Milton Sandy was standing next to her, Jake spying the little bug with the big X's over its eyes on the pocket of his overalls. Jake moved around them, nodding at Evelyn, whom he suspected knew exactly what he was up to.

He finally spotted Randy Burrows and Emma Kennedy off to the side of the group. There was no love lost for the subjects of the memorial, as they were smoking and talking to themselves and ignoring the proceedings completely. Jake circled around, pretending to be taking Barnaby around for a little walk. Barnaby rose to the occasion by marking one of the trees. Jake listened intently to what Kennedy and Burrows were talking about without looking obvious about it, but he didn't have long.

"Blackburn says we really don't have a choice. Rudd's the only one who's submitted his name that can be taken sincerely. He could seriously stymie things," Kennedy was saying, exhaling a plume of smoke. Jake inched his way closer, trying to get Barnaby the next tree over.

"Not a lot we can do about it at this point. We'll just have to make the best of a bad situation," he said, spying Jake and Barnaby.

Jake was now focused on Verna Monger, who was watching Jake as he edged his way over to Kennedy and Burrows. Jake put his index fingers in the corner of his mouth and stuck his tongue out at Monger. Kennedy and Burrows laughed, and Verna Monger abruptly turned away while the Reverend Crawford faltered in her speech. She recovered quickly, but Jake could see Sam, now standing next to his mother covering his eyes with one gloved hand while Evelyn O'Conner tried to suppress uncontrolled laughter, tears running out of the corners of her eyes. Jake quit making the face and turned back to nudge Barnaby along a little closer to Burrows and Kennedy.

Jake caught sight of Adam Haggerty, who appeared to be scrutinizing him with a bemused expression on his face. Jake pretended not to see him.

"Arrow Bay's finest detective been bugging you too?" Kennedy asked.

"Let's just say I don't like the sudden attention I've been getting from Arrow Bay's PD."

"I know the feeling," said Burrows, lighting another cigarette. "They've been breathing down my neck for weeks now."

Jake caught Kennedy giving Burrows a look like she wanted him to clam up, but fortunately for Jake, he completely missed it. Jake pressed on, trying to be delicate.

"When they run out of evidence, they try shaking trees. I suspect Haggerty's at the end of his rope and hopes if he bothers enough people, one of them will break down and confess."

"With plans like that, he ought to catch the guy in about 2050," said Emma Kennedy.

"Well, you have to wonder. I mean, obviously this service was done especially to make someone slip up," said Jake, eliciting uncomfortable looks from Kennedy and Burrows. "You didn't know that?"

"I hadn't thought of it," she said, "but I suppose that makes sense."

"Yeah," agreed Burrows.

"Well, we're all suspects in Haggerty's eyes. I mean me and Sam for not liking Leona…"

"Ha," said Kennedy in another puff of smoke. "Who *did* like Leona?"

"Or Longhoffer."

"Well, it'll make things easier on the council for you. Two of three stumbling blocks gone."

"See, that's why I can't figure out why Haggerty keeps bugging us," said Emma, clearly annoyed. "If we were knocking people off to open up the city council, why stop at Longhoffer? Why not get rid of Verna

Monger while we're at it? Alex Blackburn's father was a creep, but I wouldn't have any reason to kill him."

"I take it you didn't know about Blackburn Junior bankrolling Longhoffer's attempt to plow under Wilde Park."

"I didn't know he had anything to do with Reed until Alex let it slip at the meeting."

"Oh, the police probably put you down on the suspect list for throwing Blackburn Junior out of the Inn that night. Ready-made motive, there, the idiots," said Jake, rolling his eyes dramatically.

"That's right, you were there. You saw what he did. He punched his own son. I wasn't about to put up with that."

"Damn right," said Jake.

"I mean, sure I'd had some problems in the past with the guy. We fought tooth and nail over some of the property on Ashton Avenue, but God, that was years ago."

"I thought Blackburn died of natural causes?" asked Burrows.

"Ha, don't kid yourself. I talked to Alex about it. It was not natural causes. Our local mook is keeping it out of the press, though I gather not for much longer," said Kennedy. "Other than that night at the Inn, I hadn't set eyes on the man in probably ten years. He never came to the council meetings."

"Even with all his dealings with Reed Longhoffer?"

"He always kept well out of the public side of it," said Randy Burrows, shaking his head. "Roxy told me Junior and Reed had some land deal going, but Blackburn had to pull out of it when the company came crashing down around his head."

"I don't think even Alex knew about that," said Emma, eyeing Jake. "You're pretty good friends with him, aren't you?"

"Yes. I don't think Alex knew what his father was up to most of the time. Particularly over the last year. If it was something his father was doing outside of the company, then Alex wouldn't know a thing about it."

"That's what Roxy said. Before she came to work for me, she had her finger right on the pulse of the Arrow Bay real estate market."

"Someone told me that Blackburn Junior owned that lot you built your studio on," said Jake.

"What? Who told you that? No, that was Roxy's, free and clear. She finally agreed to sell to me after I promised her I'd try her out for a year at KABW," said Randy. "How do you think she's doing?"

"Oh," said Jake, "Fine, fine."

"There are some rough edges to work out, but I think it'll be okay," said Randy. "God knows she's interested enough in the goings on of Arrow Bay to make a career out of it."

Emma Kennedy grunted. Jake got the distinct feeling she wanted to say something more, but instead she said, "It's only for a year, anyway," said Emma, shaking her head. "Here comes Haggerty again. Probably wants to ask me where I was on the night old Longhoffer got eaten," she said, disgusted.

"He bugged me about that too," said Jake. Banding together with Haggerty's list of suspects was proving to be very useful, even if he wasn't technically a suspect. "Didn't like the fact that I was in front of a bar full of witnesses."

"That sounds familiar. I was in the basement of the Inn with my handywoman Gert. We were trying to sort out a plumbing problem. Ugh, we were there all night after the council meeting. Finally got the damn basement pumped out around two in the morning."

"And I was in Seattle," said Burrows. "Left just after the meeting, constructive bit of work that it was. Although I have to say, I didn't realize Gladys Nyberg had quite the arm on her."

They all laughed, getting another look from Reverend Crawford, who had just finished up her service and was now leading a prayer. Everyone bowed their heads accordingly, Jake, Randy and Emma all stifling their laughs. After "amen" was uttered, the crowd began to disperse. Emma and Randy bid Jake good-bye.

"Hello, Mr. Finnigan," rang Haggerty's voice from behind him. "Glean anything useful?"

"I'm sure I don't know what you mean. I was merely talking to a few acquaintances."

"I wasn't aware that you were acquainted with Mr. Burrows and Ms. Kennedy."

"It's a small town. Everyone tends to know everyone else. Although I didn't have the pleasure of meeting you until last year," said Jake, stomping down the hill toward Sam.

"Oh, brother," said Haggerty. "Please don't ever go into police work, Mr. Finnigan. You'd get shot in a heartbeat with that inability to lie."

"More likely for being a snitch," said Sam, approaching them. "Kennedy and Burrows probably think you're ratting them out," he said.

"Well, there was a big fat zero there anyway," Jake said. "Although it's nice to be able to cross them off the suspect list."

"I thought you didn't get involved in murder investigations, Mr. Finnigan?"

"I don't."

"Be very careful, Mr. Finnigan. Aside from the fact that there's a dangerous killer around, there are certain superiors in the department with suspicious minds, shall we say?"

"You mean Nelson Dorval."

"I didn't say that."

"Say, what's with him anyway?" asked Sam. "Why does he feel the need to go poking around in something that doesn't even concern him?"

"What I can say about my boss can't be said here without offending nearly everyone."

"Oh, I don't know, try me," said Reverend Crawford. "I didn't think this was a good idea, and I don't like being manipulated. I only agreed to it because I thought it might do the town some good. All it really did was point out to me how much the people of this town really loathed them."

"There wasn't exactly a Longhoffer/Weinberg/Blackburn fan club out there," Evelyn O'Conner said, wrapping her red shawl over her head.

"Let's just say my boss would be in good company with those aforementioned people," Haggerty said as Sharon Trumbo joined him.

"Adam," she said, a tone of reprimand in her voice.

"Then this was his idea?" Jake asked.

"I'm sorry, we can't comment on that," Sharon said.

"Yes. As he doesn't seem to think I'm doing my job correctly. That I haven't been able to peg down enough suspects," Haggerty said angrily.

"There's got to be better suspects out there than the lot that showed up here," said Reverend Crawford. "Occam's razor says the simplest solution is usually the answer, but I don't think that is the case here."

"Nor do I," Evelyn said.

"That's one thing we can all agree on," said Sharon. "Adam, we should get going."

"Good day, Reverend. Nice service. Thank you for being accommodating," he said, bowing gracefully before walking away with Sharon Trumbo and disappearing up the pathway back to the parking lot.

"What was that all about?" Evelyn O'Conner asked.

"I think the police are having a harder time than I thought," Jake said, "and it seems that Haggerty is bearing the brunt of it."

"Which is too bad," said Sam, resting his hand on Jake's shoulder. "I get the feeling that Haggerty and Trumbo are the best Arrow Bay has."

Jake sucked in a great breath of air, letting it out slowly. "Politics," he said, still not happy with the fact that Nelson Dorval was too keenly interested in the Susan Crane case.

"I wish I'd never gone along with this," said Milly Crawford, shaking her head. "If I had known that Nelson Dorval was going to put thumbscrews into the innocent people of this town I'd have told him to jump off a cliff. I just thought I was doing my civic duty, I suppose."

"Not your fault, Reverend," said Jake kindly. "The Arrow Bay PD is under a tremendous amount of pressure. Dorval's just letting his personal agenda get in the way." He picked his cell phone out of his pocket, hit the fifth quick dial-button, and waited until his brother picked up.

Chapter Thirty-three

"Finnigan."

"What a coincidence, this is Finnigan too."

"How'd it go?" Jason asked.

"I know who didn't do it. Though I think I'm a suspect again. At least with some people. I know you said Derek is off the story, but do you think he'd get back on the story if he had an exclusive?"

"Exclusive what?"

"Yes or no? I won't go into details on the phone."

"I can ask him. I can only assume this has to do with the case."

"Oh, yeah. I have some things he might be interested in."

"Jake," said Sam. "You're shaking the beehive."

"The beehive shook me," said Jake, shielding the phone from his mouth.

"How about dinner at my place tonight?" asked Jason. "Well, our place I guess."

"That'll be just fine. Six?"

"Better make it seven. I need to clean the joint up."

"I thought you said Derek was pathologically neat."

"He is. Let's just say some sprawl from my room is taking up some space."

"Seven it is," said Jake.

"Good. And I'll warn you, whatever you have better be good. I don't think Derek relishes the idea of spending time in an interrogation room with Arrow Bay PD again."

"See ya, J.D.," said Jake, ringing off. He shook his head looking at Sam. "Don't look at me like that."

"I'm going to start calling you Veronica Mars."

"She had a good sense of justice."

"She also didn't have any friends. And this isn't a television show. Or a mystery novel."

"No, you've got that right. If it was this loony, the killer, would have been caught by now," said Jake, dialing the phone again. "I have to ask Alex if it is okay if I talk to Derek about this."

"Blackburn."

"Hi Alex, it's Jake."

"I know. Caller ID. What can I do for you?"

"If I cook you a big homemade meal, can I ask a huge favor of you?"

"Why do I get the feeling I'm not going to like what you're about to ask me?"

"It's an easy one. Would you mind if I spilled the beans about the manner of your father's passing to the press?"

"I see. Arrow Bay PD doing something to displease you?"

"Let's just say I understand a lot more of where you're coming from this afternoon than I did a week ago."

"Ah ha. Well then. Yes, tell away. Give Mr. Brauer my best and tell him he can confirm it with me if he wishes."

"I will do just that," said Jake.

"And be careful, Jake," Alex said. "While I know your intent is good, don't forget you're not playing with someone carrying a full deck."

"Dorval may be a bit of an idiot, but I wouldn't say—"

"No, Jake. Whoever has taken their fairytales a little too much to heart. If they think you are getting too close, they may come after you next."

"Not worried. I'm playing this as 'anonymous source.'"

"Good call. And I'm holding you to that dinner."

"You're on," said Jake. "Thank you."

Sam was looking at him again as he rang off. Evelyn and the Reverend Crawford were in an animated conversation that Jake didn't get the gist of. The rest of the crowd had long ago made their way up the hill and away from the gazebo. Barnaby was tugging restlessly at his leash, wanting to go as well. Jake shrugged, interrupted Evelyn long enough to give her a hug and say good-bye to the Reverend Crawford, and then started back up to the Cruiser with Sam after he had done the same.

"I don't like it, Jake."

"I don't either, Sam, but if I am going to be accused of meddling in a police investigation, I might as well actually do it."

"Do you have any idea of who it is?"

"No, dammit. I keep thinking I missed something. Something in the way the murders were committed, something in the way something was said or done. Of course maybe Haggerty is doing it all to bolster his career."

"Ha, not a chance. That only happens in books," said Sam, pausing for a moment to allow Barnaby to mark another tree. "Not to mention Haggerty isn't the murdering type. And it violates Spievens Rule number nine."

"Cherchez la femme?" Jake asked, confused.

"I thought that was rule thirteen."

"Uh uh. Thirteen is people who have something to hide aren't necessarily guilty."

"Right. I always thought number nine was rather sexist."

"It is. But in the 1920's when Spievens was writing some of those books, it was more often than not Lady Penelope bashing someone's head in with a bust of Paris. That was right after Margot Lefftington jilted Spievens at the altar."

"Bitter much?" Sam asked.

"A tad. Can you blame him? Half the royal family was there." He shook his head. "In any event, Haggerty being the killer would violate rule fourteen, which is the most obvious suspect likely isn't."

"Huh. This cat isn't obvious at all."

"I know that and you know that. Whoever is doing this is careful, methodical, but bonkers," he said, sighing. "He's made a mistake somewhere, though. I just have to figure out what it is."

"You will."

"Why's that?"

"Because, my handsome man, you never, ever back away from a challenge."

"Thank you," said Jake, giving Sam a quick kiss.

"And you never let anything go, either."

"You just couldn't let that slip past, could you?"

"'Fraid not."

"And you were so close to getting to take me home and have your way with me," said Jake, opening the car.

"Ha, like you can resist me," said Sam. "I know you've got a weak spot for husky guys who look like Kevin Smith. You're putty in my hands."

"Well Mr. Smith, unless you come up with some creative ideas for lunch, it's tuna fish."

"I've got a creative idea," said Sam.

"Hmm?"

"Drop Barnaby off and go to the Bitter End."

"May not be creative, but it is certainly appealing."

Driving out of the iron gates of Bedford Park, Jake was once again assailed by the thought that he had missed something critical. His mind tried to grasp it, but it flitted away. He tried to push everything out of his head. After dropping Barnaby off, they went down to the Bitter End and remained there most of the afternoon until Caleb came on shift so that Sam could gloat over his latest chess move. Jake couldn't help but feel that he'd made his own move on the chessboard, and somewhere in Arrow Bay, the murderer was about to move the next piece.

❖

Adam Haggerty had been fighting off a cold for a week, but as he struggled to get up from bed, he knew it had finally reached him. Once out of bed, he made a quick phone call to Sharon to let her know he wouldn't be in for the day before making his way downstairs for his morning cup of coffee.

Head still swimming, he made coffee. As the room filled with the aroma of Starbucks, Haggerty scratched his goatee thinking, *what have I overlooked?*

He poured himself a cup as soon as the coffeemaker had made enough to fill his mug. He went into his study, where the crime scene photos and other materials related to the Concerned Citizen Killer lay sprawled across his desk.

He looked at a copy of the note left for Reverend Crawford. *For fighting the goode fight.* What was it about this particular note that was bothering him? It was manufactured the same way as the other two, still it seemed genuine to him. It didn't fit the pattern, and that was part of the reason it was niggling at him. Why send it to Crawford? It wasn't something the press could get hold of, and it wasn't something that would bring to light anything on the killings.

He took a sip of his coffee and looked at the photos again, when the colors began to swim. Glancing down at the cobalt blue mug, Haggerty knew immediately something was wrong. Suddenly feeling as if he were on a raft, he struggled to get up from the chair.

"Sharon," he said to himself, knowing he had to call for help.

Halfway back to the kitchen where he left his cell phone, Haggerty collapsed to the floor. The light flashed and sparked in front him. It hadn't been a cold coming on. He'd been progressively drugged. Unable to move, he only hoped the drugs would wear off before anything happened...

Behind him, the back door swung open.

Adam managed to roll himself over, but only just, consciousness fleeting. Before he blacked out completely, he saw the face leaning down before him and thought to himself, *I wouldn't have guessed it was you...*

❖

HAS KILLER CLAIMED THIRD VICTIM?

The headlines were less dramatic than anticipated, because Jake had decided following Sam's advice was probably best. Jake didn't want to antagonize either the police or the killer. Having gone down that particular path previously, he decided discretion was the better part of valor despite the fact that the cliché grated on his nerves.

Derek Brauer did not seem at all enthused to be back on the subject. He took notes dutifully, calling Alex Blackburn to confirm the nature of his father's death, and then, after fifteen minutes of going over his notes while Sam, Jason, and Jake talked about other things entirely, he looked up at them and asked, "What aren't you telling me, Jake?"

"I don't get you," said Jake. He cursed his inability to even tell the smallest lie.

"I understand your need to make the Arrow Bay PD look bad. They're doing a terrible job."

"No, no. Not at all. Just maybe got their one-track minds derailed."

"What makes you think they're on the wrong track?"

"Talk to Haggerty for five minutes," Jake said irritably. "Look, I can't name names, but someone down at ABPD is convinced Alex had something to do with his father's death. This same person now probably thinks I had something to do with it, even though I've got an alibi."

"I hate anonymous sources. Who is causing the problems with Arrow Bay PD?"

"Someone who wants everything wrapped up neatly," Sam said, voice somber. "I think if you asked the right questions, you'd find out who quick enough."

"This person is so busy working on trying to pin this on someone who's not guilty that he's not looking to see who else might be, and from what I understand interfering with Haggerty and Trumbo's investigation."

"And you can confirm this how?"

"Talking to the other suspects, like Burrows, Blackburn and Kennedy for one," said Jake. "Personal experience for another."

"So this was his doing? The unknown person at Arrow Bay PD? But why suppress this? Why keep it from the public?"

"Haggerty doesn't want the case taken away from him," said Jason. "And that you know. You did the complete background check on him."

The spotlight suddenly shifted onto Derek, making him shift uncomfortably in his seat. He shot Jason an *I'll get you for that later* look.

"Not Haggerty," Jake said again, but stopped. "You did a background check on Haggerty?"

"Jake," Sam warned. "Don't be a snoop."

"He did a background check on us."

"Well that's fair, I guess. Okay, Woodward, spill it."

"Born 26 April 1976, San Francisco, California, older brother Tom, older sister Jan, younger brother John, younger sister Emily. Moved from San Francisco in 1978 to Willapa Bay, then to Arrow Bay in '85. Family is all law enforcement. Mother worked for San Francisco police as a meter maid, father was a detective. Father later worked and retired from Kulshan County Sherriff's department. Oldest brother is an agent for the FBI, older sister is the first woman police chief in the city of Concrete's history, younger brother works for the San Diego police department, and the youngest sister married a cop."

"No pressure to succeed there," said Jake. "Go on."

"At twenty-seven he became Arrow Bay's youngest detective. Helped bust up the big meth ring in town that was such a problem a few years back. His young looks have been a hindrance for him, which is why he keeps the goatee. All his work has been letter perfect and airtight." He looked up at Jake. "He has worked almost exclusively outside the box, which has really helped him nab some truly awful people."

"Which is probably why he realized all the murder victims met the fate of characters in *Grimm's Fairytales* about the same time I did."

Derek looked thunderstruck. He shook his head and removed his glasses, rubbing his eyes. "Of course," he said tiredly. "The apple, the wolf and now Alexander Blackburn Junior, roasted in his own oven."

"Wolf*hound*," Jason corrected again.

"The common thread being the 'Concerned Citizen' seeing each as a threat somehow to Arrow Bay. Weinberg and Longhoffer were easy, given what they wanted to do to Wilde Park, but what about Blackburn? He was bankrolling Longhoffer, but really, was that enough?" asked Sam.

"You're kidding, right?" asked Derek.

"Okay, what?"

"Blackburn was in the process of buying up all the farm land on Dormer Window Road to plow under and build more exclusive eyesores like that faux Victorian monstrosity he built. More gated communities and fancy retirement homes for the upper crust of Seattle to come into and drive up home values."

"Wait a minute," said Jake, rushing out of the room. He returned moments later, flopping open the phonebook to look at the map of Arrow Bay. "Longhoffer here, Weinberg here, Blackburn Junior here," said Jake, indicating various points on the map. "What do they have in common?"

"Nothing that I can see," said Jason. "You've got Weinberg next door, Longhoffer out on Sky Heights and Blackburn clear across town on Dormer Window Road."

"Exactly!" said Jake, grabbing a pen. He drew a line circling Arrow Bay, making points at McDougal Lake, Barnes Bay, Smith's Pond, Palmer Lake, Orange Lake, Cultus Mountain, Castle Lake, down again the length of Dormer Window Road, out to Panama Hat Park, over to Wilde Park, then over to Jefferson Park, finally connecting the line back up to Barnes Bay.

"I don't get it," said Jason, looking at the map and frowning.

"I do," said Derek, looking at Sam and Jake. "Sky to Sea."

"Exactly. Everyone who has been killed has been a potential opponent to the inter-park trail system the city is trying to link up, a spur of which runs right behind our house here."

"Yeah, but Leona didn't oppose that," said Jason. "She may have fenced off her backyard from the trail, but it was already there long before Sky to Sea."

"Right. However, she did oppose Wilde Park. That would have broken the chain of trails," he said, then tapped at Dormer Window Road. "Blackburn developing that hillside and making gated communities would have completely chopped the trail off at the knees. The rest of the town could have been completely hooked up, but developing that property would put an irreversible hole in it."

"Are you really suggesting that someone has been killing these people off because of a bike trail?" Jason said.

"Ha, how long did you work in San Francisco, J.D.?" Derek said. "People kill for a lot less. People have murdered others throughout history for land, and who they think ought to live there and ought not to."

"We're not talking about a plot of land that two or three different cultures think of as holy ground and that God gives them a right to claim, Derek," said Jason.

"How about this country then? Didn't our government actively endorse a genocidal policy against the indigenous people of this country in order to take their land?"

"I don't disagree with either thing you're saying, Derek, I just don't think you can quite equate the two. We're talking about a *bike trail*, for Chrissakes."

"It pains me to say this, J.D., but despite all my claims over the years to the contrary, *you're sane*," Jake pointed out.

"Exactly," Derek said.

"So we've got some sort of crackpot environmentalist knocking off people via *Grimm's Fairy Tales*," said Sam, stroking his chin thoughtfully. "This cat is really warped."

"Doesn't the wolfhound contradict any environmental angle?" Jason asked. "I mean, training the dog to attack someone doesn't exactly sound like the guy would get an award from the people at PETA."

"That was a mistake," said Jake, though not the mistake he was looking for. "I don't think that they intended for that wolfhound to die. Reed Longhoffer was tougher and more resourceful than the killer anticipated."

"It's all about the symbols," said Derek. "The evil queen killed by her own apple. The financial wolf killed by his own ilk. The evil witch in the gingerbread palace cooked in his own oven."

"Technically, that's a warlock," said Jason.

"What difference does it make?"

"Well, you want to be completely correct."

"Guys, can we rope it in a bit?" Sam said. "Semantics aside, this cat is playing fast and loose with gender roles anyway. It was *granny* who got eaten by the wolf, and the witch who was pushed into her own oven."

"I wonder if that caused any consideration for method," Jason said.

"If it did, it doesn't matter much to Longhoffer and Blackburn, does it?" Derek pointed out. "I doubt very much they had much say in the issue. I can't imagine Alex Blackburn Junior was too concerned about being the wrong gender as he was being pushed head first into his oven."

The conversation had pretty much died away after that. They'd eaten, and then Derek had outlined how he was going to approach the story.

"I'll say that Alex neither confirmed nor denied the rumor," said Derek, eating a bite of salad. "I'll state my anonymous source speculated that there was a definite method to the manner of the killings, but I won't say what. It'll either shake up another note, or possibly…" he stopped, not wanting to think about what might happen.

"I think that's the best way to approach it," said Sam.

And they'd left it at that. Derek hadn't even pressed the point into a special edition. The *Examiner* was printing their usual Friday before Thanksgiving edition, so the story appeared there.

Chapter Thirty-four

Outside her office, Sharon Trumbo watched over the wall of George Culpepper's cubicle at the mirror on the wall facing her office.

"Just what are you waiting for?"

"Quiet, George. You're sure he's here?" she asked him again.

"Of course I'm sure," Culpepper said. "You should have heard him ranting when he found out Adam called in sick."

Sharon resumed watching the door of her office reflected in the mirror. Someone had been going through all their paperwork and reports at night. Sharon was positive it had been Nelson Dorval, and she wanted to catch him in the act. Dorval was not their direct superior and had no need to be poking around in their office. She knew he had an ax to grind with Haggerty, but she would be damned before she'd let him ruin Adam's career.

"What did you tell him when he called about me?" she asked.

"I told him you were out looking over the Blackburn house again. That you wouldn't be back for hours, that—"

"Shh!" she hissed. "Here he comes."

"Oh, I gotta see this," said Culpepper, turning to face the mirror.

Sharon knew she was taking a risk. She could easily be fired if what was about to happen actually transpired. She was, however, tired of having him submarine her work and interfere with both her and Adam Haggerty's careers. She should have slapped him with an accusation of sexual harassment, too, but doing so would require a lot of proof, and Dorval was slippery when it came to being caught.

The balding man walked down the hall, looking in each direction furtively. Making sure no one was around, he ducked into the Haggerty-Trumbo office.

"You're sure he'll take it?" Culpepper asked.

"As sure as I am that Imelda Marcos had a lot of shoes."

"Where did you get it?"

"Oh, they're easy enough to get if you're in law enforcement," she said. "Getting the thing set up correctly is quite another story. Adam's brilliant when it comes to a lot of things, but computers and electronics are my forte."

After a rustling sound from the office, Dorval appeared at the doorway, holding a bulky folder in his hand. He paused, looking right and left before stepping out into the hallway.

Sharon would later recall what happened next as one of her fondest memories. There was a muffled *pfffft* and a flash of blue as the dye-pack she'd slipped into file folder detonated.

Nelson Dorval let out a scream of rage as curious workers began flooding out of offices and cubicles to see what had happened.

"God damn it! What the hell!" Dorval screamed.

"I think I'll go check out the Blackburn house again," Sharon said, leaving Culpepper clutching his sides as he tried unsuccessfully to stifle his laughter.

Chapter Thirty-five

Jake took the stairs up to Sam's office. Sam was sitting at his drafting board, making a few marks. He looked up and smiled at Jake, but did not rise from the table as Jake embraced him from behind. "How was lunch with your old crewmates?"

"Good. Always nice to catch up with them after our shared trauma from last year. I'm just about to knock off here," he said, hugging Jake back. "How do you feel about a cocktail at the Bitter End and dinner?"

"Sounds wonderful." He told Sam about the panic his former coworkers experienced when discovering an abandoned vehicle on the car deck of the *Elwha* a few months earlier.

"I suspect the ghost of Susan Crane will hang about for a while," said Sam, setting his drafting tools back in their places, snapping off the light on the board.

"Do you ever dream about it?"

Sam sighed. "That night, sometimes. Being tied up, not knowing if you were going to show up. It was bad for a couple of months, but they faded away."

"You never told me any of this."

Sam shrugged. "You were usually in Friday Harbor for work, and I couldn't tell you. I never had the dreams when you were home. Go figure."

"I'm sorry, Sam. I wish you had told me."

"There was nothing you could do. I didn't want to upset you," he said, washing out his cup in the kitchenette sink. "I felt it was something I had to figure out myself. The dreams went away eventually."

Jake walked up behind Sam and embraced him tightly again. Sam grunted, gasping for breath. "Little looser, Jake."

"Sorry. I just don't want to lose you. Last year came way too close for my liking."

"You'll be pleased to know," said Sam, replacing his cup on the dish drainer, "that it was a little too close for my liking as well. A mistake I don't plan to repeat."

"Well, good. I wasn't planning on making any overtures in that direction myself," said Jake. "Did you know Nora has been planning to move back to Seattle?"

"Not exactly. I guess she and Mom had another knockdown, drag-out fight on the phone the other day. She ended the conversation saying she was going to put the house up for sale and get out of Arrow Bay."

"And I bet I know what Evelyn's reply was."

"Well, Ma has never been one to mince words. Although she was unusually calm and collected for this reply—at least to hear her tell it anyway. You know my mother when she gets upset."

"I can imagine."

"She told Nora she was a selfish, self-centered brat who had better get over her hang ups before she ended up alienating her entire family."

"You sound as though you agree with her." said Jake, rising. He stepped behind Sam and began massaging his shoulders.

"I tell myself I should rush to the defense of my sister, but I just can't bring myself to do it. I'm so angry at her for her complete dismissal of our relationship that I can't even begin to articulate it."

"Then don't, Sam. Let it go. Let her go if you have to. Nora's not stupid. She'll come to her senses sooner or later."

"That feels good," said Sam, all but purring. "I hope she does. I can't wait for her to grow up though. Aside from having my life firmly established at the age of thirty-six, I don't wish to rehash my childhood again and again with her. Mom and I have moved on, why can't she?"

"If I knew that, Sam, we wouldn't be having this conversation," said Jake.

❖

Later that evening, Sam and Jake hopped into Sam's Outback and drove down to the Bitter End. Caleb made Jake his usual Jameson and Pepsi and mixed Sam a Sea Shine, a combo of vodka, pineapple juice and green apple schnapps topped with peach schnapps. Sam sipped it while brooding over the chessboard, where Caleb had stymied him again.

"Sam seems a little down," said Caleb, bringing Jake his second drink.

"Trying to get me drunk so you can have your way with me?"

"Oh stow it, Finnigan. You know I'm too much man for you."

"I keep telling you I won't know until…"

"Yeah, yeah, keep hoping. That boat'll never sail, no matter how nice a guy I think you are," said Caleb with a sly grin. "Seriously though, what's up? I haven't seen Sam so glum since I took his last bishop two months back."

Jake turned to study his husband. Sam was looking intently at the chessboard, sipping his drink. He raised his hand to move his queen, hesitated, and then returned his hand to his lap. Jake turned back to Caleb and said, "No one can quite disappoint you like family."

"Ah," said Caleb knowingly. "Nora."

"How'd you guess?"

"Wasn't too hard. Sam and his mother are very close, it obviously isn't anyone in your family as you all seem to get along well with Jason and, of course, Ms. O'Conner and the Reverend Crawford were in here today having a similar discussion."

"Bartenders, the unsung detectives of the working world," said Jake, raising his glass.

"You left out psychologists, best friends, confessors, and sometimes boy toys," said Caleb, slipping back behind the counter to refill Sam's glass.

Sam looked up at Caleb. "You're doing this to drive me crazy, aren't you?"

"Who, me?" asked Caleb innocently. "What can I get you for dinner?"

"Steak, medium rare, baked potato, salad with honey mustard," said Sam.

"You want the steak in the Cajun marinade, the Hawaiian marinade, or pounded flat and soaked in our house marinade?"

"What's in the house?"

"Well, lots of stuff, but there's a base of Jack Daniels, onion, garlic, pepper and several other mystery ingredients I can't tell you or the cook will kill me," replied Caleb.

"I'll try the house," replied Sam. Grinning triumphantly, he moved his rook and said to Caleb, "Take them apples."

"How about you, Jake?" said Caleb, not taking his eyes off the board.

"Make it two, sir."

"Eight or sixteen ounce?"

Sam looked at Jake and grinned. "One eight, one sixteen."

"Gotcha," said Caleb distractedly, still not taking his eyes from the board. He continued to stare at it until he finally had to walk over to the pass window and put up the order.

"What did you do?"

"He wants to play a stalemate game, a stalemate game is what he is going to get," said Sam with a grin.

The bar began to fill slowly as the hour wore toward dinner. Caleb became busier and couldn't chat as often, but considered the chessboard every free moment he had. Jake and Sam had consumed dinner and were contemplating dessert when Sharon Trumbo stepped in the front door. She spotted Jake and Sam and made a beeline for their table, the heels of her shoes clicking loudly on the floorboards. She pulled off her long pale blue raincoat and adjusted the tailored gray suit beneath.

"Can I talk to you for a moment?"

"That all depends. Are you here to arrest us?"

"Mr. Finnigan, you never have been a suspect."

"Please sit down, Detective Trumbo," Sam said, offering her the empty chair.

"Thank you," she said, brushing back a lock of black hair. "I'm not sure what to do. I'm upset, but starving and I don't know how to say this without sounding like a complete lunatic."

"Start slowly," suggested Sam. "And have some deep-fried olives."

"Deep fried what?"

"Deep fried olives. They're stuffed with pepper jack cheese, breaded lightly and deep-fried. Deliciously evil, artery-clogging appetizers. You're hungry and a bit flustered, and it'll give you something to do with your hands, which usually helps me calm down," said Sam. "Come to think of it, I'm not sure if it's the hands thing or the fact that I like food—"

"Sam," said Jake cutting him off. "Caleb, can we get an order of deep-fried olives for Detective Trumbo please?"

"Huh?" asked Caleb, looking up from the chessboard. "Oh! Right. Anything to drink, Sharon?"

"I'd love a double vanilla vodka on the rocks, but I'm on duty."

"Cherry Pepsi it is," said Caleb.

"Diet, hon, if you have it."

"Diet it is."

"I have to tell you right now this is very, very awkward coming to talk to you," said Sharon. "But some of my coworkers are not the brightest lights in the harbor. None of the others spotted the *Grimm's Fairytales* element. Especially not Dorval."

"I thought it was just you and Haggerty working this case," said Jake slowly.

"It is, officially. *Unofficially*, Nelson Dorval will do anything he can to bring Adam down. He's been subverting Adam's work on this from the beginning. I found out last night he's been breaking into our office and going through our reports. Well, I should say mine as Adam keeps most of his stuff at home."

"How'd you find that out?" asked Sam.

"I've suspected it for a while. To prove a point, today I put an explosive dye pack in with my paper work. Anyone taking it outside of our office would set it off."

"Oh, my," said Sam with an approving grin.

"Did he fall for it?"

"He's going to be called 'Papa Smurf' for a while."

"You didn't get in trouble, did you?"

"Well, not officially, no. I'll receive a letter in my file for carelessly leaving the dye pack in my files. It was worth it."

The olives arrived along with her diet cherry Pepsi. She took an olive, dipped it in ranch dressing and took a bite. "These are as good as I remember," she said.

"I'm still not understanding why you're here," said Jake.

"Adam didn't come in today. He called in sick, but the message sounded strange. Not like him. Almost like he'd been drugged. When he didn't call me later, I started to get really concerned."

"He calls you regularly?" asked Jake.

"When we're on a case, always. And, well, even if we're not," she said, shaking her head. "I think Adam's kind of lonely sometimes. He doesn't seem to have many friends."

"Can't imagine why not," said Jake under his breath.

Sam gave him a kick under the table. "So did you go over to his house to check on him?"

"I did. I have a key. When he goes on vacation, I water his plants and feed the fish."

"What did you find?"

"Nothing. Adam's meticulously neat. Almost obsessive. His house was neat as a pin, nothing out of place, or so I thought," she said, finishing another olive. "When I started to look around, something was out of place. You know how something can bother you and you won't know what it is, but it's wrong?"

"I do," said Jake. He'd had that feeling for days.

"It was easy to miss. If I hadn't looked at everything carefully, I would have missed it."

"What was it?" asked Sam.

"A coffee cup. Right by his computer, right by where anyone sitting at their computer would leave it if they were on the Internet drinking a cup of coffee. That's why I almost overlooked it. Adam would never leave a cup of coffee sitting there like that. Ever. He'd take it into the kitchen, rinse it out, and put it in the dishwasher."

"Even if, say, he got a hot lead and wanted to check it out? He wouldn't just throw on his coat and run out the door?" asked Jake.

"Not a chance. If he had gotten a lead or tip or anything at all, he would have called me, either before he left or on his way."

"So what was in the cup?" asked Jake.

"Why do you think there was anything in the cup?" Sharon asked suspiciously.

"You said he sounded drugged. A leads to B."

"Half a cup of coffee. I tested it. It was full of Flunitrazepam."

"What?" asked Sam.

"Rohypnol," replied Jake. "Lady Macdougal poisoned Lady Ecksworth with it in *The Teacup Assassin*. You think he's been abducted."

"I'm positive."

Sam shifted uncomfortably in his seat. He looked at Jake and then said, "Okay, so if that's the case, why are you here? Shouldn't you report this to Sanderson or the FBI or someone?"

Sharon Trumbo sighed heavily. "It's not that I don't think I should. I *know* I should. I'm afraid of what will happen if I do. I've got to wait twenty-four hours before I can do anything, which will be tomorrow at nine o'clock. If...if you can think of anything that might lead to him, will you call me?" she asked, digging out her card and handing one each to Sam and Jake. "And I mean anything."

"I understand," said Jake.

"You think the killer has him, don't you?" Sam said.

"I am almost positive. I think Adam was getting close, and the killer decided to take him out. I just hope it isn't permanently."

"I don't think so. Haggerty wasn't an 'enemy of Arrow Bay' as the letter writer put it," said Jake. "He is Arrow Bay's protector, in fact. Far from an enemy," said Jake. "Oh."

"Something wrong, Jake?" asked Sam

"If you do think of something," said Sharon, rising and putting her coat on, "don't be a hero. Call me at once. This guy is dangerous."

"That would violate Rule Four," said Sam.

"Rule four?"

"Spievens' Rules. If you know who the killer is, never go after them yourself. Always call the police. It's rule four," said Jake.

"Well, remember I am the one with the really big gun and am trained to use it. I don't want to see either of you getting hurt, okay?" she said. "How much for the olives, Caleb?"

"On the house."

"Thanks, Caleb. And thank you, Mr. Finnigan."

"You better make it Jake."

She gave him a hopeful grin, turned, and then walked out the door of the Bitter End into the cold night.

"How did she know we were here?" asked Sam.

"Well, we're fairly predictable," said Jake. "You caught the slip about the olives."

"I did," said Sam. "As well as the fact that she addressed Caleb by name. Unless you're seeing Sharon Trumbo in some other place regularly, Caleb?" said Sam to Caleb, who had resumed staring at the chessboard.

"What? No, no. Sharon's a regular. Lunch, mainly, but she and a few of her friends sing karaoke on Saturday nights."

"Well, that explains why we never see her," said Sam. "We hate karaoke."

"Sam, I need to talk to you," said Jake, fishing out money to pay the bill.

"I thought you might."

They settled their tab and bid Caleb good night. Jake and Sam walked into the blustery, cold, but rain-free November evening. Jake took a deep breath, but refrained from speaking until they got into the Subaru.

"Spill it. Something hit you while we were there. What was it?"

"The note sent to Reverend Crawford. I told you that one was out of place. Haggerty thought so too, which is why he considered it might be a fake. So did I for a bit."

"Right, but I saw the thing. It was identical to the rest of them."

"Exactly. I know you well enough to know you're not going to make rash judgments about anything. If you say it was an identical note to the others, I believe you completely."

"Well, thanks," said Sam, turning up Dawson Road.

"I kept focusing on the note itself. What it said, how it was written, what was written, and then while sitting there tonight I realized I'd been concentrating on the wrong thing all along. Sam, what came with that note?"

"Flowers."

"You didn't tell me it had arrived with flowers."

"Oh, yes, I did. But you were so hopped up on cold meds I had to pick you up at the police station."

"Oh no," moaned Jake. "Damn, damn, damn!"

"Jake…"

"What kind of flowers?"

"There were sprigs of Western red cedar mixed in with stargazer lilies—big ones and little ones."

Jake felt the bottom drop out of his stomach. For a moment, he felt as if he might be physically ill. He leaned against the seat and let the world sway until he was completely able to gather his thoughts again. He looked desperately at Sam, who was still not sure what was wrong.

"You know who did it, don't you?" he asked.

"Yeah, I do. And I think you do too, if you think about it."

"I don't get it," Sam said. "What's the big deal about the flowers?"

"Think about what you said, Sam, about the flowers."

"Stargazer lilies? You can get them anywhere at this time of year, florists have them, you can grow them in the greenhouse—" He stopped.

"And what else did you say about them? The stargazers?"

Sam leaned back in his seat and shut his eyes. "Not small stargazer lilies. *Orchids*."

Chapter Thirty-six

"Just room for some orchids and lilies,'" said Jake, recalling a conversation in Wilde Park weeks back. "How are we going to handle this, Sam?" asked Jake.

"Are you sure, Jake? I mean, Professor Mills? How can it be? Why?"

"I don't know. You heard that impassioned speech he gave at the town meeting. You know his feelings on the environment and how much this town has come to mean to him."

"But what—is he off his rocker or something? I can't see him murdering anyone, Jake. I just can't."

"Maybe he's off his meds or something. We've got to call the police."

"I—I'm not sure, Jake. I can't...I can't just call the police on him. I've known him for so long! So have you."

Jake sighed. "Go to his house. We'll see if we can't convince him to turn himself in."

Sam fired up the Outback and slowly backed out of the driveway, both silent as they drove over to Professor Mills's. Sam stopped in the driveway and shut the engine down, looking up at the cheerful yellow Cape Cod style home with white shutters, the lower floors ablaze with light.

"What do we do?"

"We go in, we talk to him. He's not really dangerous, Jake."

"Sam, he trained a two-hundred-pound dog to turn Reed Longhoffer into a dinner snack."

"He wouldn't hurt us, Jake. I know he wouldn't."

"That is exactly what Lord Milton said in *Geneva Glaspar and The Venomous Violets* right before the Mad Baron cleaved his head neatly in two with a fire ax," Jake whispered harshly. "We're violating Rule One!"

"He won't. I just know he won't," said Sam, getting out of the car. He jogged up the narrow path up to the front door, Jake hot on his heels.

"Be careful, damn it."

Sam knocked on the door, pushing it open as he did so. The door had been left partially open.

"Rule One, Rule One. Every horror movie I've ever seen ends badly when that happens, Samuel. Now what?"

"Nice and casual. We go in."

Sam stepped into Professor Mills's tidy living room. A fire in the gas stove burned merrily, and a book off to the left, the dining room opened into the kitchen. The stairs leading to the second level were directly ahead, in shadow.

"Professor Mills?" Jake called.

"Where's Gretel?"

"Upstairs maybe?"

"I'll check upstairs, you check down here. That way if he corners one of us, the other can call for help."

"That violates Rule Three. That's a stupid idea. He could stick one of us with a needle and the other would be none the wiser."

"Okay, okay," said Sam. "Five minutes. If I'm not back down by then, call Sharon Trumbo."

They split off, Jake still feeling it was a stupid idea. After checking the closet in the kitchen and the downstairs bathroom and bedroom, Jake didn't find Professor Mills on the lower level. Sam was just coming down stairs as Jake made his way back to the foyer, where the door was still partially open.

"Nothing," said Sam. "I checked the closets. Even under the bed."

"Nothing down here, either," said Jake, examining the living room again. Next to the chair on an end table was a half consumed cup of coffee. He held his finger to the side and found it was still lukewarm. "He hasn't been gone long."

"Basement?"

"This close to the creek and the bay? Wouldn't it be flooded with the tide?"

"It's solid rock right here," said Sam. "Pillow basalts millions of years old. Same land that's under the *Chinook*."

"I didn't know that."

"Are we going to actually go in the basement or talk about geology all night?"

"I was considering my options," said Jake, walking around to the backside of the stairs. A somewhat smaller door with a black china knob was set into the wall. Jake looked at Sam and then slowly pulled the door open.

Light came up from the basement. Against every fiber in his being, Jake forced himself down the steps. He nearly jumped out of his skin when he saw a figure with its back turned to him sitting in a chair in the corner of the room in front of a television set which was turned off.

The top of its head looked familiar. He walked around the figure, where he came face to face with a bound—and sleeping—Adam Haggerty. A piece of duct tape was over his mouth, but he appeared no worse for wear.

Jake poked him sharply in the shoulder. "Wake up, Sleeping Beauty," he whispered sharply.

Haggerty's eyes flew open and he jolted back in fright. He then saw Jake, and his head dropped, slowly shaking.

Jake thought for a second before he quickly yanked off the duct tape, taking a fair amount of Haggerty's goatee with it.

"Ouch!"

"You could look a little happier at being rescued, you know," said Jake.

Haggerty gazed at him dejectedly. "You'll pardon my disappointment. I had hoped one of my coworkers would figure this out and be the one rescuing me."

"I can always leave you here if you'd like," said Jake, watching Sam come down the stairs.

"No, don't do that. Have you called Sharon and the police?"

Jake and Sam looked at one another.

"Well, no," Jake said. "We know Professor Mills. We think we can talk him in to turning himself in."

"I don't like it," Haggerty said. "You may have a point, though."

"Where is the Professor?" Jake said.

"I'm not sure. I've been out of it for quite some time. He dosed me pretty good on something."

"Rohypnol in your coffee," said Jake, while Sam worked on Haggerty's ropes.

"That would explain why I can't remember anything after breakfast. I woke up about two hours ago, and here's this squirrely little guy telling me he's not going to hurt me, but he has to keep me out of the way for a few days. I hadn't seriously pegged this guy for the killer. I dismissed him for lack of strength."

"That was a mistake," said Jake. "Had you asked me, I could have told you about the time Professor Mills hauled a large potted Japanese maple out to my car single-handedly. You suspected him?"

"Only just," Haggerty said. "It was that note to Milly Crawford."

"You examined the flowers that came with them?"

"Yes. I didn't think much about them at first. Just stargazer lilies. You can get them at any supermarket."

"You missed the orchids. Professor Mills specializes in them."

"I knew that," Haggerty said. "About the orchids. And Mills. It was in his dossier. I was actually going to check with him about the species they were."

"Which is probably why he kidnapped you," Jake said. "You were getting too close. Not being an 'enemy of Arrow Bay.'"

"I think I know why he's doing this. Aside from the enemy of Arrow Bay angle—"

"Damn it, I can't get these knots undone," said Sam. "Is there something to cut the rope with?"

Jake fished out his Swiss army knife and handed it to Sam. Thinking for a moment, he said, "He's got to be in the greenhouse, Sam."

"Can you wait until I am done?"

"I'll be right back," said Jake, heading toward the steps. "I'll just see if he's in there."

"That's an extraordinarily bad idea," said Haggerty. "This man is very clever. He could easily get the drop on you."

"Could, but won't," said Jake, and headed back upstairs, not entirely sure he believed his own words.

He left the basement door open a crack, so as not to arouse suspicion if Professor Mills returned. Jake walked down a short hallway through the back door, emerging on a short porch. Down a concrete path, a small greenhouse blazed with light.

He walked down the path toward the greenhouse, his heart thudding in his chest. He stopped at the greenhouse door, which was thick with condensation, and slightly ajar. He eased it open and looked inside. There was no one to be seen. The length of the room ran thirty feet and was no more than twenty across. However, every table was crammed full of the most beautiful array of orchids and lilies Jake had ever seen. He stepped carefully inside, pausing to look at an orchid that was so like a stargazer in miniature, breathing in the soft fragrance of the delicate flower.

"Yes, I thought it might be you."

Chapter Thirty-seven

Jake whirled around. He had somehow walked half the length of the building. Professor Mills now stood between him and the door.

"Professor Mills."

"Dear Jake," said Mills, his voice suddenly taking on a very definitive edge, a hardness Jake had never heard before. "If you have a fault, Mr. Finnigan, it is that you are entirely too trusting of people."

Mills had strapped an explosive device around himself and was holding on to the detonator in his right hand, his thumb above the trigger.

"Where's Gretel?"

"I've left her with my housekeeper. Poor Minerva has no idea what I've done. I don't suspect you have either until fairly recently."

"I figured out your method some time ago, Professor," said Jake. "I have to admit, that was very inventive."

"I thought it was creative, though I am truly sorry about the wolfhound. Magnificent creature. I hadn't intended for him to get killed by that miserable bastard. He was in such poor condition when I found him. I had hoped to give him the feast of his life, but Reed Longhoffer proved to be every bit as difficult in dying as he was living. And that's quite close enough, Jake. You're more than strong enough to overpower me, but I've got enough explosives here to level this building and completely obliterate both of us. As I'm rather fond of you, I'd rather not do that."

Jake stopped moving forward. He had been creeping toward the professor, intent on getting the detonator away from him.

"I suspect you know why I chose to do what I did? And why it had to be done?"

Jake nodded. "The Sky to Sea trail."

"Well, that was merely part of it. I was eliminating those who were attempting to destroy the very thing I spoke so passionately about at the first town meeting. They were working to destroy the uniqueness of this city. They were going to crush it and make it like every other little bland suburb in the state. The Sky to Sea trail is a part of that, a grand vision for blending the community in with the natural world around it, something very unique in this part of the northwest that has lost so much of its natural heritage. Wilde Park was going to be the crown gem of the entire system.

"But then Longhoffer and Weinberg tried to make sure that we'd have another faceless corporate box store forced upon us. I knew there were probably no legal grounds for it, so I decided to take care of things myself."

"But why, Professor, after Leona...at the second town meeting, Reed had been thwarted by the documents Baldo Ludich produced. There was no need to..."

"To kill him? My dear boy, you do exhibit some of the tendencies of that annoying Pollyanna character."

"I do not."

"When it comes to human nature, you do. Do you really think that Reed Longhoffer would let something like a little piece of paper stand in his way? Particularly with the unlimited resources of Blackburn behind him? He and Blackburn were already looking into ways to overturn that, and believe me they could have done it."

"But..."

"No, Mr. Finnigan, I know what you're going to say. There was no other way. Blackburn, aside from being a truly loathsome individual, was poised to take over some of the last bits of original farmland within the city limits and develop it into some gated monstrosity. I was not about to wait around to see which would happen first—his mind collapsing or his succeeding with his plans."

"His mind collapsing?"

"Surely Jake, you do not think that punching one's son out in public is the action of a rational man? No, Alexander Blackburn's mind was rapidly deteriorating. Had been since young Alex took over the company. He had been prone to violent rages and irrational behavior for months.

It was only a matter of time before Vivian Blackburn would have been forced to put him away. I chose not to wait that long."

"No, you chose to bake him at four-fifty for several hours."

"He was already dead, dear boy. I couldn't see actually cooking him *alive*. That was beyond even me."

Jake sighed, knowing what he was about to say was probably the lamest thing he could possibly utter. His inner English major rebelled at such a clichéd notion, but here he was, faced with the criminal again. He knew he had to give it a try even if it was just for Sam's sake.

"Professor, you have to turn yourself in. Please, it's the only right thing to do."

"On the whole, I think not," said Mills. "You see, well intentioned as you may have been, you did interrupt my work. There were at least six more viable threats to this city I had planned to dispose of, but alas, I don't think now I shall get to that. I also do not see myself going to jail. I don't particularly fancy another long stay at the state hospital, either. No, on the whole, I think this is the best solution."

"What are you planning to do?"

"Simple enough. You shall see. When I tell you to run, you will do so, right past me, out the door and up my back porch and into the house, slamming the door firmly behind you. You should have just enough time. Do not dawdle, Mr. Finnigan. You're a fine, handsome man, and I do not wish any flying shards of glass to harm you." He depressed the plunger on the bomb. "I'd suggest you run, Mr. Finnigan."

Jake tore past Professor Mills without a second glance. He ran out the greenhouse door and up the path, nearly tripping up the stairs. He threw the back door to the house open and slammed it shut, sinking to the floor, his hands over his ears.

The roar was deafening, the explosion immediately followed by a high-pitched crystalline sound as the greenhouse shattered outward. The entire house shook, the plaster of the walls cracking. All the windows at the back of the house smashed, and Jake's ears began ringing. He had felt several solid thumps into the door behind him. Outside in the driveway, Sam's car alarm went off, as did several others up the block.

Then all was still. The basement door flew open, Sam bursting through it. Seeing Jake crouched behind the closed door, he swooped down upon him and took him into his arms, saying repeatedly, "Are you okay? Are you okay?"

"Sam, you're squeezing me to death. I'm fine, I'm fine."

"What happened?" Sam asked, as Jake slowly got back up to his feet.

Jake sighed and slowly turned around, facing the door. He opened it cautiously. As he opened the door, he saw a dozen or more shards of glass embedded in the wood. Stepping out onto the porch, he looked at the backside of the house, which was peppered with shards blown into the siding by the explosion. Jake turned, his eyes following the concrete pathway that now terminated at the smoking black crater.

Just then, something landed on his nose, making him flinch. He reached up and pulled off the material, expecting it to be ash, but it wasn't. The fragrant smell of stargazer lily hit him and he realized that it was a piece of Professor Mills's plants. Another piece softly landed on his shoulder, and Sam said, "Look!" pointing upward.

The sky was filled with the soft fragments of flowers now falling back softly to the earth. Jake watched them fall slowly toward the ground, feeling a hollow pit in his stomach. He sighed and said, "Good-bye, Professor."

❖

This time there was no way to keep Jake's name out of the papers. He was being described by most papers as a hero for ending the reign of terror in Arrow Bay. Jake, for his part, gave all the credit to Detective Haggerty, saying he'd only made the discovery about Professor Grover Mills by accident when he'd dropped by to see Mills that evening to ask him about a plant related matter.

Haggerty, for his part, remained quiet about the entire incident, not wishing to discuss his drugging or abduction by Professor Mills. Jake told Randy Burrows on KABW that Haggerty had been on the Professor's trail and that Mills had come after him before Haggerty could put a stop to his plans. Haggerty had watched this in a bemused fashion, with a Mona Lisa smile, then turned and left the studio quietly. Jake had not seen him since.

Jake refused to let his photo be taken and refused interviews other than to the *Examiner* and KABW. He and Sam had retreated home and let Barnaby out to bark at anyone who approached. After a few days, the people pressing to see and speak to Jake dwindled as more important news stories took over the headlines. The nut who had killed a few people and blown himself up in a small town in the San Juan Islands faded away, and Jake's fifteen minutes of fame diminished quickly.

Notes from friends had arrived in a sudden flurry of mailings. Gavin had called from San Francisco and given both of them a thorough talking-to about getting involved with homicidal maniacs. They couldn't disagree with him and only after getting the promise of a visit to see both he and Jeff soon had they been able to mollify him.

On the plus side, Jake had been moved from the pariah list in Port Jefferson to most notable local celebrity. He suspected his mother had something to do with that. When the principal of William Henry Harrison High School asked him to speak at a school assembly, he politely declined. He was also asked to relate his experience to the Arrow Bay Book Club, the Arrow Bay Writing Club, and for reasons he wasn't quite sure why, the Arrow Bay Plant Society. He declined them all.

Jake was having problems sleeping. Every time he closed his eyes, he could see the Professor in the greenhouse, surrounded by orchids, the bomb strapped to his torso, looking for all the world normal as can be, then hitting the button and exploding into a shower of stargazer lilies. He'd awakened from these dreams in a cold sweat, wondering what had happened to turn the mild mannered and seemingly gentle professor into someone who murdered three people.

"I don't understand, Sam," Jake said in bed one night. "Professor Mills was just the sweetest man. I wouldn't have thought of him being remotely capable of something like this."

"Me either, Jake. I really thought I knew the man."

❖

On the Wednesday before Thanksgiving, Alex stopped by, and with him was Miranda Zimmerman.

"You look tired, Jake," Alex noted.

"Haven't been sleeping very well. Sam and I were also up late last night, finishing my new office," Jake said, motioning to the open door where his newly painted and newly furnished writing room was.

"Looks very nice. I'm looking forward to reading some of your work."

"What can I do for you today?"

"Your other half called me the other night," said Alex. "He said you were understandably upset about Professor Mills and what happened. I asked Miranda to do a little checking. I knew the name was familiar and although I knew who he was, I only actually met the man the one time with you when we went to see his place in the foothills."

"I couldn't figure out why the name resonated with me either, so I checked back through some of our older publications," said Miranda.

"And you found he'd spent some time in a mental institution," said Jake. "Specifically Western State."

"Yes. How did you know?"

"I've been wracking my brain for the last few days trying to think of why there was such a sudden personality change in the Professor. It finally came to me," said Jake, laughing tiredly. "When I was trying to convince him to turn himself in, he talked about not spending any time in jail, or that he 'particularly fancied another extended stay at the state hospital.'"

Miranda nodded and took a notebook out of her satchel. "I found this." She opened it to the front page, and staring at Jake from a newspaper clipping, dated in October, 1978 was a photo of Professor Mills. He was considerably younger, but as ever was wearing the tweed suit and ascot. The headline next to the photo read: NOTED SCHOLAR SUFFERS BREAKDOWN.

Jake read the article quickly. Professor Mills's wife had been killed in a hit and run traffic accident while crossing the street in Seattle. Unable to cope with the loss of his wife, Mills had completely broken down one day while teaching. He was sent to Western State Hospital.

"How long was he there?"

"A while. He finally came back to the UW in the mid-1980's," said Miranda, turning the page, which had another article, this time from the UW newspaper about the Professor's "return to health" and resuming his teaching duties.

Jake read the story quickly, looking for something to confirm his suspicions. One phrase in the second story suddenly stood out as if illuminated by neon lights. He read aloud, "'I owe so much to the doctors and medications for the return of my health.' Well, that explains it."

"Explains what?" asked Alex.

"If you have Detective Haggerty check, I think you'll find that a while back, Professor Mills quit taking his medication. One of the last times we saw him, an alarm went off on his watch. He seemed disconcerted by it, and when I asked him what it was, he said, 'Oh bah, it's nothing. Just a reminder to take my...well, I certainly don't need to worry about *that* anymore.' And I bet you'll find that he was probably prescribed some pretty heavy mood stablizers."

"That would explain a lot," Miranda said.

"It helps to reconcile things," said Jake sadly. He re-read the second story again, focusing on the paragraph that said Professor Mills had taken up growing orchids as part of his therapy. Jake and Sam had always wondered how the professor, a stellar engineer, had gotten into growing such fantastic flowers.

"Where's Sam?" asked Alex.

"Seattle. He should be home any time now."

"Well, we won't keep you," said Miranda, rising. She stepped out into the foyer, leaving Alex a few steps behind.

"If either one of you need anything, just call me, okay?"

"I will, Alex. Thanks," said Jake, giving Alex a hug.

"You're welcome."

Chapter Thirty-eight

An hour later, Sam arrived back from Sea-Tac Airport. Jake opened the front door. He was nearly knocked over as Rachel Parker jumped into his arms, locking him in a bear hug.

"I'm so glad you're okay," she sobbed.

"I'm glad you're okay too," he said.

Rachel pulled back, brushing back a long lock of hair from her face. "You big dope. Rule One. Don't you know you *never* go into the killer's lair? Particularly the basement. I mean, what you have been reading Spievens all those years for anyway?" she said, bursting out in fresh sobs.

"It was a greenhouse, actually," said Jake.

"Oh, whatever."

Sam walked in, carrying two large suitcases. "I think Rachel's home," he said with a grin.

❖

Thanksgiving the next day was a festive event. Jake had risen early to get the turkey in the oven, delighting in the opportunity to torture Rachel when she wandered down the stairs. Rachel was even less of a morning person than he was. Once she was fully caffeinated, she and Jake talked and talked as they always had, as if Rachel hadn't been living clear across the country for the last eight years.

In the afternoon, Evelyn and the Reverend Crawford arrived, along with Caleb Rivers and Betty Newmar from the Duty Free store. Jake had invited those he knew would be alone for the holiday as he had every year.

Still, he was saddened not to see Nora and Ben. He paused in the doorway of the living room as if looking for them, gazing down sadly at the bowl of snacks he was holding. Somewhere he could almost hear a door being shut.

Rachel was regaling Caleb and Betty with her tales of Washington D.C., including Tony Graham. The good doctor had already sent a letter and, of all archaic things, a fruit basket with a note of congratulations to Jake. Jake was setting the bowl of almonds on the table when he heard Caleb say, "He wrote what?"

"An essay called *The Constitutional Right to our Foreskin*. That was the first essay that really got him noticed, anyway. From there it was like a rock rolling down hill," said Rachel.

"I remember that," said Jason. "That was right after he left the NFL. Caused quite a stir."

Sam looked at Jake, eyebrows raised. "Constitutional right to what?"

"Foreskin," said Rachel. "Why is it a constitutional right?" Sam said.

"Tony was always very passionate about the subject. He equated circumcision to mutilation and called for it to be stopped," Jake said.

"Most guys are circumcised when they're babies, so they don't really remember it, do they?" asked Caleb.

"Beats me," said Jake, shrugging. "I know I don't. Do you?"

"No."

"There you have it," said Jake, sitting down on the sofa. Out in the dining room he could hear Betty, Evelyn, and the Reverend Crawford laughing while the smell of turkey filled the house.

Knowing he was blushing, Jake just grinned and smiled, then hastily picked up the *New York Times* Crossword puzzle and began working on it, while Sam and Caleb continued to lament their lost foreskins.

"Did you have to bring that up?" he asked Rachel.

"Well, you know, you might want to get used to having Tony around again," said Rachel slowly.

Jake set down the crossword puzzle. He turned his head and looked Rachel directly in the eyes. "Rachel, what haven't you told me?"

"I told you he got hold of my email."

"Yes."

"And how he suddenly feels like he's my best friend, right?"

"Yes, you did mention that," said Jake.

"Well, just before I left D.C., I got another email from him. He was going on and on about his new book that was coming out...you know, typical egotistical Tony..."

"To the point, please?"

Rachel took in a deep breath. "Okay. At the end, he was talking about how happy he was to have found a job as a professor. He said it was at a very progressive private college. He said it was in a beautiful place, on a little island all of its own..."

"Oh, no!" said Jake. "No, oh come on, no!"

"He's going to be a writer in residence at Considine University," said Rachel.

"What? He's coming here?" asked Sam.

"I'm afraid so."

"It doesn't get any worse. First Amy and Hector Suggs, now Tony."

"Uh, Jacob, what do you mean 'first Amy and Hector Suggs'?" asked Sam, one eyebrow sharply raised over his right eye.

"Um. Well. Remember that vacation we were planning? We might want to take it sooner than later," said Jake.

Rachel and Caleb looked at Sam, then Jake, then back to Sam and burst out laughing. Jake smiled and shrugged as Sam shook his head. Sam got up, kissed Jake on top of the head, and said, "I love you, you know that, you nut?"

"I do, Samuel Patrick O'Conner. And I love you back."

❖

Just before they were about to sit down to dinner, the doorbell rang. Jake looked to his brother and said, "You expecting anyone?"

"No."

Shrugging, Jake went to the door and pulled it open.

"Detective Haggerty," Jake said, surprised.

"Hi," Haggerty said. "Um, sorry to interrupt. I just thought, well, it's Thanksgiving and all. I was thinking about things to be thankful for, and I realized I hadn't actually said thank you for finding me." He shuffled his feet a bit. "So, thank you."

Jake smiled. "You're welcome, Detective. However when it comes right down to the pointy pin cushions of the matter, I don't think he would have hurt you."

"Pointy pin cushions?"

"That's Jake's way of avoiding using the hackneyed 'brass tacks' and failing at it," said Sam.

"Best I could come up with on short notice," Jake said. "And I still don't think he would have hurt you."

"I don't think he would have either, really. I think he just wanted me out of the way for a while. I think he was working on getting out of town when things got too close and he took another way out," Haggerty said sadly.

"How are things for you?" Sam asked. "Sharon let us know about Dorval…"

"Ah, well. Your husband throwing as much of the credit as he did at me went a long way with the department. Dorval is letting the matter go. He's not happy someone outside the department figured it out, but as Chief Sanderson pointed out, you and Sam had a special relationship with Professor Mills that gave you some insider knowledge the police couldn't possibly have."

"At which point I'm guessing Dorval said we should have come forward sooner, I bet," said Jake.

"Well," said Haggerty scratching the back of his head. "There was some mention of that. However, I was quick to point out that you didn't have access to the information we had and that putting the pieces together had kind of been an accident." He sighed. "I'd still watch out for Dorval if I were you." He shrugged, looking up for a moment. "Actually Sharon and I will be keeping an eye on him, but you didn't hear that from me."

"Hear what?" Jake asked.

"Would you like to come in? We've got more than enough food for everyone. You'd be more than welcome."

"Thanks, I appreciate that, but I'm actually on my way to Sharon's. She does a little thing for Thanksgiving every year. I appreciate the offer, though."

"You're always welcome," Sam said.

"Unless you think we're suspects again."

"Stow it, O love of my life."

"Well, I'd better be off," Haggerty said. "Thanks again, Mr. Finnigan. I owe you one."

"You're welcome, Detective Haggerty. Happy Thanksgiving," said Jake, watching him go. Haggerty had just gotten to his car when Jake thought of something. "Hey!"

Haggerty looked up. "Yes?"

"Misty Snipes. She doesn't exist, does she?"

"What makes you think that?"

"Snipes...snipe hunt?"

"That would be a bit obvious, wouldn't it?"

"Rule Twelve: Don't overlook the obvious because it is obvious."

"Let's just say 'Misty Snipes' was a useful diversion for another case we've been working on, and it provided some wonderful entertainment at the town meeting," he said with a wink.

Jake waved as he watched Haggerty pull out of the driveway. He smiled as the car disappeared down High Street, a trail of the Crenshaws' leaves in its wake.

❖

Twenty minutes later, they dug into Thanksgiving dinner. Turkey overflowed the platter, stuffing and mashed potatoes rose high above the bowls, fruit salads and rolls took up every bit of space.

With every bite, Jake counted the things he was thankful for: his health, his family and friends, and the family they had created together. He then slipped his hand under the table, took Sam's hand and looked deeply into Sam's eyes, counting the thing he was thankful for most of all.

"You've got that sappy look again," Rachel said in his ear.

"I've got all the ones I love around me," said Jake. "I can't be happier. Well, nearly," he amended. "Gavin and Jeff aren't here."

"Gavin was making Jeff take him to Maui for Thanksgiving in exchange for being forced to endure Christmas with the rest of the Gilmores," said Rachel.

"Indeed."

"Well, let's see, your ex is moving into town, your best friend has moved in and she's unemployed with absolutely zero job prospects..."

"Shut up and have some turkey, Sadie McKee," said Jake.

"It is awfully good."

"Besides, who said anything about Tony moving into town? Considine is a good twenty miles off. He'll be far enough away."

"Still close enough to be irritating," Jason chimed in. "Mashed potatoes, please."

"Frankly I'm more worried about Amy and Mr. Musings-On-The-China-Door Knob or whatever it was," said Sam. "Spending time with them is like having all the oxygen slowly sucked out of the room. You don't realize you're in peril until it's too late."

"Sam!" said Evelyn, shocked. "You shouldn't say such things about your in-laws!"

"Have you ever met our sister and her husband, Evelyn?"

"No," she said. "But honestly…" She stopped. "I was about to say they couldn't be that bad, but I of all people should know better."

"I suppose this is where I should pipe in with some wise quote from the Good Book," said Reverend Crawford. "But I've got a brother who's a right pain in my ass, and I'd be a complete hypocrite if said otherwise."

The entire conversation ground to a halt. Oblivious, the Reverend Crawford continued piling stuffing onto her plate before reaching for the green bean casserole. Catching everyone's expression, she said, "What, did I take too much?"

Everyone at the table roared with laughter.

About the Author

Steve Pickens was born in Seattle, Washington. He has spent his entire life in the land of Bigfoot, strong coffee, ferryboats, heavy rain, and active volcanoes, all of which have influenced his work.

When not writing, he can be found tending and photographing flowers in the garden, taking trips into the Cascades, or wandering along the shores of Puget Sound. He and his husband live in northwestern Washington in a town that bears more than a passing resemblance to the one in his mysteries with far too much ferry ephemera and two spoiled cats.

Books Available from Bold Strokes Books

Sinister Justice by Steve Pickens. When a vigilante targets citizens of Jake Finnigan's hometown, Jake and his partner Sam fall under suspicion themselves as they investigate the murders. (978-1-63555-094-8)

Club Arcana: Operation Janus by Jon Wilson. Wizards, demons, Elder Gods: Who knew the universe was so crowded, and that they'd all be out to get Angus McAslan? (978-162639-969-3)

Triad Soul by 'Nathan Burgoine. Luc, Anders, and Curtis—vampire, demon, and wizard—must use their powers of blood, soul, and magic to defeat a murderer determined to turn their city into a battlefield. (978-1-62639-863-4)

Gatecrasher by Stephen Graham King. Aided by a high-tech thief, the Maverick Heart crew race against time to prevent a cadre of savage corporate mercenaries from seizing control of a revolutionary wormhole technology. (978-1-62639-936-5)

Wicked Frat Boy Ways by Todd Gregory. Beta Kappa brothers Brandon Benson and Phil Connor play an increasingly dangerous game of love, seduction, and emotional manipulation. (978-1-62639-671-5)

Death Goes Overboard by David S. Pederson. Heath Barrington and Alan Keyes are two sides of a steamy love triangle as they encounter gangsters, con men, murder, and more aboard an old lake steamer. (978-1-62639-907-5)

A Careful Heart by Ralph Josiah Bardsley. Be careful what you wish for…love changes everything. (978-1-62639-887-0)

Worms of Sin by Lyle Blake Smythers. A haunted mental asylum turned drug treatment facility exposes supernatural detective Finn M'Coul to an outbreak of murderous insanity, a strange parasite, and ghosts that seek sex with the living. (978-1-62639-823-8)

Tartarus by Eric Andrews-Katz. When Echidna, Mother of all Monsters, escapes from Tartarus and into the modern world, only an Olympian has the power to oppose her. (978-1-62639-746-0)

Rank by Richard Compson Sater. Rank means nothing to the heart, but the Air Force isn't as impartial. Every airman learns that rank has its privileges. What about love? (978-1-62639-845-0)

The Grim Reaper's Calling Card by Donald Webb. When Katsuro Tanaka begins investigating the disappearance of a young nurse, he discovers more missing persons, and they all have one thing in common: The Grim Reaper Tarot Card. (978-1-62639-748-4)

Smoldering Desires by C.E. Knipes. Evan McGarrity has found the man of his dreams in Sebastian Tantalos. When an old boyfriend from Sebastian's past enters the picture, Evan must fight for the man he loves. (978-1-62639-714-9)

Tallulah Bankhead Slept Here by Sam Lollar. A coming of age/coming out story, set in El Paso of 1967, that tells of Aaron's adventures with movie stars, cool cars, and topless bars. (978-1-62639-710-1)

Death Came Calling by Donald Webb. When private investigator Katsuro Tanaka is hired to look into the death of a high-profile lawyer, he becomes embroiled in a case of murder and mayhem. (978-1-60282-979-4)

The City of Seven Gods by Andrew J. Peters. In an ancient city of aerie temples, a young priest and a barbarian mercenary struggle to refashion their lives after their worlds are torn apart by betrayal. (978-1-62639-775-0)

Lysistrata Cove by Dena Hankins. Jack and Eve navigate the maelstrom of their darkest desires and find love by transgressing gender, dominance, submission, and the law on the crystal blue Caribbean Sea. (978-1-62639-821-4)

Garden District Gothic by Greg Herren. Scotty Bradley has to solve a notorious thirty-year-old unsolved murder that has terrible repercussions in the present. (978-1-62639-667-8)

The Man on Top of the World by Vanessa Clark. Jonathan Maxwell falling in love with Izzy Rich, the world's hottest glam rock superstar, is not only unpredictable but complicated when a bold teenage fan-girl changes everything. (978-1-62639-699-9)

The Orchard of Flesh by Christian Baines. With two hotheaded men under his roof including his werewolf lover, a vampire tries to solve an increasingly lethal mystery while keeping Sydney's supernatural factions from the brink of war. (978-1-62639-649-4)

Funny Bone by Daniel W. Kelly. Sometimes sex feels so good you just gotta giggle! (978-1-62639-683-8)

The Thassos Confabulation by Sam Sommer. With the inheritance of a great deal of money, David and Chris also inherit a nondescript brown paper parcel and a strange and perplexing letter that sends David on a quest to understand its meaning. (978-1-62639-665-4)

The Photographer's Truth by Ralph Josiah Bardsley. Silicon Valley tech geek Ian Baines gets more than he bargained for on an unexpected journey of self-discovery through the lustrous nightlife of Paris. (978-1-62639-637-1)

Crimson Souls by William Holden. A scorned shadow demon brings a centuries-old vendetta to a bloody end as he assembles the last of the descendants of Harvard's Secret Court. (978-1-62639-628-9)

The Long Season by Michael Vance Gurley. When Brett Bennett enters the professional hockey world of 1926 Chicago, will he meet his match in either handsome goalie Jean-Paul or in the man who may destroy everything? (978-1-62639-655-5)

Triad Blood by 'Nathan Burgoine. Cheating tradition, Luc, Anders, and Curtis—vampire, demon, and wizard—form a bond to gain their freedom, but will surviving those they cheated be beyond their combined power? (978-1-62639-587-9)

Death Comes Darkly by David S. Pederson. Can dashing detective Heath Barrington solve the murder of an eccentric millionaire and find love with policeman Alan Keyes, who, despite his lust, harbors feelings of guilt and shame? (978-1-62639-625-8)

Slaves of Greenworld by David Holly. On the planet Greenworld, the amnesiac Dove must cope with intrigues, alien monsters, and a growing slave revolt, while reveling in homoerotic sexual intimacy with his own slave Raret. (978-1-62639-623-4)

Men in Love: M/M Romance, edited by Jerry L. Wheeler. Love stories between men, from first blush to wedding bells and beyond. (978-1-62639-736-1)

Lightning Source UK Ltd.
Milton Keynes UK
UKHW011837081118
332017UK00001B/136/P